VILLA D'ESTE

VILLA D'ESTE

Margaret Pemberton

SEVERN
SH
HOUSE

This edition, complete with new material from the author,
first published in Great Britain 1995 by
SEVERN HOUSE PUBLISHERS LTD of
9–15 High Street, Sutton, Surrey SM1 1DF.
Originally published 1979 in Great Britain by Robert Hale Ltd.
First published in the USA 1995 by
SEVERN HOUSE PUBLISHERS INC of
595 Madison Avenue, New York, NY 10022.

British Library Cataloguing in Publication Data
Pemberton, Margaret
  Villa d'Este. – New ed
  I. Title
  823.914 [F]

  ISBN 0-7278-4767-8

Typeset by Hewer Text Composition Services, Edinburgh.
Printed and bound in Great Britain by
Hartnolls Ltd, Bodmin, Cornwall.

For my children, Amanda, Rebecca, Polly,
Michael and Natasha

Author's Note

VILLA D'ESTE was first published under the title VENGE-ANCE IN THE SUN, in 1979. It was my third novel and lots of other novels, in many different genres, have followed it. Why, then, am I so happy to see this early book enjoying a new lease of life? In the seventies, when VILLA D'ESTE was written, romantic suspense was the most popular genre in women's fiction. Though fashions change in fiction as in anything else, romantic suspense is *still* the most popular genre for many writers, (and I am one of them!), as well as a whole host of readers. In an icy British winter, or a too cool British summer, imaginative escape to the Mediterranean areas in which so many romantic suspense novels are set, is sure to prevail. The hero, (the *true* hero!), will not prove to be a heel. In a world of increasing uncertainties, the values inherent in romantic sus-pense are, for many people, to be more than ever welcomed.

Re-reading VILLA D'ESTE, on a chill February day in London, brought back many happy memories for me, for the book is set in Majorca, and Majorca holds a special place in my heart. I fell in love with it when I first visited it, nearly twenty years ago and now, with Spanish members of my family living there, return at every opportunity. Unlike many other beautiful places, the mountainous north coastline which provides the setting for VILLA D'ESTE has changed very little. Though the villa of the title is fictitious, the promontory it imaginatively overlooks, is not. It is a place that is still as beautiful, and as wild, as when I first saw it. I hope it always remains so.

Margaret Pemberton 1995

ONE

Below me Majorca's tiny airstrip shelved into view, shimmering beneath a heat haze. I took a deep breath and fastened my seat belt. It was no use going back. There was nothing to go back to. I clenched my fists at the memory of Max. Damn him. Damn him. Damn him.

The wheels touched ground and the heavily built man sat next to me, mistaking my anguish for fear, said: "It's all right. We're down now. Nothing to worry about."

I smiled mechanically and reached for my hand luggage.

"Here, let me." Good-naturedly he lifted my overnight bag from the rack. "No fun travelling alone, is it?"

"No," I said with a tight smile, squeezing after him into the aisle. And if it hadn't been for Max's faithlessness I wouldn't have been travelling alone. I followed an expensive smelling Frenchwoman down the steps and onto the tarmac. I should never have become engaged to him in the first place. I should have known it wouldn't work. Max liked his women as fast as his cars and I was well rid of him.

"Have a nice time," my cheerful companion from the plane said, heaving his suitcase from the conveyor belt, then turning and disappearing amongst the crowd.

"Yes," I said grimly, alarming the woman stood next to me. "I will."

I walked out into the dazzling sunlight, pausing hesitantly as uniformed couriers herded their holidaymakers into mini buses and the elegant Frenchwoman stepped into a waiting limousine. Mrs Van de Naude had said I would be met at the airport. The throng around me thinned and trickled away and still there was no-one looking for an English girl travelling alone. I sat down on my case and prepared to wait.

It was midday and the sun was bright, the air sharp with

7

the tang of orange and lemon trees. Beyond the smudged green of the hillsides the sky was a deep, unbelievable blue, high curling clouds trailing wispily towards the bone-white outline of mountains. On the verge of the airfield the stark silhouette of a windmill creaked motionless in the heat. I closed my eyes. Perhaps my rash act in flying to Majorca wasn't going to be so disastrous after all. Here there would be no constant reminders of Max. No repetition of last week when I had walked into Lacey's, our favourite restaurant, and caught Max holding hands with a half dressed French girl. They had been so engrossed in each other that they hadn't even been aware of my entrance. And that had been only weeks before we were due to be married! I was well rid of him and it was time I stopped thinking about him.

The trouble was, I had known Max too long. We were cousins, and I had spent all my school holidays at Crailsham Place with Aunt Katherine, Uncle Alistair . . . and Max.

He was the older by six years, and the first holiday I had spent there, when he was eleven and I was five, he had nick-named me Brat, told me not to be a nuisance and not to get in his way. Mournfully I had trailed round after him, until he had said condescendingly that I could run after his cricket balls, fetch his kite back, and even watch him ride, on condition I didn't tell any tales. Gradually a bond grew between us and we became inseparable. For the next six years, all through the summer, Max took me everywhere with him, teaching me to ride and swim and fish and even, to Aunt Katherine's horror, shoot. After he had seen his first motor race and begun single-handedly building his own car, I stood for hours with oil and grease on my hands, handing him his tools, always having a rag at the ready. Wherever Max went. I went. Blissfully content.

Then, when he was seventeen, he no longer returned to Crailsham Place in the summer, and the holidays were long and tedious and nothing seemed as much fun as it used to.

Max had begun to race professionally . . . and have girl friends. My mother said he was wild and that Aunt Katherine was too indulgent with him, but I thought Max's flamboyant success as a driver and the flare he had for

8

hitting the headlines the height of glamour and secretly kept any press cuttings I could find to show to my envious friends at school.

When I did meet him again I felt strangely shy. My precious hoard of cuttings hadn't prepared me for the drastic change in him. He was tall, over six foot, and powerfully built with strong shoulders and the easy grace of an athlete. His colouring betrayed his Italian grandmother who, my mother said, was no better than she should have been. He was even darker than I remembered, his hair a black, curling pelt, his complexion swarthy, only his brown eyes, gleaming and full of laughter, were familiar.

"Hello Brat," he had said, as though it were the school holidays and we were children again. And, old habits dying hard, I slipped back into my role of worshipful admirer. Around when he wanted me, uncomplaining when he didn't. Then, suddenly, everything changed.

Max was spending a week with some friends in Cornwall surfing. Uncle Alistair said he was going down to join them for a weekend and asked if I would go with him. It was tea-time when we arrived, and there was the smell of rain in the air. I had the uncomfortable feeling that Max had rather we hadn't gone, his attention being taken up with Claudette Claustre, a beautiful film actress he had recently been spending his time with. Uncle Alistair seemed not to notice his son's coolness and was his usual bland and genial self, and there was no reason why I should have minded. After all, I was only cousin Lucy. But when Max excused himself from the proposed boat trip after dinner and said he was taking Claudette into Polperro, there seemed no pleasure left in the expedition. There were seven of us altogether. Giles Fulbright, an old friend of Uncle Alistair's. Gwen Fulbright, his wife. Jim Shernham, a racing driver friend of Max's, and his girl friend, a pretty brunette called Kay, and Danny Collins whose boat we were to go out in.

Uncle Alistair had expressed doubts even before we had reached the boat-house. The sky was darkening and the waves were high. Danny had been emphatic that it was nothing but a squall, but as a spray of foam showered us, Kay had taken Jim's hand and said she preferred not to go.

9

Staring out over the heaving sea Gwen Fulbright had been the next to cry off. Uncle Alistair had said:

"Come on, Lucy. Let's go back and warm ourselves with a drink. No joy in going out in weather like this."

But I had no desire to spend the evening sitting in the cottage brooding about Max and Claudette. So Jim Shernham, Giles Fulbright, Danny Collins and myself put to sea. Within minutes there came the ominous roll of distant thunder and I gritted my teeth as the small boat pitched and rolled, struggling for the headland. The turbulence of the waves and the smack of the foam against our faces as we reached the open sea was exhilerating at first, but soon became touched with fear as the sea gripped the boat, plunging her deeper and deeper amongst the white horses. Acknowledging defeat, Danny strained to turn the boat and battled towards the shore. We didn't make it. Twenty yards from the jetty a giant wave lifted the boat, smashing it leewards into the icy sea. Ten minutes later, frozen and exhausted, I staggered out of the water behind Giles Fulbright and collapsed on the beach.

"Lucy!"

I don't remember seeing him running over the sand. One moment I was sick and shivering, the next Max was down beside me, his face white in the darkness.

"Lucy! Look at me! For God's sake! Lucy!" His arms were round me and he was kissing me in a way that had nothing cousinly about it. I clung to him, oblivious of Uncle Alistair and the dripping figures of Jim Shernham and Danny Collins. His hands gripped my hair savagely as he lifted his face from mine, saying in a voice that was almost unrecognisable:

"Don't ever frighten me like that again, understand?"

I nodded, unable to answer as his mouth came down hard on mine and then, eternities later, he said hoarsely:

"God, what a fool I've been. I thought I'd lost you, Brat."

And he picked me up in his arms and carried me gently across the wet shingle to the house. After that, for a full year, Max wasn't seen in the company of models, actresses and society girls. Only me.

Aunt Katherine said it was too good to be true and it was.

A few weeks ago I had begun to hear rumours that Max was seeing Claudette Claustre again. I had ignored it as malicious gossip until the day of my birthday. We had arranged to go to Paris, but Max phoned me, full of apologies, saying they were having trouble with the car he was driving next season and he wouldn't be able to get back from testing it till after the weekend. I had gone to Crailsham Place, had dinner with Aunt Katherine and Uncle Alistair, and waited for him to return.

The next day the papers had a photograph of Max and Claudette Claustre. It had been taken the night before at a party held for Fedor Katchorsky, a visiting Russian composer. He had written the score for a film Claudette had recently appeared in, hence her presence there. The reason for Max's was, presumably, Claudette.

He was all sweet reason when he had returned and I had showed him the photograph.

"It's nothing to get upset about, sweetheart," he had said, pouring himself a drink.

"But it is, Max. You lied to me. . . ."

"No I didn't," he'd said firmly. "When I telephoned you I told you the truth. I had to go down to Oatlands to test the car. I didn't know then I would be seeing Claudette. . . ."

"It was my birthday," I'd said stubbornly, feeling myself weaken as he put his drink down and moved purposefully towards me.

"It was my love . . . and I hadn't forgotten." He lifted a delicate pendant of gold and lapis lazuli from his pocket. Two tiny cherubs floated heavenwards against the deep blue surface. "Like it, Brat?" he asked softly, fastening it around my neck, pulling me against him.

"Yes," I said. "But Claudette. . . ."

"Forget Claudette," he'd said, the dark eyes gleaming as he held me fast, silencing my protests with kisses.

Then last Sunday I had swung happily into Lacey's to be met by the sight of Max and Claudette at a corner table. They were sat close together, hands clasped, and Claudette's eyes were radiant. Sick and trembling I had turned, running blindly up the street, knowing the truth and knowing what I must do.

11

Max did not want to marry me. Had never wanted to marry me. His rash proposal had been nothing but reaction when he had found me half-drowned on the beach. He was still as unable to resist the company of the beautiful women who flocked the racing circuits as he ever was. I had an old magazine clipping of an interview he had once given, where he was quoted as saying 'I like having lots of beautiful women around me', when asked about his playboy image. Well, I wasn't beautiful. Pretty, yes. Beautiful in the way of film stars like Claudette Claustre, no. Max had made a mistake and been too kind to admit it. Admitting it was going to be up to me.

It hadn't been easy. Max had merely laughed when I had handed him my engagement ring back.

"Don't be ridiculous, Brat," he had said, leaving it where it lay on the table.

"I'm not being ridiculous," I said, my throat painfully tight. "I've given it a lot of thought and I'm not marrying you."

"Well I'm damn well marrying you!" he had said, his eyes flickering dangerously as he made a grab for me. Once in his arms I knew my good intentions would be gone forever. The telephone began to ring and as he glanced towards it I pushed him, knocking him off balance, darting under his outstretched arm, slamming the door behind me as I flew from the room. Suicidally I ran into the street, the sound of the telephone still ringing in my ears as I frantically flagged a taxi and scrambled into it, seeing Max hurtle out of the house and stand, panting and cursing in the dust behind me.

That evening I had answered Helena Van de Naude's advertisement for a nanny for her daughter, the attraction being the chance to leave Max far behind me and start life afresh. Helena Van de Naude had rung me immediately, and three days later I had gone to see her at the Dorchester and now, only a week later, I was on my way to the villa D'Este and my first meeting with Danielle.

I opened my eyes, looking around me. Another plane was circling the airport and a couple of mini buses had drawn up ready to ferry more tourists into Palma and the resorts nearby. The villa D'Este lay in another part of the island, high in the mountains. Helena Van de Naude had stressed to me how remote the villa was but I hadn't cared. All I had wanted was to get away from Max and Crailsham Place, to be spared the misery of seeing him and Claudette together and knowing I had been right, for in all that long, never-ending week, Max had neither written nor telephoned me.

I had liked Helena Van de Naude immediately. She was in her late thirties, tall and athletically built. Her skin was darkened by the Mediterranean sun and her hair was thick and wavy. She wore it swept away from her forehead, accentuating hazel eyes and glossy winged eyebrows. She was full of energy and vitality, the wide mouth smiling easily and often.

"Have you been a nanny before?" she asked pleasantly.

"No. . . ."

"Is it something you have always wanted to do?"

"No," I answered truthfully, feeling the job slipping away from me.

"You want the opportunity to travel, perhaps?"

I thought of the past jet-setting year with Max. Monaco, Japan, Germany, South Africa. . . .

"No," I said.

She stared at me in amusement, then said directly: "You look like an educated girl who would have no difficulties in getting a good job. What are the attractions in burrowing yourself away with a six year old girl? You will have very little company, you know."

"I don't want company."

The perceptive eyes flickered to the naked white band on the third finger of my left hand.

"Divorced?"

I shook my head. "No. It was an engagement."

She stretched her long legs. "And I was to be your refuge?"

"Yes," I said, standing up and picking up my shoulder-bag. "I'm sorry I've wasted your time, Mrs Van de Naude. Goodbye."

She didn't move. "You haven't wasted my time, Miss Matthews. Quite the reverse. There is every chance in the near future that my family will be moving to Africa. A new nanny may not find the idea of Africa as congenial as that of Majorca, and so whoever I engage may only be with us for a short time. I think you would suit us very well."

"You mean I can have the job?"

"Can you drive?"

I nodded. She motioned me to sit down again.

"Then if you want it, the job is yours." She curled her legs beneath her on the sofa. "We are very isolated. The villa is on a headland a good three miles from the nearest road, and that's only a mountain road that leaves a lot to be desired. Danielle has a tutor. A Mr Lyall. He will have care of her in the mornings, your duties will start after lunch. My housekeeper is English and her husband, a Majorcan, speaks excellent English so you will have no language problems. Mario is our gardener and odd job man. He will meet you at the airport when you arrive. The only other member of the staff is Miss Blanchard, my secretary."

I wondered why a married woman living in isolation should need a secretary.

"Now that I have found someone I shall fly straight back home. There is a ten-o'clock flight on Saturday morning which I shall book for you. If you run into any problems telephone the villa." She rose to her feet and handed me a card embossed with the name of the villa and telephone number and several ten pound notes. "These should tide you over until you arrive," she said generously. "My husband spends a lot of his time away from the villa, but he is there at the moment. I am sure you will fit in with us very well. We are a very casual household." Her large hand gripped mine firmly. "Till Saturday then. Goodbye."

"Goodbye," I said, slightly dazed. "And thank you."

It was Uncle Alistair who cast the first ripples on the apparently smooth surface of life at the villa D'Este.

"Van de Naude?" he had asked vaguely. "John Van de Naude?"

"Yes. Do you know him?"

"Know of him, m'dear. Fellow's a South African, lives in exile now. Made a fortune in mining or diamonds . . . or are they both the same? I know he couldn't take his wealth out of the country. I only hope you know what you're doing . . . seems a bit drastic to me . . . haring off to Minorca. . . ."

"Majorca."

"Just because you and Max have had a tiff."

"It wasn't a tiff. I never want to see Max again."

"Quite, quite," Uncle Alistair said, totally untaken in by this lie. "When is the wedding? Never did have a head for dates?"

"There isn't going to be a wedding," I said for the hundredth time.

"Bad as that, is it?" he said sympathetically. "Well, well, still think this jaunt of yours is a mistake. Where there's smoke there's fire and all that."

"All what?"

"Nasty business, remember thinking so at the time."

"I haven't the slightest idea what you're talking about. What was a nasty business?"

"The whole thing. Him being a politician as well. Wasn't on m'dear. Wasn't on at all."

"Uncle Alistair," I said patiently. "What are you talking about?"

"You mean you don't know?"

"No," I said, wondering if it wouldn't be better to put the telephone down and forget all about it. "Tell me."

"He was a widower with a young son when he met this second wife of his. A high ranking government minister. Couldn't have been worse."

"What couldn't?"

"Marrying her."

I counted to ten slowly. "Why?"

"I should have thought that was obvious when you met her. I mean, if someone is black as the ace of spades you notice, don't you?"

"Generally. Helena Van de Naude isn't."

"Rubbish," Uncle Alistair said crossly. "Of course she is. That's what all the fuss was about. Can't go marrying who you want in South Africa. Against the law."

"She's hardly any darker than Max."

"Can't help that. She's coloured and that's that. It was

the ruin of Van de Naude. Lost his wealth and became an exile. I think they said at the time she was a communist, but governments always say that if they want to discredit someone. Only hope you know what you're letting yourself in for. Don't mind her being coloured," he said generously. "But don't want you coming back a communist. Your Aunt Katherine wouldn't like it. She's set her heart on becoming a Justice of the Peace!"

"Then I'll try not to jeopardise her chances. Don't worry about me, Uncle Alistair. I shan't come to any harm!"

TWO

A car horn tooted loudly. The driver slammed his door behind him and walked across to me, a wide smile on his face.

"Miss Matthews?"

I nodded, rising to my feet. He was a big man with a head of untidy hair and friendly eyes, wearing a white tee-shirt that had seen better days and a pair of creased cotton trousers.

"Mario Arteche," he said, shaking my hand vigorously and picking up my case, throwing it easily into the rear of a battered cream-coloured estate car. "I am sorry I am late."

We swerved recklessly out onto a sun bleached road: "Is this your first visit to Majorca?"

"Yes."

"The villa D'Este is not near the tourist resorts. It is high in the mountains. A little lonely perhaps, but very beautiful. . . ."

I leant back against the musty leather of the seat, content to let him do the talking, enjoying the sun and the sounds and smells of a new country. Trying not even to think of Max. . . .

"In another few minutes we will be among the mountains," Mario said, pointing ahead to where white granite peaks rose sheer against the vibrant sky. With an ear splitting blast on the car horn he scattered a group of laughing children and the dust blown streets were left behind us as the land fell away steeply at the roadside and we began to climb.

Soft green trees, silvered in the brilliant light, gave the otherwise barren mountain-sides a milkish hue. Waist high pampas grass brushed against the car as the road narrowed in its tortuous ascent, winding tirelessly round curve after curve, each fresh view one of blinding blue sky and searing white rock.

"Daniella is looking forward to meeting you," Mario said, the wheel spinning beneath his large brown hands.

"Good. I'm looking forward to meeting her too."

"She is a nice little girl. You will like her. And," he turned and gave me a dazzling smile, "she will like you."

"What about the others? Mrs Van de Naude's secretary and Danielle's tutor. Are they easy to get on with?"

"Miss Blanchard is very sophisticated," he took his hands from the wheel, to show that she also had a very good shape. "Mr Lyall is . . . quiet." Mario dismissed Mr Lyall with a shrug. "The next lot of hairpin bends are known as the Devesas. Lots of accidents happen here," as he spoke the car swung dizzily to face nothing but sky and, far below, the glittering turquoise of the sea. "It is best to drive slowly round here," Mario said unnecessarily, "especially at dusk."

The road swung briefly away from the sea, leading into a narrow gorge between the mountains. Soaring slabs of rock plunged us into shadow, only the higher flanks catching the golden glitter of the sun. We climbed even higher, and then the gorge widened and we shot off the road onto a sun scorched promontory, the mountains closing in behind us. Ahead of us the headland jutted out over the sea and doll-like, poised precariously with nothing but a background of sky and cloud, stood the pale bleached walls of the villa D'Este.

We bucketed over the rough grass, weaving expertly between shoulders of serrated rock as the courtyard walls loomed nearer. Then we swept through wide gates and into a riot of colour. In the centre of the courtyard a bronze fountain sprayed a mist of water over a pool full of water lilies. On three sides were shaded colonades and delicate archways, and everywhere there were flowers. They wound up the white pillars, massed the balconies and covered the walls, the scent thick in the heat. Helena Van de Naude stepped towards me, her hands outstretched.

"Welcome to the villa D'Este, Lucy. I hope you will be happy here."

"I'm sure I will," I said confidently.

"Take Miss Matthews' case to her room and ask Peggy to bring drinks out to the pool, Mario. Come this way, Lucy. It's rather a maze at first but you'll soon get used to it."

We stepped under the arcade and into the coolness of a high ceilinged corridor with pretty tiled floor and brilliant white walls. Walking quickly past innumerable doors and then up a flight of shallow steps, the tiles gave way to polished floors of pale gold wood, the walls hung with big, bold paintings, all with an African theme. An open door gave a glimpse of deeply piled carpet and silk lined walls and then we were once more in the heat of the sun. A long terrace stretched the length of the villa with sun-chairs and loungers around the edge of a large swimming-pool.

A plump dark-haired woman with a tray of drinks came towards us. She set it down on a glass topped table, looking at me with friendly curiosity.

"Peggy, I'd like you to meet Lucy Matthews."

Peggy shook my hand warmly. "Very pleased to meet you I'm sure. Danielle's been doing nothing else all morning but talk about your arrival."

"Where is she now?" her mother asked, glancing towards the villa.

"Mr Lyall let her finish her lessons early and she's gone to change her dress. Not that it needed changing, but she would insist on putting on her best to meet Miss Matthews."

"Mario has already taken Lucy's case upstairs. I thought I'd let Danny show Lucy to her room. She'll enjoy doing that."

"She certainly will," Peggy said, giving me another warm smile. "She helped me dust and put fresh flowers in there only this morning."

"She's a nice woman," Helena Van de Naude said as Peggy disappeared back into the villa. "She'll be a great help to you." She scooped ice into a glass of fresh orange, saying: "Does it come up to expectations?"

"The villa?"

She nodded, handing me my glass and pouring a drink for herself.

"It's beautiful," I said truthfully. "Absolutely breath-

19

taking."

Behind the villa was the broad sweep of the headland and beyond that, the mountains rising stark against the cloudless sky, the ridges of barren rock silvered in the sun. In front of us, beyond the terrace, the wooded cliffs fell steeply to the Mediterranean. The sea shimmered translucently, creaming gently against the cliffs, a small breeze tossing up flying scuds of spray, stirring the sleepy scent from the pines that hugged the cliff. Wherever one looked there was sea and sky and rock. And silence.

"We've lived here for ten years and I still love it. The only necessity is a car. There is a Fiat and an Audi in the garage which you can use whenever you wish. There is also that disreputable wreck that Mario insists on driving if the other cars are not available."

There came the sound of running footsteps and a little girl ran out of the villa, a piece of paper clutched in her hand. She ran to her mother, flinging her arms around her waist, burrowing her head in her lap so that all I could see of her were two skinny brown legs and a mop of mousy hair.

Helena Van de Naude patted her shoulder. "There's no need to be shy, Danny. Miss Matthews has come a long way to be with us. Aren't you going to say hello?"

Slowly she raised her head. She was smaller than I had expected, with none of her mother's blatant vitality. The mousy hair was straight, her face plain, but there was a gentleness in the wide spaced grey eyes that was attractive and appealing.

"I've done a drawing for you," she said, smiling shyly, still holding on to her mother with one hand as she held out her piece of paper.

A matchstick figure with a riot of yellow curls and triangular skirt of red and blue was surrounded by birds and butterflies and a sun like a giant cartwheel.

"Thank you, Danielle. That's lovely," I said, smiling and holding out my hand to her. She came hesitantly, saying:

"I like drawing pretty ladies. Do you like drawing?"

Thankful I had one talent that pleased, I drew as near a likeness to her as I could. She watched me, eyes wide, then said uncertainly:

"That little girl looks like me."

"It *is* you. Look . . . she's even got one tooth missing, just like you!"

"You *are* clever. I'm glad you've come. Will you draw me a horse and. . . ."

"Later, Danny," Helena Van de Naude said laughing. "Miss Matthews has to unpack her things yet, and have lunch."

"Can I help you?" she asked, the drawing held tight in her hand.

Her mother nodded, and I said: "Yes. I think if we look hard enough, we'll find something in my case for a little girl."

"For me?" her grey eyes shone.

"Peggy has left a cold lunch for you in the dining-room, Lucy. Danny will show you the way. Spend the rest of the day getting acclimatised."

My room was lovely. A large, airy room overlooking the sea.

"The bathroom is next door and then my bedroom," Danielle said chattily, the last of her reserve melting when I had given her my small present. It wasn't much. Humpty Dumpty figures that couldn't fall over, but she played happily with them while I unpacked. There was a soft knock on the door. I opened it to Peggy who said apologetically.

"Could I have Danielle please? She has a dental appointment in Palma and Miss Blanchard is taking her. Mrs Van de Naude had forgotten all about it."

Danielle pulled a face and left reluctantly. I finished my unpacking and then decided to make my own way to the dining-room and my late lunch. The corridor overlooked the terrace and the swimming-pool, and from an open window I could see Peggy clearing away the empty glasses from the table and caught a glimpse of Mario disappearing round the corner of the villa, a bucket and a washleather in his hand.

"*You should have told me!*" a man's voice said suddenly from behind a nearby door. I increased speed, not wanting to hear more, but Helena Van de Naude's voice, taut with strain, carried clearly behind me.

"She's here now. . . ."

"*Too bloody right she is!*" the voice rose, and as I turned the corner of the stairs, I heard him say harshly:

"*It's no good, Helena. She'll have to go. And soon!*"

THREE

I hurried down the remaining stairs. Peggy was crossing the hall. She looked up as she heard me, saying: "Are you ready for your lunch now?"

I nodded, feeling more in the need of a stiff drink. She led the way to a table set out on a low balcony.

"Mrs Van de Naude prefers eating out here at lunchtime. Danielle has gone to the dentists in Palma with Miss Blanchard, and the rest of the day is your own. If you want to use one of the cars the keys are hanging up in the hall, though Mrs Van de Naude thinks perhaps you would like to rest."

"Thank you Peggy, but I think I'll go down to the beach. Is it safe to swim?"

"Mr Van de Naude and Mr Lyall swim down there, but it's a steep climb back." She sat down, preparing herself for a chat. "Do you play tennis as well?"

I nodded.

"Then you'll fit in very well here. They're all tennis and swimming mad. Janet was just the same."

"Janet?"

"Danielle's previous nanny. Such a nice girl she was. With her ever since she was a toddler."

"Did she leave to get married?"

"Oh no," Peggy's good-natured face was shocked. "She was killed."

"Killed!"

Peggy lowered her voice. "Suicide. And her only nineteen as well."

"How . . . dreadful," I said inadequately.

"Such a nice girl she was. Always had a smile and a cheery word. It was just over a month ago. She went into Palma and never came back," her voice shook and she fumbled for a handkerchief. "She just walked into a block of flats in Ria Square and threw herself from the fifth floor."

"Dear God. . . ."

"Danielle took it ever so badly. So did Mrs Van de Naude come to that. Not that it was her fault. A nicer lady you couldn't wish to work for. Very attached to Janet she was, seeing as how Janet had been with her ever since she left school. The day it happened Janet came into me in the kitchen and said she was going into Palma and did I want anything . . . and then, three hours later, there's a telephone call and Mrs Van de Naude went chasing off like a woman demented." She drew in a shuddering breath. "Terrible it was. Little Danielle asking and asking for her. Then there was Mr Bradley here as well. First time the family had been all together and a tragedy like that happens. . . ."

"Mr Bradley?"

"That's Mr Van de Naude's son by his first marriage. He lives in South Africa but he was over here earlier in the year. Gone off to London or Paris or somewhere now." She moved towards the door. "I wouldn't say anything to Mrs Van de Naude. About Janet I mean. She took it very badly. Best wait till she tells you herself. I expect she wants you to settle in first."

The path wound dustily beneath the pines, zig-zagging the cliff face in crumbling steps till it reached a sickle of golden sand backed by the soaring backdrop of cliff and pine. There was a small jetty with a dinghy bobbing at anchor, and swaying magnificently in the centre of the bay was a sleek white yacht, its carmine-red sails furled and the name 'Helena' painted boldly on her prow. I ran down the last few steps sinking ankle-deep into the soft sand. Within minutes I was in the water, swimming out in the direction of the yacht, then turning over onto my back, eyes closed as I soaked up the glorious sun, the only sound the soft suck and slap of water against the 'Helena's' prow. After a little while I rocked back onto my stomach, swimming through the smooth water towards the shore, the sun almost blinding as it dazzled off the glittering surface of

24

the sea.

I swung my towel round my shoulder and began to walk along the sand until I came to a small rowing boat, upturned and disused. Stretching my towel in its shade I lay down and closed my eyes.

It was the muted sound of sandalled feet that woke me. I sat up, shielding my eyes from the sun. In the distance the unmistakeable figure of Helena Van de Naude in jeans and open necked shirt ran lightly across the sand and into the shallows to the dinghy. Behind her was a leanly built man with a shock of red hair. He took the oars, rowing strongly out towards the yacht. If it was Mr Van de Naude he wasn't nearly as old as I had been led to believe.

I rose to my feet, wondering again why he had been so angry at my arrival, and when I would be asked to leave.

When I reached my room I closed the shutters, took a disprin for my throbbing head, and tried to sleep. It was Peggy who woke me.

"It's a quarter to eight," she said. "I didn't think you would want to be late for dinner, not on your first evening."

"Thanks Peggy, I'll be down in five minutes." Hurriedly I changed into a long velvet skirt and silk blouse, but by the time I reached the dining-room everyone else was seated.

"I'm sorry I'm late," I said awkwardly. "I fell asleep. . . ."

"There's no need to apologise," Helena Van de Naude said with her wide smile. "Sit down and let me introduce you to everyone."

"I'm John Van de Naude," the powerfully built man at the head of the table said, standing up and shaking my hand. "I'm sorry I wasn't here to meet you, but I hope you will be very happy with us, Lucy."

"Thank you," I said as my hand was crushed in his. He was a strikingly handsome man with steel grey hair that waved thickly and deep lines running from nose to mouth. He must have been nearly sixty, but there was no spare flesh on his body, only solid muscle and bone. John Van de Naude was a man who kept himself fit.

"Leonie Blanchard, Helena's secretary," he was saying,

25

and I had a swift impression of silky blonde hair and glossy lips. "And Ian Lyall, Danielle's tutor."

The man I had seen earlier boarding the yacht with Helena Van de Naude, said pleasantly: "I'm very pleased to meet you."

I managed a smile, grateful for the intervention of Peggy with a laden tray. So it was Danielle's tutor who had shouted at Helena Van de Naude. . . .

"Helena tells me you have already made friends with Danielle," John Van de Naude was saying. "You will find her an easy child to handle. She can be a little stubborn at times, but she is very sweet-natured."

Leonie Blanchard's eyes rested on me thoughtfully. She was in her mid-twenties with a beautiful heart-shaped face and curving mouth. Her eyes were a brilliant, feline green, lustrous under rather heavy lids, and the slender gold bracelets on her wrists and the deceptively simple chiffon dress she wore, indicated she was not totally reliant on her salary as secretary. She toyed with the stem of her glass, saying in a husky voice: "Excuse me asking, but I'm sure I recognise you. Aren't you engaged to Max Wyndham?"

"No," I said, the blood rushing to my face.

She leant her head against the high carved back of her chair. "How strange. I could swear I've seen you with him. It was at the Monaco Formula one race last year."

"I *was* engaged to Max. I'm not any longer."

There was a ripple of interest around the dinner table and I inwardly cursed the smiling Miss Blanchard.

"How is Max?" she asked intimately. "I haven't seen him for ages."

"I've no idea."

"A magnificent driver," Ian Lyall said unexpectedly. "I saw the Monaco race on television. Finished in the third fastest time if I remember rightly."

I remembered the Monaco race. A long, laughing week in the Riviera heat.

"I thought your face was familiar," John Van de Naude said. "Must have seen it in the papers a dozen times."

"And your engagement is off, is it?" Leonie asked, her eyebrows raised delicately.

26

"Yes," I said shortly, "and I would really rather not discuss it."

"Of course not," John Van de Naude said hastily, "foolish of us to have discussed it at all. It was just the surprise. . . ."

"Prawn cocktail or melon?" Helena Van de Naude asked practically, breaking the awkward pause.

"Melon."

"Peggy tells me you play tennis?"

"Yes," I said, forcing back the memory of a soft autumn day and Max teaching me on the familiar courts at Crailsham Place.

"Good," John Van de Naude said smiling. "Leonie doesn't play and Ian's playing is atrocious. . . ."

Ian Lyall laughed. "Atrocious or not, I still won the last set we played. . . ."

The light-hearted bantering continued throughout dinner. Employees at the villa D'Este were certainly not made to feel their place. Afterwards we sat out on the lamplit terrace with our coffees, the purple silhouette of the pines deepening slowly to black against the night sky.

Ian Lyall, who had been deep in conversation with Leonie, came across with his drink and sat next to me.

"You look a little tired," he said considerately. "All a bit much in one day. New job, new people."

"Yes, I am rather," I agreed, finding it hard to believe that the quiet spoken young man beside me had, only hours ago, sworn angrily at his employer's wife. And about me.

"If you're tired, have an early night," Helena Van de Naude said. "You'll feel better for it tomorrow."

"Thank you," I said gratefully. "I will."

As I walked away from them, towards the French windows, I could see their reflections in the dark glass. Ian Lyall's head turned, watching me thoughtfully.

All trace of friendliness had left his face. His mouth was a thin line, his eyes narrowed. I shivered. Ian Lyall had not wanted me to come to the villa D'Este. But why? What possible difference could my arrival make to him?"

FOUR

In the next few weeks I settled down into a comfortable routine. There was no talk of my leaving, and the Van de Naudes seemed happy with my work. The mornings were my own and I spent them mainly in swimming and sun-bathing, occasionally taking the car into Palma to shop. The afternoons and early evenings were spent with Danielle. Ian Lyall continued to be pleasant to my face and to watch me unnervingly when he thought I wasn't aware of it. Despite his friendliness I avoided him as much as possible. Leonie I saw very little of. She drifted into dinner each evening with a half smile on her lips and lazy amusement in her eyes, and though Max's name was never mentioned again, I knew that she knew him, and knew him well. The knowledge didn't help our relationship.

Peggy and Mario I liked, the Van de Naudes were more like friends than employers, and Danielle was a pet. It was three weeks later that the accident happened and I first met Steve Patterson.

It had been a lovely day. We had gone for a picnic at Cape Formentor, sharing our sandwiches with some friendly goats at the lighthouse. Later, we had motored down to the beach and Danielle had played in the surf, gathering strands of scarlet seaweed and trailing them in the sea behind her. When she had finished we had raced each other along the sand back to the car and bought ice-creams before heading back to the villa.

As we approached the treacherous Devesas, I saw that the sun was touching the mountain ridges, the light smoking with the first hint of dusk. I increased speed, not wanting to be caught on the wrong side of the headland in the dark.

28

The road narrowed, twisting steeply between wooded slopes and the sickening plunge to the sea. In the distance I heard the sound of a car, and from the whine of the engine he was coming fast. Too fast. I slowed down, climbing round the first of the hairpin bends, and through the serried ranks of pines saw a large Cadillac speeding recklessly behind me. The dusk was deepening, the shadows lengthening across the road. Apprehensively I pulled over as far as I could. Seconds later he screamed round the bend behind me, not giving an inch. With a cry of alarm I spun the wheel, swerving out of his way as he roared down on me, metal rending against metal. Danielle was screaming and the force of the other car as it scraped alongside us sent me skidding off the road. For what seemed like eternity we leaped towards the abyss of sky, rock and sea. There was blood in my mouth and a thundering in my ears and then the tyres finally gripped ground, the brake pedal responding at last. The front wheels smashed into rock, shattering the windscreen and the car slithered to a halt, rocking wildly.

Above Danielle's terrified sobs came another sound. Another engine. A sports car hummed round the bend, careering dizzily as it saw us. I was still clinging to the wheel, the world spinning blackly, when he wrenched open the door.

"My God! Are you all right? What the hell happened?"

"Miss Matthews! Miss Matthews!"

I stumbled from the car, flinging my arms around the sobbing Danielle.

"Danielle! Are you all right? Oh Danielle! Danielle!"

Her terrified hands clung to my neck. I hugged her fiercely.

"It's all right baby. It's all right. Are you hurt? Let me see. . . ."

With trembling hands I felt her body, crying with relief at finding only bleeding knees and cut forehead.

"Thank God for seat belts," my rescuer observed dryly. "Do you think you could stop scaring the hell out of me and walk back onto the road?"

I looked around me. We were only inches from the cliff

29

edge and the hundred foot drop to the sea. I felt violently sick.

"Don't mind me," my rescuer said. I smiled waveringly.

"It's the shock."

"Have a cigarette."

"Thanks."

He carried Danielle, and on shaky legs I followed him across to his car. She raised a white face to mine.

"That was very silly, wasn't it?"

I smiled weakly. "It was Danny, it was."

"Did that man try to kill us?"

"No, darling. He was drunk. He must have been drunk. I don't think he even saw us till he forced me off the road."

"Feel like a candy?" our rescuer asked her.

Danielle brightened considerably. "Yes please. I was very brave, wasn't I?"

"Sure were," he agreed gravely. She turned to me.

"Will you tell Daddy I was very brave?"

I squeezed her tightly. "Of course I will, my love."

"And can I have a bandage on my knee? A big one?"

"Anything you like, Danielle. Anything at all."

Satisfied, Danielle put another sweet in her mouth and began to look rather pleased with herself.

"How about me giving you a lift back to where you're staying?"

I looked at him properly for the first time and smiled. He was an American, somewhere in his mid-twenties, with untidy fair hair and friendly face.

"What about the car?"

"Leave it," he said. "You're in no state to drive and your car is in no state to be driven."

"It isn't my car."

He grinned. "Then I don't envy you the explanations. What the hell happened?"

"I don't know. He must have been drunk. He came hurtling round the bend as if he was on a speedway track, and then he just kept on going, didn't pull over, didn't slow down, nothing. If I hadn't swerved he would have rammed straight into us." I looked at the tyre marks where my car had left the road, burning their way over the coarse grass to the cliff edge. "Only there was nowhere to swerve to."

"Except the sea," he said grimly. "Come on, let's get you home."

"Are we going in that speed buggy?" Danielle asked interestedly, pointing towards the sports car.

"Sure are, and with a bag of candy," the American said, settling her in the tiny space at the back, saying to me: "Resiliant little things, aren't they? If that had happened to me I wouldn't want to go near a car again. Especially a speed buggy!"

Danielle curled up with her bag of sweets and he said: "Did you get a good look at the driver?"

"No. I doubt if I would recognise him again. He was young and he was dark. That's all."

"A Spaniard?"

"It could have been."

"Are you on holiday here?"

"No, I live here."

"I reckon your husband is going to be one angry man tonight when he sees where that car is!"

"I'm not married. Danielle isn't my little girl. I'm her nanny."

"So it isn't such a bad day after all," he said disarmingly. "I'm Steve Patterson. Twenty-three. American and single."

"Pleased to meet you, Mr Patterson. I'm Lucy Matthews. English and twenty-one."

"You're going to have to do a lot of explaining to your employers!"

"Don't," I said feelingly. "I've only been with them a few weeks."

"Don't worry," he said with a broad grin. "I'll keep you company if the going gets too tough!"

Helena Van de Naude was alone on the terrace when we got back to the villa. At the sight of Steve Patterson she rose to her feet, and then as she saw Danielle's blood-caked knees and forehead her face whitened and she broke into a run.

"Lucy! What happened? Has there been an accident? Is Danielle hurt?"

"A little. She's cut herself but the bleeding has stopped."

31

Alarmed, she swung Danielle up into her arms. "Are you all right, Danny? What happened?"

"We crashed," Danielle said with satisfaction. "We nearly got killed and I was very brave and our friend gave me some sweets called candy and I like them."

"Dear God!" Her arms tightened around her. "Was it your car?" she asked, looking at Steve.

"No. I'm just the knight on a white charger who was passing by at the time. Steve Patterson by name."

"Then who. . . ."

I said: "It happened on the mountain road. At the Devesas. We were driving on quite happily when I heard this car coming up behind us. It was obviously going too fast. I'd rounded the first of the bends and slowed down and pulled over . . . he could have got past . . . but he didn't even try. He must have been doing seventy at least. It was all so quick. . . ."

Steve said: "He forced her off the road. There was all of a foot left between them and the sea."

Helena Van de Naude's eyes seemed to have sunk into her head.

"You'd better have a drink," she said unsteadily. "I'll take Danny upstairs to Peggy and join you in a minute." Still carrying Danielle in her arms she left the room.

"She seems like a nice lady," Steve observed, settling himself on a sofa.

"She is."

"No hysterics."

"No, she isn't the type."

"It wasn't your fault," he said comfortingly. "She realises that."

"I nearly killed her only child," I said bleakly.

"Rubbish. You saved her life. Another fraction of an inch and it wouldn't have been paintwork that would have ripped off the car. It would have been the whole side. Danielle's side. That was a piece of smart driving. You must have been taught by an expert."

"I was."

The door clicked open and Helena Van de Naude said: "What will you have to drink? Whisky? Brandy?"

32

"Whisky," Steve said. She poured him his drink.

"Did you see what happened, Mr Patterson?"

"No. I only saw him fleetingly through the trees. It was a distinctive car though. A powder-blue Cadillac, and travelling fast."

"He was drunk," I said. "There's no other explanation."

"Then we'll find him," she said, her mouth drawn in a tight line.

"It shouldn't be too hard," Steve said. "He took half the paint off the Fiat. His own car must be badly marked."

She looked at me. "Are you feeling better now, Lucy?"

"Yes. I'm sorry. . . ."

"Nonsense," she said crisply, the colour back in her face. "There's nothing to be sorry for. I don't hold you responsible in any way whatever."

"You'll report it to the police?" Steve asked.

"Yes. Yes of course." She looked suddenly old.

"The sooner the better," Steve said. "They may be able to pick the car up straight away."

"Yes," she rose to her feet. "I'll do it now."

"Should I have offered to do it for her?" Steve asked. "She didn't look as if she liked the idea."

"She's seen rather a lot of them lately and seeing them again will only bring back unpleasant memories."

Steve waited expectantly.

"Her previous nanny committed suicide only a couple of months ago."

"Suicide?" Steve said unbelievingly.

I nodded. "She jumped from a block of flats in Ria Square."

"Hellfire! What did she do a crazy thing like that for?"

"No-one knows. I don't think Mrs Van de Naude has got over the shock yet. Janet had been with her since she was sixteen. She came here straight from school."

"How old was she?" he asked quietly.

"Nineteen."

He put his whisky down. "Poor kid," he said feelingly. "Poor, dumb kid. . . ."

FIVE

Danielle recovered remarkably well from the accident, very proud of how brave she had been. Leonie had raised her pencil-thin eyebrows, saying: "These mountain roads are so narrow that it's possible it was your fault, Lucy. Ian thinks you didn't pull over far enough to let him pass."

I didn't give a damn what Ian Lyall thought. I said: "If I'd pulled over anymore I'd have been in the Mediterranean!"

She closed her eyes, stretching langorously out in the hammock, her face tilted to the sun. "Palma has an interesting visitor?"

I came in right on cue. "Who?"

"Max," she said lazily. "He flew in yesterday. Don't you read your papers?"

"I've had more on my mind," I said curtly, my heart beginning to race.

"I must say your Mr Patterson pales into insignificance beside him. I never did go for that fresh faced American boy look."

"Steve Patterson is very attractive," I said defensively.

The mocking smile deepened. "I'm glad you think so, Lucy."

Annoyed with both her and myself I picked up the book I had been reading and walked back into the villa, the sound of Leonie's soft laughter echoing behind me.

I was beginning to find the after dinner gatherings on the terrace increasingly claustrophobic, the only relief, Steve Patterson's company. We had gone into Palma for dinner the night of the Cadillac incident, and he was picking me up again that evening. Until Leonie had mentioned Max I had been looking forward to it. The breath was tight in my chest as I walked along the sunlit corridor to my room.

Why should Max come to Majorca unless it was to see me? Aunt Katherine must have told him where I was. He could only have one reason for seeing me. . . . I stood at the open window of my room, hardly able to breath. If he came tonight and I was out with Steve. . . . Yet if I stayed in, waiting, wouldn't that be what I had always done where Max was concerned? I turned decisively, my mind made up. I would go out with Steve. It would do Max good to find me out with another man. He would just have to come again in the morning. It wasn't a decision that brought peace of mind. For the rest of the day I was like a cat on hot bricks, my heart leaping when I heard the sound of a car, plunging again when it turned out to be only Mario returning from the market. Even Danielle noticed.

"You don't look very happy," she said as I tucked her up in bed.

"I was thinking about something," I said truthfully, sitting down beside her. "What would you like to do to-morrow?"

"Could we go to Valldemossa? I went there once with Janet and we saw where Chopin lived and saw his little piano."

"That sounds nice." I opened the book I was reading to her. my thoughts far away.

"We've nearly finished it now, haven't we?" she said pensively.

"We're on the very last chapter."

Her bottom lip quivered.

"What on earth is the matter, Danielle?"

"I don't want to finish it," she said, her eyes filling with tears.

"But we'll read another one."

"That one is special."

"It's a very nice book, but the man who wrote it wrote other books too. We can start another one tomorrow night."

Two large tears slid down her cheeks.

"Don't be a goose, Danielle," I said gently.

"I'm not a goose. But Janet began reading that book and now it's finished and Janet is dead and. . . ."

I held her close, her tears wetting my face. "Janet would want you to finish it and read other books."

"*You* won't go away, will you?"

"No, darling. I won't go away. Snuggle down under the covers and I'll hold your hand while I read."

It was half an hour before I left her. By then she was asleep, her arms around Mr Sam, her teddy-bear. I turned the light off and went back into my own room to get ready for Steve, but my thoughts were not on him as I brushed my hair and sprayed perfume on my wrists and throat. If Max had flown in yesterday he had had plenty of time to get in touch with me. What could be delaying him?

There was the distant sound of a car approaching the villa and I ran to the window, swallowing my disappointment as minutes later Steve stepped out onto the terrace, his shock of fair hair nearly blond in the dusk. What I had said to Leonie had been the truth. He *was* attractive. Tall and loose-limbed, with an easygoing friendliness that put people at their ease. I liked Steve Patterson. I liked him very much, and I wasn't going to let the shadow of Max spoil our evening. Not even if the effort killed me.

He gave me an appreciative whistle as I went out to meet him.

"That's what I call a dress. How do I live up to it?"

"Easily."

He grinned down at me. "Now I know why I like you. You flatter me."

My heels tapped metallically on the terrace and I saw Peggy's curtain drop back quickly into place. I smiled. There wasn't much that Peggy missed. We walked quickly down the corridor that led to the courtyard, the empty rooms on either side seeming to whisper with a life of their own. I was glad when we finally reached it and heard the sound of the gently falling water of the fountain. The night was warm and scented. In the darkness a frog dived with a soft plop into the lily pond, the rings of water silvered in the moonlight.

"Heard anything from the police yet?" Steve asked as he opened the car door for me.

"Not a thing."

36

The car surged forward between the bronze studded courtyard gates and dropped down to the track across the darkened headland.

"Strange. I would have thought a powder-blue Cadillac with half the paint ripped off the side would be an easy enough car to spot."

"Me too. I get the uncomfortable feeling that they think I imagined it."

"How do you mean?"

"That they think I simply overshot the road and cooked up the drunken driver story to cover myself. They haven't bothered to speak to me themselves, only Helena."

"What about what I said about the car speeding?"

"I think they've put you down as a romantic attachment!"

He grinned. "There's an idea to brighten up the evening. But from what Leonie was saying, you're still involved in one."

The car bucked off the headland onto the mountain road, gathering speed as it swooped round the first of the bends.

"Just what *did* Leonie say?"

"That you're engaged to Max Wyndham."

"Was."

"I must have heard her wrong."

"I don't think so. It's the sort of deliberate mistake Leonie *would* make."

"I thought it might be. I'm not so unobservant not to notice an engagement ring. Not that it would have made any difference. It's the little gold ones that have me running for the hills!"

I stared out of the window as we plunged into a tunnel of trees, hardly aware of him, my thoughts riveted firmly back on Max.

He drove on in silence for a while and then said: "I gather it went deep?"

I said simply: "I've known him all my life." It seemed unnecessary to say I had loved him all my life as well.

"I see."

From the tone of his voice I thought perhaps he did. The lights of a small village swam up to meet us, then streamed

37

by, swallowed in the darkness.

"How is Danielle? No after effects?"

"None at all," I said, grateful for the change of subject. "She's rather pleased she was able to show us how brave she is."

"She was as well. Have you taken her out in the car since it happened?"

"You and Helena are birds of a feather. She made me take Danielle out in the Audi the next morning. Said it would prevent us losing our nerve. The Fiat has already been towed back. Mario is still working on it."

"She was right about you driving again straight away," Steve said. "Should cure any nerves."

"Wrong. I shan't have any nerve till that Cadillac and its driver are found."

"Don't worry," he said grimly. "He'll be found. If the police don't find him, I will."

In the glow of the dashboard I saw the expression on his face and stiffened, surprised at what I saw there. His eyes met mine in the driving mirror and he smiled: "Let's forget about it for now. We came out to enjoy ourselves. Wining, dining and dancing, remember?" and he accelerated, zooming past a huddle of houses towards the bright lights of Palma.

The streets were thick with tourists and we had to slow down to a crawl as we nosed our way through a cobbled square. the trees surrounding it hung with fairy lights. A crowd of laughing teenagers surged round the car, bringing us to a standstill. Idly I wound the window down, and then caught my breath, the foot high lettering showing clearly. Ria Square. Steve turned his head.

"Are you all right?"

"Yes. . . ." I pointed to the sign and the dark block of flats soaring behind it, as I did so, he said:

"Do you see what I see?"

In the narrow entrance to the flats I saw a man standing. There was something familiar about the angle of the head and the hunched shoulders. Then, as we watched, he sauntered down the few steps to the street, stepping out into the lamplight. There was no mistaking that head of red hair. It was Ian Lyall.

"What on earth. . . ." I began.

"I take it he was the boy-friend?"

"Not that I know of. Peggy never mentioned it. I got the impression there wasn't one."

The traffic began to move again and behind us Ian Lyall crossed the square and disappeared into the shadows beneath the trees.

I shivered. "He really is the strangest man. Did I tell you that the day I arrived I overheard him shouting at Helena Van de Naude, saying. 'She'll have to go,' he could only have been talking about me."

"*Shouting* at her?" Steve asked incredulously.

"Yes. Mrs Van de Naude said something like: 'She's here now,' and he said: 'Too bloody right she is. She'll have to go.' "

"Did he, indeed?" Steve said curiously. "Just what gives Lyall the right to give orders to his employer's wife? Was anything said to you?"

"No. Everything has been sweetness and light. He *looks* at me oddly sometimes, but he's always perfectly civil."

"But not to Helena Van de Naude," Steve said musingly. "I find that very strange."

"I told you," I said, as we sped out of a narrow street and onto the brightly lit sea front. "He's a strange man!"

SIX

There were no messages for me when I returned to the villa in the early hours of the morning. Max had not been, nor had he phoned. Fighting crushing disappointment I walked quietly up the dark staircase and along the corridor to my room. He would come tomorrow. Perhaps Aunt Katherine had forgotten the name of the villa. . . .

The next morning at breakfast, Ian Lyall said: "Did you have a nice time last night?"

"Yes, thank you."

Leonie, with her cat that got the cream smile, said: "So did I."

"I'd forgotten you had gone out," he said, pouring himself a fresh cup of coffee. "Where did you go?"

"Palma."

"With the new boyfriend?"

The smile was more of a smirk. "How do you know about my new boyfriend?" she asked lazily.

"Peggy. She's infallible."

She shrugged carelessly. "What did you do?"

"Stayed in and had a game of cards with Mario."

I stopped buttering my toast and stared at him.

Leonie laughed. "Then you're a fool. That man is a blatant cheat."

And Ian Lyall a blatant liar I thought as Peggy entered with another jug of coffee. Her lips were closed in a tight line and I wondered if she had overheard Leonie.

"Good morning, Peggy," I said, with more cheerfulness than I felt.

"Good morning, did you have a nice time last night?"

"Lovely, thank you Peggy."

She piled some empty cereal bowls onto her tray. "I'm

glad of that, and I don't want you to fret when I tell you I had to go in to Danielle last night."

"What for? Was she ill?"

"Not ill exactly. More brooding if you know what I mean. She had a nasty dream and woke up crying and asking for you. I told her you had gone to Palma and wouldn't be back till late. Then she really began to cry. Saying you wouldn't come back at all, like Janet. Terrible time I had with her. I had to go for her mother in the end and she soothed her down and gave her some medicine. I've left it in the bathroom on the shelf. The doctor prescribed it for her when she was having such terrible dreams after Janet's death. Helped her to sleep better. She hasn't got over it yet, I'm sure of that. Still, it's only to be expected under the circumstances. . . ."

"Is there any more toast?" Ian asked hastily, stopping her in full flow.

She said sharply: "There's always as much fresh toast as anybody wants and well you know it!" and she whisked his plate away, slamming the door behind her.

Leonie laughed. "Thank God you saved us from another rhapsody about that wretched Grey girl." She pushed her chair from the table. "You can tell Peggy I've gone out for the day and won't be in for lunch."

Ian Lyall raised sandy brows as she disappeared along the terrace with a clicking of high heels.

"The new boyfriend would seem to be in earnest," he said, stirring his coffee and smiling across at me.

"You were in Palma last night, not playing cards with Mario," I said bluntly.

"You're mistaken," he said, his eyes meeting mine. "People are always thinking they've seen me when they haven't. It's the hair. Every time anyone sees a thatch like mine they automatically think it's me."

"It *was* you. You were coming out of the flats in Ria Square."

The pause before he answered was only a fraction of a second, but it was enough.

"You're wrong," and I knew he was lying. "Ask Mario."

Peggy came in with fresh toast and he said, changing the

subject: "Has Leonie told you about Max Wyndham?"

"No," I said, no longer caring whether he had been in Palma or not. "What about him?"

He looked vaguely uncomfortable and waited till Peggy had left the room before saying: "Apparently he's married some French film actress. They were both in the El Cid last night and Leonie says the street outside was jammed with autograph hunters and well-wishers. Lots of police around too, because that Russian, Katchorsky, was among their party. I read in the papers that Britain has given him asylum. That won't please the Russians. . . ." He put his knife down. "It hasn't come as a shock to you, has it?" his face showed genuine concern.

"Of course not," I said, my chest hurting so that I thought I would faint. "I couldn't care less who Max marries."

"Well, he's certainly chosen a looker," Ian said cheerfully. "I wonder if it will last?" and he dug his hands into his jeans pockets and left the room whistling.

I remained seated, the room swimming around me. Max married! And to Claudette! I had thought he had wanted his freedom, that Claudette was only one of many. It had never occurred to me that he would marry her. Shakily I rose to my feet, stumbling to the privacy of my room. Marriage! The word had the finality of a death knell.

I closed the shutters against the brilliant sunlight and as I did so, saw Ian Lyall and Helena Van de Naude, heads close together, deep in conversation. His good humour had vanished. He seemed angry. His face flushed, his eyebrows pulled together in a deep frown. I moved towards the bed and lay down, the rays of the sun slanting through the shutters. Now there was truly no going back. Crailsham Place could be a second home no longer. Not with Max and his bride there. The word spun in my brain, echoing and re-echoing. I began to weep, covering my face with my hands and turning to the wall.

In the afternoon, my face washed and carefully made-up, I took Danielle to Valldemossa. We walked through the village, down a steep winding track that led into meadows and a small stream. I unpacked the picnic things while

42

Danielle paddled in the icy water, screaming with pleasure.

"Ooo, it's freezing cold, Miss Matthews. Won't you come in?"

"No thanks, Danielle. Come and get a sandwich."

"I'm glad I came. I thought it might not be as much fun a second time. First time things are usually best aren't they?"

"Perhaps we could do a first time thing today as well. Would you like to visit some caves?"

"Oooh, can we really? Real caves? Under the ground?"

I nodded. Her eyes shone. "That's a *super* idea, Miss Matthews. I *am* glad you came. I only had Miss Blanchard to talk to before and she doesn't like little girls."

"I'm sure she does, Danielle."

"She doesn't like me," Danielle said cheerfully. "I can tell. Do you think Mr Lyall would like to come to the caves as well?"

"Good heavens, no. Why should he?"

"I just thought he might."

"Anyway, I meant to go to the caves today, after our picnic."

"I know you did," she said unabashed. "I thought I could go and tell him."

"We can't go back to the villa now, Danielle. There isn't the time."

"Silly," Danielle said giggling. "He's in the village. In that little shop with the red and white shade outside."

"Mr Lyall is?"

"Yes. I expect he wants to make sure we don't have another accident."

"Then perhaps we'd better have a word with him and put his mind at rest!"

Beneath a striped awning three metal tables and shabby wicker chairs waited vacantly for customers.

"He isn't here, Danielle. You must have made a mistake."

"No," she said, gripping my hand and leading me confidently into the dim interior.

Ian Lyall looked distinctly sheepish.

"If you wanted to come with us, we could have shared a car," I said, not trying to disguise my anger.

43

He smiled. "I just thought I'd keep an eye on you, that's all."

"In case I drove over a cliff?"

"Don't be so touchy."

"I *was* forced off the road the other day. I'm not such a lousy driver I'm not safe to take a child out without a watchdog!"

"No-one said you were. Stop being so over-sensitive."

"I don't like being followed!"

"For God's sake," he said good-humouredly. "I'd nothing else to do today. I just thought that I'd keep an eye on you. After all, they haven't found the Cadillac yet. I didn't want anything to spoil your day."

"Then you're too late," I said rudely. "It just has!"

He flushed, brushing his hair back with his hand. "I *have* offended, haven't I?"

"Yes, you have. We're going to see the Caves of Drach and I *don't* want a nursemaid!"

Angrily I turned my back on him and stalked across the square to the car.

"Sometimes it sounds as if you don't like Mr Lyall," Danielle said chattily. "I like him. Before him I had a teacher who was French and very strict. He didn't like it when he left. I heard him tell Mummy that she had no grounds for dismissing him."

"That's enough, Danielle. You hear far too much."

"I do, don't I? I'd much rather have Mr Lyall than my old teacher. He and Mummy are friends, you see."

"Yes," I said faintly, wondering just how much Danielle saw and heard. "Isn't that a goat over there, look . . . behind those trees."

Danielle agreed that it was a goat and went on to tell me how much she wanted one and how she might get one if only she could persuade her daddy they didn't smell.

I didn't enjoy any part of the visit to the Caves of Drach. I could think of nothing but that Max was in Palma. On his honeymoon. Bleakly I wondered how Aunt Katherine would reconcile herself to having the glamorous Claudette as daughter-in-law. And how Claudette would reconcile herself to the other side of Max. The side the gossip

44

columnists didn't know. The side that loved to tramp for miles with the dogs at his heels, to play chess in the firelight, to read for hours in companionable silence, to ride the horses across the flat country surrounding Crailsham Place, when the first snow had fallen and the world was a white wilderness.

I couldn't visualise the party loving Claudette striding around the estate with the dogs yapping around her. Or even riding for that matter. It didn't seem likely that Crailsham Place would see much of its future mistress.

When we came out of the caves, the sky was flushing to rose, the shadows lengthening. Sleepily Danielle curled in the car seat.

"That was the *nicest* first thing I've ever done," she said. "It's been a lovely day, hasn't it?"

I couldn't answer her, merely squeezed her hand and headed back to the mountains and home.

SEVEN

There was a visitor at the villa D'Este when we returned.

"David!" Danielle squealed as we stepped out onto the terrace, racing across to where her parents sat beneath the shade of a magnolia tree. "David!"

A large, handsome African turned his head, smiling broadly as she hurtled into his outstretched arms. Laughing, he swung her into the air.

"You've grown, little Danny! You're nearly as big as me!"

"Silly," she gasped. "*No-one* could be as big as you, David. You're bigger than *everyone*."

No-one seemed to notice me. John Van de Naude was in swimming trunks, his body still glistening with water. Helena had a short towelling robe over her costume, her hair wound carelessly into a knot on the top of her head, her long legs curled beneath her in her chair as she laughed across at her visitor. I turned to go to my room, but as I did so, Helena Van de Naude called out gaily: "Lucy! Please come and join us."

I walked over to them and John Van de Naude rose to his feet, saying: "Lucy, I'd like you to meet an old friend of ours, David Katjavivi."

My hand was crushed in a giant handshake. Close to, David Katjavivi was even bigger, broader and blacker, his head the magnificent leonine of the African portraits in the villa, the lines of forehead and jaw, powerful and strong.

"I've heard a lot about you," he said, and as he smiled I knew that I had seen him before. Not only in the portraits, but in the flesh . . . or was it on film?"

Reading my thoughts, Helena said: "You've probably seen David's picture in the papers or seen him on the news. He's the leader of APFO, the organisation that I work for

46

and which keeps Leonie so busy."

"APFO?"

"African Peoples Freedom Organisation," she said with a smile.

"Is the paperwork finished?" David Katjavivi asked, turning to Helena again.

"All but John's final speech. It's in its second draft. Do you want to see it now or after dinner?"

"Now I think," David Katjavivi said, putting his glass down.

"Oh," Danielle said disappointed. "What about my stories? You haven't told me any for *ages*."

"Later," he said gently. "When you are in bed, then I will come and tell you stories."

Her eyes glowed. "Promise?"

"Promise."

"It's time for your bath, Danny," her mother said practically.

She slipped off his knee, saying resignedly: "I'm *always* having baths. I have one *every* night!"

"Yes Danny, and you're going to have one tonight."

"It's not fair. When I grow up I'm not going to have baths. Not *ever*!"

She took hold of my hand and skipped across the terrace, telling me all about David's wonderful stories, the ordeal of the bath forgotten: "He knows all about lions and warriors and all *sorts* of exciting things, and he never gets tired of telling me them. I hope he's staying a long time. Then we can really have fun!"

Peggy met us at the foot of the stairs.

"Did you have a nice time?"

"*Super*, Peggy," Danielle said enthusiastically. "We had our picnic and then we went to visit some caves, absolutely *enormous*. There was one that even had a *lake* in it, and we went in a boat and there was a man singing and it was *fabulous*!"

"Well, I'm glad you enjoyed yourselves," Peggy said comfortably. "I was beginning to get worried. You were gone an awful long time."

"*Everyone* is worried about us," Danielle said with a

47

world weary sigh. "Even Mr Lyall came to make sure we were all right."

Peggy looked at me. "I thought you'd gone by yourselves?"

"We had. For reasons I don't yet understand, Ian followed us as far as Valldemossa. Keeping an eye on us was the expression he used when I asked him what he was doing."

"Dear me, what a strange thing to do. Though of course, Mrs Van de Naude might have asked him to, after the car accident you know."

"Perhaps, but I think she would have told me."

"She's a lot on her mind at the moment," Peggy said confidingly. "What with Mr Katjavivi coming and all."

Danielle had gone on up the stairs. I said: "Is he a regular visitor, Peggy?"

"Oh yes. Always here he is. He's the leader of Mrs Van de Naude's organisation."

"So Mrs Van de Naude just said. What organisation is it?"

Peggy looked slightly flustered. "To be truthful I don't rightly know. Something to do with Africa. Mrs Van de Naude is African herself though you wouldn't think it to look at her. She looks more Spanish to me. She does a lot of work though and people are always coming to stay for a few days. We had two Anglican ministers not long ago. Nice gentlemen they were. Black, you know, but nice." She glanced over her shoulder to make sure no-one was approaching and lowered her voice: "You won't credit this, but when she married Mr Van de Naude they had to leave South Africa on account of how he was white and she was coloured. Shame I call it, but there you are. That's their law and laws is laws when all said and done. Not everyone thinks alike or ever will." She shrugged philosophically. "They're happy and that's what matters. Not that it didn't make things difficult for Mr Bradley, because it did. He was over here not long ago. A very nice young man he is. He stayed on in South Africa to finish his education when his father re-married. Not that he's a schoolboy now. Twenty-two or three he must be. A nicer, more well-spoken young man you couldn't wish to meet. I took to him straight away. I said to Mario. . . ."

48

There came the sound of chairs scraping back on the terrace and she said hurriedly: "What am I thinking of? Chattering here and the dinner still to do. . . ." She bustled back towards the kitchen and I followed Danielle up the stairs. The mystery of Mrs Van de Naude's need for a secretary finally solved.

Leonie drifted into the bathroom as I was shampooing Danielle's hair. I glanced round, surprised. Visits from Leonie were unheard of.

"We have a visitor, or did you know?"

"I know."

"Yes, he's not exactly easy to miss, is he?" She leaned against the door as I towelled Danielle's hair. "The Saviour of the African race. Dinner will be just one long bore . . . and I hate being bored."

"So do I," a little voice said clearly from beneath the towel.

Leonie's green eyes flickered dangerously, but she said merely: "There's going to be a party in honour of our visitor tomorrow night. I imagine you will be asked to bring the devastating Mr Patterson."

I ignored the sarcasm on the word devastating, and said only: "Will we be invited?"

She raised her eyebrows, saying mockingly: "But of course! No class distinctions at the villa D'Este, darling. Haven't you learned that yet?" and she left the room, leaving the door open and a draught blowing on the naked Danielle. I closed it after her and as I helped Danielle into her nightdress, she said: "She *smiles* a lot, but it isn't like when other people smile, is it?"

"Into bed, or you'll have no time for a story."

"I haven't had my medicine yet *or* my hot chocolate."

"Do you really need your medicine, Danielle?"

"I'll have bad dreams if I don't," she said blackmailingly.

I laughed. "All right. Get into bed and I'll bring it in to you."

"*And* my hot chocolate. . . ."

"Your hot chocolate is by your bed, cooling."

"Goody," she said, scampering quickly into her room. I picked up her clothes and the medicine bottle and followed

49

her. My head was beginning to ache and when I had finished the first chapter I said: "No more tonight, Danny. David Katjavivi will be up to tell you a story soon. Be careful with your drink. You won't spill it, will you?"

"Silly," said Danielle affectionately. "I'm not a baby. I'm six."

I kissed her cheek. "Goodnight, pet lamb. Pleasant dreams."

I left the light on and closed the door quietly behind me. On the threshold I fell over Ian Lyall.

He steadied me saying: "Is David in there?"

"No, why?"

"He said he was going to tell Danielle a story and I'm looking for him."

I began to move away and he stepped in front of me.

"Did you enjoy your trip to the caves this afternoon?"

"Yes. You didn't follow us, did you?"

He grinned, looking disarmingly boyish. "Suspicious little devil, aren't you? No, I didn't follow you and I'm sorry if I offended. Somewhere I got off on the wrong foot with you. It isn't just this afternoon's incident, is it? You've been unfriendly with me ever since you arrived. Why?"

I was in no mood for a heart to heart talk with Ian Lyall.

"I have a headache and all I want to do is lie down in a dark room. Would you make my apologies at dinner please?"

"Sure. Would you like a disprin bringing up?"

"I have some in my room. Goodnight."

"Goodnight," he said, and I knew that he was watching me as I walked away, but what his expression was I neither knew nor cared.

It had been a long day. The longest of my life. And there was no way I could survive it any longer. Instinct told me that Leonie would mention Max's marriage at the dinner table and there was no way I could handle it. Not tonight.

I closed my bedroom door behind me, then pulled the blinds, plunging the room into merciful darkness.

EIGHT

Two o'clock found me restless and awake. Wearily I reached for my dressing-gown and padded over to the open window.

In the distance I could hear the sea whispering round the base of the cliff and from the direction of the pines there came the thin, high squeaking of a bat.

I still have no idea what prompted me to look in on Danielle. But instead of returning to bed and the vain hope of sleep, I walked quietly across to Danielle's room and opened the door.

I knew the instant I entered the bedroom that something was wrong. The curtains were pulled back, the moonlight streaming across her as she lay with her arms around her teddy-bear. I walked across to her, putting my hand on her forehead. It was clammy and damp, her breathing unnaturally shallow. I said anxiously: "Danielle! Danielle!"

There was no responding flicker of the eyelids. I reached for the light switch, plunging the room into garish brilliance, and then I saw the medicine bottle. It was on the bedside table, standing stickily on top of the book I had been reading to her. The cork was missing. The contents drained.

My heart began to slam. I shouted: "Peggy! Peggy!" at the top of my voice as I dragged Danielle upright in bed, slapping her face, frantically trying to remember how much medicine had been left in the bottle, what time she must have taken it, and what to do. Dear God, what to *do*!

She stirred feebly, making a little groaning sound. I picked her up in my arms and ran into the bathroom with her. I was still shouting for Peggy, and dimly I registered the sound of opening doors and the thud of nearing footsteps. Her head rolled on my shoulders as the door burst open and Ian Lyall hurtled into the room with Peggy at his heels.

"What the hell. . . ."

"She's drunk the medicine! Get some salt, Peggy. Quick!"

Peggy took one look at the inert Danielle and raced for the kitchen. Ian Lyall was on his knees beside me, lifting her eyelids.

"We've got to make her sick!" I said desperately.

Her eyes were flickering open now, glazed and bewildered, and then Peggy was squeezing into the tiny bathroom with a packet of salt. Ian poured some into a tumbler of water, and as I held her, poured it down her throat. She was struggling now, trying to twist her head away as he held it in a vice-like grip, the water spilling down her nightdress and over my hands. Seconds later I could feel her stomach heave and then she vomited, her tiny body shuddering, the tears streaming down her face. Ian leant back on his heels, his face ashen.

"Go for her mother," he said to Peggy. "She can't hear a damn thing from her room."

Dumbly Peggy handed me a towel and did as she was told. I wiped Danielle's face, cradling her in my arms as we sat on the tiled floor. Her hands clung around my neck, small and defenceless.

"I don't like being sick."

I rocked her gently. "We didn't like making you sick, darling. But we had to, you drank all your medicine and if we hadn't made you sick you would have been very ill."

She stirred against me. "I didn't. I didn't drink my medicine."

Ian reached across to take her from my arms, but she clung closer, her hands tightening around my neck.

"I want to stay with Miss Matthews."

I carried her out of the bathroom and into the bedroom. The empty bottle remained on the table, untouched.

"I didn't drink it, really I didn't. . . ." I kissed her forehead.

"Let me get you back into bed, my love." It was no time to start cross examining her. Flying footsteps hurtled down the corridor and Helena and John Van de Naude burst into the room.

"What's happened? Danny! Are you all right, baby?"

Danielle smiled waveringly as her mother took her in her arms.

"Sweetheart, you *have* been sick, haven't you? Do you feel better now? Would you like a drink of water?"

Danielle, remembering the salt water, shuddered. "It's horrible. . . ."

"It will make your mouth feel better, darling. Just have a little sip."

Ian rinsed the tumbler out, half filling it with tap water. Peggy began to clean the bathroom up and Ian said curtly: "How did she get hold of the medicine?"

"I don't know . . . she couldn't have. . . ."

"She did," he said, his face grim.

Helena Van de Naude turned towards us and John Van de Naude said sharply: "What medicine?"

"The medicine she takes on a night to help her to sleep. I gave her a spoonful tonight and put it away." I pointed to the bottle. "It was there when I came in the room."

"Dear God," Helena Van de Naude said, "she's drunk the lot. . . ."

John Van de Naude said bewildered: "But how? You didn't *leave* it there, did you, Lucy?"

"No," I said unhappily. "It's kept in the medicine chest in the bathroom and that's where I put it tonight."

"But she couldn't reach. . . ." John Van de Naude said, staring at the medicine chest high on the bathroom wall.

"She must have. If I had been careless and left it on the table I would tell you so. Honestly, I would. But I *didn't*. I put it back in the medicine chest."

"Do you *remember* putting it in the medicine chest?" John Van de Naude asked.

"Yes. . . ."

Helena Van de Naude said tiredly: "Let's leave the inquest till the morning. I'll stay in here and play cards with her to keep her awake for a while and make sure she really is all right. Goodnight Ian. Goodnight Lucy."

Peggy, her voice breaking, said reproachfully: "How *could* you, Lucy! How *could* you?"

"But I didn't, Peggy. I put it back in the medicine chest. I know I did."

Her eyes veered from mine. "Oh, Lucy. . . ." she said unbelievingly, walking heavy footed out of the bedroom and down the corridor. Limply I went back into my own room and sat on the bed, reaction setting in. I was trembling violently, shivering with sudden cold. If I hadn't gone in when I had. . . . But I *had* gone in. Danielle *was* all right. Unhappily I closed my eyes and tried to sleep.

The next morning at breakfast, Ian said: "Have you seen Danielle yet?"

"I went in to her earlier but she was still asleep."

"Shouldn't you have woken her?" Leonie asked carelessly.

"She was sleeping quite normally, after last night she needs her rest."

"Well, I wouldn't blame yourself too much," Leonie said with unexpected generosity. "How were you to know the silly child would drink it. Putting bottles on bedside tables is a habit, after all."

"Danielle is not a silly child," I said angrily, "and I did *not* leave the bottle on the bedside table."

"Really?" Leonie's eyebrows were raised, a half smile on her lips. "How strange. . . ."

"It isn't strange at all. Simply the truth."

"Then how *did* she reach it?"

"I don't know. But when she wakes up she will no doubt tell us. Would you pass the toast please?"

"Are you quite sure your memory isn't at fault," Ian asked, looking at me keenly. "You had a splitting headache last night."

My temper snapped completely. "I don't expect *you* to believe me, whatever I say! I'm quite well aware that you never wanted me to come here and that you'll do your best to make me seem incompetent and careless. Well, I'm not. You thought the car accident was my fault as well, didn't you? It wasn't, and neither was last night! I care very much about Danielle. I enjoy looking after her and I intend to stay looking after her!" and I swung out of the room, leaving him with his mouth wide open and a startled expression in his eyes.

Danielle was getting dressed when I went in to her. She

54

smiled sleepily.

"Do you feel all right this morning, Danielle?"

"Yes thank you. Did I really play cards with Mummy in the middle of the night?"

"You certainly did."

"Right in the very *middle* of the night?"

"Yes."

"Gosh, do you think Mummy will let me do it again?"

"I don't think so. It was because you had been sick."

"It wasn't very nice. I always cry when I'm sick."

I picked up the empty medicine bottle. "How did you get it out of the medicine chest, Danielle?"

She looked at me, puzzled. "I didn't get it from anywhere."

"But you drank it, didn't you?" I asked gently.

She shook her head. "I had my chocolate, that's all."

"Danielle, you were ill last night because you drank all your medicine. Look, there's none left now."

The grey-green eyes were wide and innocent. "I didn't. Honestly I didn't."

"It's very important that you tell the truth, Danielle. I won't be cross with you if you do, but I *shall* be cross if you fib to me. How did you manage to get the bottle out of the medicine chest?"

"I didn't."

"Did you drink it?"

"No, I didn't, really I didn't. I'm telling the truth, really I am," and two large tears slid down her cheeks. I put my arm around her shoulders. "There's nothing to cry about, Danielle. Come on down for breakfast. Peggy has made you some scrambled eggs."

She slipped her hand in mine. "You *do* believe me, don't you? I wouldn't lie to you, really I wouldn't."

I squeezed her hand. "Well, if you remember taking your medicine or how you got it, you will tell me, won't you?"

"I will, honest I will. You're not cross with me, are you?"

"Silly one, of course not. I just wish you could remember that's all."

"I don't remember. I don't remember even *dreaming* it!"

55

She was just as adamant when her father questioned her. With a sigh he let her go, saying to me:

"Last night has frightened her. She won't even admit to drinking it, let alone tell us how she reached it. I think we will regard the subject as closed, making sure in future that the medicine chest is kept locked."

Miserably I wandered down the beach. The only person who would make me feel better was Steve, and there were ten hours before I would have the benefit of his good sense and cheerfulness.

The sand was hot in the blaze of the sun and I quickly changed into my costume, wading out into the welcome coolness of the sea. I swam out towards the yacht, lonely and splendid in the centre of the bay, its dazzling white hull reflected in the clear depths of the water. A mere puff of breeze carried the sharp tang of lemon and the sweetness of the pines. I rolled onto my back, floating blissfully. . . .

Ian Lyall, in jeans and tee-shirt, was sitting on the beach when ¯ turned shorewards.

"Enjoy your swim?" he asked.

"Yes," I slipped my beach wrap round my shoulders, conscious of his eyes on my body. He stood up.

"I didn't mean to sound insulting this morning."

I didn't say anything, simply picked up my clothes and began to walk towards the cliff path. He followed me.

"It was quite a genuine question. It isn't always easy to remember distinctly doing something you always do out of habit. Do you know what I mean?"

"Yes," I said. "I know what you mean. You mean did I leave that bloody bottle on the bedside table and the answer is no!"

There was a brief silence as we negotiated the steep steps that wound up through the thickest part of the trees, then he said:

"What did you mean about me not wanting you to come here?"

I could hardly admit to eavesdropping, however unintentional. I said: "You've made it quite obvious."

"Have I?" he seemed bemused. "I thought I'd been friendly."

"You watch me behind my back."

"I like you."

"You've got a funny way of showing it."

We were rounding a curtain of sweet smelling jasmine.

"Then perhaps this is a better way," and before I realised what he intended, he had swung me round, taking me in his arms and kissing me, the white petals scattering over my head and shoulders. For a second I was too surprised to even react, then I pushed him away indignantly, saying:

"When I want to be kissed I'll give some indication of it!"

He grinned, the sunlight glinting on his red hair. "Please do. It was a very enjoyable experience!"

For a second I was tempted to slap his face, then I turned angrily away, pushing past thickets of wild roses and myrtle, letting the branches spring back against him as I increased speed. He kept pace with me easily, saying as if nothing had happened: "Helena has asked me remind you about the party tonight. Last night put it completely out of her head. She couldn't remember if she had mentioned it to you or not."

"Leonie mentioned it last night."

"When? You weren't at dinner."

"She came in while I was bathing Danielle."

"Did she? What did she say?"

"That there was to be a party and that most likely I would be asked to bring Steve."

"Will you?"

"If I'm asked."

"Of course you're asked. What do you think I'm doing now?"

"I thought it was the Van de Naude's party?" I said icily.

He laughed. "We're all one big family, hadn't you noticed?"

"Yes," I said breathlessly as we rounded the curve at the top of the cliffs and stepped out into the dappled shade of the terrace. "So Leonie told me."

"It would help if you didn't invite Steve. From a personal point of view."

David Katjavivi and John Van de Naude were sat by the

pool deep in talk. Ignoring Ian, and clutching my beach wrap round me, I walked hurriedly past them and into the villa. Ian remained standing in the shade of the pines. When I looked out of my bedroom window he was still there, smoking a cigarette and staring thoughtfully out to sea.

There was a soft knock on the door. I opened it to Helena Van de Naude. She came into the room, showing no trace of the anxiety of the previous night.

"Danielle is fine, Lucy. I let her off her lessons this morning, but you can take her out this afternoon."

She wandered over to the window and I saw her smile, but whether at her husband or Ian Lyall I couldn't tell.

"Did I ask you about the party?" she said, turning back towards me.

"No, but both Leonie and Ian have mentioned it."

"It won't be very large, but I thought it would be nice to have one while David is here and before John leaves."

"I didn't know Mr Van de Naude was leaving?" I said surprised.

She sat down on the edge of my bed, hugging her knees to her chest.

"It's the culmination of years of work, Lucy. John is going back to Africa and politics."

"Africa?" I asked amazed. The situation was never discussed in the villa, but I knew enough from what Uncle Alistair had told me, to know that John Van de Naude's career in South Africa was at an end.

"Ovambia," she said, eyes glowing. "*My* country. For years we have struggled for self rule, but always the argument has been that we are not ready for it, that we have no suitable leader acceptable to both blacks and whites. There can be no such excuse if John is Premier. The western powers know and trust him. He proved himself politically capable years ago in South Africa. The Ovambian people know and trust him. It's the perfect solution! Next week, in Lusaka, there is to be a summit conference and the other African states will vote on it. The answer is bound to be yes. Otherwise Ovambia will go on being ruled solely by whites and no-one wants that. It will only lead to eventual bloodshed. America and Britain want a peaceful solution and this way they will have one!" She rose, pacing restlessly across the room. "We've worked for this for so long I can hardly believe it's actually within our grasp!" She swung round. "You'll come with us, won't you?"

"To Ovambia?" I asked, startled.

"Yes. It's beautiful out there. There's no other country in the world like Africa."

"Yes," I said rashly. "I'll come." After all, anything would be better than Crailsham Place."

"Good! And you'll bring Steve tonight?"

"Yes."

"Super. Leonie is bringing her new boyfriend." Then she said prophetically: "I've a feeling tonight is going to be a night to remember!"

NINE

I took Danielle to Puerto Soller after lunch It wasn't too far and it was a lively sea-side resort with plenty to keep her amused. She teetered along the harbour wall, an ice-lolly in one hand, the other balancing on my shoulder.

"You know last night? When I was sick?"

"Yes," I said, hoping she was going to make a confession.

"Well I told David about that silly old medicine and he said it wasn't there when I went to sleep."

I had forgotten all about David Katjavivi's promise to tell her a bedtime story. I said: "Did David come into you last night?"

She nodded. "David *always* comes and tells me stories. He tells nice stories. He doesn't read them from a book. He just tells them."

"Then you must have taken the bottle out of the medicine chest after David had said goodnight to you."

"I didn't. I fell asleep while David was with me. I felt ever so funny and my head was heavy and I fell asleep. You ask him."

"Yes," I said. "I will."

I didn't get a chance to speak to David Katjavivi until Danielle was in bed and the party practically underway. He was stringing fairylights between the pine trees that shaded Mario's carefully arranged barbecue. "Hello," I said "I wonder if I could have a quick word with you?"

He beamed down at me. "What is it you want to talk about? Ovambia?"

In the short time he had been at the villa he had talked about little else.

"No. It's about Danielle."

"Danielle?" He threaded the last of the lights through the branches, surveyed his handiwork and said: "What

60

about Danielle?"

"You know about the medicine incident last night?"

He nodded. "I slept through it all but John has told me."

"I left Danielle about seven. I had a bad headache and went straight to bed. Before I left her, I gave her a spoonful of medicine and her hot chocolate. I put the medicine back in the medicine chest in the bathroom. It doesn't lock, but it's out of a child's reach and nothing but the medicine and elastoplast and ointment are kept in it. When I went in to have a look at her about two o'clock, the medicine bottle was on the table by her bed. It was empty. It's possible she reached the medicine chest by standing on a chair but none of the chairs were out of place and. . . ."

"Yes," he prompted.

"Danielle denies taking it. She says you went in to her after I had left her. That you told her stories and that she fell asleep while you were still with her."

"That's right," he said. "She was tired, couldn't keep her eyes open."

"Was there anything on the bedside table then?"

"Yes. A book."

"That's all?"

"That's all."

"Thank you," I said, my mouth unnaturally dry.

When I told Steve he didn't attach any importance to it.

"Stop worrying. It's obvious what happened. She woke up and began playing about like kids do. She drank the medicine all right, but when she realised how serious everyone was taking it decided the safest thing to do was play dumb. Beats me why they make kids medicine so it tastes like raspberries or whatever. I doubt if it would have harmed her much even if you hadn't gone in to her."

"She scared me to death."

He squeezed my shoulder. "Forget it. Seems like the Van de Naudes have done. What's this party for tonight?"

"No real reason. Helena thought it would be nice to have one while David Katjavivi is here and before John Van de Naude leaves for Lusaka."

"What's Katjavivi like?"

"Very nice. Danielle adores him."

"Isn't he in the thick of the Freed ,m for Ovambia movement?"

"They all are. Helena Van de Naude is an Ovambian herself. She's hoping John is going to be the next Premier."

"The next what?" Steve asked, laughing.

"Premier. The country is about to be given its independence."

"I think she's being a little optimistic," Steve said wryly. "I can't see a black African nation accepting a White South African as its first Premier, can you?"

I laughed. "It does seem a bit bizarre, but apparently the Ovambian people know and trust him, and because of his political status in previous years, so do the Western powers. Helena says it's a perfect solution."

Steve shook his head. "The United Nations established a council to administer Ovambia years ago. The system works. There's no need to change it."

"David Katjavivi and the Van de Naudes don't agree. . . ."

Guests had already begun to arrive. David Katjavivi, magnificent in a scarlet robe, was talking earnestly with John Van de Naude and Ian Lyall. As we entered the room, Ian turned, his eyes moving over me in blatant appreciation. I turned my back on him, saying to Steve: "Could I have a pernod with lots of ice please?"

"Where's Leonie and the new boyfriend?" Steve asked, as a party of four people I had never seen before, eased themselves past us towards the bar.

"I don't know. I haven't seen her since breakfast. When she does come we're bound to notice. Knowing Leonie she'll make a spectacular entrance."

"Do I detect some bitchiness?" Steve asked with a grin. "Come on. Let's take our drinks and find a quiet corner." Taking my hand he led me through the clusters of guests and out onto the terrace. We strolled past the swimming pool to the woods and the cliff path.

The music from the party drifted down through the trees as we began to walk slowly towards the sea. His grip on my hand tightened.

"I shall be leaving Majorca soon, Lucy."

I said awkwardly, knowing he wanted me to say more:

62

"I'm sorry."

The woods were still and silent now, the moonlight streaming through the branches in a trail of silver. He turned me round to face him.

"Is that all? No protests? No asking me to stay?"

"Of course I would like you to stay, Steve. . . ."

"But it's not a matter of life and death?"

I said gently: "I'm not in love with you, Steve."

The darkness of the trees hid the expression on his face. For a few seconds he said nothing, and then, firmly and strongly, he took me in his arms and kissed me passionately. For a brief second I could feel myself weaken, his kiss aroused desire in me and I liked him. I liked him very much. But he wasn't Max, and the feeling I felt wasn't love.

Gently I eased myself away from him. "It's too soon for me, Steve. I need a lot of time before I become seriously involved again."

His hand still held the nape of my neck, forcing my eyes to meet his in the darkness.

"I'm not in the habit of falling in love with the girls I take out. Now that I have done, I'm going to be very persistent. I love you, Lucy. I want you to join me after I leave Majorca."

"Join you where?"

He shrugged. "I don't know yet. It could be your choice. I'm not tied like a lot of people are." In the moonlight I saw him smile briefly. "I'm what is known as financially independent. And I'm used to getting what I want. What I want now is you. I think, given a little more time, that I can change your mind."

Pulling me closer, wrapping his arm around my waist, we began to walk silently back towards the party and the lights and the music and laughter.

As we emerged from the dark tunnel of trees, Ian Lyall's eyes met mine. The expression in them was not pleasant. He looked quickly away again, continuing to pour drinks and I was angry with myself for the reaction I felt. If I wanted to walk in the darkness of the woods with Steve Patterson, surely it was my business and no-one else's?

Helena Van de Naude, her hair wound glossily in the

nape of her neck, was dancing with a distinguished looking man with a luxuriant white beard. There was still no sign of Leonie.

"I wonder where she is?" I asked Steve. "She seemed to be quite looking forward to it when she spoke to me yesterday."

"I thought Leonie was too blasé to show pleasure in anything."

"She's bringing her new boyfriend. I gather he's quite a piéce de resistence!"

We threaded our way through dancing couples and across to the buffet.

"Can you see Katjavivi anywhere?" Steve asked. "I'd like a word with him."

"No, and that's *plenty*," I said, as he piled my plate high with prawn vol au vents and little pastries crammed with chicken and shells full of lobster and crab. He handed me a glass of champagne.

"Let's find a quiet corner to sit in. . . ."

There was a fresh outburst of greetings and an undercurrent of excitement as people's attention was focused on some new arrivals. A massive woman in a gown of velvet purple and a large fur stole stood immediately in front of me and I couldn't see.

"Who is it, Steve?"

He grinned. "Leonie, making her entrance as you said she would."

Over a fur clad shoulder I caught a brief glimpse of Leonie, her hair burnished to gold, her dress a floating swirl of pastel chiffon, looking incredibly beautiful and fragile.

"She's certainly causing a sensation."

"Not on her own account. She's brought some guests."

The buxom lady in front of me moved and I knew then why Leonie had been so looking forward to tonight.

Across the crowded room I could see quite clearly. Leonie was introducing her guest to John Van de Naude and it was on her that the attention was centred. She was tall and slim, wearing a perfectly cut black dress, her only jewels a large glittering diamond and broad gold band on her left hand. Blue-black hair swung silkily to her shoulders,

64

and as she smiled at John Van de Naude, the light caught the finely chiselled cheek-bones and the perfect curve of her mouth.

My mouth was dry, the blood throbbing in my temples. Huge dark eyes left John Van de Naude's face and scanned the room. I turned quickly, but not quick enough. Her smile widened in recognition. I saw her say something briefly to Leonie and then she was weaving her way towards me, arms outstretched, saying huskily:

"Lucy! What a lovely surprise! I had no idea you were in Majorca."

Somehow I managed a smile. "Steve, let me introduce you. Steve Patterson. Claudette Claustre." It was as much as I could say, my throat had tightened so I could hardly speak.

Claudette shook hands with Steve and flicked a wing of hair back over her shoulder.

"Why didn't you let people know where you were? Max has been going out of his mind with worry."

"He had no need to. . . ." My voice seemed to be coming from a great distance.

"We sent you an invitation to the wedding but it came back marked gone away, and even Max's mother wouldn't say where you were, though I'm sure she knew!"

In the doorway I saw the plump, balding figure of Fedor Katchorsky, he was talking to someone over his shoulder and I knew, beyond a shadow of doubt, that it was Max.

I said wildly: "Would you excuse me a moment. . . ." and pushed Steve's hand away, wriggling through the laughing cliques of guests to the terrace. Dancing couples brushed past me as I hurried the length of the villa towards the darkness of the cliff path. Then, in the shadows, I saw Ian Lyall smoking a cigarette, his back to me. I paused, trying to get my breath, my heart pounding painfully. I was outside Helena Van de Naude's study. I grasped the handle of the French window and pushed, letting myself into the darkened room. Behind me the music came muted, the laughter only a faint echo. I folded my arms around me, breathing heavily.

Dear God! to have even sent me an invitation to the

wedding! Anger, not grief, flooded through me. I didn't blame Claudette. I was the one who had broken the engagement off and Claudette wasn't to know that I still loved Max. But Max knew. Max knew what my feelings were. Max had always known. And he had the audacity to have sent me an invitation to his wedding to another woman! I picked up a cushion and hurled it at the opposite wall.

"*Hell*," I said aloud. Hell! Hell! Hell!"

"Hello, Brat," a voice said behind me in the darkness. "Having a tantrum?"

TEN

I spun round, the word strangled in my throat: "Max!"

"Yes," he agreed comfortably. "Why the game of hide and seek?"

"I don't know what you're talking about."

"Come off it, Brat. As soon as you saw me you took to your heels."

"I didn't see you," I said truthfully, edging round the back of a velvet covered chair, grasping the back of it for support.

He sighed, leaning against the windows, a dark silhouette against the moonlight.

"I want to know one thing and one thing only, Lucy. Why?"

"I should think the reason is obvious."

"Not to me it isn't."

"Then you're more of a fool than I thought you were!" I said cruelly.

When he spoke again there was an edge to his voice I had never heard before. "I think I deserve an explanation."

"Our engagement was broken off, I needed a job and Helena Van de Naude offered me one. It's as simple as that."

"Without letting me know where you were."

"It was no longer any of your affair. My life is my own now."

"Is the man you were with when I entered the room part of your new life?"

"Yes," I said, my nails digging into the soft velvet. "And he will be wondering where I am."

"*He'll* be wondering where you are!" Max said explosively. "I've been wondering where you are for the past two months! Did you know that Claudette wanted you

67

for a bridesmaid?"

"*A bridesmaid!*" I hissed.

"And what's so wrong about that?"

"If you can't see it, I can't tell you!"

"Why the hell you and Claudette can't be friends I don't know!" Max shouted exasperatedly. "From now on have it your own way. I'll keep out of your life if that's what you want. But when I get ditched for another man I like to know about it firsthand!"

"When you get. . . ." I struggled to say, choking with anger. "*You* were the one who two-timed me with Claudette! What was I supposed to do? Sit at home and read good books!"

He moved swiftly, his temper snapping completely, grasping me savagely by the wrist. "I *explained* that to you once!"

"And I was fool enough to believe it!"

He said through his teeth. "I've never laid a hand on you, Brat. But by God I'm going to do now!" and he swung me over his knee, his hand coming down hard as I kicked and struggled. I never heard Steve enter the room, one minute Max was beating me in a rage of temper that terrified me, and the next I had rolled onto the floor, and Steve had Max pinned against the wall. Max grasped his wrists, forcing them away, saying harshly:

"If you want my cousin, she's all yours!" and while Steve hesitated, torn between concern for me as I stumbled crying from the floor, and the decision whether or not to begin a full scale fist fight, Max strode from the room, slamming the door behind him, the sound of my sobs filling the darkened room.

Steve's arms closed round me, but I was too shocked, too upset to listen to what he was saying to me. At last I heard him say: "What the hell happened? What made him lose his temper with you like that?"

I laughed hysterically. "They wanted me for a bridesmaid."

He swore beneath his breath, wiping my face tenderly with his handkerchief. "Feeling better now?"

"Yes," I lied. "I'm fine."

With his arm tight round my shoulders we walked back out onto the terrace.

"I'd like to speak to Katjavivi if I get the chance," Steve was saying. "Get the low down on Ovambia."

We joined the circle round David Katjavivi, Steve bringing me a welcome brandy. Across the room I could see Max looking for Claudette. She was standing with Fedor Katchorsky, laughing at something he had said, the expression on the little Russian's face one of worshipping admiration. She turned as Max approached, putting one hand lightly on his arm, leaning towards him. He whispered to her and I saw Claudette's face cloud over and her slim shoulders shrug eloquently. Leonie had joined them now and Max was smiling, only the whiteness around his mouth showing signs of his recent fury. Fedor spoke to Max and then led Claudette out onto the terrace where couples were dancing beneath the fairy lights. It seemed to me that Leonie moved nearer to Max, her cloud of pale blonde hair seeming to brush his shoulder as her green eyes smiled up into his. He bent his head to say something to her and Leonie's light peal of laughter floated clearly across the room.

Helena Van de Naude, accompanied by the large purple clad lady, still enveloped by her stole, came up to us.

"Lucy, I don't believe I have introduced you to Lady Bingham, have I?"

Lady Bingham shook my hand saying gruffly, "I believe you're related to the racing driver chappie."

"We're cousins," I said briefly.

Lady Bingham gazed across at Max, "Where's the bride?"

"Dancing," I said, grateful for the normality in my voice.

"Uumph. Pretty girl. Shouldn't think she has any brains. Foreign isn't she?"

"French."

"Well, it won't last. Not with a husband like that. Not compatible. Any fool can see that."

"Like to dance," Steve asked, offering me escape. "Yes," I took his arm eagerly. As we excused ourselves I heard Lady Bingham saying brusquely, "Nice little thing. Reminds me of the other girl you had. Janice . . . Janet. . . ."

Claudette, head and shoulders above Fedor, danced past.

"He looks like a nice little man," Steve said, trying to ease the tension he could feel in me.

"He is. He's one of those jolly men who are always smiling and never speak an unkind word about anyone."

We continued to dance and I could feel myself freeze as Max and Claudette drifted past, so close that I could smell her perfume. Her arms were round his neck and they were laughing. Steve, understanding without being told, led me back to the buffet and more food. Through the open French windows we had a clear view of the terrace. Max still danced, this time with Leonie, her red laquered nails wound tight in his hair. I wondered if Claudette minded.

"I think I'd like to go to bed," I said to Steve.

He bent his head and kissed me, a tender, loving kiss. "Goodnight Lucy. Sleep well. . . ."

Over his shoulder Max's eyes lifted to mine. A muscle twitched in his cheek and his jaw was clenched, his face hard with controlled anger.

I lifted my mouth once more to Steve's.

ELEVEN

I went down early to breakfast in the hope of avoiding Leonie. Helena Van de Naude was sat on the terrace a sheaf of letters in her hand. She glanced up as I entered the dining-room, joining me and pouring herself a coffee.

"I'm sorry about last night, Lucy."

I buttered a slice of toast. "You mean Leonie's friends?"

"Yes. If I'd known who she was bringing I would have spoken to her about it. I gather you didn't know?"

"No. It was one of Leonie's better surprises."

She said tentatively. "I may be wrong, but I thought Max was very angry last night."

"He was. He was furious. Apparently he wanted me for a bridesmaid and I had the bad manners to leave no forwarding address."

"Are you sure that was the reason?" Helena asked doubtfully.

"Oh yes. Max has never been the most reasonable of men."

"Even so, it seems to be carrying things a bit far. . . ."

"It is," I said crisply.

The frown was back. "He couldn't be simply a dog in the manger, could he?"

"What do you mean?"

"Not wanting you himself, but not wanting anyone else to have you. He spent most of the evening simply *glowering* at Steve."

"Even Max couldn't be *so* petty. Anyhow, it doesn't matter. I couldn't care less about his reasons. Max is no longer my problem."

"If you say so," she said, not sounding convinced. She lit a cigarette. "Try not to let Leonie provoke you. It isn't worth it."

"I wouldn't give her the pleasure," I said truthfully.

She grinned. "I don't want any ill feeling either. I like a peaceful home." She glanced at her watch. "Good heavens, is that the time? I shall have to get a move on. David and John are catching the midday flight to London."

"I thought they were going to Lusaka?"

"Not till the end of the week. They are meeting with the other members of the support committee in London first."

She hurried out of the room and I could hear her taking the stairs two at a time. Peggy popped her head round the door, saying cheerfully: "My, you're an early bird after such a late night."

"I'm not the only one. Mrs Van de Naude is up as well."

"That doesn't surprise me. She's regularly up as early as seven o'clock." She hesitated, then curiosity got the better of her. "Was that the young man you were engaged to? The one with the film actress last night?"

"The very one," I said dryly.

"My, but he's a good looking one, isn't he? I said to Mario, fancy Lucy being engaged to the likes of him. Set a few heads turning last night. That Leonie. . . ."

"It was Leonie that brought him."

"Did she now?" Peggy asked interestedly. "Well I never. Has she known him long?"

"It appears so."

Peggy pondered on this thoughtfully, then said: "I reckon you're better off without him. A real ladies man. I said so to Mario. Handsome is as handsome does. Now, what you need is a nice, steady young man. Someone like Mr Patterson. . . ."

There came the familiar tread of Ian Lyall's footsteps approaching and I rose hastily, making a speedy exit through the French windows. The day would have to be a little older before I faced Ian Lyall.

David Katjavivi, soberly dressed once more in Western clothes, stood beneath the pines, gazing out to sea. I was in sympathy with his desire to free his country, but seven-thirty was too early for a discussion on the future of Ovambia. Cowardly I tip-toed round the corner of the villa.

I wanted no company. No inquisitive eyes. No curious questions. This morning I wanted to be alone.

The sun was already warm, the sky cloudless. Ten minutes of energetic walking took me into splendid isolation. I crossed the headland and began to climb the rocky foothills at the far side of the mountain road. I had often seen Max angry, but never before with me, and never anything to compare with last night. The naked fury as he had looked across and seen me in Steve's arms had been even worse than his rage in the study. But why should he be so angry with me? He had Claudette. Surely I was entitled to form new relationships, to find happiness of my own?

The ground steepened, twisting up into the foothills, trees and shrubs closing in. A stream trickled down, carving a narrow bed between the high banks of maquis. The going was more difficult now, tumbles of stones blocking my way. I sat down, leaning against a rock, looking back the way I had come. Below me was the headland, thrusting out over the glittering sea, and on its tip the sun-bleached walls of the villa D'Este. From where I sat I could see the blaze of flowers in the courtyard and the pines that clustered the cliffs edge.

I wondered how long Max would stay in Majorca. It couldn't be for long. His racing schedule wouldn't allow it. There was a flicker of movement in the courtyard and I narrowed my eyes against the brightness. Seconds later, the unmistakable red of the vehicle emerged from the gates and began its arduous crawl across the headland towards the road. Ian would be giving Danielle her lessons now, so the chances were it was Leonie going into Palma again to meet her boyfriend. I tugged at a clump of asphodel.

On seeing who Leonie's guests were I hadn't stayed around long enough to be introduced to the boyfriend. I wondered if Steve had, and what he had been like. Not the possessive type by the way she had been flirting with Max. The car edged onto the pale ribbon of road that led through the mountains towards Palma. I heard the faint hum of the engine as it increased speed, then the morning was as still, as quiet, as before. I settled myself more comfortably against the buttress of warm rock and closed my eyes. I had slept

73

precious little the previous night. The sun was hot on my face and strangely comforting. . . .

I was awakened by the sound of another car bucketing from the rough grass of the headland onto the narrow road. This time it was the Van de Naude's vehicle that skimmed away in the distance. I looked at my watch. Eleven o'clock. John Van de Naude and David Katjavivi being driven to the airport by Helena.

Reluctantly I rose to my feet and began the long walk towards the villa. There was only Ian and myself for lunch and I was spared conversation with him because Peggy came in seconds after I had sat down, saying that Steve was on the telephone. Gratefully I left the table and went out into the hall.

"Did I get you out of bed?" he asked cheerfully.

"I've been up for hours."

"What are your plans for this afternoon? Anything special?"

"I'm taking Danielle into Palma to have her hair cut."

"Great. I'll meet you. There's something I want to tell you."

"You sound very excited about it. What is it?"

"Secrets. Where are you taking Danielle to have her hair cut?"

"Juanita's on the Parade Maritime."

"I'll meet you there at three. By the way, could you ask Peggy if she has a photograph of Janet Grey?"

"A what?"

"You heard," he said good naturedly. "There's no need to tell anyone else I want it."

"But I can't just ask for a photograph of a dead girl without a reason!" I protested.

"Say you want it for Danielle. Say anything."

"But why do you want it?"

"Meet me at three and I'll tell you," he said tantalisingly. "Bye."

Puzzled I went back into the dining-room. Ian had already taken his coffee out onto the terrace and I was left in peace. When I had finished my lunch I strolled into the kitchen.

74

"I wonder if you would do me a favour, Peggy?"

"Of course, love. What is it?"

"I wondered if perhaps you had a photograph of Janet that I could borrow?"

"Well now, let me see. There was the time we both went to Can Pastilla. I took some photographs that day. I'll just go and have a look for them. Would you mind keeping an eye on my mayonnaise?"

I stirred the mayonnaise, thankful for Peggy's uncomplicated nature. She bustled back into the kitchen slightly out of breath.

"Here it is. Whole lot of them. That's one of me on the beach, and that's Janet outside the shop where we bought some pottery."

The face that looked back at me from the photograph was half smiling, the eyes steady and firm. Her hair was fair, worn casually at jaw length, the ends flicking up wispily. It was a pleasant, dependable face. I knew as I looked at it, that I would have liked Janet Grey.

Peggy's eyes were moist. "Pretty girl she was. Ever so good-natured. . . ."

I said hastily: "Thanks a lot, Peggy. I'm taking Danny to have her hair cut this afternoon, we should be back about six."

With the photograph safely in my hand I went back to my room, putting it in my shoulderbag before looking for Danielle. She was in the garage with Mario, sitting on an upturned petrol can and chatting to him as he investigated the insides of his car.

"Is it because it's an old car that you love it?" she was asking interestedly. "Mr Sam, my teddy-bear, is dreadfully old. Years and years, and I love him as well. Mummy says we should throw him away, that if she washed him he would fall to pieces, but I won't let her. Does she say that about your car?"

"She does say it's falling to pieces," Mario admitted with a grin.

Danielle saw me and jumped to her feet. "Goody, is it time to go to the hairdresser? I'm going to a *proper* ladies' hairdresser," she said proudly to Mario.

He laughed. "Don't come back blonde like Miss Blanchard, will you?"

"Silly," Danielle giggled. "Your hair only goes that colour when you're *old*!"

"Don't let Miss Blanchard hear you say that," Mario called after her as she skipped along by my side.

"Steve is meeting us after you have had your hair cut," I said, bundling her into the car.

"That's nice," she said in a voice of intense satisfaction. "I like Steve. Will he have some candy?"

"You don't like people just because they give you sweets," I said chidingly.

"I don't. I like him because he makes me laugh and he carries me on his shoulder and gives me swings."

"That's all right then."

"I sat at the top of the stairs last night and watched some of the party."

"Then you shouldn't have. You should have been tucked up in bed."

"But I wanted to see people and Mario sneaked me some trifle and cake and lemonade and sat with me and told me who people were. I had my dressing-gown on," she added defensively.

I smiled. "You win. Did you enjoy it?"

"I thought you looked *super*. Mario said you looked super too."

"Thank you," I said gravely.

"I saw the film star lady as well. She's ever so beautiful. More beautiful than Miss Blanchard. I think I'd like to be a film star when I grow up and wear pretty clothes and have a famous husband. That lady's husband is *very* famous. Mario said so. Mario said he was *brilliant*."

I decided it was time to change the subject.

"How do you want your hair cutting? Your mummy said you could have it how you wanted as long as you had your fringe short."

"I wish my hair was curly," she said with a sigh. "Curly hair is very pretty."

"Straight hair can be pretty too."

Danielle brightened. "Janet had straight hair and *hers*

76

was pretty. . . ."

Janet. Janet. It was like being followed by a ghost. I wondered what Steve wanted with her photograph. From the suppressed excitement in his voice, it was more than just idle curiosity. I glanced at my watch. Half one. Another hour and a half and I would know. Whatever it was, I hoped it would be something that would take my mind off Max. . . .

TWELVE

There was no sign of him when we arrived, but when we came out half an hour later he was leaning against the bonnet of his car.

"Hello, little one," he said, taking hold of Danielle's hand. "You look rather special."

"I've had my hair cut. Do you like it?"

"It looks great. How about an ice-cream?"

"Oooh, *super*. . . ."

"Don't you ever think of anything else but eating?" I asked him.

"Sometimes," he said with a meaningful grin. "Did you bring what I asked for?"

"Yes, but it's a little difficult at the moment," I indicated Danielle.

"Don't worry. There's plenty of time."

We began to stroll down the sunlit street, "Have you seen anything of Katjavivi this morning?"

"No. He and John Van de Naude flew to London at lunchtime."

"*London?*" Steve stared at me. "I thought they were going to Lusaka, and not until the end of the week?"

"I know. Apparently they are meeting what Helena calls the rest of the support committee in London first and flying on to Lusaka from there. Why did you want to see Janet Grey's photograph?" I asked, changing the subject.

"I wanted to show it to a friend of mine."

"But why?"

"There's a paper seller outside the Ria Square flats. He's there from early morning to late night. He says a powder-blue Cadillac used to park outside the flats regularly."

"I don't understand. Why were you asking the paper seller about the car?"

He shrugged. "Call it instinct. Whatever it was, it paid dividends. He also remembered the guy who drove it. He remembered him because of his hair."

I stopped dead, staring at him. "What about his hair?"

"It was red, interesting don't you think?"

"Red?" I repeated disbelievingly. "Are you trying to tell me it was *Ian Lyall* driving that car?"

"No. You saw the driver and you said he was dark. It couldn't have been Lyall."

"Well then. . . ."

"But it does make me think Ian Lyall knows more about things than he's letting on."

"I'm sorry, Steve. None of this is making sense to me."

"It's not making much to me," he said grimly. "But it will. Given time."

"Why do you want to show the paper seller Janet's photograph?"

"Instinct again. . . ."

Despite the sun I felt suddenly cold. "You think it was *Ian* Janet was meeting?"

"I don't know. What I *do* know, is that Janet Grey died in Ria Square and that Lyall has been very silent about the fact that he was and is a visitor there. I know something else as well."

"What?" I asked, the nerves tightening unpleasantly in my stomach.

He shook his head. "Later. After I've shown Pedro the photograph."

Danielle was hopping on and off the kerb as cars and taxis hurtled by. I hurried forward and took her hand.

"We can't *all* go."

Steve looked at Danielle. "No, perhaps not. What about you two going for an ice-cream somewhere. I shouldn't be more than half an hour, I'll meet you back at the car."

He gave my hand a tight squeeze and then turned back, striding rapidly through throngs of strolling tourists. Danielle stared after him disappointed.

"He didn't stay very long, did he?" she asked, her mouth pouting a little.

"He's coming back in a little while. Would you like that

ice-cream?"

"Ooh yes," she said, her face brightening immediately. "Can I have one with chocolate on please?"

"Yes," I said, wishing my own worries could be so easily forgotten.

What Steve was suggesting was unthinkable. The paper seller had made a mistake. He must see hundreds of people. It wasn't possible that he would remember one car and one driver. I persuaded Danielle to sit down at a street cafe and have a lemonade with her ice-cream, so that I could have a welcome cup of coffee. The heat was beating up from the pavement in stifling waves and I already had the beginning of a headache. I drank the coffee, convincing myself that Steve was on a wild goose chase. A dark shadow fell across the table, I looked up, expecting to see him, and Max said: "Feeling in a more reasonable mood today?" His voice was tight, as if he were exercising great self control in keeping his temper. He took off his sunglasses and straddled an opposite chair. A nerve twitched at the side of his jaw, and even beneath his tan I could see he was unusually pale.

"No," I said, struggling to control my voice. "Is there any reason why I should?"

"You'd try the patience of a saint, Brat."

"You hardly fall into that category!"

His eyes held mine. "No. But I've done nothing to deserve this sort of behaviour."

Danielle was listening with interest.

"Are you going to marry this boyfriend of yours?"

"What I do in the future is my own affair. . . ."

"Are you going to marry him?"

"Yes," I lied, wanting to hurt him as he had hurt me.

He stood up abruptly. "Then there's nothing more to be said, but I'm damned if I'll wish you every happiness!"

I stared at him, at the anguish in his eyes, the bitter lines of his mouth.

"Max . . . I said uncertainly, then with growing conviction. "Max!"

But he was already striding away down the crowded sidewalk. Grasping a protesting Danielle by the hand, I hastily left some coins on the table and raced after him.

The jostling tourists surged between us like a flood.

"Max!" I shouted. "*Max!*" but the noise of the traffic and laughing, chattering holidaymakers that thronged around me, drowned my voice.

He stepped free of the crowds, crossing the road with rapid strides and scant regard for traffic. Tightening my hold on Danielle's hand I prepared to follow. A lorry surged past, forcing me back on the pavement, and when it had gone, Max was already on the far side of the road. I took a deep breath, my mouth framing his name, the sound dying on my lips.

A familiar red Audi was parked at the opposite kerb. Leonie's blonde head laughed provocatively up at him as he slid in beside her. Her hands tightened on the wheel and with a surge of dust the car swung out into the main stream of traffic.

"I didn't know you knew Miss Blanchard's new boyfriend?" Danielle said solemnly.

"Neither did I," I said bleakly. "Until a few minutes ago."

THIRTEEN

"I wonder where his friends are? I'd like to see the film star lady again *and* her husband. He was nice. He sneaked upstairs to talk to me when I was sitting on the landing. He comes from Russia. That's nearly as far away as Africa!"

"Yes," I said, still staring down the crowded street, the Audi no longer in sight. "He would do. Fedor likes children."

"Mummy was awfully cross with Miss Blanchard for bringing her boyfriend to the party. I heard her saying that in the circumstances she should have told us who it was she was bringing. What do you think she meant by circumstances?"

"I really don't know, Danny. You listen to other people's conversations too much. It isn't polite."

"But it's the only way I get to *know* anything," Danielle said practically. "Mario said it was because of you. That you were going to marry him and that you changed your mind. Is that true?"

"Yes . . . no. . . ."

"Gosh, I think you were awfully silly. *I'd* have married him. Do you think Miss Blanchard will marry him now that you won't?"

"Not," I said with frightening intensity. "If I can help it!"

She skipped along beside me, holding my hand and chattering, but I was no longer listening. I had to find out where Max was staying. I had to see him. Somehow I had to explain.

"Look, there's Steve!" Danielle called out happily. "*And* he's got a doll. Do you think it's for me?" and she darted towards him. He swung her up in his arms and gave her a hug before setting her on her feet and giving her an old-fashioned rag doll.

"Ooh, isn't she lovely?" Danielle was squealing. "Thank

82

you *ever* so much. I shall call her Emmeline. She looks like an Emmeline, doesn't she?"

"If you say so." Steve took my hand. His eyes met mine, grimly triumphant and I was aware of a sickening sensation deep in the pit of my stomach. He said, lowering his voice: "The paper seller says he saw her visit the flats twice. Once with the red-haired man. Once on the day of her death."

"But that doesn't make any difference to the way she died. Ian wasn't there then!"

"To the best of my knowledge Ian Lyall has never admitted *ever* going to the Ria Square flats."

I thought back over the scraps of conversation I had had with Peggy. It was true. Ian's name had never been mentioned, and Peggy wasn't one to leave a detail like that out.

"*And* he denied being there the other night when we saw him." Steve said flatly.

I nodded unwillingly. "He was quite emphatic about it. He said we had made a mistake. That people often make mistakes about him."

"I bet they do!" Steve said.

We walked on in silence for a little while, and then I said: "What was the other thing you were going to tell me?"

He breathed in deeply, staring straight ahead of him to where Danielle skipped happily along on the pavement.

"I went to the police to tell them the car they were looking for had, in the past, been regularly parked outside the Ria Square flats."

"And?"

"They didn't know what I was talking about. No incident involving a powder-blue Cadillac has been reported to them. They have no record of Helena Van de Naude ever telephoning them. If they had, they would most certainly have wanted to speak to you themselves."

"But why. . . ." I said, completely bewildered.

"That," Steve said, "is what I'd like to know. Why indeed?"

The heat didn't help me think any clearer. It beat out of the ground in relentless waves.

"No matter how I try I can't think of a logical explanation," I said as we crossed the street and entered a small square, gay with flowers.

"There isn't one that exactly hits you between the eyes," Steve agreed.

"But there will *be* one," I insisted. "At least where Helena is concerned."

"And Ian Lyall?"

I remained silent, pondering on the puzzle that was Ian Lyall. We walked on for a little way beneath the welcome shade of lime trees, and then he said quietly: "Has it occurred to you that she may have known the car was one Ian had the use of? That it belonged to a friend of his? If that's the case she may well have been reluctant to telephone the police and get Ian involved."

"But she knew it wasn't Ian driving! I would have recognised him!"

"But if it was a friend of his?" Steve persisted.

"Her only child was nearly killed!" I said, feeling again all my rage at the unknown driver. "Dear God, it wasn't a minor traffic offence! Even if it was a friend of Ian's she would have still wanted him caught!"

"But she didn't report it."

"Then she must have had a reason."

"Like Lyall has a reason for saying he isn't in Ria Square when we both clearly see him? Like he has a reason for not admitting to the fact that he, too, often drives a powder-blue Cadillac?"

"Stop it!" I said, my nerves stretched to breaking point. "We're just going round in circles. The only thing to do is to ask Helena why she didn't report the accident to the police, and ask Ian outright about the car and the visit to the flats he made with Janet!"

Steve's mouth was set in a tight line. "Not yet, Lucy. I don't want you to say anything to either of them just yet."

"But why? The sooner we find out the better!"

"No. There's something else. Something I haven't told you yet."

People brushed past us but I was hardly aware of them. The tone of his voice froze me.

"Will you trust me, Lucy? Go back to the villa and

84

behave as if nothing has happened. I'll come out tomorrow afternoon and we'll speak to them together."

"And the thing you haven't told me yet?"

He breathed heavily, the corners of his mouth pinched and white.

"That can wait till tomorrow as well. After all, I could be wrong. I want to make sure first. Quite, quite sure."

"And you'll know by tomorrow?"

"Yes."

We carried on walking in silence till we came to the car. Then he took both my hands in his.

"I'll be over tomorrow afternoon. We'll speak to Helena Van de Naude then. Okay?"

I nodded. He bent his head and kissed me gently. "Take care, Lucy."

With my headache raging worse than ever, I drove through the busy streets of Palma and onto the mountain road home. For once Danielle was quiet, Emmeline hugged close to her chest, her breathing deepening as she fell asleep.

It wasn't only Steve's mystery that was causing the blinding pain behind my eyes. It was the thought of Max. The air of cold finality as he had walked away from me. The minute I reached the villa I would telephone all the leading hotels in Palma. It wouldn't take long to find him. To explain what a fool I'd been. And then . . . and then. . . .

The image of Leonie, silken-haired and softly laughing, made me bite my lip till I tasted blood. It was Leonie who had told Ian Max had married Claudette. Leonie who had deliberately lied, calculatingly making her entrance with him at the party in the company of Claudette and Fedor, knowing full well what I believed and letting me go on believing it. Leonie who wanted Max for herself. . . .

The car slowed as we climbed up the jutting headland to the villa. The courtyard gates were open wide and Mario, white-faced, was standing agitatedly by the fountain, waiting for us.

"Mario! What is it?" I asked alarmed, as he ran towards us.

"Peggy wants you," he said tautly to Danielle. "Be a

good girl and run in and see her."

"Has she made a cake?" Danielle asked as she began to run towards the archway. "There wasn't any yesterday, and. . . ."

"Mario! What's happened?"

"Mr Van de Naude has had a heart attack. Mrs Van de Naude is leaving immediately. We were frightened you wouldn't be back in time for her to say goodbye to Danielle."

He was already striding beneath the colonnades. I hurried after him, the late afternoon sun flooding the villa a soft gold. Peggy came running from the direction of the kitchen, her plump face tense and strained.

"Thank goodness you got back in time. How we would have explained to Danielle if she had come back and found her mummy gone I can't imagine!"

"Does she know what has happened?"

"She knows her daddy isn't very well."

Footsteps sounded on the stairs and Helena, an overnight bag clutched in her hand, said breathlessly: "Can I have a few words with you, Lucy?"

She was wearing a beige linen suit, her hair hastily scooped back into a french pleat, tendrils escaping wispily around her face. There were dark circles beneath her eyes and the usually laughing mouth was slack, making her look suddenly old.

"I don't know when I'll be back. I can't tell till I know how bad John is. I want you to take full responsibility for Danielle while I am away." Her eyes held mine, the expression tigerish. "I can trust you, can't I, Lucy?"

"Yes, of course. . . ."

Her naked intensity alarmed me. I took her hand. "I'll look after Danielle. She'll be perfectly safe till you get back. Please don't worry."

Her eyes were suspiciously bright. "I'm sorry. I'm a fool. Of course you'll look after her, and Ian will be here." Her grip on my hand tightened. "If there should be any more accidents. . . ."

"There won't be," I said firmly. "Please stop worrying. Everything will be all right."

"I hope so. Dear God, I hope so. I've left the telegram for Ian to see. Tell him I'll telephone the minute I can."

"Doesn't he know?"

"No. He's not expected back till tonight and I can't get hold of him anywhere. . . ." There was a break in her voice. "Danielle is in her room. I've tried to explain to her. Would you go to her?"

"Yes, of course."

She squeezed my hand and was gone.

Wearily I climbed the stairs, wondering what other ghastly surprises the day could hold. As I neared Danielle's room there came the muffled sound of crying and my heart sank. She was sat on the floor, her shoulders hunched, her arms around her knees.

"Don't cry, Danielle," I said gently, pulling her to her feet, putting my arm around her shoulders. "Your daddy is going to be all right and Mummy will be back soon."

I sat down with her on my knee and she cuddled close.

"Really and truly?"

"Really and truly. Remember how brave you were when we had our accident? Well, now you have to be brave in another way."

"It's hard sometimes," she said forlornly. "I don't like it when people go away."

"But think how nice it is when they come back. Perhaps we could plan a special party for when Mummy and Daddy come back, make some decorations?"

She wiped her tear-streaked face. "I'd like that. I'm good at making decorations. I made some at Christmas with Janet. Can we do some tomorrow?"

"Yes. There's plenty of crepe paper. We could make some paper flowers as well."

"Can I go and get the paper now? I know where it is."

I nodded and she slipped off my knee, her tears already drying, her thoughts now firmly on decorations and paper.

My thoughts were back on Max again. I went in search of telephone directories and stood in the sun-filled hallway, flicking through them and writing down the numbers of all the five star hotels. Peggy came across to me, a cup of coffee in her hand. I took it gratefully.

"I thought you'd be needing one. Is Danielle all right?"

"Yes. She's planning a welcome home party and busy searching out crepe paper to make decorations with."

Peggy gave a sigh of relief. "Thank goodness she's not brooding. Though when they'll be back goodness only knows."

"How bad is Mr Van de Naude?"

"The telegram didn't say. Just said he'd had a heart attack and gave the address of the hospital. Nothing else."

"Mrs Van de Naude will be there in another few hours," I said comfortingly. "She said she would telephone Ian the minute she gets there. We'll know this evening how he is."

"Oh no," Peggy looked at me in surprise. "She hasn't gone to London!"

I let the pages of the directory fall shut and stared at her.

"Not gone to London? What do you mean? Of course she's gone to London. . . ."

"No," Peggy said. "She's gone to stand in for him at the summit meeting. She's gone to Lusaka!"

FOURTEEN

It was nine o'clock before Ian Lyall returned to the villa, and I wasn't in the best of moods. I had found the hotel Max was staying at easy enough, but had been unable to speak to him. Senor Wyndham was not in. No, they did not know when Senor Wyndham would return. Yes, they would leave a message. I had stayed downstairs near the telephone, fortified by vodka and tonic and still the phone hadn't rung. As the Audi had not returned I could only assume he was still with Leonie. The thought seared like a knife.

I jumped when there came the sound of a distant closing door, waiting for the sound of high heels in a mixture of dread and hope. But the footsteps were the heavy steps of a man. Seconds later the salon door opened and Ian Lyall said briefly: "Where's Helena?"

"Lusaka."

"Lusaka!" he stared at me rigid with shock.

"Mr Van de Naude has had a heart attack. A cable came this afternoon. As he won't be able to attend the conference she has gone in his place."

"She's what!" he said disbelievingly.

"She's gone to Lusaka," I repeated again.

He strode towards the telephone. I said: "She told me to tell you she would ring the minute she could."

"She'll never get a line through!" he was talking to himself more than to me: "Of all times to have a bloody heart attack! Now! Only days away from the conference!"

I rose to my feet and as I left the room I heard him asking tautly for a person to person call with David Katjavivi in London.

Sick with suspense I paced the floor of my room, waiting

to hear the ringing of the telephone that could mean Max. Once or twice I went in to look at Danielle. She was sleeping soundly, her arms tightly around Mr Sam, her teddy-bear. Emmeline, resplendent in starched gingham and frills, had been relegated to a chair. Danielle, it seemed, had a loyal heart.

I tucked the covers over her shoulders and went back to my fruitless wait. At eleven o'clock, unable to bear it any longer, I went back downstairs. The salon was empty, but the light from Helena's study flooded out onto the terrace and there was the dim murmur of a voice. Ian was either talking to Mario or telephoning. Nervously I picked up the receiver and dialled the number of the Illa d'Orr.

"I'm sorry, madam. Senor Wyndham is not in his room. Yes, I will leave a message. . . ."

I walked over to the French windows, staring out over the tops of the pines to the silk-black of the sea. Around a distant headland a line of pale foam gleamed luminously in the moonlight.

Mario said suddenly from behind me: "Would you like a coffee?"

"Thank you, Mario. That would be lovely."

He left the room, returning minutes later with a steaming jug of sweet smelling coffee and two cups.

"You are very restless tonight?"

"I'm waiting for a telephone call."

"From Mrs Van de Naude?"

"No. A friend."

The telephone rang shrilly, and I jumped, sending scalding coffee splashing over my knees. As Mario leapt forward with a handkerchief I grabbed at it. An impersonal voice said in Spanish: "I have a telegram for you."

Fighting crushing disappointment I handed the receiver to Mario. He scribbled the message down, frowning.

"Is it bad news?" I asked fearfully.

He shook his head. "It's from Mr Van de Naude. He wants Ian to fly out to him immediately," and he hurried out of the room and along to the study.

It was three o'clock when I woke stiff and cramped on the sofa. Through the still open windows the sea whispered faintly, the house around me uncomfortably silent. With a last, bitter look at the dark shape of the telephone I padded softly up the stairs to my room.

The next morning there was no Ian, and no Leonie. Striving to keep my voice uninterested I asked Peggy if she was in. Peggy, never one to hide her feelings where Leonie was concerned, said spiritedly:

"Her bed hasn't been slept in and the car isn't back. Where she's spent the night *I* don't know, nor want to!"

With a colossal effort I turned my thoughts from Leonie and the speculation as to where and with whom she had spent the night, and said:

"Has Ian already left for London?"

"He went off on the seven o'clock flight. Are you going to tell Danielle that Mr Lyall has left for London, or shall I? There'll be no lessons for her this morning."

"I'll tell her."

"It might be a good idea to take her out for the day. The villa feels empty at the moment and she's bound to feel it, poor lamb."

"Steve said he would come over at lunchtime so it's a bit difficult." Not, I thought, buttering a slice of toast, that there was any purpose in his coming now. Neither Helena or Ian were here to talk to. The mystery would just have to be put on ice till the crisis was over.

"Mario is taking me into Soller to do some shopping this morning. I could take Danielle with me if you like."

"She'd enjoy that. Thanks Peggy."

"Anything to help. You look a bit peaky to me. Is it anything to do with the telephone call you were waiting for last night?"

"No. I'm fine, Peggy. Really."

"Well, if there's anything troubling you, you can always chat to me. That's what I'm here for you know." She was eyeing me with a faintly worried look and I smiled.

"I know, Peggy, and it's a nice feeling."

She smiled back. "That's all right then. I'll take Danielle her breakfast up to bed for a treat and we'll be off in about an hour. We should be back by one o'clock." She bustled off to the kitchen and I leant my elbow on the table and sipped my coffee, wondering whether to telephone the Illa d'Orr once again. If I rang and Leonie was there . . . I poured myself a second cup. It would be better to wait. When I spoke to him I wanted him to be alone, after all, Leonie would have to return to the villa eventually. For the first time I realised she did not know of John Van de Naude's heart attack, or Helena's and Ian's absence.

Restlessly I walked across the terrace and down the cliff path to the bay. The water was cool and silky and vaguely soothing. I let myself drift, the crescent of fine white sand gradually growing farther and farther away. I wondered what Steve would say when he arrived and found his birds had flown. I closed my eyes against the brilliance of the sun's glare, wondering what it was that he was going to tell me today, hoping his suspicions had been unfounded and that he would have no need to say what they had been. A gull fluttered noisily down some yards away, bobbing on the waves and eyeing me with a beady eye. I turned lazily onto my stomach and began to swim for shore.

By the time I had dried myself in the sun and strolled leisurely back up the cliff path, Mario, Peggy and Danielle had gone. I had the villa to myself. I padded into the kitchen, poured myself a fruit juice and scooped in some ice. There came the soft click of a door closing. I stopped, hand in mid-air. Leonie was back. My heart began to slam painfully and I went into the hall and picked up the telephone receiver. Leonie could wait. Right now I had to speak to Max. Had to put myself out of my torment one way or another. I reached out to dial and from the direction of Helena's study there came a dry cough.

A man's cough.

Slowly I put the receiver down and listened. There came the faint sound of drawers opening and closing and the metal ring as the filing cabinet was opened. I tied the belt of my short beach wrap tightly round my waist and walked quietly out onto the terrace. The french windows leading to the study were flung open and as I drew nearer I could see the figure of a strange man bending over Helena's desk, flicking through her papers. My shadow fell across him and he whirled round.

"What the. . . ." he began, stepping menacingly towards me.

Instinctively I reached out for the standard lamp and sent it crashing between us. The heavy brass ornamentation caught him full on the temple, and he slumped to his knees, buckling over full length at my feet, blood oozing stickily from his hairline and down his forehead.

Fighting down panic I tried to think clearly. Even if he recovered consciousness it was doubtful if he would have the strength to harm me. It was already one o'clock, Mario and Peggy would be back at any minute. The blood on his forehead was unpleasantly dark, his face ashen. Tentatively I leant down and parted his hair, trying to see where it was coming from. The gash the lamp had made was deep and ugly. I hurried back into the kitchen for towels and water, then began to sponge the blood away and try to staunch the bleeding. His eyes flickered open once and I stopped, my heart pounding apprehensively. The glazed eyes stared at me uncomprehendingly then closed again.

He didn't look like a burglar. He had a high cheek-boned, intelligent face and auburn hair bleached blond by the sun. The eyes that had focused hazily on mine were a smoky blue, the lashes full and thick.

I looked anxiously at my watch. It was nearly half past one and still there was no sign of Mario. I bit my lip, wondering if I should ring the Van de Naude's doctor. If the bleeding didn't stop and Mario didn't come back. . . .

With a sigh of heartfelt relief I heard the distant sound of feet and a door opening. Placing a fresh towel across his forehead I ran out along the terrace towards the kitchen.

"Mario! Mario!"

When he saw me his genial smile vanished. "Lucy! What is it? What is the matter?"

"There's a man! I caught him looking through Mrs Van de Naude's desk. . . ."

Mario was already running.

"I hit him with the lamp . . . he's bleeding dreadfully. . . ."

Peggy ran breathlessly after us, calling: "Who is hurt? What has happened?"

"A burglar," I called over my shoulder. "I caught him

93

in the study. . . ."

Mario thundered down the terrace and I raced after him, leaning weakly against the French windows as Mario burst into the room. For a long moment no-one spoke. Peggy, clutching her heaving bosom, stared horrified at the bleeding figure of the man on the floor. Then Mario said in a cracked voice: "Holy Mary, Mother of God. . . ."

Peggy sank down onto the blood stained carpet, saying dazedly: "He's dead. She's killed him, Mario. She's killed him!"

"Nonsense," I said with more confidence than I felt. "He opened his eyes a few minutes ago. If Mario rings for a doctor as well as the police. . . ."

Mario was already dialling, Peggy was holding the towel tight against the bleeding head.

"Dear God," she kept saying. "What will we *say*? What will we *say*?"

"That it was an accident!" I said, wishing someone would show concern for the shock I had been through.

"Please let him be all right. Dear God, please let him be all right," Peggy continued, rocking herself to and fro.

"Of course he'll be all right," I said crossly. "I didn't *mean* to hurt him so hard, but if I hadn't, he would most certainly have hurt me! He's a burglar, for goodness sake!"

Mario turned to me, his face ashen. "He isn't. He's Bradley Van de Naude and I think you've killed him!"

FIFTEEN

Peggy continued to staunch the bleeding. Mario had laid a blanket over him, and I sat numbly on a chair in the corner and watched. By the time the doctor arrived, Bradley Van de Naude was already regaining consciousness, no doubt comforted by seeing Peggy bending over him and not myself. Briefly I told the doctor what had happened and then, as there was nothing I could do to help, and the atmosphere was distinctly hostile, I excused myself and left.

I was shivering violently. A combination of delayed shock and a still damp swimming costume. I hurried upstairs to my bedroom and ran a hot bath. Bradley Van de Naude's blood was spattered over my legs and, quite literally, on my hands.

What would happen to me would depend to a large extent on what sort of man Bradley Van de Naude was. That I would be asked to leave went without question. There was a timid tap on the door and a little voice said: "Miss Matthews, are you there?"

I stepped out of the bath and wrapped a towel round me, opening the door to a frightened looking Danielle.

"Bradley's here and he's hurt and Peggy and Mario won't talk to me and keep telling me to go away. . . ." Her voice trembled and her eyes were suspiciously bright.

"They're not cross with you, darling. They're just worried about Bradley. Is the doctor still here?"

"Yes. He's taking Bradley to hospital for stitches. . . ."

As Danielle was talking I was dressing hurriedly.

"And Steve has just arrived and. . . ."

"*Steve has?*"

"Yes . . . and Mario said it was your fault. It wasn't your fault, was it? You won't get into trouble, will you?" and she began to cry, clinging tightly to me. "I couldn't bear

95

it if you got into trouble because you might go away and leave me and then there wouldn't be anybody. . . ."

"I won't go away," I said quietly. "Not until Mummy comes back."

It was a promise that under the circumstances might be difficult to keep, but one which I intended keeping. Whatever happened, Danielle was not going to suffer for my actions.

"Where is Steve now?"

"He's in the study talking to Bradley while the doctor bandages his head."

I breathed a sigh of relief. If Bradley Van de Naude was fit to talk to a stranger he couldn't be at death's door.

"Steve is explaining who you are. Bradley didn't know."

"Then we'd better go back downstairs. If Bradley is feeling better I need to apologise to him."

Danielle stared at me round-eyed. "Did you really do it? Did you really hit him?"

"It was an accident, Danielle. I've never met Bradley and I didn't know he was coming here. I just walked into the room and when I saw him I thought he was a burglar and. . . ."

"And you hit him with the lamp. I know. Peggy said so, but I didn't believe her. Gosh, do you think he'll be angry?"

"Very," I said dryly.

"Gosh," Danielle said again reflectively. "Still, I think it was very brave of you. It *could* have been a burglar, couldn't it? If it *had* been, everyone would have been very pleased with you I expect. It was only a mistake after all."

"Thank you, Danny," I said, squeezing her hand. "It's nice to have a friend."

"Steve is your friend too. I'm sure he'll explain to Bradley. . . ."

"I think even Steve may be finding it hard going. We'd better go and help him out."

Peggy was on her hands and knees sponging the carpet. There was no-one else in the study.

She said: "Mario and the doctor have taken him to hospital in Palma." Then she closed her lips again tightly, squeezing more cold water onto the carpet. Danielle's hand still comfortably in mine, I left her and went in search of Steve. He was in the main salon, smoking a cigarette and staring out to sea.

I said apprehensively: "Is he going to be all right?"

He spun round, a reassuring smile on his face, concern in his eyes.

"Of course he is. Nasty gash on the head, that's all. Nothing a few stitches and rest won't cure. He'll probably have a pretty stiff headache for a while."

"Oh Steve. . . ." I sat down weakly. "There was a moment in there when I thought I'd killed him."

He sat beside me, his arm round my shoulders, pulling me close.

"Hey, there's no need for tears now. I've told you, he's going to be all right. It was obvious what you'd thought. He seems a reasonable guy. I'm sure he'll understand."

"I hope so. I don't want to leave. . . ."

You said you wouldn't!" Danielle burst out. "You *promised* me!"

"Lucy isn't leaving," Steve said with calm certainty. "Now will you both pack it up? Having one female crying all over me is bad enough, but two. . . ."

It was four o'clock when Mario returned. Alone. He came into the salon where we were playing Monopoly with Danielle and said flatly: "They are keeping him in."

"How bad is he?" I asked, sick with apprehension.

Mario shrugged. "Enough. He has concussion and. . . ."

"But his skull isn't fractured?" I asked anxiously.

"No."

I breathed a sigh of relief. "Thank goodness for that. I thought I'd killed him. . . ."

"You nearly did," Mario said, leaving the room without so much as a flicker of a smile. Steve's hand closed on my shoulder.

"Don't take it so hard, Lucy."

"It's not just Bradley Van de Naude. It's everything. The car accident, Danny drinking her medicine. . . ."

"I didn't," Danielle said firmly.

Steve said: "There's some Cokes in the fridge. Fancy some?"

"Ooh, please," Danielle said, jumping to her feet. "Can I bring them in here?"

"As long as you don't spill."

Peggy had only just finished cleaning the blood off the study carpet. She wouldn't be too pleased by starting all over again with Coke. As she ran eagerly off, Steve said casually: "She didn't, you know."

"Didn't what?"

"Drink her medicine."

"Then what was the matter with her and where did the medicine go?"

"Probably down the sink."

I stared at him. "Is this a serious conversation?"

"Very. Danielle was doped," Steve said matter of factly. "Mogadon crushed into her hot chocolate."

"Is this supposed to be some kind of joke, because if it is, it's in very bad taste."

"No joke. It's a fact. I knew right from the word go that the medicine couldn't have doped her like you said it had. It was far too mild."

"Are you an expert on medicines?"

"No, but I know more than you, or anyone else here for that matter."

"Are you telling me that Danny was *doped* and you *knew* and you didn't even *tell* me!"

"It was no use saying anything until I was sure."

"But why?" I stared at him, my mind in a whirl.

"Listen," he said gently. "The medicine had disappeared and Danny hadn't drunk it. Obviously someone wanted us to think she had and that it was your fault. I found that interesting to put it mildly. The night of the party I spent a few minutes in Danielle's room. The cup was still there. Peggy had been very busy that day, remember? I took the liberty of borrowing it and having the sediment analysed."

"But who would *do* such a thing?"

"Ian Lyall," he said simply. "Do you remember telling me that he came to Danielle's room on the pretext of looking for Katjavivi? He did it then?"

"But you can't *know* that!"

"I can't *know* anything. I wish to God I could! But what

I can do is put two and two together and come up with four."

I felt physically sick. "What should we do? John Van de Naude is ill and Helena is thousands of miles away. . . ."

"Don't panic. Lyall is in London at the moment so there's no immediate cause for worry. We just keep a very close eye on Danielle until her mother returns."

Danielle came skipping back in with an armful of Cokes, saying cheerfully: "Miss Blanchard is back. Mario has just told her about Bradley and she's ever so angry. . . ."

Hours later, when Danielle was in bed and Steve had gone back to Palma, and my tired brain had given up trying to find a motive for Ian Lyall's behaviour, I finally telephoned Max.

"Lucy?" His voice was surprised.

I said with difficulty. "I'd like to talk to you, Max. To explain. . . ."

"There's no need," and this time his voice was unfamiliar and cool.

"But there *is*. You don't understand!"

"I understand enough," and for a second his bitterness showed through.

My breathing hurt me as if I had been running a long way. "You don't Max. It's all been a hideous, ghastly mistake. I thought you were having an affair with Claudette. . . ."

"Because we attended the same party and were photographed together. . . ."

"No, because. . . ."

He wouldn't let me finish, just carried on relentlessly: "So you thought you would get your own back. Have your own little affair with Steve Patterson. Well, I'm only glad your childish behaviour turned out all right. At least he wants to marry you. Lots of men wouldn't," he finished cruelly.

"I'm sorry about the things I thought when I saw that photograph. Truly I am. But that's not the reason. . . ."

"No. The reason you left me was you fell in love with someone else. I believe it's something that happens to people all the time. I just never expected it to happen to me!"

"It didn't Max. Please listen to me. I thought you and Claudette were *married*, that's why I behaved as I did at the party."

"You left me long before that, Brat. Claudette hadn't married anyone when you fled London leaving no forwarding address and no explanation."

"Max, *please*. . . ."

"Leonie did all the explaining for you this afternoon. You fell in love with Patterson and didn't have the courage to confront me with it. I thought life held very few surprises for me, Lucy. I was wrong."

"Max!"

The line was dead. Frantically I dialled again but Senor Wyndham was taking no calls. None.

I sat in the dark for a long time. Leonie had won the first fight, but she had not won the battle. Tomorrow I would see Max, make him listen to me. The temptation to march straight into Leonie's room was strong, but I resisted it. It was the sort of scene she would revel in.

Lonely beyond belief, I made my solitary way to bed.

The next morning Peggy unexpectedly brought breakfast to my room.

"That's nice of you, Peggy," I said, as she deposited the tray across my knees. She gave a small smile.

"I wanted to apologise for yesterday. Being rude to you. It was the shock, you see. Walking in and finding Mr Bradley lying there, blood all over the place. . . ."

"It's all right. Peggy, I understand."

"I thought he was dead, and what with Mr Van de Naude being taken badly and. . . ."

I took her hand. "I know, Peggy. It was dreadful. But he'll be out of hospital in a couple of days."

"I thought after what a shock it must have been to you. Quite ashamed of myself I felt. So I thought, I'll take her breakfast up and apologise."

"Thank you, Peggy. I appreciate the treat and there's no need for apologies."

She smiled. "That's all right then. I'll see you later downstairs."

When I had finished my breakfast, I dressed and went

down to the hall, one decision made. Before I drove into Palma I would speak to Claudette.

It took me ten minutes to find which hotel she was staying at, but when I finally spoke to her, it was worth it. Her voice was pleased and surprised.

"Lucee! How nice. I thought I had offended in some way. . . ."

"No, Claudette. There's been a ghastly misunderstanding."

"Between you and Max?"

"Yes," a sob caught at my throat and she said gently: "Pauvre petite. You so unhappy. Max so unhappy."

"Could you talk to him for me, Claudette? He won't give me the chance to explain."

"But of course! I would love to play the, how do you say, the go-between! But first you must tell me what went wrong and why you left England and poor Max not knowing where you were and so worried!"

"I thought he was having an affair with you," I said simply.

There was a gasp and then Claudette laughed merrily.

"Mon Dieu! With me? When all he had eyes for was you! How could you think such a thing?"

"There was gossip. . . ."

"There is *always* gossip," Claudette agreed with the air of one who expects it and long ago learned to live with it. "But Max was crazily in love with you and wanted to marry you. How could you believe such nonsense?"

"I didn't. But the week before I left England I walked into Lacey's and I saw you and Max. You were holding hands and you looked radiant and I thought. . . ."

"But that was because of Fedor! I had just heard that he could stay in Britain and we were so overjoyed. Max knew we were in love and he had done all he could to help us. He has been the best friend in all the world. . . ."

"But there was a whole week before I left for Majorca and Max never once telephoned me or came to see me. . . ."

There was a pause, and when she spoke again her voice had lost its merriness: "Then it *was* my fault, Lucy. Mine and Fedor's. The Russians did not want Fedor to stay in Britain. Two men came and took him away. I was out of my mind with fear. I thought I would never see him again. I rang Max and he came immediately. Fedor had already been given permission to stay but that would not have mattered if they could have persuaded Fedor to change his mind. Max was marvellous. He had the national press on to it, his MP, everyone. With all the publicity Max stirred up there was no way the Russians could keep Fedor any longer at the Embassy. But it was a very near thing. We owe Max, and your government, a lot."

I remembered the shrill ringing of the telephone as I had fled into the street.

"But what is the problem now?" she asked, cheering up. "You tell Max and he will understand and be so happy to have you back, and you will be together again like me and Fedor!"

"It's not that easy, Claudette."

"It seems easy to me," Claudette said simply. "You love each other. What could be simpler than that?"

"There's Leonie Blanchard."

"Ah," there was a new inflection in her voice. "Surely you are not going to wreck your happiness a second time over such a one as Leonie Blanchard?"

"Leonie has lied left, right and centre. Firstly, she told Ian Lyall that Max had married you. . . ."

"And the good Mr Lyall told you?"

"Yes," I said bitterly. "When you came to the party I thought your new husband was Max, not Fedor."

"Then that explains your behaviour! Pauvre petite, Lucy."

"There's more."

"Helas," Claudette said expressively. "What more can there be?"

"Max thinks I'm in love with Steve Patterson."

"But why should he think a thing like that?" Claudette asked indignantly.

"Because I told him I was," I said miserably.

"Mon Dieu! and Max believed this stupidity?"

"Yes. Leonie told him that Steve and I were having an affair together in London. That I was afraid to confront Max with the truth and that is the reason I ran away."

"But you hadn't met this Steve then, so how could you?" Claudette asked reasonably.

"I couldn't and didn't. But Max has listened to Leonie's lies and believes them. He won't give me a chance to explain the truth!"

"He will listen to me!" Claudette said spiritedly. "Before the day is over you will be with Max again and you will be happy!"

But Claudette was wrong. Before the day was over I was far from happy, fighting for my own life and Danielle's.

SIXTEEN

I opened the English newspaper that Peggy had left on the tray. The front page contained large photographs of both John and Helena Van de Naude. There was also one of David Ktjavivi speaking at the summit conference. The leader column had large extracts of Helena Van de Naude's speech to the delegates, pledging her husband's desire and will to lead the people of Ovambia to independence and freedom. Emphatically denying that his health had broken down, that the heart attack he had suffered had been mild and would in no way impair him from becoming an efficient head of Ovambia's government. The editorial on the middle page read:

"APFO (The African People's Freedom Organisation) is intensifying its struggle for self rule. With the promise of ex-government minister, John Van de Naude, to head the country's first black parliament, the end could be in sight. With the irony, for the Ovambians, of achieving independence and black rule with an exiled white South African as Premier. Ovambians all over the country are affirming their commitment to the idea of One Ovambia, One Nation, and their loyalty to Mr Van de Naude is overwhelming. On the international and diplomatic front APFO is gaining increased support. It has been recognised by the Organisation of African Unity and the United Nations as the authentic representative of the people of Ovambia. David Katjavivi, the founder of APFO is quoted as saying:

'We do not expect independence to end our troubles overnight, but we believe that our people are entitled to rule themselves with a leader of their own choosing. Ovambia is our country and Ovambians wish to be their own masters.'

The vote by other heads of black African countries is to

be taken on Saturday after a final speech by Helena Van de Naude. Voting is expected to be unanimously in favour. The Americans feel with Van de Naude as premier the threat of a Communist take over will be defeated. If the Africans accept John Van de Naude as leader of an independent Ovambia they will be able to count on the support of America. Let's hope, for the sake of both blacks and whites in Ovambia, that they accept him and that the threat of escalating violence is averted."

I hoped they would accept him too. If they did, it meant that Helena Van de Naude could be back in Majorca within a week, and under the circumstances, the sooner she was back the better.

I dressed slowly, with mounting tension. Sometime today, Claudette would see Max and he would listen to her and understand, and all Leonie's lies would be in vain. Holding on to that thought I went in to Danielle's room to wake her.

The sun streamed in golden bars through the shutters but the only occupant was Mr Sam, lying on his nose in the middle of the floor. Wondering where she was, I picked him up and put him back on her bed, then went downstairs to look for her. The villa was quiet and there was no sign of her on the terrace or near the pool. I went into the kitchen where Peggy was busy baking.

"My, that wasn't much of a sleep in," she said cheerfully.

"I'm looking for Danielle. Have you seen her anywhere?"

"Danielle? She's still in bed."

"She isn't. And wherever she is, she's running around with only her nightdress on. I wonder if Mario knows where she is?"

"He's gone into Soller. It's market day today." She shook her hands free of flour. "I'll help you look for her. As if we haven't enough to worry about without her being a naughty girl into the bargain!"

With the first growing seeds of anxiety we searched the villa, and then, panic growing, the grounds.

"*Danielle! Danielle!*" I called, standing at the top of the cliff path and straining my eyes for the glimpse of a little nightdressed figure. The only reply was the call of a bird as it swooped low over the tops of the pines.

Peggy ran across the terrace towards me, her face white.

"I've searched the villa as far back as the rear courtyard and there's not a sign of her!"

"She must be somewhere," I said, with more confidence than I felt. "She's hiding from us."

"I'll smack her bottom when I find her!" Peggy's voice had a break in it. "Of all the naughty girls, when she knows the worry we have. First her daddy and then Bradley and now Danny running away. . . ."

"She hasn't run away," I said firmly. "She's hiding. As soon as she is hungry she will be in the kitchen."

"Well that can't be long then. She's had no breakfast. I could tell if she had been in the kitchen and she hasn't. Where on earth can she *be?*"

"She could be nearly anywhere, Peggy. If she wants to hide the mass of rooms at the rear of the villa are a child's delight."

"But I've been through them all calling her name!" Peggy protested.

"And she's probably been giggling in a corner thinking it all great fun. Another few minutes and she'll be back wanting something to eat."

But she wasn't. By the time Mario arrived back at eleven o'clock, there was still no sign of her.

"Have you been down to the beach?" he asked, striding through the villa with Peggy and myself hurrying after him.

"No. . . ."

He broke into a run, leaping down the cliff path like a mountain goat. I flew after him, my heart in my mouth. If she was on the beach she would have heard us calling. That is, if she wasn't hurt she would have heard us calling. . . . I slipped and slid breathlessly after Mario. The last overhanging branch was pushed aside and the bay lay spread before us, still and beautiful and completely deserted. I leaned against a tree to get my breath, watching fearfully as Mario scrambled over a fall of rocks, searching every possible crack and crevice. He jumped down, spreading his hands in the air with a shrug. The fear I had fought to suppress began to take hold with a vengeance.

The dinghy, a brilliant blob of orange against the vast blue of the sea, bobbed carelessly at anchor. With sudden hope I raced across the sand to the jetty, but there was nothing in it but a pool of water and a stray piece of seaweed.

Mario, his genial face tense and grim, said: "I'll search the villa once more. If she's not there I'm calling the police."

I didn't argue with him. There had been too many accidents, too many things going wrong. If anything should have happened to Danielle. . . . I pushed the thought away. She was playing. Hiding. She was all right. Dear God, she had to be all right.

Peggy didn't even ask if we had found her. She took one look at our faces and began to cry, covering her face with her apron. Mario began his search of the villa, and I could hear angry words between him and Leonie. Then he was calling Danielle's name at the top of his voice, distant doors opening and slamming as he scoured every possible hiding place, every cupboard and chest. Breathlessly I ran back up the stairs to her room, passing a sulky Leonie as I did so. I didn't even spare her a glance. Perhaps Danielle was still in her room, hidden in the wardrobe or beneath her bed. . . .

"Danny!" there was no answering cry. Mr Sam stared desolately at me with his glass eyes. I looked again for her nightdress, checking her clothes, her shoes. All her day shoes were there, only her slippers were missing. There was something else though, something else that should have been in the room and wasn't. My eyes rested on the chair and I knew immediately. Emmeline. Wherever she was, Danny had taken Emmeline with her. I stared once more round the room. Then I saw it. The letter lay on the dressing-table, and if I had been looking for a letter and not a little girl, I suppose I would have seen it much earlier. It was not in Danielle's writing. With sickening intuition I tore it open. Neat, capital lettering said briefly:

"Danielle will be returned when John Van de Naude publicly announces his decision not to head a black government in Ovambia or have anything further to do with APFO. If the police and press are not informed, no harm will come to her."

I raced down the stairs to Mario, but I had no need to break the news to him. The telephone receiver was in his hand, his eyes glazed with shock. He said blankly: "It's Mr Van de Naude . . . they've kidnapped her. Holy Mother of God, they've kidnapped her. . . ."

I snatched the receiver from him and John Van de Naude's voice said urgently: "Lucy? Is that you, Lucy?"

"Yes. I've just read the kidnap note. . . ."

"I received one a minute ago and I imagine Helena has as well. I haven't been able to get through to her yet. Listen to me very carefully. I want you to do nothing. Do you understand me? Nothing at all!"

"But she must be still here, in Majorca. The police will be able to find her, check the airport. . . ."

"No! There's to be no going to the police. The kidnappers are in direct touch with me and I'm handling it. Is that understood?"

"Yes. . . ."

"I want the three of you to sit tight there and to do nothing, and above all, to tell no-one, and that goes for your American friend. If the press get hold of it, we might never see Danny again!"

"Can I tell Bradley?"

"*Bradley?*"

"Yes. He came unexpectedly yesterday morning. . . ."

"Let me speak to him!" John Van de Naude barked.

"He's had a slight accident. Nothing serious. He's in the local hospital for a few days. . . ." It didn't seem to be the time and place to go into explanations.

"Tell Bradley. No-one else. I want no-one screwing things up, do you understand? *No-one!*" and the phone crashed down.

Mario's face was ablaze with anger, he grabbed me by both shoulders, hissing: "How did they take her? You were supposed to be looking after her! *How did they take her?*"

"I don't know! I put her to bed last night. I heard

nothing from her room. . . ."

His large hands tightened their grip. "Always it is you! The car! The medicine! Now kidnapping! Where is she? *Where is Danielle?*"

"*Stop it, Mario! I don't know!*"

"She would have screamed. She would have called out! They could not have taken her from the villa without a disturbance! Danielle would not have gone with strangers in the middle of the night. *But she would have gone with you! You! You know where she is!*"

"*You're being ridiculous, Mario! I had nothing to do with it. Nothing!*"

"For your sake, I hope you are right!" he said through clenched teeth, pushing roughly past the still crying Peggy.

"Where are you going?" she called after him. "Mr Van de Naude said we must do nothing . . . tell no-one. . . ."

"*He didn't say we couldn't look for her!*" and like a wild bull he charged out of the villa, the doors slamming behind him.

Peggy rocked herself to and fro, the tears streaming down her face: "Oh, my baby! My poor baby! Oh dear God, what have they done with her?"

Numbly I walked into the kitchen and put the kettle on for a cup of strong tea. It seemed the only action I was capable of.

What Mario had said had been correct, in that Danielle would not have left her bed willingly in the middle of the night. Unless they carried her from the room while she was still asleep. . . . The kettle began to puff clouds of steam. Danielle wasn't a deep sleeper. . . . But if she'd been drugged beforehand. . . . The kettle began to boil and like Newton discovering the power of steam, I knew. At long last a pattern had formed. Janet Grey's death, Ian Lyall's visit to the flats, the car accident and Ian's use of the car, his following us to Valldemossa, the Mogadon in Danielle's hot chocolate. Everything was clear. The difficulty was going to be convincing people I was right. Especially as I couldn't take Steve into my confidence. With things crystal clear in my mind I took a cup of tea into Peggy.

"What are you doing?" she asked as I picked up the

telephone receiver and asked for a London number.

"I'm ringing Mr Van de Naude."

She put her cup down suddenly, tea spilling on the pale cream carpet. "You can't do that! He'll be waiting to hear from the kidnappers! He'll be. . . ."

"It's important, Peggy." The certainty I was now feeling must have showed itself in my voice. She sat silently, watching me. Eternities later an English voice said crisply: "Mr Van de Naude discharged himself today. I'm sorry, no, there is no forwarding address."

I said slowly to Peggy: "He's not at the hospital anymore. He's discharged himself. Do you know what his London address will be?"

She shook her head. "He'll telephone here when he hears . . . if he hears. . . ." She began to cry again.

"Do you know the telephone number of APFO in London?"

"No, but it will be in Mrs Van de Naude's address book in her desk . . . but you can't go in there. . . ." She ran after me, seizing me by the arm with surprising strength. "You're one of them, aren't you? That's why you want to speak to him! You're one of them!" her voice rose hysterically.

"Don't talk nonsense, Peggy."

"I'm not. It's true! Mario said so. I heard him! Oh, you wicked, cruel. . . ."

I slapped her face hard and she fell back on the sofa.

"You're hysterical, Peggy. I love Danielle and you know it."

She didn't answer, just sat in a huddled heap, crying noisily.

I searched Helena Van de Naude's desk thoroughly but found no trace of anything resembling an address book. It seemed to take forever for Continental Enquiries to give me APFO's London telephone number, and a further ten minutes agonising wait to be connected. It was all in vain. John Van de Naude had obviously given the same adamant instructions to APFO headquarters as he had to me.

There was only one thing for it. I would have to see Bradley Van de Naude. Peggy didn't even bother to lift her head up when I told her where I was going. She was still crying, her shoulders hunched, a fist pressed against her mouth. I watched her helplessly, not liking to leave her alone and yet not daring to risk a minute's delay in talking to Bradley Van de Naude. It was Leonie who came to my rescue.

She said from behind me: "You go off on your little errand, darling. I'll look after Peggy. There's nothing wrong with her a large brandy won't cure."

"Thanks," I said briefly. There was no emotion on her face. No concern or distress over Danielle's disappearance. She was as carefully dressed, as beautifully made-up as ever. She smiled lazily as she poured a brandy for Peggy and an even larger one for herself.

"I hope the son and heir will be suitably pleased to see you. I understand he has rather a bad headache at the moment."

I didn't trust myself to answer her. There was too much I wanted to say to Leonie and it would all have to wait until Danielle was safely home again.

I drove furiously into Palma, heedless of the speed limit and with scant regard for other traffic. Now I knew who Danielle was with, one fear had been eliminated. Where-ever she was, Danielle would not be frightened. Not yet.

Bradley Van de Naude regarded me with startled surprise as I burst into his room. I said briefly: "Danielle has been kidnapped."

"*What!*" he jerked himself upright in bed.

"Your father received a letter this morning in London and the kidnappers left one in her room last night. It was obviously planned some time ago."

"How much?" he snapped, swinging his legs off the bed and reaching for his dressing-gown.

"It isn't money. They want to prevent your father becoming Premier of Ovambia. He's given us strict instructions to tell no-one. Not the police or the press or anyone."

He stood up. "He's giving in to the demands then?"

"Yes. He didn't actually *say* so, but what else can he do?"

"And my stepmother?"

"I haven't spoken to her."

"I'll be five minutes. You can drive me back to the villa."

"There's something else. I know who kidnapped her but I can't get through to your father . . . ."

"*You know what?*" his whole body tightened.

"It's Ian Lyall. He tried once before. He drugged her with Mogadon but it didn't work."

"*Lyall?*" the smoke-blue eyes were incredulous. "Have you proof of this?"

"Steve Patterson has proof that her drinking chocolate was drugged. He's also found out that Ian Lyall was a regular visitor to the flats in Ria Square where Janet Grey died."

"And?" he waited tensely.

"And I think something like this has been in the offing a long time. Ever since your father first made his decision to go back into politics. I think Janet Grey knew about it."

A nurse came in, drowning us in a flood of Spanish.

"We'll talk in the car," he said curtly. "I'll be five minutes."

He wasn't. He was three. He slammed the passenger door shut and said. "Where is Lyall now?"

"He's supposed to be with your father in London."

"And my father has no idea?"

"No. He left the hospital and I couldn't get hold of him at APFO headquarters."

"If Lyall is in London your theory must be wrong. He couldn't possibly be responsible."

"Not if he *is* in London," I agreed. "But I don't think he is. I think the telegram was a hoax. That's why we must get in touch with your father, to find out."

We sped through the dusty suburbs of Palma and out past the airport.

He said grimly: "The sooner my father makes an announcement the better!" he glanced at his watch. "We should just be able to catch the news if we hurry."

I put my foot down, tearing through a village and onto the mountain road. He sat quietly beside me, his face a chilly mask of suppressed emotion. He bore very little resemblance to his father. He was tall and leanly built. His fine hair almost girlish. The smoke-blue eyes gave no sign of his feelings. I felt that even in happier circumstances, Bradley Van de Naude would have none of his father's charm and geniality.

He said suddenly: "Do Peggy and Mario know about Lyall?"

"No. Mario wouldn't believe me if I'd tried to tell him. He thinks *I'm* the one who's behaviour is suspect. He actually accused me of being one of the kidnappers!"

He gave a smile that held no warmth. "And now he's gone crashing round Majorca on a one man rescue operation?"

"He took the news very badly. He's devoted to Danielle. It would have been impossible for a man of his temperament to have sat still and simply waited."

"But that's all we can do," Bradley said. "Wait for my father to renounce the Premiership and wait for Danielle's return."

I looked at my watch. Only half an hour to go until the main television news of the day. I pressed my foot down even harder on the accelerator, streaming headlong down the narrowing road.

SEVENTEEN

We clustered round the television in the main salon. The endless musical comedy show had finished. The news flashed on. There had been a train crash in Madrid. There had been a fire in an hotel in San Sebastian injuring eleven tourists. Mario swore desperately and my nails dug deeper into the soft velvet of the sofa. In an impersonal voice I heard the news commentator mention the words African Summit meeting, and Van de Naude, but my Spanish was not good enough for me to understand the rest of his words. Then there were pictures from Lusaka. A crowded, roaring auditorium of enthusiasm and John Van de Naude, upright and broad, his shock of steel-grey hair making him look like a patriarch of old, took the stand to thunderous applause. Behind him I could make out the seated figures of Helena and David. . . . His face was stern and impassive. He raised one hand to silence the thunderous hand clapping and began to speak.

It was not necessary to understand Spanish to know what his next words were. Within seconds the delegates rose to their feet in a bodily mass, cheering and clapping.

For once even Leonie seemed disconcerted, her eyes fixed like everyone else's on Bradley's mask-like face.

Savagely he ground his cigarette out and turned on his heel. Leonie hesitated a few seconds then hurried after him and we heard the study door slam shut.

"He will telephone his father," Peggy said tremulously. "He will telephone his father and his father will explain." Her voice rose with pathetic hope. "Perhaps they already have Danielle safe. Communications are so difficult. . . ."

"Perhaps," Mario said brutally, "she is dead!" and he spat on the velvet sheen of the opulent carpet and strode from the room.

I sank back against the cushions on the sofa, and leaned my head back and closed my eyes. If only I could speak to Steve. But I had promised John Van de Naude I wouldn't, and it was a promise I could not break.

If only, I thought, my heart aching, if only I could speak to Max. To have Max take me in his arms and whisper words of comfort. Give me some of his strength. Tiredly I wondered if Claudette had spoken to him. Danielle's kidnap had pushed everything else into the background. Even Max. But now he was in my heart and mind again and I wanted him so badly that my body ached in physical pain.

The room was dark now and empty. I had not bothered to switch on the lamps and when at last my tears for Max were shed, I rose wearily to my feet and crossed to the windows. Somewhere a six year old girl would be crying too. Crying because she was bewildered and afraid. I felt ashamed at my momentary preoccupation with my own troubles.

John Van de Naude had not given in to the blackmailers' demands. He had called their bluff. It *had* to be bluff. If it wasn't, Danielle could be dead already.

In the dark, where the pines clustered round the entrance to the cliff path, something moved. A fox or a weasel. The moon sailed briefly out from behind a bank of cloud and I glimpsed it again, running behind the cover of the trees for the path. Crouching low and on two legs, not four, I froze, straining my eyes as the moon slid behind cloud and the terrace and cliff top were plunged once more into darkness. Then I turned and ran towards the study. Not across the terrace where the intruder would see me, but through the villa, the breath tight in my chest.

A light came from beneath the study door. I knocked urgently, and Bradley opened the door, his fine-boned face taut with nervous tension.

I said briefly: "I've just seen someone running under cover of the trees towards the cliff path!"

"Are you sure? You're not just overwrought?"

"No," I said shortly. "I'm not."

His eyes held mine and I said defiantly: "I'm almost certain it was Ian Lyall."

He drew in his breath quickly. "Then for Christ's sake why didn't you say so?"

"Because. . . ." My explanations were lost on him. He was whipping a torch out of one of Helena's drawers, saying tersely: "Is there a spare dinghy anywhere?"

"There's an inflatable one with a foot pump where Mario keeps his tools."

"Good," he said, sprinting out onto the terrace, and then, as I started to follow: "Stay here!"

"I will not! You might need help."

"You'll do as you're told!" he snapped.

"What about Mario? Can't Mario go with you?"

"Mario is out. He took that old car of his and headed God knows where."

"Then I'm *definitely* coming with you!"

We were in the shed where Mario kept his bits and pieces, with the dinghy tucked under one arm and the foot pump and torch in the other, he stared across at me, the expression in his eyes chilling. Bradley needed no help from me or anyone else.

"I'm going to get that bastard and I'm going to get him alone!" he said between clenched teeth, then he turned on his heel and was gone.

For five minutes I waited, then I could stand the suspense no longer. I was under no obligation to do as Bradley told me. If Danielle was somewhere out there in the dark, it was me she would want to comfort her.

The terrace was empty as I padded softly across it, gazing out across the bay to where the *Helena* lay at anchor, white and sleek and magnificent. And unsearched. Knowing at last where Danielle was added to my determination.

I slipped down the steep path between the silent woods, the only light that of the stars, the moon still blanketed by cloud. There came the sound of something moving in the undergrowth and my heart lurched painfully, but it was only a small animal scurrying for safety. The jasmine smelt heavy and sweet as I brushed past it. I remembered Ian Lyall's kiss and involuntarily wiped my mouth with the back of my hand. The path steepened, and as I rounded the last of the trees I could see Bradley paddling softly out

116

to sea. I ran down the last of the steps and stared after him. The jetty was empty. Ian Lyall would have taken the dinghy, Bradley had the only spare one. The only other way of reaching the *Helena* was to swim for it. Not an inviting idea on a dark night. Then I remembered the old rowing boat I had sunbathed against on my first day at the villa. I ran lightly over the sand, straining my eyes in the dark. It was just discernible. A dark hump against the black of the rocks. I dragged it right side up, searching frantically for oars. They were there, under the seat. Painfully I dragged the boat down to the water's edge, wading in waist deep as I floated her. Then, praying she wouldn't sink within minutes of leaving shore, I sprang aboard and began pulling strongly out to sea.

Ahead of me a silver line of foam creamed round the *Helena*'s hull, and after about fifteen minutes hard rowing I could make out the shape of the two dinghies anchored to the yacht. Through the darkness the *Helena* loomed nearer and nearer, the dull glow of lights showing behind a curtained cabin window. With a grating sound the rowing boat scraped alongside her. I had nothing to anchor on to, nothing to tie the rowing boat with. I paddled alongside until I reached the dinghies, and in the fleeting moonlight caught a brief glimpse of the rope ladder. I grasped it, the boat rocking wildly beneath me, then, letting her float free, I began to climb.

It wasn't pleasant. The ladder swung alarmingly and it was pitch black and cold. The only thing that kept my courage up was the thought of Danielle and the relief she would feel on seeing me.

Eternities later I stood on the empty deck, straining my ears for the sound of footsteps or voices. What I did hear was the distant sound of a child's crying. Carefully I began to walk along the darkened deck towards the cockpit. The cabin door opened easily. Large windows on either side gazed blankly out at the glittering sea, the faint light showing settee berths and cupboards. I walked quickly through it, past a long, narrow galley, recently used, and then another cabin with a single bunk in it. All were empty and all were in darkness. I descended a short flight of steps and the crying became more distinct. The cabin door facing me was edged with light, and ther were voices. Both of them instantly recognisable.

Bradley was saying with quiet viciousness: "I knew it was you! All along I knew it was you!"

And subdued but clear. I heard Ian Lyall say: "You bastard, Van de Naude. You number one prize *bastard*!"

Danielle was saying tearfully: "Please take me home. I don't like it here anymore. I want my mummy."

My hand tightened on the door knob and I pushed.

I don't know who was the most surprised. Danielle, who raced towards me, throwing herself in my arms. Ian Lyall, eyes blazing, or Bradley, a gun levelled at Ian Lyall's chest.

"What the hell. . . ." Ian began, his eyes widening, moving towards me.

"Stay where you are!" Bradley ordered.

Ian Lyall stopped, his desperate glance going from Bradley's gun, to Danielle, to myself.

Danielle's arms were around my waist, her face pressed close against me. I held her to me tightly, my eyes fixed on Ian Lyall's, saying in a voice I scarcely recognised: "How *could* you? How *could* you do this to her!" then, feeling myself on the verge of tears, I said: "I don't know what will happen to you and I don't care. I'm taking Danny home." With her hand clutched tight in mine I turned to leave.

"You're not going to find that as easy as you think," Ian said dryly.

I looked at him again, glad I had never allowed myself to respond to his overtures of friendship.

"I knew there was something wrong about you the first day I arrived. I heard you talking to Helena, shouting at her, telling her I would have to go. Now I know why. You were frightened I would carry out my duties too conscientiously. Make things too difficult for you! Well, you've failed. I'm taking Danny back to the villa and I'm going to find it very easy to do so. There's not much you can do now with a gun pointing at your chest!"

"There's not much you can do single-handed and unarmed, either," and he smiled. A bitter, defeated smile. "If you hadn't seen me tonight there was a chance for Danny. Now there's none."

"I don't understand what you mean."

He said, and his voice was patient. "No, I know you don't. But you will. Give or take five minutes."

I said to Bradley: "I'm taking Danielle back in the dinghy. You and Ian can come back in the other one. The rowing boat I came in is probably in the middle of the Mediterranean by now."

A familiar voice said from the cabin door behind me: "Sorry, Lucy. We can't let you do that."

I spun round.

"I'd have given a thousand dollars for it not to have happened this way, Lucy." It was the first time I had seen Steve without a smile on his face.

I said stupidly: "How did you get here?"

"He's been here all the time," Ian said. "Ever since he took Danny from her room."

"I don't believe you. . . ." The walls of the cabin were beginning to close in on me, beginning to spin. Steve stepped forward, taking me firmly by both shoulders and pressing me down in a chair.

"I'm afraid the man's right, Lucy. You should have stayed at the villa like you were told."

"*You!*" I managed weakly. "*You* kidnapped Danny?"

"With a little help from his friends," Ian said bitterly.

The cabin walls began to steady and recede. I gazed at the tableau before me. Steve, staring concernedly down at me. Ian, white-faced and defeated, and Bradley, still holding the gun.

I licked dry lips, saying to Bradley: "Shouldn't that thing be pointing at Steve? You heard what he just said."

"Yes. I heard. It seems you didn't."

"Danielle's kidnapper," Ian said quietly, though I no longer needed telling. "Is the bastard you just helped to-night."

I tried to speak but no sound came. Danielle said: "Steve brought lots of new games for me to play with, but I got tired and now I want to go home and Bradley is frightening me and I want Mummy. . . ."

I pulled her onto my knee, cuddling her close.

"Why?" I asked, looking once more at Bradley.

"Why is no concern of yours," he said off-handedly, looking at his watch. Then to Steve. "We'd better wait another half hour. The roads will still be busy with traffic from Palma."

I said inadequately to Ian: "I'm sorry."

He grinned, pushing his mop of red hair away from his forehead, looking more boyish than ever. "There's no need to be. You did a good job of looking after Danny. You foiled one kidnap attempt."

"You mean the night her chocolate was drugged?"

He nodded.

"I thought it was you that had done it. Steve told me it was you and I believed him."

"Steve had his own reasons for giving me as bad a press as he could. Firstly he didn't want you running to me if you thought anything was wrong, and secondly he was frightened of a developing relationship. He guessed how I felt about you."

My face flushed, remembering the lies I had believed so easily, the off-handed way I had always treated him.

I said to Steve: "And the second time the Mogadon was in the Coke?"

He didn't answer. He didn't have to.

"The car accident. Was that a kidnap attempt as well?"

Bradley laughed shortly and I saw Steve wince. Bradley said cuttingly: "It would have been if Steve hadn't fouled it up."

"You were supposed to go over the cliff with the car, Lucy. Brad wanted no witnesses. I couldn't do it to you," his eyes were pleading. "Everything I've said is the truth. I do love you. I wanted to finish the job, leave Majorca, and start afresh somewhere else with you. You need never have known. . . ."

I turned away, unable to bear the sight of him any longer.

"Who was driving the Cadillac?" I asked Bradley.

"A friend who, like Steve, is prepared to do anything if the money is right."

"And who did the car belong to?"

Bradley's narrow face smiled. "Lyall. Lyall had one for his work in Palma. The work he thought we didn't know about. We borrowed it. It appealed to my sense of humour. I knew Helena wouldn't report it to the police if the attempt failed. She couldn't afford to have Lyall taken in custody for questioning. She needed him at the villa. They both knew what the accident was and she thought Lyall could handle it. After all, that's what she paid him for."

I looked at Ian questioningly. He said simply: "I'm a private detective, not a tutor. Helena was taking no risks. Or thought she wasn't. She knew there were people who would do anything to stop John becoming Premier of Ovambia. She took kidnapping into consideration a long time ago. I had the use of one of the Ria Square flats. Telephone calls at the villa are notoriously public."

"And that's why Janet went there to talk to you? She suspected something and knew who you were?"

"Janet Grey," he said, his face contorted with grief. "Was my cousin, and these two smiling bastards pushed her from a fifth floor window!"

"*I wasn't there!*" Steve shouted. "*I had nothing to do with it!*"

"*You didn't exactly run to the police and tell them who did, did you!*" Ian yelled back, his face ablaze.

"And now you'll murder me, like you did Janet?" I said, turning to Bradley.

"Yes."

Steve moved forward in a gesture of protest, to be waved back imperiously by Bradley.

My throat felt so tight I could hardly speak. When I did it was little more than a croak: "And Danielle? What are you going to do with Danielle?"

Bradley smiled, his chill, humourless smile. "You'll be responsible for her death. If you hadn't told me you'd seen Lyall tonight he might have freed her. Even if he hadn't, Danielle would never have seen me. Only Steve. And arangements for Steve to leave the island were already well planned. There would have been no need to have killed Danielle. Now, thanks to you, we have no option."

It didn't seem to bother him much.

"Why?" I asked uncomprehendingly. "Why does it matter to you whether your father is Premier of Ovambia or not? Why is it so important that you're prepared to kill, to prevent him?"

He said coldly, not even bothering to look at me: "If my father becomes leader of a nation of illiterate wogs, my political career in South Africa is over. Besides, I wanted revenge."

"Revenge? Revenge for what?"

He laughed unpleasantly. "You can ask that? My father marries that black bitch, degrading my mother's memory, degrading my name and you can ask that? I've lived with the stigma of that marriage for twenty years! For twenty years I've promised myself revenge. Now I have it and no-one, *no-one* is going to take it from me!"

Violently he jabbed the gun in Ian's side. "On your feet, Lyall. We're going places."

I gave a cry of protest and Steve said reassuringly: "Don't worry, Lucy. He's going to be all right. Brad's angry, that's all."

It seemed like the understatement of the year.

I half rose to my feet as Ian passed, our hands touching briefly, then Steve knocked them apart and Danielle began to stir, raising frightened eyes to mine. I sat down again, watching fearfully as Bradley forced him out of the cabin. At the door Ian paused, looking back at me, grinning briefly: "I'm sorry about that overheard conversation. I didn't want you in any danger, that's all. At least now I know why you were so unfriendly. It's some comfort," and then Bradley dug the gun painfully in his back, sending him stumbling down the corridor.

Steve took my hand and I snatched it away angrily. His voice had thickened: "I still want you, Lucy."

"Dead or alive?"

"Brad didn't mean all that. He's just trying to frighten you. Stick with me and. . . ."

A muffled shot rang out and seconds later there came the soft drop of a body as it slid beneath the waves.

"He's killed him," I said softly. "He's killed Ian."

Steve's face had whitened, his grasp on my arm tightening painfully.

"Listen to me, Lucy. Brad's the boss, not me. He's the one with the hardware. But I won't let him hurt you. I promise!"

I could already hear Bradley's feet hurrying down the steps.

"And Danny?" I asked hoarsely. "What about Danny?"

Before he could answer the door opened and Bradley said briefly:

"I want the two of them back on the island."

"Are we going home?" Danny asked hopefully. "Now Mr Lyall has gone home, can we go home too?"

"Yes," I lied. "We're going home."

But I knew from the expression on Bradley Van de Naude's face that we hadn't a hope in hell.

There was no chance for heroics. Nothing to do but obediently follow Steve down the rope ladder to the dinghy, reassuring and comforting Danielle as best I could. The expression on Steve's face was one of intense anxiety. Whatever Bradley's plans were, it was obvious he hadn't taken Steve into his confidence.

The dinghy pitched and rolled, and Danielle and myself huddled together, cold and wet, and I tried to force my numbed brain to think. The waves dropped, slapping lightly alongside as we neared the shore, and then the dinghy bucked over the shallows and Steve leapt out, helping me after him, carrying Danielle while Bradley dragged the dinghy up the beach.

The sand was a silver crescent, ghostly in the moonlight. The woods still and silent as we began to climb. Hope began to grow within me. Mario and Peggy would be in the villa. If I could shout and attract attention, there was no way Bradley could talk his way out. Not after the things Danielle had seen in the cabin. As if reading my thoughts, Bradley said: "We'll have to gag them both. I'll make sure the villa is safe. Peggy was in bed before I left but Mario was still out. He could be waiting up for me to return. I'll get rid of him and then we take them through the villa and take two of the cars."

"That's a bit of a bloody risk, isn't it?" Steve asked, the tautness of his nerves showing in his voice.

"There's no other way to the courtyard but through the villa," Bradley said tersely. "First things first. I don't want one whisper from these two. Not one."

Danielle gave a frightened cry as Steve clapped his hand over her mouth. I was already drawing breath for the loudest scream of my life when Bradley forced a hanky in my mouth, binding it with broad elastoplast. Then he pulled my hands behind my back, tying them tightly, and with Danielle also silenced, we began to climb the last few bends to the villa.

The curtain of jasmine hung milky-white in the darkness, the heady smell filling the air thickly. As I brushed past it, the petals scattering on my head and shoulders, my fear vanished.

Ian was dead, and I was the only one who could bring his murderer to justice. And the only one who could save Danielle. To do these two things I had to stay alive myself. I was grimly determined to do so.

In the thickness of the woods, before the path emerged onto the terrace, Bradley handed Steve the gun and then slipped silently across and into the villa. The salon light was on and I guessed Mario was there, waiting for Bradley's return. My eyes sought Steve's.

His eyes held doubt and indecision, and then he moved quickly, trying to untie my hands. The knots were tight and he had no torch to see by. He blasphemed viciously and as they loosened Bradley was already sprinting back towards us. I turned desperate eyes to Steve's. He had the gun! If he acted now! His hand fell uselessly back to his side. Bradley, seeing my freed hands smiled grimly, taking the gun from Steve, pointing it at me.

"*I'll* take the girl. You take the kid," and to me, "Don't get any fancy ideas. I've told Mario you're involved in the kidnapping and he'll shoot you as soon as look at you!"

Steve lifted Danielle, carrying her a captive into her own home. I followed, Bradley's gun in my back. Coffee cups lay scattered on the glass topped tables. Mario had had a long wait. Swiftly we walked through the villa to the courtyard. Mario's old car, the Audi, the Fiat, all were there. Till then I had had no idea what Bradley's intentions were. If he wanted to murder us, it seemed simpler if he had done it at sea. He turned to Steve.

"You take the kid in the Audi. I'll take the girl. We'll meet at the Devesas."

My eyes met Steve's and understanding dawned simultaneously. Danielle and myself. In one car. Over the cliff. Steve couldn't go along with it, I was sure of that. Now he knew what Bradley's intentions were he must be thinking of a way of helping us. But he was unarmed, and spineless, as I had just found out.

As the car rocked down onto the blackened headland, Bradley leaned across and with one hand ripped the elastoplast from my mouth, saying softly: "I owe you, Lucy Matthews."

He touched his temple where the purple welt of bruising showed even in the dimness of the car. Then, with no warning, he swung his fist into the side of my face, sending me smashing into the side of the car, blinded by searing pain. It must have been several minutes later that my vision returned, for when I could see and hear clearly again, the mountain road was already showing like a thin white snake in the headlamps of the car. He laughed.

"I always get my revenge, Lucy Matthews. Even if it takes twenty years as it has with Helena."

Gingerly I fingered the side of my face, moving my jaw fractionally, grateful it still moved. For the first time emotion crept into his cold, cultivated voice. He sounded elated as he said:

"Now nothing can stop me! I've sweated my guts out for political power in South Africa. I've got wealth, talent, charm, I'm a leader, not a follower like the Steve Patterson's of this world! And one thing stopped me. Would always stop me. My father's known association with APFO. When I heard what he intended doing! Christ!" he slung the car suicidally round a hairpin bend, "That was it! Bradley Van de Naude finished for good. And why?" the elation turned to viciousness. "Because he lets that black bitch treat him like a little dog. Well she's the one who will do the begging

125

now! For her precious half-caste brat!" and he began to laugh as the car plunged through a tunnel of trees and down a steep rush in the mountainside.

I wondered vainly if knowing he was mad could possibly be of any help to me. We slashed through a tiny hamlet and I said: "But killing Danielle will make no difference to your father becoming Premier of Ovambia. If you don't hurt her, try to reason with your father, explain. . . ."

"Never," he said gloatingly. "He had his choice and he took it! Let him have his precious APFO. Every day of his life he will know what it cost him!"

Even though Bradley was driving the Fiat flat out, we had long since lost sight of the Audi. Steve and Danielle would be at the Devesas already. Waiting for us.

The road ahead veered sharp left, hurtling down to the rendezvous. He said almost conversationally: "You know she can't have any more, don't you? There'll be no more half-breeds claiming my father's name!"

The lights of the waiting Audi arched brilliantly through the night. Bradley laughed again: "This is it, Lucy Matthews. This is the end!"

EIGHTEEN

The car sliced round the first of the bends and I grabbed the wheel, tugging downwards with all my might, the car veering dizzily across the road towards the cliff face. Blaspheming, he thrust me forcefully away, struggling to swing the car back onto the centre of the road. In the crazily weaving headlights I could see the Audi parked under cover of the pines and the silhouetted figure of Steve some yards away.

All Bradley's attention was on gaining control of the car, avoiding the hundred foot drop he intended only Danielle and myself to go over. I could hear his breathing coming shallow and fast and knew that he was afraid. I flung myself across him again, wrenching wildly at the wheel. If I could smash the car into the cliff it would be the driver's seat that would receive the worst impact. This time the Fiat skidded in earnest. A black wall of rock soared up in front of us. I heard Bradley give a scream and was aware of my own terrified sobs, and then the whole world exploded in a kaleidoscope of glaring light. For endless seconds the car soared through the air, smashing and grinding and the last thing I saw was Steve standing immediately before us, his mouth gaping blackly in the white of his face. Then. as pain crushed me down into excruciating senselessness I knew the car had ricocheted off the cliff face. Was speeding backwards towards the cliff and the sea.

Light years away there came the sound of tinkling glass and the night wind on my face. Feebly I stirred, trying to move my legs, the breath choked out of me. Naked metal tore down my shin as I pulled it clear, tremblingly opening the crushed door. I think I literally fell onto the darkened grass. For endless seconds I lay there, my ears thundering, my heart pounding, aware only of the dreadful stillness. No other sound came from the car. There was no sign of Steve.

Painfully I struggled to my bloodied knees and then to my feet. Yards away, across the road, the Audi remained safe beneath the shelter of the pines. Slowly, I turned to look at the car I had just escaped from. It was in nearly the exact position it had been when Bradley had us rammed only weeks before. As I watched, it teetered, rocking majestically for a few seconds over the cliff edge and then plunging to the dark depths below. Standing in the starlight, I could hear the suck of the waves as they closed over it, spiralling it down to the sea-bed.

Unsteadily I walked back over to the Audi and Danielle. Steve's body lay crushed in the centre of the road, his head at an unnatural angle, his pulse stilled. I let his wrist fall and knelt there amongst the broken glass and the blood, his and mine. He had said he had loved me. Perhaps he had in his way. Certainly I don't think he would willingly have participated in my death. But whatever scheme he may have been thinking up as he waited for Bradley to meet him, Bradley had the gun, and Bradley was the stronger. Relying on Steve was a chance I hadn't been able to take. Gently I closed his eyes and then opened the Audi's door.

Danielle flung herself into my arms, incoherent with shock, her hands clinging round my neck, her breath coming in harsh gasps. Tenderly I stroked her hair, holding her close till her breathing eased.

"Come on, baby. It's time we went home."

"Is everything going to be all right now?" she asked tearfully.

"You'll be in your own bed, with Peggy making you a hot chocolate and Mr Sam to keep you company in less than an hour," I promised.

Every joint, every muscle, ached and throbbed. Painfully I put the car into gear, eased it round Steve's spreadeagled body and began slowly to drive back up the mountain road towards the headland and the villa.

Danielle cried quietly to herself as I drove off the road and onto the blackened headland. It had taken her a long time to get over the shock of Janet Grey's death. I wondered what indelible marks tonight's events would leave. I took the three miles to the villa slowly, easing the car round every suspicious drop of ground, the lights of the villa shining on the tip of the headland like those of a lighthouse to a distressed ship.

Gently I eased my breath in relief as the car rocked carefully onto the drive and up the sweep towards the courtyard gates. There were no lights on at the rear of the villa. The courtyard, heavy with the scent of roses and jasmine, lay plunged in darkness. With Danielle's hand safely clutched in mine, we slammed the car doors behind us and skirted the fountain and the silky ripples where a frog had suddenly dived for cover, and then entered the safety of the silent villa. As we left the tiled floors for the deep pile of white carpeting, we could hear the dull sound of voices.

"Won't they be pleased to see us?" Danielle whispered with a hint of her usual cheerfulness. "It will be a big surprise, won't it?"

"It certainly will," I said dryly.

Light flowed from beneath the salon door and I could hear Mario's voice, harsh and taut, silencing Leonie's lazy drawl. Taking a deep breath I pulled the door open and went in.

I think of the three of them, Leonie was the one who was most shocked. The glass of golden liquid she held in her hand crashed to the floor, her face draining of colour. Peggy was the first to recover. With a cry she ran forward, clutching Danielle to her bosom, drowning her with tears. Mario stared at me unbelievingly, and then beyond me.

"I said tiredly: "There's no-one else. Only Danielle and myself."

"My baby, my baby," Peggy was crooning, rocking Danielle to her, kissing her cheeks, her hair.

Mario said slowly: "Make the child some supper and take her to bed, and Peggy," she paused at the door, her eyes darting for the first time to mine. "Stay with her."

The blood running from my leg was dripping grotesquely onto the white carpeting. I knew my face was badly cut, my hands bruised and swollen. No-one moved to help me.

In complete silence I limped across the room, sitting on the brocaded sofa, heedless of the crimson trail I was leaving.

"Well," I said at last. "Don't you want to know what happened?"

"*I want to know where Brad is,*" Leonie said, the skin tight over her cheek-bones, her cat eyes brilliant.

"Bradley," I said flatly. "Is dead."

She faltered, her hands fluttering behind her for something to support herself on, her eyes fixed on mine unbelievingly.

Mario hadn't moved. "Telephone for the police," he said quietly to Leonie. "Tell them the child is safe and the woman is here."

"Mario," I said in a voice struggling for calm. "I am not 'the woman'. Whatever Bradley Van de Naude told you earlier this evening was lies. He and Steve Patterson kidnapped Danny. Steve has been with her on the yacht ever since she disappeared."

"You expect me to believe that?" Mario said, still not moving, watching me as warily as a cat a mouse. "I knew about you even before he told me! Instinct told me! But no-one listened to me. Well, they'll listen to me now. Now that it's too late. Not that you've murdered!"

"Mario. . . ." I protested.

"You tried before, didn't you? In the study. You tried to kill him then but Peggy and myself, we came home too quickly for you. . . ."

"Bradley shot Ian Lyall," I said flatly. "He shot him and threw his body into the sea."

He said stubbornly: "Mr Lyall is with Mr Van de Naude."

Wearily I shook my head. "That telegram was a hoax by Bradley to get Ian out of the way while they kidnapped Danny. Ian Lyall was a private detective hired by Helena Van de Naude for just such an emergency."

Leonie's voice, flat and strange, said: "They are on their way."

"Good," Mario relaxed perceptibly. "At least the child is safe."

The blood from my leg was soaking in ever widening circles into the pristine whiteness of the floor.

"If I had kidnapped Danielle, why on earth should I bring her back?" I asked with what I hoped was sane reason.

"Because you grew afraid," Mario said triumphantly. "You have committed murder and now you are afraid!"

"Would it be too much to ask for something to bind my leg with while we wait for the police?" I asked. "Otherwise I'll have bled to death and no-one will get any answers."

Mario looked at my leg grudgingly, then said to Leonie: "See she doesn't try to leave."

"She won't," Leonie said surely.

"Leonie for goodness sake, listen to me. . . ."

"How did he die?" she asked, her eyes glittering pinpricks, the sockets already deepening.

"It was an accident," I said bleakly, wondering when she had changed her affections from Max to Bradley. "The car crashed. It went over the cliff."

She closed her eyes, her face ashen.

I said: "What I told Mario was the truth. Bradley and Steve kidnapped Danielle."

She opened her eyes and said slowly: "They won't believe you. Mario and Peggy will give evidence about the time you drugged her before and about the other accident. They won't accept the word of a child. You're going to find yourself on a charge of kidnap and murder."

Our eyes held. Hers held complete certainty.

I said vehemently: "But I didn't do it!"

"Prove it."

I thought of Bradley's mangled body fathoms deep, and Steve's broken body spreadeagled across the road.

"Leave now. Go to Max. He'll know what to do."

I had never thought to have Leonie as an ally.

Max. I was already rising unsteadily to my feet. She reached for her handbag, handing me a headscarf.

"It's the best I can do, but it will stop the bleeding and it doesn't look too serious. Go now. I'll stall Mario. I'll tell him you're in the bathroom."

There was no time to think. What Leonie said made sense. Max, at least, would believe me when I told him what had happened. Once in a foreign jail it could be days before I could get in touch with him. With strength born of desperation, I ran across the room and down the long corridors of the villa D'Este.

The Audi and the old Estate stood side by side in the moonlit courtyard. I made for the Estate first. My years with Max had not been useless. Within seconds I had yanked the bonnet open, and even as I heard the distant ring of running feet, immobilised it in a way that I hoped would fox even the mechanically minded Mario. Then, as the running click of high heels grew nearer, I was back in the Audi, the courtyard gates a blur as I sped through them.

I switched the headlamps full on and trod hard on the accelerator, driving recklessly into the black void of the headland. It wouldn't take the police long to respond to Leonie's telephone call. I only had precious minutes, and however hard I strained my eyes to the furthermost tips of the lights, I still could not see the narrow band of grey that indicated the road.

The feet that had been racing after me had been Leonie's, not Mario's. I drove the car into a gulley, revving the engine desperately as the wheels churned, finally gripping solid earth and I jerked forward, the car continuing to bucket and rock.

Why Leonie? Perhaps Mario had come to his senses and she was telling me my flight was unnecessary. In the blaze of the headlamps the land showed clear and flat. I trod harder on the accelerator. If she had, it made no difference. I was going to Max. Nothing, and no-one was going to stop me.

But I was too late. Even as I saw the snakelike grey of the road and the grim background of soaring mountain behind it, lights flashed, and a car, driven at suicidal speed, sped round the bend, plunging off the road onto the head-land, driving directly towards me.

I swung the wheel hard over, still racing forwards, trying to by-pass him. I knew that once I reached the road I could hold my own. Max had taught me to drive and unless there were road blocks between here and Palma I was confident I could out-distance the police.

The other car swerved to block me, our headlights

meeting in a blinding glare of light. Apart from wilful suicide there was nothing to do but brake and grip the wheel with all the strength that remained in me. For a moment, as the bonnet of the other car skimmed the Audi, I thought my luck had finally run out. The jolt flung me to the far side of the car, half stunning me as the Audi's brakes shrieked to a halt. With distorted vision I saw the policeman fling his door open, running across to me, tall and formidable. Stumblingly I opened my door, half falling out onto the rough grass.

I said determinedly: "I've got see someone . . . in Palma. . . ."

"Not tonight you haven't."

Instead of in handcuffs I was in strong arms, and Max's voice, thick with emotion, was saying against my hair.

"You fool! You stupid, beautiful, unbelievable *fool*!"

Dizzily I cling to him, tears half choking me: "Max! Max it's you! Oh my God! I thought it was the police!"

Max didn't seem interested in the police. His lips were on mine, and there was nothing gentle about the way he was kissing me. Eventually his grip on me eased and he said unnecessarily: "I saw Claudette." He smiled down at me in the moonlight. "No more misunderstanding, Brat?"

"None," I said, my arms still around his neck, his body firm and strong against mine.

"No questions?"

"None whatever," I said, my fingers tightening into the thick curls in the nape of his neck.

"Good." He looked down at me. "I have one."

I stared up at him, my heart scarcely beating.

"Why did you think I was the police?"

Amazingly, for those brief, heaven sent minutes, I had forgotten the tragedy I was enmeshed in. I said brokenly: "There's been an accident. I've just killed Steve Patterson," I saw the expression in his eyes change to one of incredulity. "And," I added for good measure, "Bradley Van de Naude as well."

"Then in that case," Max said with remarkable cool. "You'd better tell me about it before the local officers of the law rob you of the chance."

With legs that felt as if they weren't my own I let him lead me to his car.

"I was coming for you. They won't believe me at the villa. At least Leonie does, but Mario doesn't. It was Mario who told Leonie to ring for the police. He thinks I kidnapped Danielle."

Max, imperturbable, raised a dark eyebrow as he began to drive towards the headland tip and the villa.

"Is she kidnapped?"

"She was. She's safe at home in bed now. Bradley Van de Naude and Steve did it. Steve stayed with her on the yacht. She never saw Bradley or knew he was involved. Not until the end, that is."

"Why should the son want to blackmail his parents?"

"Only John Van de Naude is his father. Helena is a stepmother and coloured. When Van de Naude married her he had to leave South Africa and his political career. Bradley stayed on there for schooling. Inherited all his father's wealth and wanted to go into politics too."

"And?"

"John Van de Naude's politics underwent a radical change. He has agreed to accept Premiership of Ovambia, Helena Van de Naude's natural home, it means the Ovambians will be self-governing for the first time in their history. It also meant any political career for Bradley in Southern Africa was definitely at an end. It was that, combined with his pathological hatred of Helena, that caused him to kidnap Danielle and try and force his father off the political scene for good. In his own words, Helena had degraded his father, his mother's memory, himself. If you ask me, he was mad as a hatter at the end."

Briefly, Max's hand came down on mine and squeezed hard.

"So far, my sweet, so good. How did the accident happen?"

Despite myself I felt my voice begin to break.

"I thought Ian Lyall had something to do with it. Steve had deliberately fostered that idea in my mind so that I wouldn't turn to Ian if I became suspicious of anything. Early this evening I saw him making his way down the path that leads to the beach. I told Bradley."

"And. . . ."

"Bradley told me to wait in the villa and said he would go after him."

"And you," Max said with an expression I knew of old. "Didn't do as you were told."

"No," I said miserably. "I followed him. On the 'Helena' I walked in on Danielle, Ian Lyall, Bradley . . . and Steve."

The ground was steepening, the yawning gates of the villa D'Este only a hundred yards away.

I said flatly: "Bradley Van de Naude took Ian outside. He shot him and threw his body over the side."

"What happened then?" Max's voice was almost unrecognisable.

"He said because I now knew he had kidnapped Danny that I would have to be killed. They killed the other nanny. Janet Grey. She became suspicious and Bradley pushed her from a fifth floor block of flats. He also said . . ." here my voice broke completely. "That now Danny had seen him she would have to die as well."

"I'm beginning to feel very sorry the gentleman in question is already dead!" Max said, speeding between the courtyard gates, "I could have made his leaving a lot more interesting for him!"

"Steve did try to stop it. Or would have done. I don't think he knew what Bradley had in mind. Not till it was too late. Bradley brought us back to the villa, gagged us, went inside and told Mario I was responsible for Danielle's kidnap, making quite sure I would also be thought responsible for her death, and then with Steve taking Danny in the Audi, he took me in the Fiat and arranged to meet Steve at the Devesas."

"The Devesas?"

"The hairpin bends on the highest point of the mountain road. He meant to put both Danny and myself into the one car, send it over the cliff edge, have me blamed for the kidnapping and Danny's death. What reason he was going to come up with I don't know. Knowing Bradley he would have had it all carefully planned out."

The big car slowed to a standstill beside the fountain.

"What happened?" Max asked gently.

I took a deep breath. "As we rounded the last bend I could see the Audi pulled off the road under the trees, and Steve some yards away from it. My only thought was to stop what was going to happen and I thought if I could smash Bradley's side of the car into the cliff face . . . I grabbed the wheel and the car veered and Bradley flung me to one side and tried to get control but it was too late. I flung myself across him, tugging down on the wheel again and we went rocketing into the cliff. I remember seeing Steve . . . and then nothing but colour and lights and sounds . . . when I came to I crawled out of the car. It had ricocheted back across the road to the cliff edge. Seconds later it went over. Bradley was still in it."

"Was Steve dead?"

"Yes. I felt his pulse. He hadn't stood a chance. I simply left him there, drove the Audi round him and came back to the villa.

Max's arms tightened around me.

"Then Mario accused me of being a murderess and kidnapping Danny and told Leonie to telephone the police. He left the room to get something to stop the bleeding."

"Bleeding?" Max asked sharply.

"I cut my leg getting out of the car. While he was out of the room Leonie suggested I make a break for it and go to you."

Max was frowning.

"As I reached the cars I put the estate out of action so Mario couldn't follow me. He knows this headland like the back of his hand and would easily have caught up with me. I could hear them running after me as I left."

Max said, as if he were thinking of something else: "Let's go inside and wait for the police. They're not fools. They'll listen to you, and to Danielle as well."

Tenderly he drew me to his feet, his eyes darkening as he saw the blood-soaked headsquare that bound my leg. Then, despite my not very strong protests, he picked me up in his arms and began to walk with me through the silent corridors of the villa D'Este, to the lighted rooms where Mario and Leonie waited.

NINETEEN

With my head resting on his broad shoulder, my arms clasped tightly around his neck, Max kicked open the door of the main salon and stood on the threshold. Despite the shock that immobilised both of them for fleeting seconds it was obvious that the atmosphere between Leonie and Mario had deteriorated to one of naked hostility.

Gone was Leonie's poise and elegant langour. Gone the beauty of the soft blonde hair, the upward slanting eyes, the graceful movements of hands and arms. There was no mocking provocation in her green eyes now. They were sunk deep in their sockets, glazed with an emotion I couldn't understand. She stood by the window, her shoulders sagging, her hands grasping a tumblerfull of whisky, the knuckles ugly and white.

Mario looked like a man on the point of explosion. The veins stood out in his neck, and I could see the deep track he had made across the carpeting, crossing and re-crossing, waiting for the police who still had not arrived, consumed with fury at Leonie's treachery in allowing me to escape. Now he stood, staring at me with stunned incredulity. The second lengthened and broke. I was aware of expression returning to Leonie's face and then Mario was charging across the room towards us like a wild bull.

Max dropped me unceremoniously to the floor, tripped the raging fifteen stone mountain of flesh and deftly knelt on top of him, pinioning him in a full nelson.

"For once in your life, listen you damned fool!" he shouted breathlessly to the violently struggling Mario. "Lucy wouldn't have come back here if she was guilty of anything! What she told you was the truth. Bradley Van de Naude kidnapped the child, *because. . . ."* his voice rose louder to drown Mario's roaring protests. "Because Helena

Van de Naude ruined his life by marrying his father. He hated her. Hated her for being black. Hated her for changing his father's politics. Hated her for giving him no chance of a political career of his own. With his father as Premier of a black state he stood no chance politically in South Africa, even you must realise that! Helena Van de Naude may not seem black to you, but in Bradley's eyes she was black as Katjavivi. He thought if he could frighten his father enough, his father would step down from the Premiership of Ovambia, leave politics altogether. The only weapon he had was Danielle. He wanted revenge. He wanted it so badly it twisted and warped his mind to the extent that he murdered Janet Grey and Ian Lyall, and was prepared to murder Lucy and Danielle! *Now, will you believe Lucy and listen to her, you stupid old ox!*"

Gradually, while Max spoke, Mario's struggles had lessened. He nodded, and panting Max let him go and rose to his feet.

Mario straightened up slowly.

"Is that the truth?"

I nodded. His fire and rage died pathetically. He sat heavily on a chair, burying his head in his massive hands.

I had been too intent on watching Mario and Max to take any notice of Leonie. Now Max turned to her, saying: "Telephone them again."

As he spoke there came the faint sound of a distant door opening and I heard Mario's audible sigh of relief.

"They are here. Now it is in their hands."

Max's arm closed reassuringly around my shoulders and Leonie said tensely: "I'll go and meet them. They'll get lost otherwise."

The familiar drift of Chanel drifted past me and out of the room. Max drew me closer.

"There's nothing to be afraid of, Brat. I shan't leave you. Ever." His lips found mine and I leaned against him, finding in him all the strength and love I would ever need. For my whole life through I would have Max. An army of police officers could not have shaken the joy I felt.

Seconds stretched into minutes and still Leonie did not appear. When at last she did, she was alone. She seemed to have regained control of herself and there was the faint tinge of colour returning to her cheeks. She said with her old nonchalance: "Only a bloody cat. It had got into one of the rear rooms through the fanlight and couldn't get out again."

Mario groaned and Max said: "Perhaps you would telephone them for us again, Leonie."

She shrugged carelessly and we sat in silence, listening to the repeated clicks, to her mutterings of exasperation.

"The line is dead. I can't get anything."

Max crossed the room and tried himself. When he came back he said briefly: "The lines must be down."

"But we must get through to them!" Mario said, rousing himself from his stupour. "Leonie's first message cannot have been understood. If we wait till morning they will not understand. It will look bad for us. Bad for all of us!" He stumbled to his feet. "I will go. I will drive to Palma. I will bring the police. It is the only way."

Max pressed him gently back into his chair. "I'll go," he said authoritatively. "I'm the expert driver, remember? If I can't make it to Palma and back in under forty minutes I don't deserve to ever race again!"

Our eyes met and he took hold of my hand.

"Only a little while, Brat. Then we'll have forever."

I nodded, hoping that all the love I felt for him showed in my eyes, then, with one last tight grip on my hands he turned on his heel and was gone.

Mario remained on his chair, still trying to grasp and understand what had happened. Leonie stood, her head a little to one side, the slight smile back on her face.

"We seem to be in capable hands again. What about a hot drink while we're waiting?"

"Peggy is in bed. . . ." Mario said without looking at her. "She is sleeping in the child's room."

"I think we can manage to fend for ourselves," Leonie said lightly. "I'll put plenty of sugar in them all. I think we need it."

Her high heels clicked across the mosaiced hallway and into the kitchen. I leaned back, unutterably weary. Danielle was safe upstairs with Peggy. Mario finally understood. Max had the situation in control. And Max loved me.

I opened my eyes, smiling as Leonie handed me a cup of strong coffee.

"Drink it while it's hot," she said, handing Mario his and then curling herself up on the sofa. "We're going to need it, if only to keep awake!"

I sipped the bitter coffee, thankful it wasn't one of Leonie's regular chores.

"The Van de Naudes still won't know Danny is safe," I said, gazing across the vast room to the silk lined wall and a magnificent portrait of David Katjavivi in African robes. "None of them will know."

Mario drained his cup. "They will know tomorrow. We will telegram and telephone. The police will see to it."

Leonie said smoothly : "I doubt if they are worrying to that extent. After all, they will think Ian Lyall has her by now."

I closed my eyes. I didn't want to think of Ian. Not yet. Not till my physical and emotional strength had returned. The look that had passed between us as he left the cabin to his death would stay with me to the end of my life.

I suddenly realised how tired I was. My eyelids were so heavy with fatigue I could hardly keep them open. Mario too, had leant his head back against his chair, his eyes closed, his breathing becoming deep and regular. Leonie pushed a strand of silky blonde hair away from her face and smiled across at me.

"Tired, too, Lucy?"

My head was too heavy to nod. I smiled weakly in assent. She laughed and in the brilliant light of the chandeliers I saw that her colour had returned, the cat eyes bright and glittering again.

"I expect you feel too tired to move?"

She was right. I tried to lift my hand but it remained stupidly by my side. Then she stretched herself sensually and rose to her feet.

"I have a surprise for you, Lucy. You have had your share of grand entrances lately, but never anything to beat this!" She raised her voice, her eyes holding mine exultantly. "Come in, darling! We're ready for you!"

Slowly the salon door opened. There was blood on his hands and clothes but on his face was a smile.

"Hello, Lucy," said Bradley Van de Naude.

TWENTY

I heard my breath escape in a gasp and tried vainly to rise to my feet. The narrow lips twisted cruelly.

"There's no escape this time," he turned to Leonie. "How long since he left?"

Leonie glanced at her wrist watch. "Twenty minutes, maybe twenty-five."

"Then we'll wait another five."

My eyelids were closing, weighed down by invisible weights. With a supreme effort I opened them, struggling to focus on Leonie's face clearly. She stood, hands on her narrow hips, surveying me with amusement.

I said: "You don't understand, Leonie. You can't help him. He's a murderer."

The golden head tilted further to one side, the curving lips smiling wider.

"It's you that don't understand, my sweet," She moved forward, linking her arm with his, scarlet nails digging deep into his jacket. "He's my husband."

My legs, my body, my arms, my head, were all pinioned into the chair with the power of a G force.

"Didn't it ever cross your mind to wonder who *had* drugged Danielle's drinking chocolate if Ian Lyall hadn't?"

She crossed the room, pouring herself another whisky. "I'm not in the habit of paying nursery visits. Especially where that child is concerned." For once, venom showed through the light mockery. Danielle had been right when she had told me that Leonie Blanchard did not like her. And I had dismissed it as nothing of importance. Nothing that mattered.

"You've had more lucky escapes than you realise, Lucy." She came back and perched on the arm of the sofa, crossed legs swinging elegantly. "You can't for one minute have thought I was *serious* about helping you to escape?"

"No," I said, aware that sensation was returning to my fingers and toes. "You were going to run after me and shoot me. Mario would have understood that. Shooting me whilst I was trying to escape." I permitted myself a smile that wiped hers off her face. "But you weren't quite quick enough were you? And when you got to the courtyard, the Estate car wouldn't start, would it?"

Her eyes flashed with anger and she leapt forward, smacking my face with the full force of her palm.

"Don't laugh at me! Don't ever laugh at me!"

"At least we know why the police never arrived. You never called them. That's the last thing you would have wanted. What were you going to do? Sneak quietly away during the night?"

She had regained her composure, the habitual mocking smile was firmly back in place.

"What I *was* going to do is none of your affair. It's what I'm going to do now that should interest you."

"And that is?"

Carry out our original plan. And get out of this God-forsaken place!" she glanced round the walls of the room with a shudder of distaste.

I wondered how much longer of our five minutes we had left.

"So everything APFO planned, every single piece of paperwork, went straight to Bradley?"

"And no-one suspected a thing," she agreed smirkingly. "Once or twice I wondered about Ian. . . . But I knew we could deal with Ian. We were more worried about Steve."

"Steve?"

"He made a hash of it the first time round at the Devesas. Then our second plan, that of fostering his relationship with you so that he would be spending time in the villa and would be able to take Danielle easily when the time came, that wasn't such a great success either."

"Why?"

She surveyed my face critically. "I find that hard to understand myself. You're not a beauty, are you? But Steve fell for you. Had romantic dreams of taking his cash and

143

sending for you so that you could join him in some private Eden, unsullied by his regrettable deeds of the past."

"He was a bloody nuisance about her!" Bradley said suddenly, his voice cold with contempt. "Thank God the idiot's dead. He was nothing but a risk from beginning to end, and in case you've forgotten," he turned to me. "*You* killed Steve Patterson. Not me."

It wasn't something I needed reminding of.

"And now? What happens now?"

"We go back to the Devesas. The Fiat is fathoms deep, its doors flung wide, the sea empty of bodies. We simply rectify it." He turned to Leonie. "Go get the kid, we've wasted enough time already."

As he glanced away from me I snatched a look at Mario. His mouth gaped open, the cup beside him drained. Mine, down at the foot of my chair, was only half empty. Tentatively I tried to move my fingers and felt them respond. The drug was beginning to wear off. If I could delay him a little longer. . . .

"How did Leonie know you were still alive?"

"She didn't. Not till she heard me enter the villa. After all, she knew it couldn't be the police. She'd never telephoned them in the first place. I stayed in one of the rear rooms while she fobbed you off with the story of a cat and then made the coffee and drugged it. I cut the telephone wires, knowing full well that your brainless world champion would go haring off to Palma like the twelfth cavalry, and waited for the drug to take effect."

There were movements from the bedrooms. I said: "How did you get here?"

His pale blue eyes held mine, filled with anticipation and pleasurable cruelty.

"When the car crashed I was flung clear and unconscious. It was very dark and you must have been stunned. Leastways you couldn't have looked for me. If you had, it would have been an easy enough task to have helped me over the edge. Assuming you could have done such a thing."

"Don't worry," I said fervently. "I'd have had a jolly good try!"

"When I regained consciousness both cars had gone and Steve was dead. I dragged him into the undergrowth to delay any police activity, and began to walk. I stole a car, empty while its occupants went for a moonlight stroll in the woods, drove here, parked it in the darkness at the foot of the drive so that no-one leaving the villa would see it, and made my entrance. None of it improved my temper. All the time, the thought that kept me going was the thought of finding you again!" He moved closer to me, his shadow falling across me. *"Of making you pay!"*

There was spittle at the corner of his mouth and his eyes were glazed. I could feel the beads of perspiration break out on my forehead.

"People get mutilated in accidents. Horribly mutilated." He ripped the makeshift bandage from my leg. The cut had congealed, the flesh on either side swollen and raw. "We could start here. Not very big, is it? We could make it a lot bigger. Say from here," his index finger touched my kneecap, "to here." He drew a line to my ankle. "Scream as much as you like. It won't bring help from Leonie."

From his inside pocket he drew a short, sharp knife. I sucked in my breath and as it quivered in his hand, saw that he was smiling. He held it high, the knife gleaming in the light, the rapier point poised exactly over my kneecap, his grip on it one that would slice my leg open as easily as a butcher cleaving meat. Then he laughed and the knife plunged downwards. I closed my eyes and screamed.

TWENTY-ONE

"If you so much as nick her skin I'll cut your throat from side to side!"

Bradley whirled round, the knife still held in his hand. Max filled the doorway, his shoulders tense, his hands clenched into fists.

"To do that," Bradley said breathlessly, "You need a knife."

"Yes," Max said with certainty. "Yours."

They stood measuring each other up and then Bradley laughed.

"You'll never get it! I'm going to give you the pleasure of seeing your girlfriend die in the most painful way I can devise. Drowning is too good for her. And you."

With sudden momentum he rushed towards Max, the knife held high, its point piercing downwards towards Max's heart. Struggling to move I saw Max side step, but not soon enough. The knife missed, but Bradley's body lunged into his, sending them both crashing across the salon, coffee tables and object d'art scattering in their wake. Max hit out with his fist, catching Bradley on the chin, sending him sprawling, the knife still gripped in his hand. As Max hurled himself upon him, Bradley forced the knife blade upwards. Max had both hands on Bradley's wrist forcing the wavering tip aside, while Bradley's muscles strained to their utmost to keep his grip firm, the knife unyielding.

Helplessly I watched, pushing up with all my might to stand. To do something. Anything.

Grunting and cursing Bradley kicked Max off him, sending him sprawling, only to be knocked half senseless as Max leapt back, seizing the knife and forcing Bradley's arm back till the knife fell in a silver crescent to the floor.

He had no chance to reach it himself.

They were locked in a bloody, swaying fist fight. The cut on Bradley's temple had re-opened, blood pouring down his face, and blood gushed from Max's lip, smearing the walls, the carpet, as they lurched and swayed about the room, only inches from Mario's inert body, and feet from where I sat, my breath hurting my chest, screams rising in my throat.

Both of them were panting, their clothes torn and ripped, and then Max kneed Bradley in the groin and as Bradley's hold on him slackened and he groaned with pain, Max thrust his arm forward with a sharp right to the chin, and then another and another. Reeling, Bradley fell back against the wall and then, his face a mask of blood, he seized the whisky decanter, hurling it into Max's face, lunging down on top of him.

My eyes were fixed on the knife lying near the open doorway, still out of Bradley's reach. If I could only force myself to move, to crawl round and get it myself . . . but though feeling and movement had returned to my arms, my legs would still not support my body and I sat useless and helpless as Bradley rained blows down on Max's head, forcing him onto his back, reaching for his throat. I could see the expression on Bradley's face. The blazing triumph beneath the blood and sweat.

Then Max gouged viciously at his eyes and Bradley's grip loosened for the fraction necessary for Max to twist away, and as both men stumbled to their knees, Max sent Bradley flying backwards with a hard punch just below the heart. Bradley lay where he fell, his breath rasping, saliva running from his mouth and as Max tensed for one last spring, Leonie said silkily: "Very entertaining. Would you like to see the little surprise I've got?"

Danielle's eyes were glazed and uncomprehending. I remember thinking thankfully. She's drugged. She doesn't realise. Leonie stood behind her, her left arm reaching across Danielle's body and grasping Danielle's right wrist. In her right hand she held the knife. It's tip rested unwaveringly at Danielle's throat.

Max took one look at the expression on Leonie's face and froze. Dazedly Bradley heaved himself first to his elbows, then to his feet, gasping lungfuls of air.

"Out to the cars," he gasped painfully, clutching his chest, kicking viciously at my legs.

"I can't move," I lied, aware of feeling easing down my veins, spreading in tingling warmth.

"Then stay here and be burnt with the villa and the rest of them!" he said, still struggling for breath. "Do as you're told Wyndham or we'll kill Danielle here and now before you all!"

Danielle began to cry. Slowly Max turned to me. My eyes flickered, sending an unspoken message across the room in a way we had done for the past fifteen years when speech had been impossible. Then, it had been the harmless understanding of Uncle Alistair and Aunt Katherine we had sought to avoid. Now our lives depended on that unspoken oneness of minds.

He turned from me, his body sagging as if in defeat, stumbling across to the open door, Bradley only feet behind him. Danielle stood in her nightdress, her eyes wide and frightened. Leonie, svelte and confident, still held the knife at her throat with tapering, well manicured nails. Bradley's narrow shoulders as he walked away from me, were those of a victor. Every movement he made betraying the triumph he felt.

As Max reached the doorway and Danielle, I summoned up all my strength and with a prayer on my lips, sprang from my chair, leaping for the light switch, plunging the room into darkness.

There were screams and cries and the sound of fist meeting bone, and I was running wildly to where I had last seen Danielle. A silk clad body reeled past me in the blackness and I could feel Leonie's long fingers clutching desperately for something to break her fall. My skirt rent and I was screaming, *"Danny! Danny!"* and then she had hurtled into my arms and I was clasping her to me and sobbing, and now it was Leonie who was screaming, and in the dark the two men lurched and swayed and I caught the deadly flash of steel held high but could not see whose grip it was held in. Feverishly I ran my hands over the blood-smeared walls. The light switch! Dear God! The light switch!"

Leonie's hysterical screams tore the darkness as the men grunted and gasped for control of the knife. Briefly, as they fell against the windows, I glimpsed Bradley's face, the blatant murder in his eyes, the knife in his grasp as he tried to force it down into Max's chest, and Max, his wrists grasped round Bradley's, forcing it away, his face and neck distorted with strain. Then they were in the dark centre of the room again and there was the sound of falling furniture as they fell to the floor. Then a brief gasp. Then nothing.

Sobbing, my fingers closed on the switch, plunging the room into garish brilliance.

Bradley lay on the carpet, face down, impaled by the weight of his body on the knife he had held. Blood seeped from beneath him, soaking into the carpet, spreading in ever widening circles.

Leonie was a woman transformed. White and haggard she huddled in a corner, staring with transfixed eyes at the body of her husband, making no movement towards him. Making no movement at all.

Max walked wearily across to her, leading her unprotesting from the room. She stood in the shadowed hallway, gazing from one to the other of us, saying like a frightened child: "Can I go? Please let me go?" her voice a mere whisper.

Max nodded, letting his hand fall from her arm. With one last, glazed look at the closed doors behind which her husband lay dead, she fled down the darkened corridors and out of the villa.

"She won't be able to get away, will she?" I asked Max, as his bloodied arm closed round my shoulder.

"No. The police will pick her up tomorrow. And the air here, will be a little purer tonight."

I said hesitantly: "The night she spent away from the villa . . . were you . . . was she. . . ."

"Lucy, Lucy," his voice was thick with love. "No, she wasn't. My only reason for even passing the time of day with Leonie was the chance it gave me to see you. To know what you were doing."

"And she told you nothing but lies."

"Leonie would have been incapable of anything else. God

knows what will happen to her now."

I remembered the knife tip at Danielle's throat.

"Whatever it is, she'll deserve it," I said, feeling no compassion for her at all. My arms closed round the shivering Danielle. "What happens now?"

"First you put Danny back to bed and then," he grinned at me grotesquely through a sea of blood, "then I really *do* go for the police!"

TWENTY-TWO

With Danielle finally asleep beside the still drugged Peggy, we had hauled Mario out of the carnage of the main salon and onto a chair on the terrace, covering him with a blanket. Then, while Max had taken a much needed shower I had made coffee and now, two hours later, we were sat in the peace and stillness of Helena Van de Naude's study.

"What made you come back?" I asked, feeling the hot liquid steadying my overwrought nerves, relaxing after what seemed an eternity of fear and tension.

"I never left, Brat. I knew Bradley was still alive."

"How? I'd *told* you he was dead. I was *sure* he was dead."

"And you were sure Steve's body was still lying in the road."

"Yes. . . ."

"Which was very strange," Max said, ruffling my hair. "Because when I drove round the Devesas a short time later there was no body at all. Not a thing I would be likely to miss."

"Bradley had already moved it?"

"Yes. He was probably still legging it up the road when I drove past."

"So you knew. All along you knew!"

"I guessed."

"And the bit about going to Palma for the police was all bluff?"

He nodded. "I was damn sure it wasn't coincidence that the telephone wasn't working, and when Leonie came back into the room her eyes gave her away. I knew Bradley was there. Just waiting for me to make my exit before he showed himself."

"Well, I wished you'd let me know!" I said feelingly. Another second and I would have been a cripple for life!"

"My timing," Max said firmly, "is always perfect." And proceeded to prove it.

Much later he said huskily: "I love you, Brat. I've always loved you. I always will love you."

My arms tightened around his neck. "I've been a fool, Max. But I never stopped loving you. Not for so much as a second!"

"Just see that you don't!" and he pulled me to him, kissing my eyelids, my mouth, my throat.

Gradually the pearl grey of early morning filled the room with ethereal light and he said at last.

"Time I woke Mario. I'll be back with the police in under the hour."

Mario was sleeping soundly. He stared, puzzled and tousel-headed as Max woke him, gazing at his surroundings uncomprehendingly.

"We had to put you to bed out here," Max said with a grin. "No easy task I can assure you!"

"I wasn't drunk!" Mario began indignantly. "I never get drunk!" he stared down at his clothes and then his expression changed. "The police! You were going for the police!"

He stumbled to his feet, his eyes alarmed. "What has happened? Why did no-one wake me?"

Max laid a restraining hand on his shoulder.

"The coffee Leonie gave you last night was drugged. It knocked you out completely, and then you fell into a natural sleep."

"Drugged?" Mario stared at Max as if he were mad.

"She was his wife," Max said, and then, seeing that the bewildered Mario still did not understand, said again: "Leonie was Bradley Van de Naude's wife. That cat she said she heard was Bradley. He was flung from the car before it went over the cliff."

Mario swallowed hard, his brain struggling to keep up with Max, his eyes registering Max's bruised face and torn shirt.

"He came back," Max said simply. "There was a fight and in the dark he fell on his knife."

"Is he dead?"

Max nodded. "So now I'll go for the police and you can take care of Danielle and Lucy."

Mario hurried after him, saying: "Leonie. Where is Leonie?"

"She got away," Max said briefly. "It was all very confused. . . ."

"But she must be caught. . . ." Mario protested excitedly. "She must be made to tell what happened. . . ."

"Don't worry," Max said reassuringly. "She'll be caught. Without Bradley, Leonie isn't going very far."

Pacified, Mario went into the kitchen to start cooking us all a substantial breakfast, and I went upstairs and gently woke Danielle. She complained of horrible nightmares, but otherwise seemed her usual, cheerful self. Peggy was impossible. For a start, despite a raging headache, she wouldn't believe that she had been drugged. Even Mario couldn't make her understand, and it took him all his strength and marital authority to prevent her from unlocking the salon door to see for herself.

"I don't believe it," she repeated time and time again. "I simply don't believe it!"

At seven o'clock, with Danielle playing ball on the terrace, Peggy still repeating that none of it was possible, Max and the police arrived at the villa.

For the next couple of hours Mario came into his own. Translating and re-translating, whilst Bradley's body was covered with a sheet and removed on a stretcher. Peggy watched, her face bloodless. Then, hesitantly she walked to the open door, surveying the destruction and carnage of what had been the most elegant room in the villa.

"Now do you believe it?" her husband asked grimly.

She nodded her head, and with unusual tenderness he helped her away, sitting her down on a kitchen chair, pressing a cup of hot tea into her hand.

A squad of men had already gone down to the bay and a tight lipped officer came back with the news that Ian Lyall's body had been washed ashore with the morning tide and that there was a single bullet through the heart.

Peggy began to cry quietly and I took Danielle upstairs on the pretext of looking for Mr Sam, while the police toiled to bring Ian's body up the steep cliff path, through the villa and into the waiting ambulance in the courtyard. Then, murdered, and murderer were driven off together.

The officer was surprisingly kind. Gently he questioned Danielle, making her repeat time and time again what had happened to her. Who had been with her on the yacht? How long had she been there? What had she seen when Bradley arrived? What had she seen and heard when I had arrived? What had happened to Mr Lyall?

Then, with Mario as interpreter, I repeated as clearly as I could the succession of events that had led to the deaths of Steve Patterson and Bradley Van de Naude.

The officer's face was expressionless as Max gave his evidence of how Bradley had died. How Leonie had come down with the knife at Danielle's throat, how I had plunged the room into darkness, and how he had wrested the knife from her grasp, only to have Bradley leap on him and wrench it from him. How they had fought. How they had overbalanced and Bradley had fallen with all his weight on the knife in his hand.

Danielle told of her 'nightmare'. Of Miss Blanchard going to cut her throat and Bradley frightening her and everything going black till she found herself in my arms, and of how there was blood everywhere and then of how she had woken up in her own bed, not the yacht, and could she go back and play ball again as she was getting rather good at it and needed to practice.

Grimly our statements were taken down, the salon searched minutely and locked, and then the officer asked that we go with him down to Police headquarters where we would be questioned yet again.

Mario turned to me with a reassuring smile.

"It will be all right. The little one's evidence will see to that. They will match the bullet with the gun owned by Bradley. All will be well."

Max looked at his watch. "Nine-thirty. Would you ask the officer if we have time for a fifteen minute detour on our way to Police headquarters, Mario?"

Mario, no longer puzzled by any request, asked. The officer frowned.

Mario said to Max: "He wants to know the reason. Cannot it wait till later."

"Afraid not," Max said, not sounding the least regretful.

Mario and the officer conferred again in rapid Spanish.

Mario said: "He wants to know where it is you wish to go that is so important?"

"The British Embassy."

The officer was voluble in his assurances that the Embassy would be immediately informed of the circumstances its nationals unfortunately found themselves in. But there was no need for Max to go there before going to Police headquarters. As officer in charge he must insist. . . .

"Tell him," Max said unperturbed, "that our reason for going to the Embassy is not to complain or seek help."

Mario did so. The officer grew more and more puzzled.

"He wants to know for why?" Mario said, raising his hands palms upwards in a gesture of bewilderment.

Max glanced at his watch again. "Tell him that in exactly two hours, Miss Matthews and myself are due to be married at the British Embassy and that our witnesses will be awaiting our arrival."

I tried to speak and failed. Mario tried and succeeded. The officer's frown became less prominent, the conversation more excitable.

I said at last: "You can't be serious, Max!"

"I've never been more serious in my life," he said, grinning down at me. "The minute Claudette spoke to me I asked the British Ambassador to arrange the quickest wedding he could. He has done and it's going to take place in exactly one hour and fifty-five minutes so perhaps you'd like to change your dress!"

I didn't wait to hear if the officer had given his permission or not. I was already racing up the stairs to my room and scrambling into the prettiest dress I owned.

Peggy and Danielle rushed after me, Danielle jumping up and down and squealing: "Oh *do* let me be a bridesmaid! *Please* let me be a bridesmaid!"

"Yes," I gasped, zipping my dress up, brushing my hair, searching for sling backed high heels.

There was a knock on the door and Mario came in,

sheepishly holding a posy of hastily picked flowers.

"It is all right. The officer understands. He and his men will have to attend the ceremony and then you will both have to go straight to Police Headquarters, but he will allow the marriage. . . ."

"How on earth did Max persuade him?" I asked breathlessly, applying eyeshadow and mascara.

"He is a romantic man," Mario said grinning. "Besides, he is a racing fanatic. How could he refuse the future world champion permission to marry!"

Danielle had her party dress on and Peggy was brushing her hair, incoherent with excitement.

Hand in hand we ran down the wide sweep of stairs to where Max, surrounded by pistol hipped police, waited.

The dark curls were as unruly as ever, and the brown eyes gleamed with an expression that sent my heart racing.

"I'm ready," I said simply.

"Not yet, Brat. Not yet." From his hip pocket he drew a delicate necklace. The gold and lapis lazuli one he had given me for my birthday and which I had so pettishly left behind me. The two cherubs soared upwards against their background of blue. I felt tears prick the back of my eyes as he gently fastened it around my neck.

"And this."

The interested policemen crowded round and Peggy began to dab at her eyes as Max very gently and very firmly, slipped my engagement ring back into place.

"Now, Brat. Now you're ready."

"Oh Max," I said. "I do love you."

The officer cleared his throat. "There is not much time. . . ."

Max smiled down at me. "Claudette and Fedor are going to be a little surprised when we turn up under police escort!"

"Oh goodness," I said. "Your mother!"

"My mother?" Max asked mystified. "What about my mother?"

"She wants to become a Justice of the Peace. Uncle Alistair asked me specifically to keep out of any trouble!"

"Then all I can say," Max said, looking round at the

squad of policemen, "is that we'd better not have any wedding photographs taken!"

And regardless of our audience he took me in his arms and kissed me.

Friday N

Harry Ritchie was born in Kir... author of *Success Stories*, *Here We Go* and *The Last Pink Bits* and has edited the anthology *New Scottish Writing*. He lives in London.

Praise for Harry Ritchie:

The Last Pink Bits

'Consistently engaging, good-tempered and funny'
The Spectator

'Written with colour, pace and sharp intelligence'
Sunday Telegraph

'Entertaining pieces of information are scattered throughout the book, along with throwaway lines, sentences of laugh-out-loud humour and bursts of potted-guide-book history . . . His style is that of Bill Bryson. Both writers throw light into dark corners of obscure foreign parts, making you laugh and think simultaneously' *Scotsman*

Friday Night Club

'Harry Ritchie proves once again that he can spin a fine yarn, turn a mean phrase and crack a good gag' *Arena*

'The pace here is breathlessly fast and the writing sprinkled with gentle wit' *Herald*

'Harry Ritchie tells a lot of good jokes, is a dab hand at cutting observation and knows how to turn on the charm' *Guardian*

'Cutting, amusing and affectionate'
Times Literary Supplement

HARRY RITCHIE

Friday Night Club

FLAME
Hodder & Stoughton

First published in Great Britain in 2002 by Hodder and Stoughton
A division of Hodder Headline
This edition first published in 2003

A Flame paperback

1 3 5 7 9 10 8 6 4 2

A CIP catalogue record for this title is available
from the British Library

ISBN 0 340 82223 6

Typeset in Sabon by
by Palimpsest Book Production Limited,
Polmont, Stirlingshire
Printed and bound in Great Britain by
Clays Ltd, St Ives plc

Hodder and Stoughton
A division of Hodder Headline
338 Euston Road
London NW1 3BH

Acknowledgments

With thanks to Rachel Calder, Stephan Chambers, Paul Davis, Lizzie Dipple, Phil Harmer, Nick Hornby, Sharon Maguire, Marta Roman, Toby Morison and Roland Philipps. Special thanks to Tracey MacLeod.

Part One

Part One

1

'PLEASE, PLEASE, PLEASE'

Thursday morning

'Thirty-four.'

Blimey. Come *on*.

'Thirty-five.'

Alastair squeezes his eyes shut. His arms tremble as they straighten and lock. He takes a deep breath and gradually lowers himself down again until the tip of his nose touches the rug. Then, slowly, slowly, he pushes himself back up, his arms beginning to shake now. 'Thirty-six,' gasps Alastair, and he flops to the floor. Given the chance, he'd very much like to stay collapsed on the rug but slacking is not allowed. The slow press-ups finished, Alastair clambers to his feet to do the stretching. When he has completed twelve bends to the right, twelve to the left, and twelve where his palms have to touch his toes, he straightens up and shakes himself loose.

'Righty-ho,' Alastair says to Susie, who has poked her head round the door, checking on his morning regime as per. 'A cup of tea and an orange juice.' Twisting his neck from side to side, Alastair follows Susie downstairs but takes a detour to the front door when he sees that there's post waiting for him on the mat – a Visa bill, something incomprehensible about his pension plan by the looks, and a thin brown envelope addressed to 'Eck Carr'. Alastair opens the envelope and sees, instead of a letter, two ten-pound notes. He drops the envelope into the bin that lives under the hallway's little mahogany table and stares blankly at the two tenners, holding them as if they are tickets.

Ah. They'll be from Rob. It's the twenty quid he lent Rob last Friday Night Club. When Rob was so stoned he couldn't remember his PIN number at the cashpoint on Shaftesbury Avenue. He should have known it was from Rob by the Eck.

Eck, thinks Alastair as he places the money on the table before making his way through to the kitchen. Eck. Well, it's no wonder. Alastairs, reckons Alastair, should be imposing, well-fed chaps with public-school hair, obedient, luxuriant hair, hair they can sweep back and forth in thick flicks. Alastairs aren't supposed to be wee, freckly, gingery, baldy blokes with the cheekbones of a turnip. Which goes a long way to explaining for this Alastair why he has answered to a wide variety of names throughout most of his thirty-six years – Ginger (obviously), Carrot (obviously), Jasper (as in Jasper Carrott), Algernon (briefly), Jimmy (as in Johnstone and not so briefly), Al (only more recently and only at the *Chronicle*) . . . and Eck. Short and ugly, no better than it should be. The one that's lasted since primary.

Susie's waiting for him in the kitchen. 'Bit of brekker,' announces Alastair as he fetches the carton of orange juice from the packed fridge, cheerily enough because the reminder that he's Al at the *Chronicle* has perked him up and started him thinking about the day ahead – there's a bit of the Arts section to finish off, then most of Lifestyle to knock into shape for press day tomorrow. If all goes well, he might be able to leave early tomorrow, zip over to Soho, make the most of Friday Night Club for a change.

Graham is watching Jenny as she wriggles out of her little black dress. The dress falls to the floor.

Now she is wearing only high-heeled shoes, black stockings and teensy black knickers. Jenny steps over the dress and towards a man. Who is the man? Graham can see just the man's thick, stubby fingers fondling Jenny's teensy-knickered rump. Jenny responds with a blissful moan. 'Please,' she says with a pout and a squirm. 'Please, please, please.' Jenny drops to her knees and nuzzles the man's bulbous, trousered crotch. 'Please, Alastair,' says Jenny.

Graham whimpers and twitches his head. He has been sleeping for only two hours. It will be another four hours before he is woken by the drilling of a sewage repair crew – long enough for him to have forgotten this dream, but not the one that will be abruptly halted by the first blast of the sewage repair crew's drills, the one where he'll be sprinting hopelessly along Old Street, pursued by the Chancellor of the Exchequer, the Right Honourable Gordon Brown, MP.

Sticky eyed, furry mouthed and fuzzy headed, Ian is standing in the tiny, shambolic kitchen, hoiking his long, tattered, red jumper down over the cartoon rhinoceros on the front of his boxer shorts and reflecting, as he frequently does at this time, that maybe he should invest in a dressing gown, a big, white, woolly dressing gown, the kind you probably get in expensive hotels. Ian is waiting for the kettle to boil. No, he reminds himself, he is waiting for the water inside the kettle to boil – for the kettle itself to boil would require a temperature of perhaps thousands of degrees. Ian sighs, because he has often inflicted this thought on himself since his return to the land of kettles, and he has pissed himself off each time. He stares morosely at the kettle, until the water inside begins to boil, then he pours that water on to the ground coffee pouched in a filter paper which is beigely unbleached, on account of Claire wanting to save the planet.

Claire. She'll need something to eat. How much would a big, white, woolly, five-star-hotel dressing gown cost? he wonders, while he reaches unseeingly inside the cupboard for a bowl and the storage jar of cereal. A hundred quid? Two hundred quid? Who knows. Ian opens the fridge and reaches unseeingly inside for the carton of yesterday's milk, which he pours unseeingly into the bowl full of uncooked pasta. Mind you, there'd be precious little need for a big, white, woolly, five-star-hotel dressing gown in Barcelona or Istanbul or Paris.

2

Thursday lunch-time

'Yeah, Graham, you there, yeah? No? Yeah, Chaz here. Might have a little something for you, man. Give us a bell at the mag.'

Chaz? Who the *fuck* is Chaz? Because he has yet to put the heating on and is still wearing only his dressing gown, Graham is shivering as he examines his answerphone with a bleary, truculent frown. 'Chaz, Chaz, Chaz,' he mutters to himself . . . Chaz! Youth with the goatee who hangs out at the Cantaloupe. Art director at some magazine. Yes, but which magazine? Come on, *think*. It's a commission, for fuck's sake. Money. Remember that?

Graham stumbles stiff ankled out of his study and back next door into the bedroom, where he hauls the duvet off the bed, scattering photographs of Jenny in the process, and gathers it round his shoulders. He has an idea. Quite failing to predict that the duvet's train will knock over the metal bin full of paper, crushed beer cans and pencil shavings, Graham lurches back to the study, picks up the phone and dials 1471.

After the phone's slow drum-roll of clicks, that posh robotic matron comes on. 'You were called. Today. At. Eleven. Forty. Two. Hours. We do not have the caller's number to return the call. Please hang up. Please hang . . .'

Fuck.

Ian swallows another yawn.

Meanwhile, the sales director of a prospering computer-supplies company, alumnus of the Fontainebleau Business School, proud husband and father and, by his own admission, one of the most respected members of the Nantes Rotary Club, is studying a picture in a textbook on the desk in front of him. The picture shows a woman in a shop pointing to a row of red dresses. The sales director, alumnus, husband, father and Rotarian is tapping the picture reflectively with a Mont Blanc pen. 'Zih laydee,' he says eventually.

Ian tries to sound encouraging. 'Yes, Marcel?'

There follows yet another long and puzzled silence while Marcel examines his textbook. Ian gazes out of the window, although the view is not one that can easily distract, consisting as it does of a fire escape and the back of the Krazee Kost-Kutter Klothes Kompany on the north side of Oxford Street. The location of the London Oxford School of English doesn't, in Ian's opinion, explain or excuse the school's title, but, then again, five of the English-language schools where Ian has taught have had 'Oxford' in their titles, and one of the others was the Oxbridge English Centre, which consisted of two rooms above a dry-cleaner's on the outskirts of Ankara.

'Zih laydee.'

'Yes?'

'Zih laydee bize . . . zih laydee bize zih cloazez.'

'Very good, Marcel,' says Ian. 'But remember – is buying, Marcel. She is buying clothes. And the next one?'

The Mont Blanc pen slides along the textbook and begins to tap at an image of a beshorted figure licking an ice cream. 'Zih boy,' announces this computer-sales supremo, who likes to boast to Ian about his two-million-francs-a-year-plus-bonuses salary, when he's speaking French, and who has managed to tell Ian, when he's been speaking English, that he has a big job.

'Zih boy . . . zih boy . . . eeets . . . zih boy eeets zih glass.'

Ice cream. Jesus. More to the point, twenty hours of extra-expensive one-to-one tuition and the man still doesn't understand that English has two present tenses. Is eating, Ian says to himself. Is buying and is eating, you dim twit. Should he have yet another go at pointing out the existence of the present continuous or should he have a shot at sorting out the vocabulary? Ian sneaks a check of his watch. Four minutes to one. Hell with it.

'Excellent, Marcel. Very good indeed.'

'*Vraiment?*'

'*Oui, vraiment, c'est formidable.* Remember – in English, Marcel. So, yes, very good.'

'*Bon, nous avons finis?* Um, wee . . . wee . . . feeneesh . . . wee feeneesh?'

'Yes, for today. I will see you tomorrow at eleven.'

'And mah . . . mah ack . . . mah acksentuh?'

'Excellent.'

I have made more coffee. I have eaten my bowl of serial. I have flossed my teeth. I am sitting at my desk. I turn on my Mackintosh. Nothing happens. I dial the number of the computer company. I try and explain that I must write and file my column. I think to myself that I

Alastair shakes his head and scrolls down his screen until he reaches the finale.

Having cudjilled my brians, the phone rings. It is the computer company to tell me that my modem and my Mackintosh are now okay. Hopefully, they are right. Otherwise you, dear reader, are not reading this column, because it and therefore you, dear reader, do not exist.

Alastair sighs. 'Barry?'

A bald and bespectacled head pops up over the computer facing Alastair's. 'Yip?'

'How come it's always my turn to sub Josh?'

Barry, the chief subeditor (Arts, Books and Lifestyle), pulls at an earlobe. 'That bad, eh?'

'No worse than last week. Or two weeks ago. But that's my point – I've done three Joshes in a row, Barry. It's not fair.'

'Hmm. The thing is, Al, my hands are tied, because Josh specifically asked that you sub him. He thinks you're great. In fact, Josh told Bluebottle that he doesn't want to be subbed by anyone else but you. Nobody else but you. Poo poop dee doop.'

'You're kidding me.'

'Yes, I am, actually. But look around. Everyone else is busy, hewing at the coalface of the Lifestyle section's prose.' Barry gestures expansively at the small huddle of fabulously untidy desks which comprises the Arts, Books and Lifestyle subs department, and where Derek, Yvonne and Mad Alice are all making a great performance of peering intently at their screens. 'Sorry, Al, but it looks like you're Joshing.' Barry checks his watch. 'Bloody hell. Gone one. High time we all skipped off to the canteen.' Barry stands up and flings his arms wide. 'Hi ho, hi ho,' he sings.

On cue, Alastair, Derek and Yvonne, though not Mad Alice, spring from their chairs.

'It's off to lunch we go,' Alastair sings back.

'With a bucket and spade,' trills Yvonne.

They turn and point at Derek, who chants, 'And a hand grenade.'

'Hi ho,' they sing in chorus. 'Hi ho, hi ho, hi ho.'

3

'I AM LOOKING FOR TWO FRENCH GIRLS'

Thursday evening

His last class of the day has just meandered out of the room and Ian is busy tidying up books and papers when there's a rap on his door and his employer rushes in.

'Ah, Ian, ah, might I, ah . . .'

In a display of dedicated efficiency, Ian pats a small pile of course books on his desk into a neat cuboid. Then he looks up and says, 'How can I help you, Dr Foxsmith?'

'Yes, ah, yes. I.' As he always does during any conversation with his boss, Ian notes the irony that the man runs an English-language school. Such is his employer's bumbling incompetence with his native tongue that Ian invariably finds himself becoming smoothly deferential in his presence, Jeeves to Foxsmith's Wooster.

'I was, ah, yes, in point of fact, I,' says Foxsmith.

Ian nods respectfully.

'There is, ah, a matter. Two young Frenchwomen. At present, they are but not being, as it were, stretched, so on, after, on, due to, due consideration, they will.'

'. . . Be joining my advanced class, Dr Foxsmith?'

'Quite, ah, quite. So.'

'No problem whatsoever. I'm sure they and indeed the rest of the class will benefit from their addition. Can I just say that Dieter and Stanislaw are making particularly encouraging progress.'

'Good, very. There is one other, ah, one.'

'Another pupil, Dr Foxsmith?'

'No, no, that is, ah, the same, ah, Frenchwomen. Another, ah, problem. Of an, of, that is, accommodation.'

As he offers the merest hint of a bow, Ian realises that he's also got his hands clasped in front of his groin. Maybe he's taking this Jeeves thing a bit too far. 'Perhaps I could have a talk with them, Dr Foxsmith,' Ian says, while unclasping his hands and putting them to work by picking up a stray copy of Osborne & Foster's *English Grammar*. 'Chat to them about moving up to the advanced class and see what the trouble is with their digs.'

'Excellent. Ah, kill, ah, two, ah, yes.'

'Might I ask if it's one of the school's recommended host families?'

'Indeed, ah, unfortunate as, indeed.'

'And are the students concerned still on these premises?'

Wisely forsaking words, Foxsmith grimaces then head-flicks an imaginary ball to his left.

'They're in the common room?'

A single firm nod this time. Keeping the ball down, a goalie's nightmare.

Ian sneaks a glance at the wall clock behind his employer. Six-thirty. He had planned to take advantage of Claire's early-evening visit to Briony's and pop down to Soho for a drink, with Rob if he's around. But this chat with two disgruntled French girls shouldn't delay him too much, and it'd be useful brownie points. In any case, the popping-in-on-Rob plan is probably a non-starter because Rob hasn't replied to the messages Ian left on his answerphone yesterday and today. Which is mildly annoying because he could do with a laugh and a chat with Rob – one to one, cool guy to cool guy, man of the world to man of the world, rather than the usual banter and patter of Fridays when it's Rob plus the others. Yes, these times when he's popped down to Rob's flat in Soho and it's been just the two of them shooting the breeze have turned out to be a surprising boon of London, where surprising boons have been, let's face it, thin on the ground. Ian places the stray copy of Osborne & Foster on top of his neat cuboid pile and announces, 'I'll have a word with the two students now.'

'Ah, I, I'm ah,' says Foxsmith as he backs off and away.

He has been working for twits like Foxsmith for the best part of the two decades since he gave up on university. Ian takes a deep breath to banish this thought and heads down the corridor to the common room, which would pass muster as a common room in a low-security prison. He looks around for a pair of disgruntled-looking French girls but the room's only occupant is slumped in the least rickety orange-patterned armchair by the window. Ian processes the following information and, as far as can be judged, in the following order – female, hasn't seen her before, podgy face, enormous, custard-yellow spot on her chin, mousey hair cut in a crap bob, twenty-one, twenty-two maybe, a real mistake to wear such a short skirt with those sausagey legs, no way can she be French. For the want of anything else to do, he approaches her and gives her a smile, feeling good about himself as he does so.

'Hello,' he says. 'I am looking for two French girls. Have you seen them?' That shouldn't be too difficult for her to understand, unless she's a real beginner.

'Oh. You are Mr Murray?'

The fat girl begins to lever herself out of the armchair, but gets as far as leaning forward before she notices that Ian is already perched on a neighbouring chair (the one remaining piece of furniture in the room which he trusts to hold an adult's weight) and holding out his hand ready for her to shake it. She's clearly a timid sort, for even this gesture seems to discombobulate her.

'Yes, I'm Ian Murray. Ian.'

'Oh. I am Monique.' She glances over at Ian then down at her trainers and then at the door. 'I and my friend are the two French girls who . . .'

Ian waits for a moment until he realises that she's not

13

searching for her friend or an elusive phrase but has finished speaking for the moment. He smiles encouragingly at the top of her bob. 'Dr Foxsmith told me that you are having trouble with your class and your accommodation. Well, the problem with the class is very easy. You and your friend are obviously far too good for the intermediate level, so you can both come to my advanced class, starting Monday at two. I'll tell Dr Foxsmith's secretary about the change. So what's the other problem?'

She risks making eye contact for a second. 'Acne.'

Ian manages not to look at her chin. 'And what's the problem with Hackney?'

She sighs. 'It is very bad. And the house is small and dirty, the landlady does not talk to us, the street is not nice and I am afraid when I walk there, and the food is . . .' She frowns and pouts. What a truly unattractive girl.

'*Dégueulasse?*' Ian suggests.

She laughs with a nervy snort and her hand flies up to cover her nose and mouth. '*Oui*,' she mutters from behind her hand. '*Dégueulasse.*'

'That is very unfortunate. But don't worry. I will sort everything out.' All he has to do is put up with her and her pal joining his advanced class, despite the fact that this one at least is almost certainly not as good as she thinks she is, and scribble a note for Moira, Foxsmith's secretary, who'll organise an immediate change of their digs. But he's hardly going to tell this fat lass that and disabuse her of the notion that he is one terrific fellow.

Which, going by the way she's beaming bashfully at her trainers, is exactly what she does think. All being well, that should be him receiving a couple of badly needed glowing assessments when she and her pal complete their course. She hauls herself up from the chair, seizes his hand and gives it an anxious shake. 'Thank you, thank you much,' she says to her trainers, before she hurries off. Ian gazes at the back of her sausage legs, a pained grin stuck on his face until she's trundled out into the corridor. Then he releases a soft groan as he opens his palm, which is indeed streaked by a slither of her snot, and wipes it down the side of the orange armchair.

I deeply reccomend the Sandy Bay Hotel to be one of the top hotels in the Carribeean. Especially it's view of the sea. A dance would be held their that very night Albert the sweet manadger told me as he giuded me round my complementery sweet with it's marbel bathroom deeply impresive bedroom and sitting room with all the things a gal could of wished for including a wellstocked miny bar where I was to spend a hole welldeserved! week of luxury. After changing into my white Versace, Albert giuded me round the Sandy Bay Hotel.

Alastair scrolls down his screen. Six-forty. Too late to start rewriting Tamara now. Two clear hours on this tomorrow morning and he'll make sure page three of the Lifestyle section carries some printable words to accompany the photographs. And that'll be one less obstacle in the way of Lifestyle going to press earlyish tomorrow evening and him making it to Friday Night Club at a reasonable time.

'Al.' Barry's bald head has popped up over the opposite computer.

'Barry?'

'Any sign of Tamara's World yet?'

'She's just filed. I've got it up on my screen.'

'I'd better message Bluebottle with the good news. So what's it like?'

'Not too bad.'

'How many deeplys?'

'I've only glanced at the intro, Barry. Just two so far.'

'What's the matter with her?'

'Don't fret. The rest is up to scratch. According to Tamara's grammar, there's going to be a dance in the sea, she's about to spend a luxurious week living in the minibar and the hotel manager is a transvestite. Barry?'

'Al?'

'Seeing that I've already been Joshed, can you not give Tamara to someone else?'

'Sure. You can swap with Derek if you like.'

Alastair leans round his computer. 'What are you doing, Derek?'

'Centre spread. Going to be the cover as well. Top-level piece.'

'You mean the fashion story?'

'Oh yes.'

'Oh God.'

'Apparently, orange is really in. Any ideas for a headline gratefully received.'

'Um . . . Something about my darling clementine?'

Derek rubs his chin. 'Not too bad. You want to take over?'

'No ta.'

'You had your chance, Al,' says Barry. 'So, as the song says . . .'

'Tamara belongs to me.'

'Exactly.' Barry's bald head ducks back down behind his computer. There follows a racket of rapid thumping as Barry hammers away at his keyboard, using his index fingers only and the violence of someone whose formative typing was done on a sit-up-and-beg Olivetti.

Moments later, MESSAGE flashes up on Alastair's screen. Alastair goes to Alt Screen then presses Receive. It's from Barry, as he thought. 'thanks, al,' the message begins, 'you're a hero. and now i have another favour to ask of you. don't worry – nothing to do with josh todd. thing is, we have a new chap joining us tomorrow and i'd like you to show him wot's wot. doubt if he'll know wot he's doing – he's just left university, so he comes to us equipped with the one vital qualification of being b/bottle's stepson.'

Alastair taps out his reply. 'well, all right, barry, but by the sounds of it he won't even know our computer system. so i'll have to spend lifestyle's press day working like a maniac and looking after the lifestyle editor's stepson at the same time. that's just about impossible.'

'correct.'

'blimey, barry. you owe me one.'

'correct once more.'

Barry's head pops up over his computer again. He gives Alastair a wink. 'Cheers, Al,' he says. 'Bloody Bluebottle, though. Right. It's a quarter to seven and it'll be a late night tomorrow.' He slaps the top of his terminal decisively. 'We should call it a day.'

'The computer?'

'What computer, Al?'

'You want us to call the computer a day?'

'Ah. Very good.' Barry slaps his forehead theatrically. 'Bloody fool that I am. Something else I meant to talk to you about but I really have to scoot. You in tonight?'

'Should be.'

'Not out carousing with your trendy Soho mates, then? I pictured you and your pal Rob in a chic nightspot. Sipping martinis. Leggy blondes nuzzling your ear.'

'I'm saving that for tomorrow, Barry.'

'Ah. The famous Friday Night Club. Of course. Well, seeing as how you're having a rare evening in, I'll call you later.'

'Anything I should worry about?'

'Yes.'

'What? What? Barry, you can't just leave it like that. You have to tell me. You have to tell me now.'

'Al, relax. I was kidding.'

'Oh. Sorry.'

'We'll talk later. And don't worry.'

'You sure?'

'Positive. Everything's fine.'

17

'Honestly?'

'Honestly.' Barry smiles reassuringly then stands up, claps his hands for attention and says, 'Now then, people.'

Alastair stands up. But Derek is still muttering at his screen, Yvonne is still huddled over a page proof and Mad Alice is still rummaging around in the carrier bags she's gathered around her chair.

Barry tries again. 'Come on. Look lively, staff.'

Mad Alice continues to rummage below her desk but Derek and Yvonne have taken their cue and stood to attention. Barry places his right foot on his chair. Now he extends his left hand, like a Roman senator making a speech, while his right hand appears to stroke his torso as he strums an imaginary guitar. 'It is time,' he chants with approximately rising notes.

Derek, Yvonne and Alastair sing back into fists for mikes, 'For us to stop.'

There is a brief pause before Barry chops his hand down to conduct them.

'All. Of. Our. Subbing.'

'Kicking idea, man,' enthuses Chaz. 'Godda cool vibe to it.'

'Glad you think so.' Graham checks his watch. Ten to seven. He decides to go for the bluff. 'I've just about completed the rough. I could fax it over in half an hour or so.'

'No worries, man,' says Chaz. 'Godda split. Gimme good fax tomorrow, yeah? Then I'll send over a bike for the finished artwork, yeah?'

'You sure?'

'Yeah.'

It takes several moments after the line goes dead for Graham to guess that Chaz probably considers himself too busy and basically too fucking tremendous to deliver formal farewells. Graham puts down the phone with exaggerated care, tells himself to be calm, then picks up the sheet of paper that contains all the work he has done on the illustration since

Chaz phoned back to commission it four hours ago. So far, the sheet contains one rectangle. But Graham has his idea and he knows exactly what's going to happen to that rectangle. A few hours' work and the whole thing could be done. Then post off the invoice for two hundred quid.

Two hundred quid. Ten, twelve years ago, he'd have told Chaz to roll that two hundred quid into a tight wee tube and get the Vaseline out. Well, the times they have a-fucking changed, and this two hundred much-needed quid buys another week of work on the Big One next door.

Graham scrapes back his chair and pads through to the bedroom for another check on the work-in-progress. He'll allow himself a ten-minute think about it, fucking *maximum* ten minutes, then back to the study and the rectangle. Graham stands in the bedroom doorway to appraise the installation that occupies most of the floor space not occupied by the bed but which, thanks to Nigel at CDQ, will soon be occupying a corner of the foyer of an advertising agency. Okay, so it's not exactly a top gallery, but more than useful as an advert for himself and a welcome hark back to the old days when he seemed to spend half his life dealing very profitably indeed with admen called Nigel and agencies called by initials.

Months of work he's looking at here. Months. And it could all amount to nothing but sad rubbish. Or something good. Aye, or something really good. Who's to say, though? The idea's a cracker, there's the skill of the pen-and-inks, the whole thing seems to work with the photos rainbowing over the duvet below. It's even got its own private structure (three bottles and four paint-brushes scattered on the duvet cover, the three and the four combining so that there are seven rows of photos, twelve in each row) – although why this particular structure and whether or not an installation like this needs a structure, however private, are questions which he cannot answer. How much easier it all was with those brooding oils of urban landscapes that first made his name (in a small, Edinburgh-only, just-out-of-art-college sort of a way), paintings which he knew, even as he worked on them, would be halfway decent if not actively good. But brooding oils of urban landscapes were already dodgy in 1982 and now they're just not on, unless he wants to wave the white flag, become a weekday suit and an artist every Sunday.

Those Polaroid self-portraits . . . fair enough, they complement the pen-and-inks below but . . . On the other hand . . . On the other *hand*, if he used photos of Jenny rather than himself . . . He feels the jittery excitement he used to feel quite often in the old days when he'd stroke a brush over canvas and surprise himself with the rightness of the result. Use photos of Jenny instead! Of course, of course . . .

Sod's law, by Christ. Weeks on end, his work has amounted to staring out at the window and, come five, then four, then three, then two o'clock, the day's first refreshing ale. And now the first commission and the first real progress in fucking *ages* and they come at the same time.

Well, he'd better get used to work making awkward demands if his career's to get back on track. If. Aye, if. But what about all those ifs that could have prevented him getting into this state? If his fucking agent, to name but one obvious example, hadn't paid a ridiculous sum for canalside offices and hadn't started overcharging art directors and hadn't gone bust and hadn't done a bunk owing him seven grand which he'd never, ever see . . . If he hadn't been so completely screwed by the recession which brought a sudden end to those lucrative advertising jobs . . . If he hadn't been tempted by Col's example but had stayed put in Edinburgh, where he might still be tootling along all right, doing two, three illustrations a week . . . if the newness and excitement of London hadn't given him itchy feet, if he hadn't got in with the Shoreditch crowd, if he hadn't felt disgruntled by the sight of Rob gallivanting round town, if he'd remained content with Jenny . . . Anyfuckingway, and if gallery owners weren't so fucking prejudiced against art done by artists who also happened to be illustrators rather than some Goldsmiths' bum chum of Damien fucking Hirst's . . .

Graham forces himself back to the study but he can't quite face sorting out the rectangle just yet. He picks up the phone, telling himself that he'll find out what's been arranged for this week's Friday-night bash and then he'll show that rectangle who's boss.

No luck. Rob's got his answerphones on, home and mobile. Ian's off out somewhere according to a snippy-sounding Claire. No answer even at Eck's work.

Nothing for it. Graham takes a deep breath and starts to work on the rough.

4

'HI, HONEY, I'M HOME'

Thursday night

'Susie! Susie!'

Still no sign of her. She's probably pottering around in the garden. Alastair opens the back door, pokes his head out and tries again. 'Susie!' That's a minor third, Alastair reflects – the same interval, he continues to reflect, that fans use when they chant, for example, 'Scot-land, Scot-land', or that you hear in the siren of an ambulance. And maybe even the difference created by the Doppler effect of an ambulance as it zooms past. Can that be right? Where could he look it up? Ach, it'll have to wait or the food will get cold.

'Soo-zee!' he calls again, more to enjoy the minor third than anything else. He waits for a moment before closing the door and returning to deal with their supper. He shoves on a blue mitt, reaches down to his gleaming oven and pulls out a baking tray loosely covered in a sheet of foil. 'Tah-rah,' says Alastair as he lifts off the foil to reveal three baked Marks and Sparks rainbow trout fillets. 'Poifict,' says Alastair in what he reckons is a pretty good New York accent. Waiting to accompany the trout fillets on one of the Oiseaux de Paradis plates (his favourites) are a handful of Marks and Sparks new potatoes and some Marks and Sparks spinach dressed in a good skoosh of Marks and Sparks Tuscan extra-virgin olive oil.

Alastair transfers two of the rainbow trout fillets on to his plate and sets aside the third for Susie. He tops up his glass of Marks and Sparks Chardonnay, checks that he's left the kitchen in good order, and carries plate and glass through to the front bit of the main room. 'Poifict,' says Alastair again, as he puts the glass down by his feet, perches on the edge of his red-and-white candy-striped sofa and balances the plate on his knees. That nature programme is still on. 'Beautiful,' says Alastair at a swooping aerial shot of the Highlands. He pops a new potato into his mouth, reaches for the remote and thumbs up the volume. 'In the high glens,' David Attenborough is saying, 'autumn takes hold.' Alastair swallows the potato and spears some spinach. A pine marten clambers up a tree and into its snug nest. Alastair takes a sip of his Chardonnay. 'Mmm,' he says.

The back door rattles and a moment later Susie appears.

'Hi, there, Sooz,' says Alastair. 'There's a fish waiting for you in the kitchen.'

Susie just gives Alastair one of her looks.

'I've ground some pepper on mine, but I left yours as it is. That okay?'

Susie pads over and starts rubbing her neck against Alastair's shin.

'Come on, then. Let's get your fish.' Alastair puts his plate down on the floor so that he can carry Susie through to the kitchen. 'There you go,' he says, as he picks up the spare fillet and plops it on to her saucer. ''Scuse the fingers.'

When he returns to his own meal, two pine martens are gnawing at the throat of some small woodland creature, so Alastair distracts himself by consulting the newspaper folded by his side. There's this, then *Seinfeld* and *Frasier* on Paramount, then *Newsnight*. Splendid.

The pine martens are preparing for winter and he is relishing his meal's final, special forkful – a slab of trout, a bit of squidged potato and the last of the spinach – when the phone rings. Alastair is tempted to let the machine take the call, but then he tells himself not to be so lazy, especially because it'll probably be his father asking him how to switch on the oven or what to do when the rubbish bin's full. Nearly two years his father's been coming up with queries like that so the son and heir is beginning to suspect they're really excuses to chat. Or – *or* – could be Rob. He hasn't been in touch since Friday. So Alastair still doesn't know where this week's Friday Night Club is convening. It'll probably be the Pig and Whistle, as per, but Rob had mentioned Soho House as a possibility last time. Maybe Soho House could become a regular Friday-night venue, now that Rob's got his membership. Alastair pushes himself off the sofa and over to the phone.

'Hello?'

'Hi there, Alastair. It's . . .'

'Jenny! What a nice surprise.' And it is a nice surprise, although one that still requires him to push aside the feeling that, by talking to Jenny as Jenny on her own rather than as the Jenny half of Graham and Jenny, he's somehow cheating on Graham. "How *are* you, Jenny?' Ah. That came out wrong, like a ham-fisted attempt at suave rather than friendly and interested. Oh dear. Oh well. But surely there has to be some kind of statute of limitations on talking to a pal's ex? Especially if you've known the ex since way back (ten, twelve years ago, in fact, when they were all still up in Edinburgh) and were getting to be pretty friendly with the pal's ex in her own right before she became an ex. Maybe so, but it's an awkward business nonetheless, so that he's had to dare himself to see Jenny, and only the once and only recently. And not very successfully either, with Jenny picking up on his doubtlessly desperate awkwardness, so that it seemed like they were the ones who'd split up and were trying their best to be civilised about it.

'I'm doing okay, Alastair. It's been ages, though.'

'Not since the works summer do,' Alastair says, frowning at a stab of guilt because that makes it four months he hasn't been in touch. And to think that in the good old days of Graham and Jenny he'd have had a great time with her at the summer bash. He'd been just as tongue-tied next morning, when Barry and Derek had teased him about that being his latest girlfriend and him being a sly old dog. Alastair shakes off a shiver of embarrassment at the memory.

'So I was thinking,' says Jenny in a bright and apparently unconcerned voice, 'that it's high time we caught up. And I was wondering if . . . Oh, damnation. That's Megan at the door. Pie eyed, no doubt, and forgotten her keys again. I'd better go. Call you soon for a proper chat. And maybe we could meet up some time?'

'That'd be great,' says Alastair, persuading himself that it might be if he got his act together for a change and they played safe by going to see a film or something.

They exchange their see-yous and take-cares. Why does it have to be so bothersome and complicated? Alastair wonders as he puts down the phone. Which immediately starts ringing again. He's Mr Popular tonight. If that's Rob, he'll definitely ask about Soho House.

'Al.'

God. How could he have forgotten that Barry said he'd call? And what's the reason for the call? Oh God. 'Barry.'

'Well done. This an all-right time for you?'

'Fine, Barry, fine.'

'Excellent. And you're okay about nursing the new boy tomorrow?'

'Well, it's not ideal, but I'm sure it'll work out.'

'Good man.'

'Barry?'

'Al.'

'Barry, when you say "new boy", does that imply he's more than a casual or a work-experience type?'

'That's one of the reasons I wanted to call you. Too difficult to explain at the office, but basically, yes, barring some catastrophic error on his part, I think it's planned that he'll be joining us as a perm rather than a temp.'

'What's his name? And, anyway, planned by who?'

'Bluebottle's idea. Whom.'

'Is there no escape from your subbing?'

'None. A chief sub's job is his life. Which brings me to the second item on my agenda.'

Oh God. Alastair feels his palms moisten with sweat. 'Item two,' he says, for something to say.

'Just so. Now that there's probably going to be five of us, I've put it to Bluebottle that he lend his support to my campaign with the management that our rapidly expanding department acquire the new post of deputy chief sub. I'm also going to ask Bluebottle to support my proposal that said deputy chief sub be you.'

'Three subjunctives in a row.'

'I was hoping for a more conventional reply. Something along the lines of, Thanks very much, Barry, you're a great boss and a prince among men.'

'Sorry, Barry. Only this is a big surprise. And thank you. Very much. You are a prince among men.'

'Marvellous. I'll give Bluebottle the good news tomorrow. Al, I have to go. Kate's out for the evening so I've got Rachel and Dan all to myself.'

'Lucky you.'

'Yeah, lucky me. Thomas the sodding Tank Engine . . . I don't need the books any more, I just recite them.'

Alastair coughs. 'Well,' he says, 'I'd better leave you to it.'

'Annie and Clarabel were feeling exhausted. "We're dreadfully tired, we're dreadfully tired," said Annie and Clarabel.'

'The trials of fatherhood, eh?' Alastair pauses then clears his throat again. 'So – I'll see you tomorrow, Barry. And thanks again. Really. Cheers.'

He is immediately lost in a daydream about telling Rob the good news tomorrow, cracking open a bottle of bubbly maybe, in Soho House even, so that it's only after putting down the phone that he realises he didn't think to ask Barry if the promotion means a pay rise. And he still doesn't know the new chap's name. Ah well, all in good time. Now, though, he's on for a little celebration and to heck with the washing up. Alastair picks up his empty plate and strides into the kitchen. He puts the plate in the basin of warm water to soak with the saucepans and the baking tray, rubs his hands and takes out the wooden box from its hiding place behind the coffee jar.

Several painstaking minutes later, Alastair replaces the packet of King Size Rizlas, the pouch of Honeyrose Special herbal tobacco and the bulging bag of home-grown back in the box and appraises this first joint of the night.

There are times, he thinks, when things are all right. One of the secrets is in getting on with it and doing good work. Graham drains the can of McEwan's and inspects the nearly finished artwork on his desk. What was a rectangle has become a dancing photocopier, which has come along nicely. Perhaps a little reminiscent of Saul Steinberg, he might grant you that, but only a little, and would Steinberg have come up with that magenta background? He appraises the artwork once more. Yes. This definitely will be the best thing he's done for weeks. Young Chaz at *Business Matters* will love it. One evening's inspired toil and he's already earned a good part of that two hundred quid.

Graham lobs the can towards the metal bin. The can hits the bin's lip and clatters to the floor. Graham leans back in his chair and clasps his hands behind his head. He'll have one more can. That'll make it four for the night. Four and no more. Then bed by twelve, a gentle, relaxing flick through an art book and definitely no staring at photos of Jenny. Then a good night's sleep and up at a normal time, fax the rough, finish the artwork, get it biked over to Chaz in Camden, and he'll be all set for a proper Friday night out with the boys tomorrow. Easy. Easy fucking peasy.

Here's Ian, walking – a little unsteadily, if truth be told – down the ammoniac tunnel which leads out of Vauxhall station and up to the six-lane racetrack that is South Lambeth Road. Usually, Ian has a free spirit's disdain for such things as pedestrian crossings, but at this junction the alternative to waiting for the permission of the green man is a sprint that might be a bit risky – in the sense, he notes to himself, as he always notes to himself at this junction, that eating an unpinned grenade might be a bit risky. So he has to linger until the first three lanes of traffic come to a halt and he can move on to the traffic island, where he has to linger again while a second set of cars charges straight at him before deciding at the last minute that it's not worth the court case and veering sharply to the left and round the corner.

Now that he's reached the precarious safety of the island, Ian turns his back on the oncoming traffic and watches a trashed train clatter along over the arches and on to the bridge which has been decorated with a twee silhouette of a choo-choo, presumably a prettifying measure and every bit as effective as slapping a smiley sticker on the Oval's gasometer.

There are times when London's resolute ugliness depresses the crap out of him, not least because the six months he's lived here have offered him far too many opportunities to appreciate that, quite unlike anywhere else he's laid his hat, the only way you can avoid horribleness in this city is by spending hilarious sums of money, and if you don't have the cash, then you end up doing things like standing in a traffic island in the middle of an inner-city M6 on your way home to a run-down, one-bedroom sublet with sheets for curtains.

Of course, there is the obvious factor as well as the extra-ordinary fact that his next birthday will be his thirty-seventh, but it is London which he blames most for making him question, for the first time really, the wisdom of dodging around Europe teaching English. Instead of sticking at some godawful career that would have given him a salary and a mortgage and stuff. Because it is London which mocks his two hundred and forty quid a week with its contemptuous extortion, its sneering prices and smirking bills, its airily dismissive manner of shoving a series of noughts on to the cost of anything that might just offer the faintest glimpse of a decent quality of life. 'An edible meal out with okay wine? That'll be a squillion pounds. Sir.' Not only has he begun to see the point of what Rob has done – slaving away in the unthinkably terrible world of investment banking but for an inevitably huge pay packet – he's even found himself envying Rob's lot. Until he arrived in London, he would still have scoffed at the very notion that he might feel jealous of Rob's club-class trips to luxury hotels, Rob's MG, Rob's tailor-made suits, Rob's credit cards, and Rob's Soho pad. But now that he has an inkling of just how much any kind of life here costs in this Weimar-priced city, and just how little of a life anyone can buy for two hundred and forty quid a week, he has sometimes felt not only a grudging admiration for Rob and Rob's ability to assume that money is just there to be used and enjoyed, but also the curious suspicion that not choosing a normal career could have been one very big and ghastly mistake.

No. Hell with it. He's in no mood to give in to self-doubt. Ian presses the back of his hand against his nose, has a rattling good sniff and senses the petrolly aftertaste of cocaine. Yeah, think of all those people who are too afraid to do anything but daydream about what he's done for real. He has lived and worked in Paris, Athens, Berlin, Paris again, Madrid, Ankara, Istanbul, Barcelona, then Paris for a third time – an impressive CV, for sure. Yeah, pretty impressive, and there's no way he should start beating himself up.

The second set of traffic jolts to a halt and Ian finally makes it to the other side of the road. He walks alongside the kind of new office building that has puzzled him since he returned to Britain. When did they all spring up, those supermarkets and schools and health centres and offices, with their brightly coloured brickwork and their Legolandy bits and bobs? Now, if he'd only played it safe, he could be spending every weekday, nine to five, in an office just like this, with nothing to look forward to except holidays and the prospect of a farewell carriage clock in forty years' time. Make that twenty-nine years.

Maybe he really would have ended up in an office like this, if he hadn't decided, on the spur of the moment when he was twenty-one and driving a van for a wine merchant and forty-eight quid a week, to take up that TEFL course in Edinburgh. No, that's crap, because the start of it was the year before, when he'd gone abroad for the first time, inter-railing with Graham for a couple of months before they returned to a wet and windy Edinburgh August, Graham to begin his last year at art college and Ian to chuck in his history degree and muck about on the dole. Yeah, it was the interrailing that did it. Made him realise that there were countries in this world where the sky didn't usually look like old washing-up liquid, where there were cafés and boulevards, and where raven-haired temptresses were two a centime.

Of course, Ian concedes in what strikes him as a mature, considered, generous-spirited sort of a way, there have been occasions in the fifteen years he's spent wandering from foreign city to foreign city when the going's got tough and he's felt lost and adrift. But the bad spell in Berlin belongs to the past, as does Madrid and the strange, brief glitch that was his marriage to Cristina.

Ian wipes a liquefying nostril. Well, he muses, nobody can get to this age unscathed and his scathings have been few and light. And if Cristina was a mistake, then it's one he's learned from, isn't it? Lesson number one – don't settle for somebody who isn't attractive enough to stop him hankering after other women. Lesson two – find someone who doesn't devote all her energy to telling him off. Lesson three – if a woman wakes him up, the morning after the third date, by playfully running a fingernail round his nipple and asking if she's special, that third date will be the last. Schoolboy errors, schoolboy errors, schoolboy errors. But he's eliminated them from his game. Hence Claire. Who has made him immune to hankering. Who is not only sweet natured but twenty-four years old, and therefore impressed even by his first-hand memories of punk. And who'd never in a million years give him any nipple-circling nonsense. Although she has been getting a bit tricky recently, seeming very young at times . . . and doing a pretty good job of making him feel that he's not pulling his weight. Which is to ignore some fairly important shit. Look, for example, at the way he handled her news last month. And before that as well – she wanted to quit Paris and what happened? They left Paris. She wanted to return to her home-town, and where are they living? Correct. When she told him her news, did he go mental? No, he did not go mental. He handled it with cool maturity . . .

Claire. Even in Paris, she turned heads. Sometimes they'd be walking along a street and he'd hang back a step or two, to notice any signs of hunger or pained yearning on the faces of men who'd checked out this passing gamine with her astonished eyes, her cropped blonde hair, her long legs, her tight bum and startling breasts. Unlike every other beautiful person Ian has ever known, Claire seems quite unaware of her own beauty and the effects it has (just as well, in his opinion, otherwise she'd probably be every bit as dull and self-centred as most beautiful people, who've never had to work at being liked), but Ian's radar has kept up a vigilant scanning for beeps of male lust. And of envy, because there've been a fair few times he's caught men checking him out as well, doubtless wondering what kind of a bloke could get a girl like this, and discovering that the answer is a tall, slim, handsome man of the world with a male model's bone structure and a full head of thick, ink-black curls. Times he'd be lying in bed, his hands stroking her honeyed thighs, Claire arching forward to dip a remarkable breast into his gaping mouth, and he'd think of those men and how they'd never know such erotic ecstasy, doomed as they'd be to the joyless humping of some roly-poly missus. While he knows exactly what it's like to watch Claire lowering her impeccable, creamy bottom on to his face or feel her running her hard little tongue round and round his ear and whispering, 'You can do anything. Anything you want.' If those men only knew . . . Christ, they'd lynch him.

Yeah, things are going to be just fine. Look at the way the job's improved since the bad start (though why that Polish student had to register a complaint still beats him). Helped in no small measure by this renewed hobby with the coke – an excellent teaching aid. And it keeps him on his toes, ready and waiting. For what he couldn't say exactly, but *something*, as if, round the next corner or after the next drink, he'll find himself invited to a party in a chic apartment where there'll be champagne in a bucket and a couple of girls with bodies so firm he could chop out top-ups on their tummies . . . Yeah, take coke and say goodbye to banality, regain that buzz of excitement he used to get as a teenager, for no reason, when he'd be just walking down the road or staring into space, and as an adult when he'd just moved to a new city or started a new affair. *Also*, there's something so beguiling, so secretly naughty, something so undefinably glamorous about the whole procedure, from unfolding the wrap, trying to guess which bit of which glossy magazine the wrap has been made from, then tipping out a tiny heap of powder, chopping into the little lumpy bits, pushing and patting it all into a couple of fuzzily thick lines . . . And no side effects to speak of, although the first toot of the day can have him scooting off, rectum twitching, to the shunkie, and there are times, like now, when his nose suddenly runs like a two-year-old's, a few others when his chest aches like his tubes are sore, and some mornings he could do with a sculptor's hammer to clear an airway through his nostrils. But he's got it under control, stuck to his rules, resisted the temptation to start on the ciggies again (no small achievement) and he can stop it any time he wants, just as he did in Barcelona when he was mucking about with that bunch of well-heeled drop-outs who were tonked off their tits half or indeed most of the time, and marvelling at the way they could each neck a bottle of brandy and stay alert with a couple of grams.

Another good thing – strange at times though it feels to be mucking about again with Rob and Graham, and Eck (and there are times when Ian has to gag the little voice in his head that tells him this is a sad regression), the regular Friday-night shindigs mean that he's found a ready-made social life here – and one that features guys he's known for ages rather than people he's just met and whose friendship won't, despite everyone's protestations, survive his next departure. Weird, though, especially now that he looks like a retired drummer, all paunch and flabby face, to be able to remember Graham at primary, spruce, Brylcreemed, shy and his bestest friend. Or first year at the high school, Graham shuffling up one breaktime and not so much introducing as explaining the gangly but curiously confident boy by his side: 'This is Rob. He's at the same dinner table as me. He's kissed Kirsty Barclay.' Despite his jealousy (Kirsty Barclay being an object of hopeless desire for every male in the year – except, of course, for Derek Paterson, who, last Ian heard, had opened his own salon in Sydney), he'd taken an instant liking to Rob. But then that's what people have always done to Rob, with his jauntiness and his affability, his air of being permanently on for a good time. Like in the mushroom gag – a fun guy to be with. Which would explain, come to think of it, why Rob was accepted by the school's various adolescent tribes – the sporty lot, the arty mavericks who hung around the music department, the ones who'd soon become mild punks, the posher decadents of the tennis club, even the hard men who sucked on their fags and joints behind the school library – and why Rob could then recruit people from different groups for what was to become the first Friday Night Club. Daft name, Ian's always thought – even at the time it struck him as the sort of thing a swinging vicar might call his Bible studies group – but an excellent institution, as he and Graham realised after Rob plucked them from the fringes of the hard smokers' crowd and invited them to a party, where the dozen or so core members of the FNC turned out to include Kirsty Barclay's successor, Fiona Macgregor, the babe of the fifth year. Never mind that it was Steve who got to Fiona first, because there were other girls and those were good times – alfresco sessions with cider and Pomagne, the trip to Aviemore, parties at Steve's and at Keith's when he'd be dressed up in his best army surplus to dance to Bowie and swig lager from cans with bikinied dolly birds, the eager if inept romps with Joanna. Yeah – happy days. When the world was brand new and waiting to be played with. And he was, ludicrously, half the age he is now.

And now here the four of them are, twenty years later, brought together by London and marriageless freedom, unlike the rest who all disappeared long ago into their own lives, their spouses and their kiddywinkles and their pension plans. In contrast to him and Graham and Rob, even Eck, because they can still muck about, just like in the old days, except this time round without the likes of Fiona and Steve and Bill and Keith and Joanna, and in Covent Garden and Soho instead of Kirkcaldy High Street or the Beveridge Park.

Ian boots aside a still-full carton of takeaway curry. Okay, so London's a toilet, but he won't stay here long – he enjoys a flash of his current fantasy where he and Claire are swinging a sunhatted toddler between them as they stroll down a hot and deserted stretch of Greek beach – and there are compensations, like British telly . . . and easier access to the Rovers' results . . .

These final concessions are a real tribute to an unexpectedly fine evening on the charlie. After the chat with the fat French girl, Ian had sauntered down to Soho and Rob's flat in Bateman Street, even though Rob hated people dropping in on him unannounced. In any case, Rob had been out, or quite possibly in and too busy seducing to answer. The prospect of an early and defeated return to Vauxhall had threatened to get Ian down, until he reminded himself that he was but twenty yards from the Pig and Whistle, and that the Pig and Whistle boasted a clean, refurbished shunkie. A pint of lager and a line had bucked him up no end. So he'd been in great form when he'd seen Paolo from the advanced class mooching about outside Ronnie Scott's. Turned out that Paolo had been dissed by some other student he was after. Also turned out that Paolo was generous with his cash, liked a drink, and was quite a boy for the coke as well – amazing, really, because, in Ian's experience, young Italian blokes tried their very best to live up to their reputation as a bunch of spoilt, preening mummy's boys who would never touch cocaine, on the grounds that (a) it was illegal and (b), and far more pertinently, it might fuck with their skin-care regimes. Not so young Paolo. Into his football, too.

Between them they'd had, by his uncertain reckoning, one packet of salted peanuts, ten pints, four brandies and six huge lines (him supplying the charlie, Paolo most of the cash), then next thing it was quarter past nine and Paolo had to get back to his landlady in Wood Green. No problem – another trip down to the Pig and Whistle's bogs had set them both up for the journey home. In fact, he had seriously considered walking back, the scenic route over the Mall, down Horse Guards Road and through Westminster, but by Piccadilly Circus he'd thought fuck it, and got the Tube.

So here he is, back in Vauxhall betimes, feeling no pain and wondering if he might do a uey and slip into the Royal Oak for a swift one before facing up to Claire.

Nup. Needs must, there's a bottle of Sainsbury's brandy in the kitchen, but it won't come to that because, by luck rather than cunning, he has achieved that so-often-elusive goal of balancing drink and drugs. All he has to do is not screw up and be cool with herself. No problem there.

As Ian turns left into Vauxhall Grove, it occurs to him that when he and Claire first lived together, he used to bound up the steps of the Métro and quick-march down the rue de la Réunion, resenting every second it took him to reach their sweet little flat. That was only two years ago . . . The road twists round into the hippie enclave of Bonnington Square, where vast plants and dustbins jostle for space on the pavement. A slight stumble makes him think it might be an idea to step behind the enormous fern on the left and take a last, invigorating pinch of coke. Just a little dab . . . He takes out his wrap, licks his finger, places the finger on the powder, pushes the finger up his nose and sniffs . . . Excellent.

He's at the corner of the street. Now he's at the front door. Shit, the wrong key. No. The right key after all. Now he's climbing the dishevelled flight of stairs, and now he's outside the door of the flat. He pauses for a moment, puts a smile on his dial and opens the door.

'Hi, honey, I'm home.' That came out nice and normal. He's fine.

'Through here,' comes her voice from the main room, but when he walks in, it's to find the main room empty.

'Behind you.'

He swivels round too quickly and has to throw out a hand against the armchair to steady himself as he looks down on Claire, who is lying behind the sofa and on the rug Omar gave him in Istanbul. 'There you are,' he says.

'Here I am.'

'You all right?'

'A bit yucky.' Claire winces as she pulls her head up and struggles to support her back with her hands.

'Can I get you anything?'

'No, it'll pass.' Claire closes her eyes and seems to swallow bile. 'How was work?' she asks after a while. 'Hard day at the office?'

When has he ever had a hard day at the office? He has

devoted his entire adult life to avoiding anything like a hard day at the office. 'It was a bit,' he says. 'A hard evening as well. I had to calm down a fat French girl about her digs and then Foxsmith asked me to take Paolo and a few others from the advanced class out for a tour of historic Soho.' Almost faultless delivery.

Claire raises her eyebrows. 'In other words, a tour of historic Soho's historic pubs.'

It seems to be just a tease so he gives an appreciative snort of laughter and blows out a white speck of coke on to the back of the armchair. 'Yeah,' he says quickly in case she notices, 'but at least I got a couple of free pints out of it.'

Claire smiles. 'And how many paid-for pints?'

He returns the smile, using this brief pause to consider the best number to select. 'None. How was your day?'

'Oh. All right. Well, not really. And I didn't make it to Briony's.'

'Ah.' Ian's mouth twitches because he's remembered one of Paolo's punch lines. 'This guy tonight, Paolo, I don't know if I've told you about him, he had this cracking Carabinieri joke, you know how the Italians have the police like the French have the Belgians or we have the Irish, anyway, there's this young policeman from Naples, right, and . . .'

'Ian.'

'What?'

'Aren't you going to ask me why I didn't go to Briony's?'

'Oh. Okay. Why didn't you go to Briony's?'

'Because I've been feeling terrible all day and I . . .'

'Sick?'

'Sick, dog tired, dizzy. And in a bit of a state, really.'

She certainly looks all four. Aren't women supposed to bloom and blossom with pregnancy? Look great, feel fulfilled, carry their neat, round bumps with pride and panache? Not Claire, though. Just three months gone and the fit, lithe, stunning girl he once ran home to and who turned Parisian heads is looking more and more like a victim. If she washed her hair, which, as usual these days, is coated with an oily, jaundicey sheen, wouldn't that help? Surely to Christ it would at least cheer her up.

'I left a message for you at the school this afternoon.'

Ian shakes his head, although he does now recall Moira popping in during the advanced class and handing him a note which he put on his desk and immediately forgot about because Paolo and Dieter were giggling at some mistake of Stanislaw's.

'So I tried Briony instead and she came round.'

I must to study more. That's what Stanislaw had said to set Paolo and Dieter off. 'And how's Briony?' Wrong tone. He tried for a neutral sound but has struck a note of polite sarcasm. Small wonder, though, given that the question had to feature that name.

'Oh, Briony's fine. After all, she isn't the one who's pregnant.'

'Come on, Claire. It's not an illness.'

'Well, it felt like one today.' She grunts as she makes, he thinks, an ostentatiously brave effort to sit up straight. 'It's not that, though, Ian. It's . . . Look, Ian, I'd really like to have a talk. I'm getting a bit scared by this.'

'Ah, don't worry, Claire. Who wouldn't be? I mean, it'll be like trying to shit a basketball, but if it frightens you too much maybe you can get a thingummy.' She seems to swallow bile again as he searches for the word. 'Yeah, a Caesarian.'

'That's not why I'm scared.'

'Okay, well, this sickness thing is just a phase. Another couple of . . .'

'Ian. Please just listen to me, will you? I know you're off your face and everything but please, can you not just let me say something?'

'Come on, a couple of beers.'

'Ian, I'm not your mum. I'm not going to give you a row, but I do want us to have a talk.'

'Fair enough. Let's talk, then. But first things first. I am not off my face, okay?'

'If you say so.' She looks steadily at the back of the sofa. 'Okay, well, this has to do with one of the things I want to say.' She frowns at him. 'I don't think you can keep on doing this.'

'What? What can I keep on not doing? Not keep doing.'

'Acting as if nothing's happening. I'm pregnant, for God's sake, and you're still going out all the time, getting hammered, getting wired . . .'

'I told you, I'm not.'

'Spending money we don't have.'

'Aw, okay, I see, so it's all my fault for not having a fucking trust fund.'

'No, Ian. I mean, I'm not saying we don't need the money because we do. And the translating might not bring in much, but I won't be able to do even that in six months' time. But what I'm really . . .'

'This is Briony, isn't it?'

'I haven't said anything to Briony. This has nothing to do with Briony. This is about me and you.'

'Or about me not being a fucking millionaire.'

'Can't you just listen to me, Ian?'

'Listen to me. Now listen to me.'

'What?'

'*The Ipcress File*. It's what the guy says when he's trying to washbrain Michael Caine.'

Claire examines the sofa. 'This is hopeless,' she decides. 'I'm going to take a bath.' She gets to her feet and heads for the door.

'Make it a red real letter day for the diary and get the shampoo out,' says Ian to her back. He holds his breath until she's left the room and shut the bathroom door behind her.

Then he sighs, with as much frustration as a sigh can manage. What's he done to deserve all this crap? He falls on to the sofa and glares at the pile of newspapers and the two poly bags of empty bottles beside the telly . . . Ah. He forgot to take them round to the recycling. Is *that* what's bugging her? Ian forces his gaze away from the recycling pile and round the rest of the room – his Jacques Tati poster listing on the wall and revealing a blob of Blu-tac which should be attached to the poster's top-right corner, the cushions he picked up in Clignancourt scattered on the floor, the unironed washing heaped on the card table. Christ, couldn't she have tidied up a bit? . . .

Right. She's deliberately left everything in a tip to make a point. Well, two can play at that game, and he could have the room looking spick and span by the time she gets out of her bath.

Hell with it. He has a much better idea. He tiptoes up to the bathroom door and listens for the telltale sound of Claire immersed in what is bound to be one of her longer soaks. She's stopped running the hot water. He hears a soft splash, then a little grunt. He tiptoes back down the hall and into the kitchen, where he treats himself to a slash in the sink before settling down at the Formica picnic table with a tall glass of tap water, a half-full bottle of brandy and, resting on the back of a small, rectangular mirror, a nice little line of cocaine.

5

Friday morning

Dearie me. Talk about feeling the burn. The thirty-six slow sit-ups were bad enough but by slow press-up number twenty-five he'd felt like going back to bed. However. That's the regime completed for the day.

Alastair carries his cup of Earl Grey out into the garden. He squints up at the cloudless sky. Either it's unnaturally bright or he might have a bit of a headache. He bends down, takes a pinch from the lavender bush and sniffs it. Together with the scent he registers a dull twinge where his hairline used to be. He does have a bit of a headache. 'Damn,' Alastair tells the lavender bush. 'And it's a Friday.' He sips his tea and thinks of the day ahead, which promises to be a typical Friday nightmare. There's Josh and Tamara to finish off, the new boy to nurse, his promotion to discuss, and then the whole fraught fandangle of getting Lifestyle off to press. Be lucky if he gets out of Canary Wharf by ten.

Alastair frees a crisp packet from the bed of heather, twists it into a long, thin, scrunched-up strip, folds one end over the other and pulls until it looks like a psychedelic bow tie. Then he drops it on to his instep and sends it flying with an ambitious volley. At the end of its high parabola, ten feet away, it plummets straight into the empty plant-pot by the kitchen door. 'Goal,' says Alastair, just as Susie appears, on the off-chance that the crisp packet might be tormentable. 'I should still make Friday Night Club, even if it's later on,' Alastair tells Susie as if passing on gossip. 'At Rob's flat maybe. Or Soho House. He's

41

a member now. And I've never been.' Alastair takes another sip of tea and wanders back inside, having first picked up the squidged crisp packet from inside the plant-pot and dropped it in the bin. 'Yes,' he says thoughtfully to the bin, 'Soho House.'

Graham's right leg twitches under the duvet, which is spattered with photographs of Jenny topless in France. He is playing for the school team but he is twenty years older than everyone else on the pitch. And he's forgotten his school strip, so there he is, standing in the centre circle in jersey and jeans, surrounded by seventeen-year-old team-mates who are trying to ignore him because they are all the right age and wearing the proper kit. But then he sees Rob, wearing the school strip, looking happy and confident and running into the box. Rob is yelling for a pass. Who has the ball? Graham looks around, perplexed, then realises that the ball is at his feet. Two of the schoolboys approach him, shaking their heads in disgust. 'We didn't want to pick you,' says one. 'You're thirty-six.' 'Where's your sports kit?' asks the other. 'Pass it,' Rob shouts. 'Over here.' But Graham has forgotten how to kick. He swings a stiff right leg and manages to toe-poke the ball with his Timberland boot. The ball starts off travelling towards Rob but it soon veers away in a wild slice to the touchline, where Jenny is looking on, hunched into her long raincoat. She traps the ball and flicks it disdainfully to Rob. Rob laughs and the school bell rings to mark the end of the games period. It keeps on ringing. And ringing. And ringing.

Graham awakes. It's the dodgy alarm at number twenty-three. He groans into the pillow and keeps his eyes clamped shut as the alarm clatters on and on. 'Please,' he mumbles into the pillow. 'Please, please, please.'

'How many lines did you have after I went to bed?'

'Jesus, Claire. What time is it?'

'Ten to eight. So. Tell me. How many lines?'

'None. Honest . . . Is there coffee?'

'So you just decided to stay up till half past three pottering about in the kitchen. Sure. And no there isn't any bloody coffee because there was hardly any left because you said you'd do some shopping yesterday and didn't do any and because I've drunk what little we had because I woke up so early because I was feeling sick and because you were bloody snoring like a . . .'

'Walrus? Elephant seal?'

'Like a bastard.'

'Ah, Christ, Claire, give me a break, will you?'

'No, Ian, you give me a break. As if it's not bad enough trying to get to sleep when I'm worried sick and I'm turning into a . . .'

'Walrus? Elephant seal? Come on, Claire, you're not putting on any weight. And I can't help it if I snore.'

'. . . a bloody Michelin Man, I have to lie there listening to you. And you can help it, because you only snore like that when you've been doing a lot of coke.'

'So because maybe I snored a bit, this is you getting your revenge by waking me at the crack of dawn to give me this fucking shit. And no coffee.'

'Fuck the coffee. Fuck you.'

'Ah, fuck off.'

'No, you fuck off.'

'Fucksake, Claire, this is what you're like when you miss out on half an hour's sleep, what kind of state are you going to be in once you've had it?'

'It! It! It!'

'Okay, what the fuck are you going to be like once you've had him stroke her? Christ. And how come there's no fucking coffee?'

'Shut up. Oh no, not again.'

Claire throws off the duvet, puts a hand over her mouth, and lurches off towards the bathroom.

6

'YOU ALL RIGHT?'

Friday lunch-time

Look on the bright side, Graham tries to persuade himself. He's hung over, he's had four hours' sleep, thanks to number twenty fucking three's alarm, and he feels like he's recovering from minor surgery, but check out all the work he's done. Faxed through the rough, finished the artwork (including lots of fiddly balloons and streamers to decorate the dancing photocopier), phoned Chaz to arrange a bike, washed his brushes, cleaned up most of the workbench, and it's still only twenty to one.

Graham leans back in his chair and yawns. Why oh why did he move on to the whisky last night? He was fine after those four cans. Aye, but that was the problem. It's impossible to imagine now but it had also been impossible to imagine feeling sleepy come midnight, so he'd decided to have a little nightcap and before he knew it the nightcap had turned into tumbler after tumbler of Johnnie Walker Black Label. And, to be perfectly honest about it, those tumblers had all been pretty fucking full. Fuck. Ah well. There's always the chance, the usual ambient racket of the usual road-repair team permitting, of a nap after the bike arrives. Aye, but then he'd be back in the old routine of being wide awake and wandering round the flat at four in the morning, thinking about Jenny, nursing yet another hefty tumbler, trying to fend off yet more images of Jenny naked and lying on a stranger's bed, or Jenny naked and kneeling on a stranger's carpet, or Jenny naked and . . .

Stop that. Only one thing for it and that's to keep going. And maybe make a couple of calls to tout for more work. Nobody's saying it's going to be easy, though, because somehow he seems to be feeling worse than he did when he woke up, and he felt fairly fucking mince then.

Okay. First things first. Get rid of the rest of this litter on the workbench. He sifts through a pile of magazines, fly-sheets, delivery menus, sheaves of doodles and empty envelopes. Nothing there to keep unless he wants to try ordering one of Pizza Planet's Euro 96 specials – the Gazza, maybe (large, thick-crust, double pepperoni) – a year late. His attention is drawn to another component of the litter – three sheets of paper stapled together. What in the name? . . . It's one of those round-robin happy-family letters. Graham frowns as he recalls that he received several such letters (addressed to him and Jenny, which proved that the senders were either very distant acquaintances or sadists) at Christmas, and solemnly set each alight in the kitchen sink. This one must have fled the flames.

1996 was of course the Year of the Conservatory!!?! More of that saga later!! When he's not been chasing the builders, Keith has enjoyed his new responsibilities as head of the department at Fife College but the workload means that the bad news is that his handicap has rocketed to six. Keith has cut down some clubs for Cameron and Jasper and Cameron already boasts a fluent swing and some pinpoint accuracy with his long irons although we also have high hopes of Cameron as the new Gavin Hastings! He captained his side to triumph in the mini-sevens this year and celebrated by scoring two tries in the final!!! We're still a wee bit concerned about Jasper but at least his eczema has got much better with the steroid cream and who knows it might help him build up those muscles before he goes to school next year!!!! But we're all very proud as well of Cameron's success at the 16th Fife – where I can forget all about the dratted builders and the new conservatory's underfloor heating as Akela and where Cameron's badge count has

'Cunts,' says Graham. 'Fucking cunts.'

When he reaches the bottom of the first page and Cameron's scout badges, Graham scrunches the three sheets of paper into a tight ball and shoves them into the overflowing bin. Just how much of a fucking *arsehole* do you have to be to write such a document? And haven't these people any notion of tempting fate? Or that some of their readers could be unemployed or grieving over a stillborn baby ... or struggling away in a one-person family after their partner has gone? Anyway, who the fuck *are* these cunts? Who is Keith? Who is I? Fife College? ... The Tech, in other words. This Keith is probably one of those who has taught plumbing to morons for a decade and now calls himself a lecturer in sanitation studies at the University of South Kirkcaldy. Obvious that they're a right pushy pair, and it's safe to say that Jasper is suffering under the stress, and with a name like that the wee guy doesn't have his troubles to seek. Mind you, even in Kirkcaldy, Jasper's future colleagues in Primary One will probably be called things like Swithin or Starchild.

What's so wrong with normal names? Elizabeth. If he and Jenny'd had a kid, Elizabeth would have been a great name for a daughter. Tea's ready, Lizzie! Fancy a trip with Daddy to Legoland, Beth? John for a boy. Jack, even.

Maybe he should do his own round-robin letter this Christmas. Graham and Jenny are still split up!! And Graham's 'friend' Col did mention recently that Jenny might be seeing someone else these days!!?! Graham is finally getting it together again workwise, which is just as well because he still owes the taxman £12,000. But he's also finding time for his favourite hobby, so business is booming in Finchley's Thresher's!!!

Enough. Graham forces himself up and out of the chair but immediately has to grip the workbench for support ... He really does feel mince. Graham shuts his eyes and gulps in air as though he's preparing to swim a length underwater. After a moment, the wave of nastiness recedes. Having risked opening his eyes to the extent that he can peer at the dancing photocopier, Graham pushes himself away from the bench and, slowly and unsurely, makes his way out of the study and next door to the kitchen.

The kitchen is Graham's favourite room – or least unfavourite room – in the whole benighted flat, since it is the room least haunted by the ghost of Jenny, who was never a one for the cooking. The sitting room at the front, that's a terrible place, full of memories of the times they'd eat the dinner he'd made, plates on their laps and *Brookside* on the telly, and of course of that one time in particular when she stumbled in, squiffy after a work do, kneeled in front of him as he sat on the sofa, peeled down his zip, hoiked out his flummoxed cock and, demonstrating unexpected skill, applied her mouth to it until he cried out and came as he'd never come before, with helpless, juddering anguish. No, the sitting room is a dangerous place. Not as bad as the bedroom, obviously, although that has improved a bit since he painted the walls a very unJennyesque, Colman's-mustard yellow, sold their bed, made do with a mattress on the floor, bought a new duvet cover and recycled their old one in the installation. But more dangerous than the bathroom, even with the significant gaps on the shelves where she used to keep her Body Shop stuff, and where the vanilla whiff of her skin cream seems to linger still. In fact, at the minimal cost of not watching television, Graham has rather given up on the sitting room, which now functions like the front room of a pre-war working-class family, as a place to receive guests, and that's something Graham does rarely, or never, these days, even if he counted Rob, Ian and Eck as guests, which he wouldn't.

So here he is, back in the kitchen, slumped at the long wooden table, gazing out through the French windows at the tiny patch of overgrown garden, and trying to remember just what he thought he was doing at exactly this spot last night, slurping at tumbler after tumbler of Johnnie Walker Black

Label. Hadn't he come up with some scheme? Ah yes. His whisky-inspired brainwave – to stop his occasional night-time trips to Jenny's street in Notting Hill (when he's in the area and like as not drunk and can't resist), quit scanning her windows, put an end to wandering and wondering and driving himself crazy with the thought that she might be in there with another man . . . to stop all that and do it properly, rent a room opposite and use it as a surveillance HQ, so that he can find out once and for all if the rumour Col passed on really could be true and she really is being fucked by some bastard.

The thought of Jenny being fucked, of Jenny opening her legs and inviting, actually inviting, another man's veinous, purple-helmeted erection to pierce her most precious, most secret . . . Last night, by the time of the third or fourth tumbler, he'd convinced himself that if he could only see it happening, perhaps through binoculars trained on her conveniently but improbably uncurtained bedroom window, he'd be able, somehow, to cope with the terrible reality instead of not coping with the many and various appalling images his brain creates to cause its owner such sharp pain.

Now, for example. God alone knows where this scenario originally came from and why it should be quite so vivid and convincing, but here he is picturing the one with Jenny in a hotel room in Leeds – why Leeds? – wearing only a pair of black stockings, lying face down on a floral valance, a pillow under her groin, offering herself to the businessman who has just finished chatting her up in the dead hotel bar.

'Oh no,' Graham moans into his hands. 'Please, please no.' He reminds himself that he's got his health and his friends and that he'll be seeing Audrey on Saturday night, but, as usual with such reminders, each one seems as effective a morale-booster as remembering that there are people starving in Africa. Weakened by exhaustion and the hangover and now the thought that even Cameron and Jasper's shitey parents have got it together to build normal lives for themselves, he can't stop the moan building into a pulse of dry, racking sobs, and then into a fully blown greet.

He's halfway through a long and uncathartic wail when the doorbell rings. Graham jolts upright. In fact, he comes as near as he'll ever come to jumping out of his chair. He gives his eyes a quick rub and yells, 'Just a moment' in the vague direction of the front door.

Composure, he reminds himself. Composure. Having blown his nose into a wodge of kitchen towel and thrown some cold water over his face, he judges that he's just about fit to be seen in public. He paces steadily to the door, like he's measuring the distance, and opens it. 'Courier from *Business Matters*?' Graham says brightly.

It's only now that he registers the curious figure standing in front of him, a person kitted out in a dark, visored helmet and perv's black – zip-covered jacket, leathers, boots, the lot. Unfortunately, the figure is so tall and thin that he looks less like a biker than someone attending a fancy-dress party as a biker. Or, now that he's standing to attention, a thoroughly burnt match. The figure flicks up the visor and exposes a pair of cheap-looking, rectangular, black-framed spectacles whose lenses are so thick they make the eyes behind them obscenely large and watery.

'Pick-up from Anderson,' says the courier. Then he peers down at Graham. 'Here. Are you all right?'

One of those London accents that are all vowels. Eeah. Ah ewe awe wigh. There is a pause while he tells himself to get a grip. He has always felt weepily vulnerable at moments like these, ever since he was of an age to scrape his knees or be stung by wasps and his mother would ruin his resolution not to burst into tears by telling him he was her poor wee thing and her brave little soldier. The temptation to cry into this long streak of misery's leather shoulder is there now, but he resists. He will not lose it in front of anyone. Especially a specky wimp who's too soft to use consonants. Graham glares up at those marmoset's eyes and, reminding himself to broaden his own accent so that he'll sound hard, says, defiantly, 'Ah am abso fucking lootly splendid. Pal.' He turns and heads back to his study, where he waits for a moment, rubs his face again, and picks up the artwork.

Back at the door, the courier tucks the dancing photocopier under his arm and proffers a clipboard in return. 'Just sign there, mate.'

Theh mye. Maybe the face-rub hasn't worked, or perhaps there's a catch in his voice when he says, 'There you go,' as he scribbles his jagged signature on the pad and hands it back. Whatever the cause, the courier wrestles off his helmet, leans farther down towards him, like an adult quizzing an infant, and says, 'Sure you're okay? Anything I can do?'

Shaw. Anyfink. And just what the *fuck* is going on here? 'Oh, aye,' Graham says, as he senses with real gratitude the anger swelling inside. 'That's just what the fucking doctor fucking *ordered*. A hand-job from an eight-foot, eight-stone twat wearing welder's fucking goggles. Soo fucking *perb*. That'll be fucking *right*.'

It's the accent. Works every time. The biker takes a step back. 'I was only . . . Tell you what, mate, you should see someone, bit of professional help, that's what you need.'

'Is that fucking right? Well, I tell you what, pal.' (The courier has put his helmet back on and casually flicked down his visor.) 'You don't fuck off out of it pronto, you're going to need.' (The courier has turned his back and is ambling calmly away and towards a vast bike gleaming beside Graham's rotting Golf.) 'Professional fucking help from a.' (The courier has mounted the bike. Now the courier kicks the bike into roaring life. Just as well, because Graham was running out of steam and would probably have fucked up the final bit about a casualty ward or a surgeon.)

After he has closed the door, Graham leans back against the wall. Fucking hell, he thinks. Things can't go *on* like this. Things have to fucking *change*.

*   *   *

'You on for the usual?'

'I'm up for that.' Ian feels something stab him in the small of his back. He swivels round to see a grinning Paolo walking backwards down the corridor and giving him the finger. 'You okay, Graham? Sounds like you've got a cold.'

'Nah. I'm fine. Just went a bit overboard with the sauce last night. Out with a couple of people.'

'Snap. I've got a fair-sized hangover on the go after a sesh at the Pig and Whistle. Then getting all sorts of grief from herself. Here. What's the best thing about fellatio?'

'Go on, then.'

'Ten minutes' silence.'

'Very good. So what do you reckon – Soho?'

'Oooh, sir. Suits me, sir.'

'What's that?'

'Come on, Graham. *The Fast Show*. You must have seen it.'

''Fraid not . . . Where will we go?' A rising note of what could be petulance or anxiety in that question, which Ian puts down to the fact that Graham's taken it on himself to make the arrangements for once – and probably also resents not having the chance to moan about whatever time and place Rob has sorted out. 'You were at the Pig last night.'

'Doesn't mean we have to kick the habit.' Ian swallows a yawn. 'Pig's fine by me. Eight?'

'Done deal . . . I'll give Rob a bell, by the way. You heard from him?'

'Nup . . . But he'll be around. Friday night, for Christ's sake. He gives you any crap, tell him he can always shag supermodels some other time.'

'Too fucking right. Oh, and I suppose I'd better call Eck as well.'

'Oh yeah. Eck as well. Here. Why are Italian men small?'

'I don't know, Ian. Why are Italian men small?'

'Because when they're young their mums tell them that once they're big they'll have to leave home and get a job.'

'I don't get it.'

'Oh, come on, Graham. It's a cracker.'

'Sorry.'

'It's referring to the way Italian guys always live with . . . Oh, stop me. Nothing worse than explaining a joke. Which reminds me. I've got a class of Germans in ten minutes. I'd better go and fish out my list of gerunds for them to memorise. Christ knows where I've put them but the hunt'll be worth it, because, believe you me, a class of Germans with a long list to learn by heart is a happy class.'

'Give the buggers hell. See you at eight.'

'*Au revoir*, my man.'

Ian yanks out his phonecard, turns round and collides with the sausage-legged French girl. 'Hello, there. All yours,' he says, and points to the booth.

'No,' says the girl . . . Monique, that's it. 'I do not want the telephone. I want to speak with you.'

'Oh. Right. Well, that would be nice, Monique, but I have to prepare for a class.'

She does her shoe-inspecting act. Hang on a minute. Is she blushing? Oh yes – definite beamer there. 'I want to say,' she tells her trainers, 'thank you for the help. We had a conversation with the secretary of Dr Foxsmith and it is okay, today we move to a new place.'

'Good news. Where's the new digs . . . I mean your new place?'

'Bow.'

'Good. And where is it? Sorry, Monique,' he adds, when he sees that she hasn't got his translingual quip. 'That was supposed to be a joke. So.' Ian beams down at this dumpy little creature while he tries to think of something else to say. 'So. You will join my advanced class at two o'clock on Monday?'

'Jaw in?' Dearie me. She really is crap. She'll be completely out of her depth with the likes of Paolo and Dieter in the advanced lot. Ah well, the customer's always right. She looks up at him with a face so scrunched up by bafflement she could win a girning contest. 'Ah. Join. Yes.'

Ian takes a step back. 'So, Monique, I am glad you feel better. But if you will excuse me, I have a lesson to prepare . . .' He is about to head off to the shunkie before scouring his desk for gerunds when he notices that the top of her bob is gently vibrating. She can't be . . . yes, she's crying. Ian bends down in an attempt to make eye contact but she turns away to wipe her tears on a chubby forearm. What on earth is the matter with her now? Ian inches forward and gives her a couple of awkward pats on a hefty shoulder. 'Shoosh, shoosh,' he murmurs. 'Shoosh, shoosh.' He's remembered. The gerund list is in his teacher's copy of the *Advanced English Primer*. Still. He can't hang around here for ever waiting for this one to calm down. 'Now then, Monique, what's wrong? Is there anything I can do?'

She gives her bob a brief shoogle. 'No,' she whispers. 'You are very kind. It is just . . .'

'Yes?'

'Everything.'

'Everything?'

'Everything. I am here a week and I am so . . . nostalgic?'

'*Je crois que tu veux dire* homesick.'

'*Oui, c'est ça.* Ohm seek.'

'But now that you have a new landlady, perhaps you will feel better.'

She yanks out a crumpled tissue from under the sleeve of her blouse, blows her nose with unexpected vigour and returns to watching her trainers. 'Yes, that is better I hope but also I think it is because I do not like . . . I am sorry. It is not important.'

'No, tell me,' says Ian, although he already has a good idea of how the rest of her sentence will go.

'I am sorry but it is here. Not the school, I mean, but this city, this country. It is so different than Toulouse. Dirty and cold and . . .'

'*Dégueulasse?*'

'*Oui.*' The hint of a smile.

Ian gives the hefty shoulder another couple of pats. 'Don't you worry, Monique. But there are good things here too. The . . . well, lots of things. Pubs . . .'

She glances up from beneath her fringe. 'Pubs? I have not visited pubs.'

Is that a come-on look she's just given him or just her being coy and shy? Surely to God it's shyness, because she can't genuinely think that he . . . Mean to say . . . Got to be shyness. Even so, best to play it safe. 'Okay. Well, I usually take the advanced class on a tour of a few pubs so you can come along. Next week some time. And you can bring your friend too.'

'Chantal?' Monique performs a Gallic pout-and-shrug.

What's he said now to put her in a huff? Ah, maybe it was mentioning the friend that did it. She must have been after a hot date after all. Steady on. Why, then, does he give her his crinkly-eyed sexy smile and her shoulder a little squeeze when he says 'See you at two' before heading off to the bog?

'Force of habit, my man,' Ian tells the empty gents'. 'Talking of which.' Ian sidles into the cubicle, where he whisks out his little mirror and assembles a quick line.

'Okeydokey,' he says a moment later. Yeah, life is fine and it's all going to work out. 'Now then,' he mutters, 'time for the Jerries' gerunds. Yes, yes, yes, indeedydoody.'

Alastair is stumped. This being the third week in a row that Josh Todd has devoted his column to the difficulties he has experienced in filing his column, Alastair cannot come up with a third consecutive punning headline about Josh's Macintosh and modem after last week's 'Not OK Computer' and 'Only connect' the week before that. 'E-mail chauvinism' is Alastair's least bad effort so far, but that's only because the one other phrase that he has scribbled on his notepad is 'The art of modemism' – lame and only works visually, if at all. He is busily scoring heavy black lines through both phrases when his phone rings.

'Subs.'

'Eck.'

'Oh, hi, Graham. How are you?'

'I feel like shite warmed up but don't let that worry you. Nothing a drink tonight won't solve. You on for it?'

'Yes. Absolutely. Looks like I'll be turning up late again, though.'

'Oh, aye, right. Giving the Arts bit its jammies and putting it to bed.'

'Lifestyle, actually.'

'Is that the bit with that Josh Todd in it?'

'Alas, yes.'

'Now he is a cunt and no error. How much does that cunt get for that shite?'

'Eighty grand a year, I heard.'

'Jesus fucking *Christ*. Eighty fucking thousand fucking notes . . . Fucking *hell* . . . He must be knobbing that bloke, the Fly.'

'Bluebottle. Yes, that was one theory we had as well. Anyway, Graham, sorry to be a bit abrupt but I'd better get on. Where tonight?'

'Pig. If there's a problem, try my mobile or Rob's.'

'Great! You've got hold of him.'

'No such fucking luck. Left a message on his machine, though.'

'Here's hoping,' says Alastair with a casualness that is feigned because a meeting of the Friday Night Club without Rob isn't what he had in mind. What he did have in mind is the residually embarrassing image of the four of them propping up a chic bar in Soho House (one that might even have a black marble counter and gantries that jutt out from a long mirrored wall) and bantering away in a lively yet sophisticated manner, like chaps in a Gillette ad. Then they'd adjourn at, say, one to Rob's flat where they would, as per, continue the crack with the help of Rob's mightily strong grass and Rob's drinks table and stereo. Ideally, a bit more civilised than usual, to be honest. Though they've been jolly, sometimes, in their way, these new FNCs. Different, of course they are, from the old FNCs. And from more recent days when it was just him and Rob, and Rob always on such good form, with his stories about some caper in the City or his latest romantic imbroglio, so that Alastair had often found himself wondering what on earth he'd unwittingly done to deserve such entertainment. But a Robless FNC would be . . . well, it wouldn't be the FNC at all. Just him inexplicably out on the town with Ian and Graham. He is wondering whether or not to mention the possibility of Rob getting them into Soho House when he sees Barry striding towards him, a pale and small youth in his wake. 'Er, Graham, sorry about this but I really had better get back to work. See you all later. Maybe tennish.'

'Whatever. 'Bye, Eck.'

''Bye, Graham,' Alastair says to his phone, and 'Hi, Barry' to his boss. Assuming that the pale and small youth in tow is the new sub, Alastair gives him what he hopes is a warm and welcoming smile, but the youth fails to respond, being too busy examining the surrounding jumble of computers and desks and litter with the fearful suspicion of an American tourist hopelessly lost in Cairo. His edginess is apparently infectious, because Barry looks quite ill at ease and fails to perform any introductions.

Instead, he says, 'Al, my pal,' and tugs an earlobe. 'Got a minute?'

Much as he would like to correct Barry's social oversight, Alastair can't catch the youth's eye and Barry is already on the move. Puzzled, Alastair follows him over to the table strewn with proofed pages. Barry surveys the mess of paper and gives his earlobe another pull. 'Maybe this'll be the historic night when we won't manage to get Lifestyle off to press. How's Josh?'

'Tosh. Never mind that, though, Barry. What's going on with the new chap?'

'Him? Bloody hell.' Barry looks at a proof of the cookery column as though he's been libelled in one of the recipes. 'I should have bloody known that Bluebottle would land us in it.'

'What?'

'You'll see, Al. And while I'm on the subject, we'd better all remember to ditch our *nom de guerre* for the Lifestyle editor while his stepson's around.'

'Ah. Of course. Richard it is.'

'One more hint. We'd better go easy on taking the piss out of the new boy as well.'

'Come on, Barry. Subs' solidarity. Why would we be nasty to him?'

For a moment, Alastair wonders if Barry is about to spit. 'How long have you got? But one obvious reason is his name.'

'What's he called? Ivor Bigun?'

'Very amusing, Al. And not so far off the mark. His name is Bond. James Bond.'

'No, really, Barry.'

'Yes, really. He is James Bond. Thatsh hish name. Oh oh sheven.'

Alastair can't help a snort. 'Blimey. Sho heesh a shub.'

'Eggshackly. Well, except he's not.' Barry picks up a proof of the cookery page and makes a show of scanning it. 'A sub, I mean. Nor does he have any desire to sub. Bloody Bluebottle. So keep an eye on him, Al, and make sure he doesn't screw up.'

'Righty ho. But why is he starting at the end of the week and on our busiest day? Why not wait until Monday?'

'God alone knows. My guess is that Bluebottle wants to impress him with the wonderful excitement of a press night.'

'Really?'

'Either that or Bluebottle has even less of a clue than we dared suspect. Yes. That's got the horrible ring of truth about it. Anyway, see what you can do with the youngster. And remember, hard though it might be, go easy on the Connery stuff.'

'Of course, Barry. Poor chap. He must have been persecuted his whole life. What were his parents thinking about? Surely, if your surname is Bond, James has got to be the last thing you'd call your son.'

'You're right. Definitely worse than Brooke or Basildon.'

'But what about him?' muses Alastair. 'I mean, I know your name can be just one of those things you're stuck with, like having a big nose or sticky-out ears. But if it's that bad, then why not go for the equivalent of plastic surgery? If your name was James Bond, wouldn't you change it by deed poll, or even just call yourself Jim, or by your middle name, or anything for that matter?'

'Well, you know, Al, I think it might be a bit like you and me being up front about being bald, rather than opting for a sad pretend hairstyle like the Bobby Cha . . . Oh, bugger. That's Derek arrived and he's already nobbled young James. Remember what he was like with the work-experience guy from Oxford?'

'Did James go to Oxford?'

'No.'

'Then he should be all right.'

'Cambridge.'

'Oh dear.'

Alastair looks over at the subs' desks, where the new boy is looking even paler and smaller as he is loomed over by Derek, who seems to be ominously jovial. And now he's slapping little James on the back and laughing.

'Bloody hell,' mutters Barry. 'What is that big lump saying?' Barry and Alastair hurry back in time to hear a delighted Derek telling a distinctly crestfallen James Bond, 'because he sounds like the character in the Goons, he buzzes around to no effect and he loves shit'.

'Now then, Derek,' Barry announces. 'Isn't it your turn to get the tea?'

'*Jawohl*.' Derek clicks his heels together. 'And what can I get *you*, James?'

'Coffee, please.'

'Milk, sugar?'

'Just black, please.'

'Shaken but not stirred?'

'Just black, please.'

Derek narrows his eyes, nods sagely and whispers, 'An excellent choice, Mr Bond.'

Oh dear, thinks Alastair. Oh dear, oh dear, oh dear. 'I'm Alastair,' he says abruptly to James, and busily shakes his hand. 'While Derek's doing the tea run, perhaps I could show you what we do here.'

James shuffles reluctantly towards Alastair's desk, while Alastair calls up his partly subbed version of Josh. Barry gives Alastair a wink and makes his way to Bluebottle's office, to talk about the new arrival or even, it occurs to Alastair, the frantic day ahead.

'How *strange*,' says James in a voice even higher and squeakier than his stepfather's, and Alastair marvels yet again at how his social betters really seem to have no idea how grating their voices can be.

'What do you mean, James?'

'It's all squiggly down the right-hand side.'

'Ah, yes. Well, that's just the way text appears on the screen. The computer will do the justifying when it's printed.'

'Justifying?'

'Um, where the words all line up straight at the sides. So, James, have you done any editorial work before?'

'I have done quite a bit of journalism for the college mag, actually. Theatre reviews, mainly.'

'Good, good. And any subbing? Subediting? Copy-editing?'

Alastair looks over his shoulder to give James another encouraging smile. James replies with the wary grimace of a schoolboy who's being told about felching.

'Okay,' says Alastair. 'Good. And has, ah, Richard told you much about what you'll be doing here?'

'Actually, he said I'd be learning the ropes . . .'

'Excellent.'

'. . . before I start to write things. I mean, that's why I'm here, actually. Not . . . *this*.'

While he tries to outstare his screen, where the cursor is blinking beside the word 'cudjilled', it occurs to Alastair that he may have got it slightly wrong about James being nervous and overawed.

'Excuse me, Alan, but shouldn't that be brains? It says brians.'

'At the moment,' says Alastair, pleasantly. 'I haven't finished this piece yet. You see, it's our job to make sure these errors don't creep into print. There's another one just after the comma of brians. Can you spot it? "Having cudjilled my brians, the phone rings."'

James gives his shoulders a token shrug. 'Seems fine to me, actually.'

'Okay. Good. Well, what we have here is a dangler.'

'Got Al to show you his dangler?' The returning Derek wiggles his eyebrows and plonks the cardboard tray of polystyrene cups precariously on top of Alastair's terminal. 'I thought you'd be a ladies' man, Mr Bond.'

'In fact,' Alastair continues hurriedly, 'quite a classic dangler. You have to watch out for them with Josh Todd. Oh, and Tamara as well. All of them, really. You see, James, what he's got at . . .'

'Your coffee, Mr Bond. Black. With the merest twist of vermouth.'

'. . . the moment is a subject in the second clause that relates erroneously to the verb in the first clause, that's to say a dangler. "Having cudjilled my brians, the phone rings." You see, at the moment, this means that the phone was attacking Josh's head with a cudgel.'

'If only,' says Derek. 'Wotcha, girls. What time do you call this?'

Mad Alice scurries towards her workstation, places her lucky crystal on the desk and switches on her computer. Yvonne, by contrast, flings her handbag on to her chair and stands over it, pursing her lips and noisily blowing air out of her nose. Evidently too preoccupied to acknowledge the fact that she is in the company of a pale and small youth she hasn't seen before, Yvonne shakes her head and growls. 'That fucking *wanker* Bluebottle,' she says.

'Yvonne,' says Alastair.

'Bluebottle only comments on us coming in late.'

'Yvonne.'

'Today of all days. When Bluebottle's usual fucking incompetence . . .'

'Yvonne.'

'. . . will no doubt mean we'll all have to stay here till tomorrow morning.'

'Yvonne.'

'Honestly, Bluebottle is such a fucking *arsehole*.'

'Yvonne.'

'*Fucking* Bluebottle. Hello,' she says to the new and open-mouthed person who is staring at her.

'Yvonne James James Yvonne,' says Alastair, before directing a dry cough into his fist. 'Yvonne, perhaps you should know that James is . . .'

'A shpeshull agent,' says Derek.

'Richard Marshall's stepson,' says Alastair.

'With a lieshensh to kill,' says Derek.

Yvonne's eyes dart around, as if she's a burglar outflanked by the cops.

'Yes,' declaims Derek. 'This is the new bug. Who has joined us directly from the University of Cambridge. And his name is Bond.'

'James,' says Alastair.

'James Bond,' says Derek.

'Right, then,' says Alastair briskly. 'If you'll excuse us, I was talking to James here about subbing Josh.'

Alastair does not have a very good feeling about any of this.

7

'WHERE THE BLOODY HELL IS
THE BLOODY THING?'

Friday evening

Here's Ian, drinking lager and feeling completely cream-crackered, despite the after-hours nap in his classroom and the two slices of takeaway pizza from Caffé Nero. Or maybe because of. Anyway, if the Pig and Whistle wasn't so crammed and noisy and sulphurous with smoke, he could quite easily have another little snooze.

'Excuse me, is this seat taken?'

Ian looks up to see a bulky bloke in a stupidly hooped rugby shirt pointing to the adjacent chair.

As if. Would Ian Murray really be sitting in a pub, on his own, on a Friday night? 'I'm keeping it for someone,' Ian says blankly. 'He's late.' As usual with Graham, who'd turn up late for a free dinner with a young and bare Sophia Loren. On account, Ian suspects, of Graham's urge to come across as a head-in-the-clouds artist and bohemian, although, as far as Ian can see, it's just Graham being crap. Mind you, the man's reliable unpunctuality does have its advantages . . . Ian turns to the young couple to his left and asks them to watch his two seats, then he gets up to begin insinuating himself through the throng and down to the basement shunkie.

Thank you, Jesus, that there's a travelcard, a straw and a good wrap in his back pocket to sort him out, and that the cubicle is free. And that the cubicle has a door which locks. Damn. He must have left his little mirror in his desk drawer.

Ian pulls down the seat lid, gives the (wooden – not ideal but okay) surface a cursory wipe with a fist of loo paper, hunkers down, fetches out the wrap and prepares a long, thick line.

Now that is a sight for sore, red, knackered eyes. He takes a good blast up each nostril. Woah. Oh yes, yes, yes, indeedydoody. He licks a fingertip and passes it over the wooden seat, picking up a few stray flecks of coke and (Ian always thinks this and always battles to dismiss the thought) countless millions of molecules of unpleasantness. He rubs the fingertip over his gums. Now then. Time for a drink.

'By fuck, do I need this pint. Fucking Northern Line, by the way. Know what it said when I got to the platform? Morden fifteen mins. On a fucking Friday bastard evening. They're all there at Tube HQ, wondering how can we fuck over the punters tonight? Tell you fucking what, we'll put on a skeleton fucking service using the oldest fucking carriages. Fucksake, the one I squeezed into should have had gas lamps. Adverts for the new Charles Dickens. Having a good fucking laugh down at Tube HQ, I tell you. Fucking fifteen mins. You wired?'

'Nup.'

'Come on, Ian. Look at the fucking state of that.' Graham points to the ashtray, which is brimming with the remains of a beer-mat Ian has shredded into stamp-sized pieces.

'It was something to do while I was sitting here for' – Ian checks his watch with a hammy flourish – 'oh, going on half an hour. And I'm not the person who has just gone off on one, ranting and raving about the Northern Line. Anyway, it's not exactly news that the Tube's rubbish, is it? I mean, if you compare it to . . .'

'The fucking Paris fucking Métro, fucking don't fucking tell me.'

'Well, yeah, but it's true. Hey, have I told you the one about the guy trapped on a desert island with Claudia Schiffer?'

'And he makes her dress up as a man and he says, "Hi, Frank, you'll never guess who I'm shagging." Aye, Ian, you told that one last Friday. Not that I'm surprised you've forgotten.'

'When last Friday?'

'Back at Rob's . . . Any word from him?'

'Nup. Maybe he's gone on a trip. Or it's some new babe.'

'Aye.' Graham purses his lips into the silence. Would Ian's absence be as disappointing? he wonders. Probably not. It's a thought which leads Graham to asking himself why it took a good few years of him being down in London before he got round to seeing Rob on a regular basis, which leads immediately to the pangful answer – Jenny. Jenny and him ensconced in their own world out in Finchley.

Ian flicks at a shred of beer-mat. 'Rob told you who he's bedding these days?'

'No. Who?'

'Nup, this is me asking.'

Graham shrugs.

'I suppose,' says Ian, 'it'll just be the next one in the queue of oiled bimbettes. Way Rob goes on, it's like he's got one of those things outside his flat going up to his bedroom window, filled with girlies. You know, one of those old kind of lifts like conveyor belts where you get on it while it's moving. A paternoster. Yeah, a paternoster, filled with oiled bimbettes and the queue to get on it stretched along Bateman Street. Maybe he has a . . .'

'Ian.'

'Graham.'

'Shut the fuck up.'

'Sorry, was I . . . ?'

'Yes. Back to the real world.' High time for a change of subject, thinks Graham, but then he's stumped when he tries to think of a subject to change to. Football, he decides, if only because that should stop Ian blethering about Rob. 'So who've the Rovers got tomorrow?'

'Hamilton away.'

'. . . What're Hamilton like these days?'

'Search me. The usual west-coast mix. Psychopaths with tattoos on their teeth in defence. Up front a pair of wee ginger blokes with scurvy. Hey – Eck could have got a game with that lot.'

'Fair dos, Ian, he was a good wee player was Alastair.'

'What was it? Two seasons for the university and a couple of games for Lochgelly Albert? Come on.'

'More than you or me could have done.'

'Yeah, but Lochgelly Albert? Christ, it doesn't even sound like a team. A notorious local sex offender, yes, but not a football club.' Ian sniffs. 'Eck coming along?'

'Aye. Said he'd be late, though.'

'Got a date, has he?'

'Settle.'

'Maybe there's a convention of Swedish porn stars in town and Eck's on call to pleasure them with his expertise.'

'Just how much of the marching powder have you had, Ian? You are blethering shite.'

'None. Mind you, I'm more than a wee bit fatigued. A trip downstairs would be just the thing. Excellent suggestion, Graham. You want to accompany me?'

'That'll be right.'

'Maybe I can persuade Rob to partake of a wee line later.'

'Doubt it. And I couldnae get hold of him.'

'Ah. Damned shame. Rob is around, isn't he?'

'The fuck am I? His fucking secretary?'

'Just asking.'

'Where is it? Where is it? Where the bloody hell is the bloody thing?'

'Found it, Barry.' Alastair waves a photograph of a young blonde woman naked but for a tiny bikini, arm in arm with an improbably muscled black man who is wearing no more than a gold posing-pouch and a smile.

'Thank God for that. Where was it, Al?'

'In among the proofs.'

'No information on the back, I suppose?'

Alastair flips the snap over. 'Sorry, Barry. That's definitely Tamara, though.'

'Well, yes, but who the bloody hell is her Caribbean consort?'

'Doesn't say.'

'Oh God. So we don't know if he's a passing fisherman or some famous cricketer or the local prime minister's son. Oh, bloody hell. Bloody hell. Bloody *hell*.'

'Doesn't matter, Barry. We can wing the caption.'

'Looks like we'll bloody have to. Why the bloody hell we have to run that dim Sloane's holiday snaps as well as the drivel she supplies as copy I do not bloody know. Yes I bloody do. Because Blue . . . Okay. Al. And James. James? Hello, James? Good. Two minutes to think of a caption. A pun. Something witty. Across three columns. And James? Could you maybe sprint over to Design with the photo so they can get it through the system?'

James shrugs, picks up the photograph, then slopes off.

Barry tugs at an earlobe. 'Then,' he mutters, 'we might just have a chance of getting this bloody section off to press. No thanks to that little . . .'

'Barry?'

'Prick. Al.'

'What about something like "On the beach" or "Life's a beach", colon, then just some vague stuff about Tamara gets to grips with the locals?'

'In run-of-the-mill circumstances, Al, I'd say it was bollocks, but at this time of night . . . Will it fit across three columns?'

'Should do, with a bit of tweaking.'

'Then it's sheer bloody genius. What headline did you get for Josh?'

'Still blank.'

'Sorry, Al, I don't get it.'

'No, Barry, I'm saying we haven't got a headline yet.'

'Bloody hell. Bloody *hell*. That page should have gone bloody *ages* ago. What are the contenders?'

'Um . . . E-mail chauvinism?'

'Yuck. Shove it in.'

8

'YOU KNOW WHAT I HATE ABOUT CEEFAX?'

Friday night

First thing he does when he gets back is slam his mobile down on the table. If the mobile had some self-repairing device, he'd smash it against the wall. The fuck is Rob playing at? 'Called him up but got the answerphone, even broke the golden rule and went over to buzz on his door. Fucking zilch,' he says.

'Damned shame,' says Ian. 'Tell you what. If he's not turned up by eleven, we'll try him again, maybe do a tour of the drinking clubs, see if he's around, and even if he isn't we'll have made a night of it.'

Graham takes a deep breath. Composure. 'Possible,' he says. 'See how I feel. Maybe I shouldn't have a late one.'

'What's this, what's this, what's this? A health drive?'

'That'll be fucking right. Nah. Just that what with Rob not turning up . . . And I've got this thing in Shoreditch tomorrow night and I want to be on good form for it.' Graham glugs down a good half of his pint. 'Especially as,' he says. 'I may be. On for. A spot of. Shagging.'

'Really? You're joking. Or are you? Are you joking?'

'Yes, really. And no I'm not.' Graham fiddles with his mobile. 'Fucksake, though, the last time I had sex was . . .'

'During the Cold War.'

'Last October. Fucking last October.'

'And that was on your own.'

'Remember Audrey?'

'Audrey, Audrey, Audrey. Nup.'

'Aye. Audrey. You met her at the Cantaloupe. The time when you and me went on to a do at Marty's place.'

'Hee hee. One of Marty's parties.'

'Fucksake, Ian. Those trips to the basement are really doing your brain in, by the way.'

'What did we eat? Smarties?'

'Christ. Anyway. Audrey. Dyes her hair a kind of red. Almost vermilion. Nice. Knows the people I shared the studio with in Curtain Road. No? Col, Tim, Amanda, Jason, all that lot. Three, four years back.'

'Before my time. I'd be, let's see, yeah, yeah, yeah, I'd be in Barcelona. Or maybe, just maybe, Paris. That would have been about the period when . . .'

'You fucking did meet Audrey. Definitely. Fucksake. The point is that Col reckons she might be on for a wee spot of hochmagandy with yours truly. There'll be a whole crowd of us at the Cantaloupe. Kind of an old studio reunion. Col'll be there, a few others you've met. Come along if you want.'

'No can do, my man, no can do. Claire's having a little soirée with a couple of her pals. At ours, so I've got to be there. So that's my Saturday night well and truly down the pan.'

'So that's my Saturday night well and truly down the pan.'

'Suit yourself, Ian. By Christ, a man could die of thirst waiting for you to get a round in.'

'Okay, okay, hud yer wheesht.' What am I saying? Ian asks himself. Hud yer wheesht? How is it that he occasionally can't resist being infected by Graham's dialect schtick? And how is it that each time it happens, he sounds like he's auditioning for *The Broons*? Odd when you think about it, thinks Ian, given that he's the one who was brought up in a grey box on a windswept council estate and Graham's the one whose daddy's a doctor and whose accent has been slaloming down the social scale ever since he used to get beaten up at primary for sounding English, i.e., not brought up on a windswept council estate. Maybe not so odd after all.

In case Graham decides to take the piss out of the wheesht, Ian gets up in a hurry and starts to make his way through the crowd to the bar. As he takes up a position behind a bloke in a suit who is either coming to the end of a massive order or is in the middle of buying drinks for the entire pub, he tries to recall an Audrey. Dyed red hair. Nup. The trouble with Graham's trendy-wendy Shoreditch crowd of artists and photographers and designers is that they all look the same, all of them with daft hair and all dressed for a guerrilla mission or a shift at a construction site. 'Glamourflage', Claire calls it. Ian catches the barman's eye and orders two pints. Mind you, a night out with a bunch of urban warriors he barely knows strikes him as much better than a night in, on best behaviour, with Briony and Co.

Ian squeezes back to the table, the two pints clutched to his chest and surviving a jolt as some oaf nudges him in the back just when he's about to place the drinks on the table. 'You watching Ceefax tomorrow?' asks Ian.

'Maybe.'

'You know what I hate about Ceefax?'

'Believe me, Ian, I haven't a fucking clue what you hate about Ceefax.'

'Page 311,' says Ian eagerly, ignoring both the faint recognition that this urge to say something has little to do with the importance of the content and the never-to-be-mentioned suspicion that Graham's not into his football as much as he should be. 'Now that we're not in the Premier we have to share a page that's divided into three kind of sub-pages. Last season all we had to do was keep it on page 310, and there it was, no problem, all the Premier results on the screen together. Unless there were millions of goals and people being sent off, so that they ran out of space and had to continue on a second page. But now with 311 there's the First Division on the first page, the Second Division on the second page, and the Third . . .'

'Ian. I get your drift.'

'Okay. So you know what I'm saying.'

'Fucksake, it's no exactly one of life's big traumas, is it? And all you do is keep the First Division bit on hold on page 311. End of problem.'

'But I keep thinking if you put it on hold it won't show the latest scores. Just the scores as they were when you put it on hold. It's not that, though. It's a sign.'

'Of?'

'Our decline.'

'Yes. They got relegated.'

'Much more than that, though, Graham. Just think. We're back to sharing page 311 with Brechin and Stenhousemuir, and it was only two years ago, almost to the day, we were going mental at half-time in the Olympic Stadium and that massive scoreboard above us saying Bayern Munchen 0 Raith Rovers 1.' As he says this, Ian indulges in a memory of the screaming pandemonium after that goal. A great trip that was, two years ago, when the Rovers' improbable success had inspired a militantly genial binge in Munich by several thousand supporters, including him, Rob, Graham and Eck. A prototype of the FNC Mark II, as it turned out – the four of them converging for the occasion at Rob's urging, Ian from Paris, Eck and Graham from London, Rob himself cutting short a business trip in Japan, and Ian gaining ample opportunity throughout those three days to marvel anew at the thickness of Rob's wallet and the reliability of Graham's disdain.

'Trust you to think that the very best thing was the Rovers playing abroad.'

'Come on, Graham, second round of the UEFA Cup, that scoreboard at half-time, you're not going to argue that wasn't the highest point ever.'

'I suppose. But we knew it wouldn't last. We even knew they'd lose that match.'

'Remember when we hit the side netting just after the break? Could have made it two.'

'Aye, right, and Bayern had no fucking chance, by the way, only two–nil up from the first leg and with numpties like Klinsmann.'

'Okay, but that's not my point.'

'So what is your point?'

'My point, my point is that, yeah, you're right . . .'

'Way hay.'

'. . . we knew at the time we were going to get knocked out and that would be it. I mean, Bayern Munich, we had no chance. But it's one thing knowing at the time that this would be as good as it ever gets, and another thing having to live through the bit afterwards knowing that that really was as good as it gets and from now on in it'll be page 311.'

'Fucksake. So you would have been a whole lot fucking happier if they'd never got into Europe and never played Bayern Munich?'

''Course not. But you know what I'm saying.'

'I do. And it's shite.'

'Terrific news,' says Derek dolefully, after he's wandered back to his desk. 'Bluebottle's having trouble with the editor.'

Barry narrows his eyes. 'What kind of trouble?'

'Oh, nothing much. Just the Lifestyle cover.'

'What! The Kate Moss!'

'That's the one.'

'Mother of Jesus. If the bloody editor changes the cover, Bluebottle will probably have to ditch the fashion centre spread. Bloody hell.'

Alastair coughs. 'It might be all right, Barry. You never know with the editor.' While Barry slumps in his chair and groans, Alastair looks up at the clock. Five to ten. Just when he thought they were about to send Lifestyle off to press. And Yvonne's already gone home in a pointed protest at Bluebottle, Mad Alice left early for a session with her homoeopath, young James has long since sloped off . . . Judging by the way he's gathering together his bag and coat, Derek isn't too keen to stay either. Just be him and Barry, then. Unless this turns out to be a false alarm, he's going to miss out on Friday Night Club and have most of his Saturday scuppered too, since he'll have to spend the best part of the weekend recovering from being here until three or four in the morning.

'Bad time and all that, Barry, but I really have to shoot,' says Derek, shrugging on his raincoat. 'I promised Edith I'd be . . .'

'Sure, Derek, don't worry. It won't take three of us. See you Monday.' Barry slides farther down his chair. 'Suppose I should call Kate and tell her I won't be home till the kids are up. Oh, bloody hell.'

'Cheer up, Barry. At least we might have something to add to the editor's list.' Even as he's speaking, Alastair realises this is a fairly silly thing to say, but he felt he had to make some kind of chirpy contribution, to cheer up Barry, who looks like somebody's stolen his scone. Plus he just couldn't pass up a chance to refer to the editor as 'the editor'. Ritual use of the title rather than the person's name, save when addressing a newspaper's editor face to face, is one of the few Fleet Street traditions which have survived in Canary Wharf, so 'the editor' is a phrase that he finds almost as evocative as 'Hold the front page', which, he knows full well, he will never, ever have the chance to say. Mind you, gauche though his remark undoubtedly is, it seems to work. Barry grants him a rueful smile and reaches out in mid-slump to the top drawer in his desk. A rummage later, he pulls out two photocopied sheets of paper.

'So. We can add Kate Moss to the editor's list.'

'Barry, we don't know that for sure.'

74

'Yes, we do. Kate. Moss,' says Barry while he turns a page then scribbles down the name. 'There you go,' he says, and sits up straight to hand the document over. 'That's three more today. Ballet Rambert, kiwi fruit and now Miss Moss.' Barry resumes his slump.

Alastair scans the list – compiled by Barry, Bluebottle, Nicholas the Arts editor and Davina in Books, the subs, in fact just about everyone at the paper's shallow end – of all the subjects on which the editor has poured scorn, as hilariously arcane or as the implausible figments of his underlings' diseased imaginations, in the four months since he was briskly and unforeseeably transformed from 'Jonathan in News' to 'the editor', thereby filling the vacancy caused when his predecessor took a risk and filled the front page with that unsourced story about Peter Mandelson. The list's first fifty-odd entries, down to the middle of page two, Alastair could just about recite by heart, but he hasn't seen it for a week and now page two is nearly full. Glastonbury, Mr Bean, Ruud Gullit – no, these are old. But Marco Pierre White's a new one. Philip Glass, the Superbowl, Ted Hughes. Yes, these he hasn't seen. Anthea Turner, Our Price, salmon farming, continues the list. E.M. Forster, Real Madrid, Pizza Express, *Blind Date*, skunk, Francis Ford Coppola, aromatherapy, the Mercury Music Awards, Kim Basinger, CenterParcs, Ballet Rambert, kiwi fruit, and now Kate Moss.

'Well,' says Barry, 'no point just sitting here and waiting for the bad news to hit us. Fancy a trip to Design?'

'Why? Because the editor will be there?'

'No, Al, because I want to play Nintendo on the Apple Macs. Because I want to drop my trousers and sit on the light-box. Because I'm going to mount a daring raid on their bloody biscuit supply. Of course it's because Bluebottle and the editor will be there. Where else would they be looking at the Lifestyle cover?'

It's not much of an outburst and by the standards of the

rest of the office would almost qualify as a pleasantry, but this is Barry and the subs desk and they're all supposed to stick together and . . . Alastair clears his throat as if that will somehow also clear his head, but his only thought is that he's cowed and hurt, just like all those years ago when he was picked on at primary.

'Apologies, Al. It's late and I'm pissed off and you must admit you can be . . . No, look, I'm sorry.'

'Don't worry, Barry. Honestly.' Pull your socks up, Alastair orders himself. He taps the Save button on his keyboard and raises his head over his terminal to show Barry that he's smiling. 'All righty. Let's hit Design.'

'I'd rather hit the editor. So,' says Barry as he re-extricates himself from his slump and beckons Alastair to accompany him down the office, 'how did you get on with the charming oh oh sheven?'

What Alastair wants to say is that James Bond and Derek's incessant baiting of James Bond have helped make this one of the worst working days of his career, and that everything, just *everything*, about this dismal nepotism has demeaned a skilled and demanding profession. However. 'Not bad. He knew a few of the basics and he picked up on the computer really quickly.'

'That's something, especially given the steam-driven system we've got here. But you would have thought with a name like that he'd be . . . Never mind. Good work, Al. I'll tell his stepdaddy. Why,' he adds under his breath, as they near the Design department, 'speak of the devil.' They move slowly towards the desk where Bluebottle and the editor are standing to inspect the screen of a large Apple Mac. 'We can hang about over at the light-box,' Barry whispers. 'Try to look busy.'

Alastair picks up a fawn folder and flicks through the photographs inside. 'Why have the Picture Desk sent down the file for Carrie Fisher?' he whispers.

'Filler pic for the satellite TV pages,' mutters Barry. 'Apparently, the editor said he wanted more glamour in the listings. Said he was fed up with all those pictures of American films and series none of our readers had heard of.'

'Like what?'

'Like *Cheers*. Oh, and *Baywatch*.'

'Two more for the list. And isn't Carrie Fisher an . . .'

'Shush, Al. I want to hear what's going on.'

Keeping their heads lowered, they both cast furtive glances over at the small group gathered round the computer screen. What is going on isn't very much. Young Tania – lovely, sweet, beautiful Tania – is hunched in her seat and busy pushing the mouse around its mat. Bluebottle is now gazing out of the window, possibly in an attempt to convey the air of a man at peace with himself and the dark, twinkling world outside and twenty-four storeys below, but succeeding only in looking like a man about to travel down those twenty-four storeys by the quickest route. The editor, a fleshily overweight man in his mid forties, is standing behind Tania, his pink paws resting on her shoulders.

'Try it in black and white,' he barks. 'At least give it a bit of class.'

By leaning to his left, Alastair can just see Tania whizzing the mouse around the mat. The image on the computer screen changes, the strikingly bright image of Kate Moss bedecked in a tangerine-coloured gown and shimmying down a catwalk giving way to a grey, grainy picture of Kate Moss walking down a catwalk.

'Christ,' mutters Barry. 'The whole point of the piece is that orange is the new black. And now he's . . . oh, bloody hell.'

The editor swivels round to turn to Bluebottle. 'You see, Richard. It's just not working. Even in black and white. What happened to the cover you promised me at conference? The one with the glamorous girl?'

'Well, I . . .'

Despite his anxiety level – because he is nervous whenever he is near the editor, because of the editor's size and sudden authority and already notorious bad temper, and because this impending cover crisis is clearly going from bad to worse – Alastair is entranced. So this is why Bluebottle and Nicholas and Davina return to the shallow end each Tuesday morning from conference, spluttering that they can't defend themselves against the editor's attacks because their only option is to offer explanations so basic and insulting that their next move would be to collect their P45s.

Credit to Bluebottle, though, for he's giving it his best shot. 'But don't you think that this being a big fashion story and this being a, well, a fairly celebrated model and that the original, as it were, colour version has . . .'

'No. No. No. A thousand times no.' The editor lifts his right paw from Tania's shoulder and holds it up, palm outward, in a stop sign. 'Richard, I have spoken on this matter.' The editor performs another ungainly swivel which brings him round to face Alastair. 'Now then,' he proclaims at Alastair, 'let's see what we can rustle up by way of a proper Lifestyle cover. A cover our readers will want to see.' Alastair is under the uncomfortable impression that he should be a large audience. 'A cover our readers will like. A cover our readers will *understand*. What have you got there?'

Before Alastair knows what's happening, the editor has loped over to him and snatched the fawn folder from his grasp.

'Ahah! *This* is more like it. *This* is our cover. *This* is the stuff.' The editor has thrust a paw into the folder and hauled out a large monochrome photograph of Carrie Fisher, with her headphone hair, as Princess Leah. 'Marvellous,' bawls the editor. 'There you are, Richard. *Star Trek* Style. Even given you a cover line.'

Alastair is aghast but he reckons he must be the picture of mental health compared to Bluebottle, who looks like he has been paralysed in mid-shout. There is a short but eerie silence which is broken by the soft chirruping of Tania's phone. She clamps a hand over the mouthpiece and looks uncertainly behind her. 'It's your secretary, um, Jonathan.'

The editor slaps the folder down on the light-box and marches over to grab the phone. '*Yello* . . . I see . . . Uhuh . . . When? . . . Fantastic.' He hands the receiver back to Tania and surveys the middle distance for a moment. 'Look, Richard, I have to dash. TV crew in my office. Completely slipped my mind.' He stretches his neck as he fiddles with the knot in his tie. 'Being interviewed for Channel Five News.'

'So . . . the cover?' asks Bluebottle.

'Cover? What? Yes. The cover.' The editor rubs a paw over his forehead. 'The thing is, Richard,' he explains with the heroic patience of a remedial teacher, 'I can't do fifteen things at once. Okay, okay, *okay*. We'll go with your one but I want to see *this*' (he brandishes the Carrie Fisher photograph) 'on the Lifestyle front next week.'

As the editor marches off, Bluebottle manages the merest hint of a nod. 'Tania,' he says, when the editor has gone, 'do me a favour and put Kate Moss back in colour, for God's sake.'

'Richard?'

'Barry.'

'Does that mean we're done?'

'By the skin of our teeth.'

Alastair looks at the clock. Twenty past ten. He might still make it.

9

'LIKE ANKLES'

Friday night

'No. Farther along the bar.'

'The one with the blue top?'

'No. The one next to her. Grey jumper.'

'Got you. What about her?'

'Superb tits.'

'Fucksake, Ian.'

'Serious, man. Just superb. Wait till she turns round a bit and she's in profile. An amazing shape to her jumper. You just know they're going to be perfect.'

'Or that she's got scaffolding for her bra.'

'No way, my man, no way.'

'Get the bra off and you could be looking at a pair of spaniel's lugs.'

'No way, Graham. That shape is tight. You can always tell.'

'Like ankles.'

'How do you mean?'

'Ankles. You can always tell what a woman's legs are going to be like by her ankles. You've got to have a really defined tendon at the back, and that hollow either side. Fucking convex.'

'Concave. And you're wrong about the ankles. I mean, it's one of the things people say, although in fact, and I've spent some considerable time thinking about this, as you can imagine, the ankle is an important but not foolproof indicator of a good leg. For instance, you could have a . . .'

'Aye, but see if the ankles are fat or don't have that delicate shape, you know the legs are rubbish.'

'What a little cracker she is. Young girls now? The number of them with big tits? It's extraordinary.'

'Aye, but that's because they're eating Big Macs all the time. Fat, that's all.'

'No way. Telling you, we should have been born in the seventies. You should see some of the talent at the school. And remember I went to that party with Claire couple of months back?'

'The one that turned out to be some sort of rave?'

'Kind of. In a warehouse. Yeah. It was Claire's pals who were giving the party, right, so they're all early twenties, twenty-six tops, and I couldn't believe it, man. The number of beautiful women there. All with shiny hair, great teeth, tall, thin, with big tits, it was extraordinary.'

'That's just you turning into a dirty old man, by the way. You want to start wearing a greasy mac.'

'No chance. Telling you, Graham, women are just getting more beautiful. Fact. There's statistics to prove it. Like the average bra size is getting larger, more people with fewer fillings. That party, they were all dancing away to that house music – what a racket, man, it was like being in the middle of a steelworks – and I just stood there not believing my eyes.'

'And wanking under your mac. Fuck knows how Claire puts up with you.'

'Tall, dark, handsome, superbly hung, brilliant in bed – yeah, fuck knows.'

'Give me fucking strength. You want another one?'

'Struggling with this.'

'Have a short.'

'Go on, then. Calvados.'

'They got that?'

'Brandy if they haven't.'

*   *   *

'There you go.'

'Cheers.'

'I did ask for Calvados. Boy looked at me like I'd ordered a Babycham. I mean, this is a pub in London, not some fucking bistro in Normandy.'

'Calm down, calm down.'

'What's with the accent and the wiggling hands?'

'Come on, Graham. Harry Enfield's Liverpudlians.'

'Never seen it. By the way. Talking of parties.'

'Were we?'

'A minute ago, aye. Fucksake. Anyway, Marty, right? Did I tell you what happened at his last bash?'

'When the cops arrived and everyone thought they were in fancy dress?'

'Nah, that was months ago, Ian. This was a week or so back. Col was telling me. So Marty was out of it. Six in the morning, something like that. He'd been doing E or maybe acid. Anyway. The boy was lying out on the window ledge, and mind, this is two storeys up. He falls asleep, right? And . . .'

'Don't tell me.'

'Topples off. Maybe thought he was in his bed, who knows. So, he topples off . . .'

'Jesus. Was he okay?'

'On to the top of a parked car. And he's lying there flat on his back for about three hours before anyone spots him.'

'Nobody see him fall?'

'Obviously not. Eck!'

'Eck. You're here.'

'Ian. Graham. Hi, there. Sorry I'm so late. No sign of Rob?'

'Nah. I tried him on the fucking mobile but no luck. Last orders, by the way. You want a pint?'

'The bar's closed, I'm afraid.'

'Have the rest of this lager if you want.'

'I wouldn't mind a sip, Ian, ta muchly.'

'Sorry, Eck, I'm just finishing this story. You met Marty? No? Anyway, Ian, the thing is, he was fine. No bones broken, absolutely okay, didn't even wake up.'

'Kidding.'

'Straight up. He was so fucking out of it he just fell on to the car roof, no problem. They think that was what saved his life, him being so relaxed.'

One sip of lager, that's what his Friday Night Club is going to amount to. One sip of somebody else's tepid lager. However. You never know. Rob might be in or they might even catch up with him if they go on to Soho House. And at least he's not stuck in Canary Wharf, with nothing to look forward to but manically subbing some cobbled-together piece on Carrie Fisher. Graham and Ian are still talking about this bloke he's never heard of. Something about the chap not killing himself. Which drugs he may or may not have taken. Ian's fine but Graham seems pretty pissed. Not that he's slurring his words or anything but he's got the heavy eyes, drooping jaw and booming voice of Graham when he's had a few. Right, then – that's both of them finished their drinks at last.

'Shall we try Rob's mobile again?' asks Alastair.

10

Saturday afternoon

'Come on. Answer.' Ian rubs a finger down each side of the telephone's 3, 6, 9 and # buttons. His fingertip is grey with dust. He remembers not to rub his gums.

'Hello?'

'Oh, you *are* there.'

'Ian. Fucksake . . . What's up?'

'What's up? What's *up*? You haven't been watching it, then.'

'No. No, I've been working. So, what's happening?'

'One–nil down.'

'Still. Plenty time left.'

'You kidding, Graham? It's gone half past four. I've been watching that zero by our name since three o'clock and it's still going to be there at quarter to five, believe you me.'

'No need to shout, by the way. It's a phone, Ian, no a fucking loudhailer.'

'You'd be worked up too if you'd been staring at page 311 all afternoon.'

'And if I'd been hoovering up a couple of lines in the meantime.'

'Not at all,' says Ian, feeling genuinely aggrieved.

'Aye. That'll be right.'

'*Shit.*'

'Oh, pardon me, Ian, I mean, what on earth would have made me think that . . .'

'No, I said shit because it is shit because Hamilton have got a second.'

'Oh.'

'*Fucking* Ceefax. *Fucking* Rovers. Why wasn't I born in Milan?'

'. . . You heard from Rob, by the way?'

'Shit. What? No.'

'Maybe give the boy a call, find out what happened to him. Phone me back at full time.'

'Yes, Master. *Toute à l'heure.*'

'What are you like? Okay. Oh fucking rivwar.'

The line goes dead. Ian decides that he will try Rob – something to do as well as staring at Ceefax. He stabs the seven numbers, shakes his head at the television, then tucks the phone under his ear just in time to hear Rob saying 'at the moment, but please leave . . .'

'Shit,' Ian tells the phone, and bangs it down. Still two–nil. And Ruth and Briony coming round later. This has all the makings of one crap Saturday.

At least, and despite the usual Saturday-afternoon hangover, mind you, he's done something with his day, even if that something amounted to no more than the couple of hours he's just spent tinkering with the installation – still, he's got more to show for his Saturday than an afternoon watching Raith Rovers lose on Ceefax . . . Only typical, mind you, of that waster.

Odd. Ian's return, seeing Ian once a week instead of once a year, you'd have thought that he would have made more of an impact. As it is, this new Friday Night Club caper has turned out to be, well, usually a good piss-up, in its defence, and it is something to do on Friday nights . . . But really it's Rob rather than Ian who has been proving the easier to get along with – Rob not quite so full of himself as he used to be, plus he's acquired that air of metropolitan chic as well as of glitzy bachelordom. Rob's done stuff. Like gone to a Damien Hirst launch, met Jay Jopling at a party . . . So he can chat to Rob about the Shoreditch scene, all that, even the installation a bit. And, to be fair to the boy, he's been gratifyingly interested.

Anyway, another date in the diary for tonight, and not only a date but maybe a date date into the bargain. Aye, *this* is more like it.

Weeds in his left hand, trowel in his right, Alastair ambles back to the kitchen, leaving Susie to sun herself beside the forsythia. He stops at the back door because he's begun to fret again about the promised promotion. If 007 isn't going to be a sub after all, will there still be a need for a deputy? And if there isn't, what should he do? Stamp his foot, call up one of the subs he knows at the *Telegraph* or the *Observer*? Why, though? Where else is he going to find a subs desk as jolly and friendly? It's the kind of problem he should know how to tackle by now. Ach, but even if he did know what to do, would it be worth all the worry and bother? He'll deal with it on Monday. Somehow. And forget about it in the meantime. Alastair chucks the weeds in the dustbin, slips off his garden shoes, tugs off his garden gloves, and replaces the trowel in the garden cupboard.

Now he appraises the kitchen. Nothing much to be done here. Actually, it's looking pretty good – everything neat, clean and tidy, without being sterile like a show house. The vase of white freesias on the table, the triangle of softening Brie and the small cylinder of *chèvre* under the cheeseboard's clear dome, the gathering of pans gleaming on their hooks above him . . . yes, it's all just about as it should be.

Alastair walks up the three steps and into what used to be a poky little dining room and is now the back bit of a main room whose varnished wooden floor extends all the way to the bay window at the front. The only drawback with the main room is that Alastair can never quite decide where he should stand to gain the best view of it. Probably here, at the entrance from the kitchen, because he can survey the room's entire length and admire the back bit's mahogany Victorian dining table and its four mahogany Victorian chairs (reupholstered in cream), as well as the red-candy-striped sofa (and the coffee table, carefully strewn with the current editions of *Time Out*, *Men's Health* and *World of Interiors*) which dominates the front bit. But even this vantage point, his favourite, fails to afford a decent view of the front bit's side walls – the three framed Doisneau prints partly hidden to his right and then the marvellous left-hand wall, whose pair of alcoves each holds five shelves of his best-looking, mainly hardback books and whose centre boasts, thanks to Alastair's redecoration, a tiled fireplace, marble mantelpiece and a large, gilt-framed mirror.

Fair enough, so it's not flash like Rob's flat, and N4 is three digits off the ideal postcode, and he doesn't have a huge basement kitchen with white fitted units, discreet spotlighting, beech-wood floor and kids' paintings on the fridge, but this main room in his two-up-two-down in Finsbury Park is as near as Alastair reckons he'll get to living in one of the perfect town houses he used to peek at during his entranced night-time walks around Islington – from Noel Road and St Peter's Street over to Theberton Street and then Barnsbury – after he swapped the subs' desk of the *Scotsman* for the subs' desk of the *Evening Standard* and arrived in London all of (blimey!) nine years ago.

Twenty-five to five. Ten minutes to go. Maybe it's sunny and they're two up. Or it's cold and rainy, three down, and people are shouting abuse as yet another simple pass goes astray. Or maybe Keith Wright has a hat-trick and they're all singing 'Take My Hand' . . .

Righty ho. He has ten minutes to do something, anything, to keep busy and not give in to lazing on the sofa and watching the latest scores. He'll take the duster upstairs, do the study and the guest room, Jif the bathroom if there's time.

11

'OUR MAN IN MARBELLA'

Saturday night

'Skeeble dibble dee. Skip dibble doodle. Skibble dabble doo . . .'

He's singing under his breath but Graham still cuts short his version of 'Strangers In The Night' as he turns into Rivington Street and sees a girl carrying a portfolio case coming towards him. The night ahead, not to mention the pair of big tequilas he had back at the flat, may have put him in a strangely jaunty mood, but it'll take more than a few tequilas and the prospect of a shag for him to risk making an exhibition of himself.

Especially in front of a, yes, a very pretty girl. As she trudges past, her eyes flicker at him for a fair fraction of a second. Here. Did she fancy him? Or was she checking him for a weirdo? Maybe she did fancy him. Now why's a pretty girl like that lugging a portfolio case around Shoreditch at nine on a Saturday night? She should be out with her mates. Having a well-earned rest after the weekly grind. She should take a tip from him. Under the pretence of being about to cross the empty street in strict adherence to the Green Cross Code, he looks over his shoulder to clock her arse. Fucking hell. Aye. He could definitely teach her a thing or two.

Now he's reached the building where Hermann used to have that fucking disgrace of a studio with a bit of wall missing and which Marty has been tarting up to house the offices of his company, D:Zine. Another sign that Shoreditch might be coming up in the world. Not something Graham could have predicted when he first rented his space in the Curtain Road studio seven years ago and found himself dodging around a dark district of clothing wholesalers, obscure printing works, and run-down studios for artists and illustrators who'd yet to make it big.

Maybe Marty's about to make it big. He and D:Zine are obviously doing pretty well for themselves at the very least. Last time Graham was down Rivington Street – three weeks ago, a month? – the ground floor was filled with rubble. And now look at this. Big, swish reception area, complete with vast plants, a wrought-iron spiral staircase, aerodynamically efficient, sunshine-yellow chairs and a grandly curving reception desk. Knowing Marty, weekdays that desk'll be manned by some teenager who looks like he should be pouting sulkily for a *GQ* fashion spread rather than telling folk he's putting them through. Marty, eh?

Graham moves on, skirting the racket of some indie shite from the juke-box in the Bricklayers – a pub that used to function as the Shoreditch crowd's staff canteen until they all decamped farther down Charlotte Street when the Cantaloupe opened a couple of years back. Odds on that they're going to have to find another place soon, because the Cantaloupe has begun to attract hordes of suits from the City, out for an evening in Bohemia. Looks okay tonight, though, the suits all necking their Budweisers back home in Essex.

Taking a sly keek through the window, he spots Col, Tim, Amanda, Hermann, Jason and Sue sitting at a table back left. No sign of Audrey. Then he notices a flash of purply red hair. She's sitting behind Hermann. As Graham looks on at the old studio crowd sitting at the table, it dawns on him that the half-hour he spent dithering at his wardrobe was a thirty-minute countdown to disaster. White T-shirt, dark blue blazer and faded blue 501s? What was he thinking about? Look at the others. *Black* T-shirts for Tim and Jason, and, doubtless, black Dockers for breeks. Col looks as if he bought his rubbery-looking jacket, with its insignia and its red, white and black stripes down the sleeves, from Halfords. And as for Hermann's outfit – fantoosh raspberry shirt with vast, flappy collar, sleeveless jersey with a yellow-and-blue golfer's-style diamond check, mainly red and green tartan trews – well, the boy would raise eyebrows at a clown school. Not counting a business suit, or perhaps tennis whites, it would seem impossible to commit a sartorial faux pas in such company, but strict rules, which he has never learned, govern this apparently wild, devil-may-care spurning of convention. And now he fears that, with what he suddenly realises is his wincingly orthodox, smart-but-casual get-up, he might just as well walk in with a placard announcing that AIDS is the work of God's justice. But he's never got the arty thing right. You'd think it was enough to be able to draw and paint, but, as he found out at art college, that was only part of the whole shebang. And since he's come down here, he's begun to suspect that an ability to draw and paint is completely irrelevant. A drawback even. Put up a tent filled with names of folk you've shagged, make shapes out of elephant shite, call it art. Long as you're in with the Goldsmiths' in-crowd and folk think you're cool. Not much danger of that for him. Graham takes a deep breath, keeps his stomach sucked in, tells himself to stay calm, and walks in. Judging that there's enough people to offer him cover, he then heads straight to the bar – no messing and, besides, no risk of a crippling round.

A minx of a barmaid with a stud in her navel gets him a pint of Guinness and a big, straight tequila. He pays the minx, downs the tequila and steels himself to carry his Guinness over to the table. Don't worry, he thinks. I worry too much, I always worry too much.

There's a spare seat by Audrey but that would be too obvious. Wouldn't it? Or would it? He decides to play safe and stand. 'Hi, guys,' he says.

'At last,' says Col. 'Our man in Marbella. Where's your Rolex?'

'Left it in the Bentley outside,' says Graham, mustering a smile. 'What have I missed?'

'The usual,' says Jason. 'Tim and Hermann had a fist fight. Some lesbian action with Aud and Sue.'

'Heard Jason's news?' Tim asks Graham.

'What, he feels he's trapped in a man's body?'

'Funny guy,' says Jason. 'Very funny guy. But if I was, at least now I could afford the surgery.'

'What's this?'

Jason leans back in his chair expansively. 'Do the words "British" and "Telecom" mean anything to you?'

'Oh no,' says Audrey, without looking round. 'Don't get him started on the blah blah blah.'

Jason reaches over to pat her thigh. 'I shall cover you with rubies, my princess. Anoint you in oriental potions.'

Graham tries not to think about Jason anointing Audrey, who's gone back to chatting with Sue, in oriental potions.

'Oh yes,' says Jason. 'Commission from BT. Big campaign. *Big* campaign.'

Graham puts down his Guinness. 'How big?'

'Big. Newspaper ads, posters, maybe telly. Twelve grand minimum.'

'Fucking hell. Confirmed?'

'Absolutely. Twelve big ones.'

'Drinks are on Jason,' says Hermann. 'In fact, they will be on Jason if he does not belt up. Can we please talk about something else?'

'What could be more interesting than me?'

'Tim's exhibition,' replies Hermann. 'The do at Marty's place later. Niall in LA. Marty and Niall splitting up. The weather. Graham's jacket. Anything.'

'Seat free over there,' Col says to Graham. 'Haul up a pew.'

Graham nods. He drags a wooden chair across to the table and nudges himself into a space between Tim and Col. He tells himself that it's only because of Jason's news or them taking the piss out of his jacket, but he knows, definitely, resolutely, with an unshakable certainty, that this sinking feeling in his gut is nature's way of warning him that, whatever happens tonight, he's going to find it difficult to chat to, far less up, Audrey, who's still ensconced with Sue. By this time, a swordsman like Rob or Ian would be sitting beside her and making her wide eyed and wet with some spiel. But how is it done? What do you say? Can I get you a . . . What's a lovely lady like you . . . What do you want for breakfast? Will the keys to my Porsche fit in your handbag? Graham finishes his Guinness. Twenty years on, and he still doesn't have a fucking clue. He gives the table a couple of slaps. 'Come on, then, Jason,' he announces. 'Tequilas all round.'

'I mean, how can they need a second runway?' says Ruth.

'Bizarre,' says Ben.

'I mean.' Ruth screws up her face. 'Manchester.'

'Bizarre,' says Ben.

'I didn't even know they *had* an airport in Manchester,' says Ruth.

Ben studies his wire-thin roll-up. 'It's bizarre,' he says.

Briony, who's been getting a bit twitchy, on account of not having said anything for nearly a minute, gives her jowls a quick shake of outrage. 'Just typical,' she mutters.

Of what? Ian thinks. The military-industrial complex? A cement-addicted patriarchy? Manchester? He pushes his chair back. ''Scuse me,' he mutters. 'Loo.' Ian smiles to show that this isn't an obvious pretext to escape. Which, of course, it is. Similarly, as he passes Claire, he gives her shoulder a gentle squeeze to show that he's not at all pissed off.

When he reaches the bathroom and closes the door, Ian shuts his eyes and expels a sigh. Not for the first time tonight, he thinks about the wrap in his wallet. He mustn't and he won't. One, it would be against his rule of charlie-free weekends (or at least Saturdays and Sundays, though not including Sunday evenings, obviously); two, he's vowed to be extra nice to Claire tonight; and three, if he had a line now, there's every chance he'd pick an argument with Ruth or ask Ben why he is such a tosser or tell Briony to do everyone a favour and get herself laid.

Ian has a dribbly piss, for form's sake, then gives his hands and face a long and thorough wash. His performance this evening has been, though he says it himself, nothing short of heroic. Two and a half hours of looking concerned and amused and *interested*, as Claire, Ruth and fucking Briony exchanged news and views about their contemporaries at Sussex, before Ruth and Ben, Ruth's new boyfriend, took charge to lament the pollution levels in eastern Europe, then to provide a day-by-day report on their recent holiday (presumably after a journey by eco-friendly clipper or canoe) in Bali, and now to debate the destruction of the Lancashire rainforest.

But it's not just the sheer, screaming boredom, Ian reflects, as he applies the towel to the skin between each finger, of listening to those three twerps congratulate themselves for being the first people, in the entire history of Western civilisation, to be truly enlightened and caring. It's not just the boredom, is it? Or even the background anxiety about Claire being pally with them. No. It's not. It's also that this evening, he, who has never felt intimidated by or estranged from youth, for he is just about the coolest person he knows (with the possible exception of Rob, but Rob's cool in a designer-suity sort of way), has been made to feel like a backbench Tory. Even when the conversation turned, briefly, to music there was no respite. He'd ventured a liking for the Prodigy – cool enough, you'd think, but no, there had been an uncomfortable silence and Briony had looked at him as if he'd just sung the praises of capital punishment or the M25.

Truth to tell, another hour of this lot and he'll be all set to campaign for the return of National Service. He already wants to tell Ruth (allegedly an actress/singer), Ben (who describes himself as a film-maker, if you please) and Briony (who has an undefined and part-time involvement in a holistic bakery) to get off their arses and find proper fucking jobs, in a building society or a shoe shop. Yeah, but why should they do that when there are mummies and daddies to fund Ruth's workshops, Ben's supply of beanie hats, Briony's eating disorder?

It's almost time to leave the sanctuary. He folds the towel into a neat rectangle and carefully adjusts it so that it hangs over the rail in equal lengths. And, come on, admit it – there's another thing below and beyond all that. Yes. There is. And it's the inescapable fact that when Briony, Ruth and Ben – and Claire, let's not forget Claire – uttered their first cries of dismay at being ejected into a wicked, Sunblest-eating, tree-felling, tarmac-loving world, he could already recite the verbs that take *être* and all the words on *Transformer*. So it is within the realms of biological possibility, perfectly conceivable in fact, that all four of those people crammed around the card-table could be his children.

Time to go back.

'Which is what I'm saying,' Ben is saying. 'If you think about it, it's really bizarre.'

Ian smiles broadly and sits down. 'What're we talking about?'

'*Friends*,' says Claire.

'The people who were at Sussex with you?'

'No,' says Ben patiently. 'It's a series on television.'

Be cool, he thinks, because this is a chance to show willing. He's seen *Friends*. He knows *Friends*. He likes *Friends*. 'Great,' he says. 'The sharpness of the script in *Friends*, you just don't get that in . . .' He's spotted Briony rolling her eyes at Ruth.

'Ah,' says Ruth.

When Briony speaks, it is with some show of doing so more in sorrow than in anger. 'Ben was just saying how *Friends* is actually really racist.'

Ian tries to catch Claire's eye but she's studying the remains of her *salade niçoise*. 'There aren't any black characters in *Friends*,' says Ian, bamboozled.

'Bizarre,' says Ben, who is being ironic.

Excellent, thinks Alastair, who is lying on the sofa and still savouring the memory of his main course – half a Marks and Sparks broccoli quiche, Marks and Sparks new potatoes, Marks and Sparks rocket salad with shavings of Marks and Sparks Parmesan. And the Fleurie turned out to be a really good choice. Went well with the quiche, and it'll be downright splendid with a few slithers of the Brie and the *chèvre*. Alastair pours himself a second glass which will last him the hour before *Match of the Day* at half-ten.

With his tummy full and his current favourite (*Northern Exposure* 2, mixed by Sasha and John Digweed) on the CD player, Alastair could quite happily spend the next hour stretched out on the sofa. Then again, a wee wander out to the garden might be just the thing. Ooh, yes. A wee wander.

Alastair swings his legs round and on to the floor. He picks up his glass of wine and the ashtray with its one spent joint. Now he walks slowly, and with heartfelt appreciation of the back bit's table and chairs, through and down into the kitchen. The pans are glistening on their hooks. The freesias look and smell terrific. And the garden . . . well, he considers as he steps outside, the garden is in fine form. He has another sip of the Fleurie and gives his shoulders a little squirm of pleasure. Mind you, it's not warm, is it? However, that could promise a clear, starlit night. He looks up at the sky, hoping that he might be stoned enough to get that feeling of staring into the endless black space of this little part of the universe. But there's only one dot of light, low to the south. Must be a planet. No sign of the moon yet. Nights like this must have been really scary before electricity.

As it is . . . Alastair looks back at the spotlit kitchen, which provides a sight so cosy that, just for a moment, he can't resist imagining the picture being completed by a woman, a sweet and beautiful woman, standing at the window and beckoning him in ... But such moments are dangerous, so Alastair reminds himself to count his blessings. Health, home, some sort of peace of mind ... And if his emotional life might sound a bit threadbare to some – no wife, no partner, no girlfriend of any description, no children, no siblings, one parent four hundred miles away – then at least it's not the tangled mess some chaps his age have blithely created. And he does have his friends. Rob. Barry. Keith and Joanna back home. Bill (another Friday Night Clubber, though long since emigrated to York, so very much a phone and now e-mail friend). Gary, even since he swapped the subs desk at the *Chronicle* for a snazzy office in Soho as chief sub of a travel glossy. A few others. Ian and Graham now, in their way. Mainly Rob, though. Who's always been a talented entertainments officer and anecdote-teller, but who has, in more recent years, also acquired the abilities – rare in men, Alastair reckons – to ask and listen. Which no doubt helps explain Rob's ever-burgeoning popularity, probably his salary hikes too, and definitely the swoonings of his women. Rob's just one of those people who have a gift for friendship, and that he has bestowed that gift on him, Alastair, has always seemed an enormous stroke of good luck. And this London part of their friendship, with Rob letting him in on his life of snazzy bachelordom, has almost let him not notice the lack of a close female friend, like Fiona was at school or Cathy. (Yes, and who's he got to blame for that lack? Nobody but himself.)

Maybe it's him getting so accustomed to this life, but it's got to the point where it's no longer a girlfriend but a girl (new word) friend he's after. Although, granted, there are those times when he aches with frustration or worries what to do for holidays, or daft things even, like having to go to parties on his own and walking in and fearing that people will look at him and think, Which is it? Little boys? Rubber frocks? Farmyard accident? But at least he's safe now, safe from harm, and November 1988 is nearly a nine-year-old memory, old enough for him to remember the split-up with Rhona and the Incident with Cathy, and not spend the next hour rocking back and forward and moaning to himself. No. It's all right. It's okay.

Alastair gives himself a shake, does a couple of stretches and lets the joint kick in again. Sure enough, the pang soon gives way to a rush of happiness so full that it almost aches. Last night might have been disappointing, even by the standards of the new FNC – five minutes in the Pig and Whistle, five minutes watching Graham fail to get Rob on the mobile, five minutes hanging shiftily around the reception area of Soho House before they had to accept that Rob wasn't there, that his membership couldn't have been processed yet and that there was no way past the girl in reception, and forty minutes on a grim Tube filled with young, loud drunks – but this more than makes up for it.

Maybe he should have another joint and get really stoned before *Match of the Day*. Ach, but then he won't remember half of it. No, a top-up of Fleurie, that's the ticket. And go back inside to the warmth.

He reaches the sofa in time for the CD to have reached 'Reeferendum' by someone or some people called Fluke, a track which can, if he's not in quite the right mood, sound a bit samey, even to him, but which can often, as now, inspire complete joy. Those drums, that bass line, and now those high arpeggios . . . just as well the curtains are closed, for he's up off the sofa again and dancing.

Who would have thought it, thinks Alastair, as he sets the CD-player for a second go of 'Reeferendum' and puts the volume up another notch. Him at thirty-six and a fan of house, dancing like a maddie around the sofa. A fan from the moment he first heard the thudding bass, when Rob persuaded him along to a club in Clerkenwell, his first year down here that must have been, early '89 maybe, and, despite feeling like a vicar at an orgy, he found himself quick-marching on the spot and nodding as if in eager agreement with the sternum-shaking beat.

Now what would the Alastair of fifteen or even ten years ago have thought about the 1997 Alastair's devotion to this music? It's a question that brings 1997 Alastair to a halt and back on to the sofa. 'This is the sound of the future,' he explains to 1987 Alastair. 'Machine made. And you see,' Alastair expounds to his former self, 'the beauty of house music is that it's simple and formulaic but in a way that allows for complexity. Basic hammering beat but lots of beats within that, basic chords but layers of stuff all kept in place by the simple patterns. Like baroque. Except baroque doesn't make you want to dance.'

But then, 1997 Alastair reflects, snuggling deeper into the sofa as the daydream conversation promises to develop as it usually does, that's what life is like now. Modern life is brilliant, isn't it? He settles into an even comfier position, for this is his favourite theme, one he can warm to at the most mundane moments, let alone a blissed-out Saturday night with *Northern Exposure 2* on the CD and *Match of the Day* coming up. There's a rattle at the back door and a moment later Susie pads into the room.

What it is, he reckons, is that we're all so used to thinking that things are getting worse and worse, and will only continue faster and faster down the slippy slope to global cataclysm, that nobody's noticed that things are actually getting better and better and better. And if anybody has paid attention to the development of democracy or anaesthetic or the near-doubling of the average lifespan this century, then nobody gets fully enthusiastic about it because optimism sounds foolish or, at the very least, like it's asking for trouble. Susie settles down by the telly, shoves a hindleg in the air like a gymnast and embarks on some energetic grooming.

'It's all a matter of social evolution,' Alastair tells Susie. 'Despite everything that everybody assumes, life is gentler and nicer than in the old days, because we're not desperate for food or shelter, so instead of stealing each other's livestock or walking around with our sword arms free, we get on with each other because we've got more to lose by being nasty.' Yes, and more to gain by taking part in the great venture of a civilisation that has given even someone like him, Alastair, the opportunity to live in complete comfort, earn an annual salary of thirty-six thousand of your Earth pounds, eat great food, drink wonderful wine, smoke quality spliff, watch brilliant TV, and listen to great music courtesy of an eminently affordable piece of technology which reproduces that music perfectly. Key question: is there any other time in the history of humankind when he, Alastair, would rather have lived? Only possible answer: absolutely not. Of course, he wouldn't mind having a go at living in the future, because now that we've reached the stage of peaceful, co-operative, scientifically advanced social democracy, things could really take off from here. Yes, everything's on schedule for the millennium. This really could be the dawning of a new era.

'So ask me,' Alastair demands of the room and 1987 Alastair, 'about what things are like now.'

'All right,' he replies. 'What about politics?'

'Thatcher's long gone and out of her box, Reagan likewise, Labour's in on a landslide, it's looking good for peace in Northern Ireland and devolution back home.'

'Foreign affairs?' he asks himself.

'The Lebanon's fine so it just disappeared from the news one day, the hostages were all freed, Arafat's for peace, Nelson Mandela was released and now he's President.'

Impressive enough, but now it's time for the big one. 'The USSR?' he asks.

'No such thing,' he replies. 'The Soviet Union collapsed, so now there's Russia and a million separate republics, no more Iron Curtain, there were people's revolutions all over eastern Europe when democracy triumphed and hardly anyone died apart from the Ceausescus, the Berlin Wall came down, Germany's been reunified, there's no more Warsaw Pact and in fact they all want to join NATO.'

'Goodness,' he says as Stunned of 1987. 'So there hasn't been a nuclear war?'

'No,' he says. 'And there's no longer any threat of one. Okay, granted,' he concedes, 'there could well be a local disaster or a loon like Saddam Hussein might explode a nuclear device, but the end of the world isn't nigh.'

He stops to consider this point. No, the end of the world isn't nigh and the nightmares he used to have – of sleek, black bombers overhead and four minutes to find his way home – are a thing of the past.

'You know what people are really worried about now?' he asks.

'Tell me,' he says. 'The ozone layer?'

'A bit,' he says, 'but even that's not as worrying as it used to be.'

'So what's the anxiety now?' he prompts.

'You wouldn't believe it,' he says.

'Try me,' he says.

'I mean, it's so ridiculous it proves my point.'

'Okay,' he says, 'what's the big threat?'

'Asteroids. Hiya, Sooz.' Alastair dangles a hand for her to rub her cheek against. 'Oh, yes,' he says, for the CD is segueing into 'Purple' by Gus Gus and that fantastic vocal line which he has to sing along to. 'Ooooh oooh ah hah wah ha ha.' And *Match of the Day* in half an hour.

12

'SO YOU HAD HALF A BOTTLE'

Sunday morning

'Yeah, right.'

'Honestly, Claire, I wasn't anywhere near drunk. What were the empties? One bottle of claret, two bottles of white.'

'Yeah, like I was really knocking it back.'

'That still leaves four of us. That Ben guy had his fair share, and Briony isn't one to hold . . .'

'Don't you start about Briony.'

'I'm not starting about Briony. All I'm saying is . . .'

'You've said quite enough in the past about Briony.'

Not true, Ian thinks. Not true by a damned sight. 'Hey,' he says brightly, 'do we need any washing-up liquid?'

''Course we need washing-up liquid.' No sign of the vile mood she's been in for the past few days disappearing. He might as well have asked her if they need to breathe air.

'I think it's back a few aisles. You stay here, I'll go and fetch it.' Times like this, Ian thinks, a cigarette would help – and he'd be able to scoot outside and leave her to do the Sainsbury's thing on her own.

He walks back, past walls of bread and bog rolls and biscuits. When he returns, Claire is holding up a large bottle of extra-virgin olive oil and scrutinising it from every conceivable angle.

'Can't afford it,' she decides, and bangs the bottle back on the shelf. Next thing, she'll be over at the pyramid of baked beans on special offer, yanking out a couple of cans from the bottom row.

'There you go,' Ian says, placing a tube of Fairy into the trolley.

'Okay, so you had half a bottle. But you certainly made the most of it.'

'Claire, what does that mean?'

'It means, Ian, it means that there has got to be a song and dance about the wine, hasn't there?' She holds a hand in front of her mouth, four fingers circling to her thumb. 'Noat as gid as the eighty-tooo,' she squeaks, 'but ah think yeel bee amyooosed by the noaz.'

He retains enough self-control to wonder if an accurate piss-take would make him feel crushed rather than enraged. As it is . . . He spends a few moments surveying the contents of their trolley. Pasta, coffee, apples, bananas, a bag of spinach, four pink bricks of salmon, a cellophaned box of potatoes, the tube of Fairy . . . 'Claire, it's not often we get the chance to drink nice wine, and I haven't had a good Bordeaux for . . .'

She puts her head to one side. 'Aye, aye, fur a gid fyoo yeerz.'

'Please, Claire. Don't do this.'

She must judge that she's gone far enough because she begins to pay particular attention to a nearby jar of mustard. Although she does make sure that he can overhear her muttering 'eighty-two' with a smirk of contempt.

He has to be big about this. 'I'm sorry, Claire. I did try my best. I know they're your friends and I . . .'

'Hah! That reminds me.'

'What?'

'Nothing.'

Neil Hamilton has no chance of a new career on telly. Dublin is urging the IRA to keep to the ceasefire. Kirkcaldy's great man in number eleven plans a surprise bonus for the elderly. American economists are talking about a golden age of low inflation and high growth.

Alastair is eating toast and scanning the Sunday papers spread out in front of him on the sitting-room floor – his weekly concession to chaos, but it's a jumble that he can easily tolerate because he'll have cleared it all up by four. By which time he will also have done the vacuuming, had a look-see round the garden and phoned his father. Because by four o'clock, according to Alastair's traditional Sunday plan, he'll be back lying on this sofa, a glass and a bottle of Highland Spring on the coffee table, an ashtray on his tummy and a joint in his hand, ready to watch Liverpool–Newcastle live on Sky.

Now he takes another bite of toast and has a quick look at the *Sunday Mirror*. Ginger Spice has been wearing a partly see-through dress. Alastair discards the *Mirror* and picks up the *Observer*. 'Aitken to face trial,' says a headline. Alastair sips his Earl Grey. This is the life.

'Is this Graham?'

'Eh . . . yeah.' Christ, where did that growl come from?

'Friend of Bobby's, right?'

Graham yawns, rubs his eyes and tries to force his brain into action. It's some woman, she's got one of those Londonish accents that vaguely posh English folk acquire in an effort not to sound vaguely posh, and he hasn't a fucking clue who she is or what the fuck she is on about. 'Aw-way,' he says through another ear-popping yawn. 'Christ,' he says when the yawn is finally over. 'Bobby. Who's Bobby?'

'Oh, *damn* it.' Whoever this woman is seems to take a deep breath. 'Is this oh one eight one, three four two five eight nine one?'

'Eh, yes. Aye, it is.' Graham scoops gunk out of the corner of each eye, but he still can't focus. He shuts his right eye and peers at the can of Spray-Mount beside the phone. Okay. Now he closes his left eyelid. The lettering on the can of Spray-Mount and everything else in the world blurs. Some- one's smeared Vaseline over his right eyeball. Then shat in his mouth. He shies away from the phone to avoid the reflection of his own halitosis when he says, 'What do you want?' He immediately regrets the rather brusque tone, because he's just had a startling thought. 'Wait. I'm sorry. Is that you, Audrey?'

'Audrey? No, no, my name's Louise. Louise Turner. You might have heard about me from Bobby.'

Count to ten, Graham urges himself. He reaches four and gives up. Losing his rag won't help him get back to sleep, but there's no other option. 'Look,' he says. 'I haven't heard of you, I don't know any Bobby, you've got the wrong number *and* you've woken me up *and* I've got a fucking terrible fucking hangover. So, please, please, *please*, whoever the *fuck* you are, fucking fuck *off*.'

'Don't hang up, don't hang up. All right, Graham, you don't know me, but I've got your telephone number here and you do know Bobby. Bobby Mackenzie. Scottish, lives in Soho, good chum of yours, *that* Bobby Mackenzie.'

Until this moment, Graham had thought that the act of holding the telephone away to examine it when being told surprising news was one of those things people did only in films, like leaving a car unlocked or falling in love with a suspect. He returns the phone to the side of his face. 'You mean Rob. Rob Mackenzie.'

'Whatever. Jeez. Yes.'

'What about Rob? Oh, fuck, wait a minute, is he all right?'

'That's the thing. I really don't know.'

Part Two

1

'VERY ODD INDEED'

Sunday lunch-time

It's a joke.

It's because of him being the fretful sort. And Bateman Street looking unusually empty. And Friday Night Club, or three-quarters of it, meeting up on a Sunday afternoon. That's why he feels that someone has blow-dried his mouth and scooped out his stomach with a spoon. Certainly not because he's suddenly acquired a paranormal ability to detect impending doom. No, this definitely has to be a practical joke.

Alastair crosses the narrow street yet again to look up yet again at the three windows of Rob's flat. He can still see only a tiny corner of the sitting room's ceiling.

However. This is some sort of a prank, no more than that. Like the time when Rob spiked Jimbo's tea.

Still only twenty to. Perhaps he could kill some more time by getting himself another coffee at Bar Italia. No. He'll wait for the others in the pub, order a rare lunch-time pint, and grab a table at the back where they'll be able to talk in peace.

It's definitely a joke.

This makes absolutely no sense whatsoever. *Nada. Rien.* Were he a betting man, Ian would lay a couple of quid on this being the result of Graham being crap, as usual. Some woman phones up and Graham gets the wrong end of the stick, grabs the stick and starts whacking people round the head with it. 'Fucking Rob's done a fucking bunk. Meet me at the Pig at one' – what kind of a message is that to leave on an answerphone? A normal message, Ian supposes, if your brain has been addled by alcohol and self-abuse. Or maybe Graham actually got a ride off that girl he was seeing last night and his synapses exploded with the shock.

Ian turns into a strangely underpopulated and carless Old Compton Street. He overtakes a Japanese couple dawdling without a clue about how to occupy the long hours of a tourist's London Sunday and dodges past a group of bleary young ravers wearing jumpers with zips and hoods. Whatever they've been on to keep them swigging from their little bottles of Evian until ten to one the next afternoon, he could fair go a shot of it. And not a care in the world, the lucky little bastards.

He's early and Graham is bound to be late and an espresso would hit the spot, so Ian loiters for a moment outside the Bar Italia but then he picks up the pace again. He's edgy enough after this morning's performance by Claire. Plus he has the feeling that simply by being in the Pig and Whistle he'll somehow get this daft business over and done with all the sooner. Ian hurries up Frith Street and into the pub.

'Ian.'

'Oh, hi, Eck. Get you a drink?' Ian says from the bar.

'Grassy arse, but I'm fine with this.'

'Sure? Pint of lager, please . . . So. Any sign of Graham?'

'Not yet.'

'Big surprise.'

'It's a wind-up. Like when Rob spiked Jimbo's tea. A wind-up.'

'Ah. Got you. So Rob hasn't turned up yet and this is your theory, that it's a practical joke.'

'Has to be.'

'Some joke. This mystery woman, is she coming?'

'According to Graham. He said she'd be a bit late, though.'

'Probably beat Graham to it by a good day or two. Rob ever say anything to you about her?'

Alastair shakes his head. This wordless reply seems to set a precedent. Ian settles into refining his fantasy monologue wherein he puts Claire to rights ('You want us to spend a Saturday evening with your pals so I spend a Saturday evening with your pals. You want me to go to Sainsbury's with you, so what happens? Correct.') so the silence is ended only by one of Alastair's coughs. 'It's all very odd,' Alastair says.

Ian replies with a nod. '*Then*,' continues the monologue inside his head, 'you spring the news on me that we're to be trekking up to Stanmore for Sunday lunch with your parents, and for once I say no, because (a) it's the first *I've* heard of it, (b) how am I supposed get from Stanmore to St John's Wood in time for my freelance class and (c) there's this Rob business to deal with.'

'Very odd indeed,' says Alastair eventually.

'Yes,' says Ian. He flips a beer-mat. Maybe it's just the pregnancy. Weird hormones or something. Well, whatever's up with Claire, he could really do without it.

Just what the fuck is Rob playing at? And just who the fuck is the bird on the phone? And how the fuck is he supposed to get through the day feeling like microwaved shite? As if his life isn't full enough of questions – what's he going to do without Jenny? Is she being screwed? Who by? – that make him feel like he's been hoiked in off the pavement, the crook of some bastard's umbayfuckingrella round his neck, and forced to sit an algebra exam. But you never know – maybe a pint and a chat is all it'll take to sort out his hangover and this Rob thing. If only the big ones had such straightforward answers. Graham pushes open the door and sees Ian and Eck staring glumly into space at the back of the pub.

'Graham, you're only five minutes late. This must be serious.'

'Hi, Graham. Any news?'

'Eck, what am I? The magic man? We'll have to wait on this bird to turn up.'

'It's a wind-up. Like Jimbo's tea.'

'The fuck you talking about, Eck?'

'The time when Rob put a tab of acid in Jimbo's tea.'

'Uh-huh.'

'And Jimbo started tripping when he was refereeing a rugby match. Remember? He tried to swim down the pitch because he thought the second fifteen were sharks.'

There are times, and this is one of them, when Graham wonders if anything has happened to the wee man since 1978. 'Aye, Eck, I do mind that, oddly enough, but I don't see that there's much fucking comparison between spiking a gym teacher's tea and doing a fucking runner. If that's what Rob has done. Fuck knows. Only thing I know for certain is that I'm off to the bar. Anyone? No? Suit yourselves.'

While he waits for his pint, Graham tells himself to stop being het up because there's got to be a simple explanation for all of this. That bird has to have something to do with it . . . He'll look back on this moment and wonder at how daft he was not to realise what was going on. This part of the proceedings is just like whenever he lost something as a kid and could only assume that the object had been stolen with a top-secret ray gun.

Graham carries his pint back to the table with a relatively steady hand. Ian's flipping a beer-mat. Eck looks like he's trying to add up several six-figure numbers in his head.

'Right, then,' says Graham, because somebody's got to take charge here. 'Time to compare notes. I haven't seen Rob since last Friday. Or heard from him. Anyone improve on that?'

'Nup,' says Ian. 'I've left a few messages on his answerphone, but I haven't heard from him since we left his flat and took him to the cashpoint.'

'I'm surprised you remember that much, fucking state you were in.'

'Same with me, Graham. I haven't had any contact with him since last FNC. Well, not Friday's Friday Night Club but the Friday before that, the last proper one. I mean . . . And he was fine then, wasn't he? In fact, he was on pretty good form, as I recall. Before he lost it. He was going on about the football on Eurosport, remember?' Eck lets out a nasal laugh. 'And a man jumping,' he quotes, in a poor approximation of a commentator's expectant tone. 'In the air.'

Graham samples his pint and suppresses a shudder. 'So none of us have seen or heard from him for over a week. Nine days if you include today. And none of us had a scooby that anything was amiss, right?'

'Right,' says Ian.

'Let's suppose,' says Eck, 'that Rob has gone away somewhere. Where would he go? And why?'

'Christ knows where,' says Ian. 'But if he really has gone away some place for longer than a fortnight, and that's a very big if, the why part would be pretty obvious.'

'Is that so? And what obvious fucking reason is that, oh sudden expert on missing persons?'

Ian shrugs. 'The reason most people do a bunk. They're pissed off with the life they have so they decide to have a shot at another one. Guy has enough of doing the same thing day in day out, tells the wife he's popping out for a packet of fags, comes back twenty years later to say he's been shacked up with a series of nymphets in the Seychelles. Happens all the time. Thousands every year.'

'Aye,' says Graham, 'but why should Rob be one of them?'

'*If*,' says Eck with unEckian emphasis, '*if* he's done this for real, then he must be in some serious trouble. Why else would he just give up all the things he's got? His flat, his friends, his . . . his *life* . . .'

Graham has another go at his pint. That's better. 'What I think is this,' he says. 'It's got to be woman trouble. Specially with a champion shagger like Rob. He'll turn up in a day or two with a story about being chased by some husband with a shotgun. Tell you one thing. I bet this female knows a lot more than she let on to me.'

Ian nods his head. 'Here's my theory, right? Rob's written her a letter to give her the push and she's got it completely wrong. Wouldn't be the first time a woman has mistaken being chucked for the end of the world. Won't be the last.'

'Well,' says Graham, 'this looks like our chance to find out.'

Ian leans forward. 'The girl that's just come in? How do you know it's her?'

'Male intuition,' says Graham. 'That and the fact that she's the only bird in the place. Aye. Must be her. Either that, or Eck's just pulled.'

'Excuse me, are you three Bobby's friends?'

Bobby again, notes Graham. Bobby. Yeuch. Mind you, Rob was a fairly noncey name for the man to pick for himself as well. Why not be like the other Roberts from back home who were Rabs or Rabbies or . . . Roberts? Eck's stood up and offered a hand for her to shake, registering too late that she is holding a little bag in one hand and a bottle of Becks in the other. Graham looks on benevolently as the wee man tries to adapt the gesture by gallantly beckoning her towards the spare seat. That's the great thing about Eck – he can make every bloke in his vicinity feel like Omar Sharif.

His footering around has also given Graham the chance to size this one up. Only five two, five three, something like that, and a bit of a skinnymalink, so she's much smaller than he assumed that, for no reason other than that she's one of Rob's, she would be, but she's got a nice enough face framed by dark, wavy hair, biggish brown eyes, slim nose, and, unless she's sooking a secretive sweetie, good cheekbones. Not a stunner, by any means, but she wouldn't frighten any horses. Black, high-lapelled jacket, white T-shirt, black clingy trousers with a touch of the flare about them. How old is she? Time was when he could confidently pinpoint someone's age, particularly a female's, but that's a knack that seems to have disappeared as he's got older, together with an ability to run more than fifty yards and first-thing-in-the-morning hard-ons, to name but two, and he has to settle for mid to late twenties. She sits down beside him and raises her bottle in an ironic toast.

'Hello. My name is Louise,' she says. 'And I'm an alcoholic.'

Lassie's obviously joking but the Eckster's all over the shop. 'Oh,' he says. 'I'm. That's.' Fucksake.

She gives Eck a quick smile. 'Not really.'

'Oh. Right. Ha. Well, it's very good to meet you. Though not under such . . . I'm Alastair. And this is Ian. And this . . .'

'Is Graham,' says Graham.

'Charmed, I'm sure. Well.' She puts her bottle down. 'This is a to-do.'

Eck coughs. 'Graham mentioned a note,' he says. 'I don't want to be rude but do you think that you might, that we could . . . have a look at it? I mean, if you haven't got it, that's fine, but . . .'

'Don't worry. Sorry, Alexander, is it?'

'Alastair.'

'Alastair. Dizzy little thing that I am, by some miracle I did remember to bring it.'

'Sorry. I didn't mean.'

'Chill. It's in here.' She pulls her bag up on to her lap. It's a little leather backpack, of the kind that's obligatory in Shoreditch and which Graham always thinks would do just fine for a hiker who is three years old. She fiddles around in the miniature rucksack. 'There you go,' she says. 'For what it's worth.' She flourishes a scrap of paper with little ripped ribbons still clinging to the perforated edges and waggles it with a grimace. 'All the charm of a square of loo roll. Then again, I don't suppose I was ever going to have it framed. Here.' She hands the scrap to Graham. Ian and Alastair move in from either side so that they can read with him.

Louise – I can't go on. By the time you read this I will have started a new life with a new name in a new place. Don't waste your time trying to find me. Any queries, ask my lawyer – he's called Maddox. 826 3436.

Ian is first to look up. 'That's it?'

'Yip.'

'Where did you find it?'

'Shoved under my door. First thing I saw when I got back this morning. I'll say this for Bobby, his timing's pretty good, because this has cured my jet-lag. I'm just in from New York,' she explains in reply to Ian's unspoken question.

'Wait a minute,' says Graham. 'Can you talk us through exactly what happened?'

'I might skip the bit about waiting in a long queue for a taxi, if you don't mind, but here goes. I get back from the States, okay? Must have been about nine by the time I opened my front door. This note was lying on my hallway carpet, no envelope, no nothing. I figured it must be some kind of pissy joke so I went up to Bobby's flat to, I don't know, give him a fright back or . . .'

Ian's shaking his head. 'Let's put the brakes on. You say you went up to Bobby's, Rob's flat?'

'Spot on, Sherlock. That'll be because his flat's the one above mine.'

'Oh,' say Ian and Graham. Eck's too busy looking at her blankly to say anything.

'Oh,' she says in return. 'I see. Not only have you never heard of me, you didn't know that his girlfriend has the flat downstairs?'

It's as Graham suspected. She does think that she's Rob's girlfriend.

'You went up to his flat,' Ian prompts quickly, presumably in case Eck says something obvious and devastating.

'Yeah, up to his flat, and everything was normal except there was no sign of Bobby. At first I assumed I wasn't thinking straight, with the jet-lag and all, so I went back to my place, made myself a cup of tea and read the note about a thousand times. Then I phoned Barbara.'

Ian raises his eyebrows. 'And Barbara is . . . ?'

'My mother.'

'Right.'

'And she said if I was so bothered, why didn't I phone the police. So I did. There's a copper coming round to see me later. More of an exercise in being seen to be nice than anything else, I imagine. The man I talked to, he must have been the desk sergeant or something, he told me not to worry, happens all the time, give Bobby a couple of days and he'll be back with his tail between his legs. But he would say that, wouldn't he? . . . Then I went back up to Bobby's to have a look around.'

Ian swirls lager round his glass. 'And what did you find? I mean, is there anything unusual or odd about the place?'

'No. That's just it.'

'What's just it?'

'I didn't find anything unusual or odd or, weirder still, missing.'

'But that has to be a good sign,' Eck says eagerly. 'Maybe he's just popped out. Or gone away for a couple of days.'

She takes a deep breath. 'A tremendously good point. If you ignore the existence of this shitty little note. And if you were popping out or going away for a couple of days, what would you take with you? I'll tell you what you would take, Alastair. You would take your wallet, yes? A change of clothes. Your passport if you were popping out to a foreign clime. Maybe your shaving stuff and things to clean your teeth. But his wardrobe's full and all his stuff is still there. Keys, wallet, credit cards, passport, cheque book, razor, the lot. 'Course, he could have packed a suitcase with a couple of shirts and a book or two and I might not be any the wiser, but it would have to be a new suitcase since the three I know about are still under the bed. Far as I can make out, everything of Bobby's is still there. Intact. It's as if he's just vanished. Or been abducted by those aliens with big heads and slanty eyes.' She takes a sip of her Becks. 'Being a great one for looking on the bright side, I like to think that the note at least proves that he isn't having a medical on an intergalactic spacecraft. So next thing, I spotted his address book. I decided to go through it, see if there were any names I recognised or at least of people I could call, and there under A was an entry for someone just called Graham in capital letters, so I guessed that person had to be a fairly good friend. Then I phoned. And here we all are.'

Aye, well. One thing, she's certainly keen on the sound of her own voice. 'What about this Maddox?' Graham asks. 'Has he told you anything?'

'No, be . . .'

'Fucksake. I bet he gave you some confidentiality shit. Could you not have asked him questions that were kind of indirect? Or maybe waited till he went out the room and had a peek at his files?'

'Not possible, I'm afraid.'

'How come?'

'This is Sunday.'

'Ah.'

'I thought that the event fell into the long-queue-for-a-taxi category, but first thing I did when I got this . . . note was dial that number, but of course there was only an answerphone saying the office was closed. I'll give him a call first thing tomorrow morning. Now, can I take my turn and ask you chaps a question?'

'Hey. Sure.'

'Fucking bash on.'

'Fine, of course, we'd be glad to be of . . .'

'Do any of you have any idea what the hell is going on?'

'Well,' says Graham, 'us three really are completely in the fucking dark.'

'Really? Bobby never said anything? Didn't give any of you the teensiest hint that something was wrong?'

'Nup,' says Ian. 'Like we were just saying, he was fine when we saw him last Friday. There's been no sign that he was about to do a Reggie Perrin. I mean, we're not hiding anything from you if that's what you think.'

She gives Ian a bemused look. 'Reggie who?'

'Thing is,' says Graham quickly to prevent Eck launching into what would probably be a comprehensive summary of Leonard Rossiter's career, 'thing is, we don't know anything about what Rob's done or why. We've never even known anything about you. And until this morning, you didn't know that us three existed. Or that your Bobby is actually called Rob. Far as I can see, none of us know anything about anything.'

She delves into her toddler's backpack again and brings out a packet of Marlboro, removes the last cigarette and crumples the packet slowly in her fist. 'Then again,' she says, 'that's just our starting point, isn't it? From here on in, all we can do is learn. And not only what's happened to Bobby but, perhaps, valuable lessons about ourselves. From this experience, we will grow. As friends and as human beings.' She drops the packet in the ashtray and lights her cigarette.

They all study the mangled packet. 'You're joking, right?' asks Ian.

'Duh.' She blows out a thread of smoke which whorls into a shaft of sunlight. 'Now, I don't want to come on too strong to you boys, but what do you say we all finish our drinks and go on somewhere else? I know a little place just along the road. A flat belonging to our mutual and absent friend.'

2

'WAS IT SOMETHING I SAID?'

Sunday afternoon

Over two hours now they've been pottering around Rob's flat and all for nothing, as far as Ian can see. The place is exactly as it always is – tidy, clean, tasteful in a clutter-is-so-uncool, minimalisty way. And the only thing missing is Rob. Being in Rob's flat without Rob there definitely got to everyone at first – the four of them moving slowly and together from room to room, surveying the few items of furniture with an inhibition that reminded Ian of a Romanian tour group he once saw shuffling through Versailles. But then, to his astonishment, the other three got into their stride, and before you knew it were ransacking cupboards like they were detectives with a warrant. Well over the top, if you ask him, and when Rob turns up in a couple of days' time, he's going to be really thrilled about having his flat turned over by a search party. Ten minutes it took them to trans-form Rob's two spruce bedrooms into sites for a jumble sale.

As if chucking shirts and jerseys and shoes all over the place would help solve a problem that doesn't exist. Because Rob's going to call up from Barbados or Sri Lanka and tell them about the wobbly he threw or the bender he's gone on. Or the grief he's been getting from this Louise. Because that's what's happened, he'd bet on that – Rob's had enough, just as he had enough when Cristina launched into a screaming fit of hyperneurotic violence spectacular even by Cristina's high standards, and he couldn't be arsed to reply but quietly and calmly packed his bags, shut the door gently behind him, and left Cristina to it.

Horse walks into a pub, orders a pint. Barman goes, 'Why the long face?' Fair enough, what Rob's done, if he really has done it, will take a bit of getting used to, but it's not as if the man is dead. And he'll probably be in touch soon when the dust has cleared. Or when he gets bored. But to look at Graham, Eck and that Louise, you'd think they'd found Rob in the shunkie, a bottle of whisky and a service revolver by his side, half his head staining the shower curtain. If you ask him, the others are maybe even getting off on this glum, fretful atmosphere, in the self-important way that people do get off on misery.

Behaviour that is all the more obviously ridiculous in a place where it's always been party time. Presumably there has been the odd occasion when Rob's had a quiet night in watching the telly but that's as easy to imagine as – he tries to think of something really unthinkable – okay, Eck pole-dancing.

Ian flumps down on the couch. By the sounds of it, the in-depth investigation has moved through to the kitchen. How much more of this is there going to be? And what should he do to keep himself occupied? Ian gazes at the room's only other item of furniture, not counting the TV or the sound system or the empty vase on the floor – the glass-topped coffee table in front of him. Granted, it's a Sunday afternoon and therefore, strictly speaking, against his rule, but this is kind of a special occasion. And this glass table might as well have come with a free razor blade and a rolled-up twenty. Not that Rob has ever been a great one for the cocaine, but he's certainly got the table for it.

Ian fetches out his wrap and tips a tiny pile of powder on to the table. There really is nothing quite like cutting out a line or two on a fuck-off, posh glass table. The man was into his grass, though. Jamaican weed, Thai stuff, skunk . . . God, yes, the skunk. Ian pauses, the straw held in his fingers like a pen as he remembers his first Friday night out in London with Rob and Graham. Eck popping in later. The first meeting of the new version of FNC, come to think of it. The night he also got chatting to that Spanish girl in the Pig and Whistle. Mih something? No. Meh, moh, mah, mah . . . Ian starts to sift the tiny pile into a pair of lines. Margarita? Maria? Nup . . . Marta – that was it. Marta. Very tidy little number. Marta. Anyway, the skunk. Just a couple of pencil-sized joints back here and they were all giggling like schoolgirls. Five minutes it had taken him to get up from the floor and stagger through to the shunkie (for what turned out to be a record-breaking piss), so he'd really had no option but to accept Rob's offer and stay the night in the spare bedroom. Sheets so clean and smooth that, according to his rather hazy memory of the event, he spent his few remaining minutes of consciousness gently writhing with the pleasure of their touch. Claire, of course, had gone ballistic the next evening when he finally made it back to Bonnington Square. Fair enough, so maybe he should have phoned, but the way she'd gone on he might as well have spent the night with his head clamped between that Marta's thighs. Now that, thinks Ian, is a thought.

Now that, thinks Graham, is a pretty fucking good view.

She's looking through one of the drawers in the sparse and spotless kitchen. Fortunately, the drawer is the second-lowest of the three in the unit beside the stainless-steel Tardis that is Rob's fridge, so she is bending down, allowing Graham to appraise her legs and arse. She is too thin, he decides, but at least the legs are straight and the arse has got a wee bit of a curve to it. Not enough shapeliness going on, though. Unlike, say, Jenny, who had excellent legs and a proper bum, one that could really fill a skirt . . . It got so that it became one of their bits of patter, her going all wide eyed and mock coquettish, twiddling an index finger against a cheekbone then bending from her waist to pick up a pretend something from the floor . . . Somehow, this thought soon evolves into a picture of Jenny doing her bending-over routine with someone else, which is such a fucking terrible image that he has to clutch hold of the shiny kitchen top for support.

With a triumphant 'ah-ha!', she pulls herself gracefully upright and turns round to show him her trove – a packet of ten cigarettes. She bends from her waist again, but only slightly this time and in profile as she lights one of the cigarettes on the shining black hob. She takes a puff, examines the packet, then looks enquiringly at him. 'Maybe you can tell me,' she says.

'Bash on.'

She shakes the packet. 'What exactly is the point of these?'

'Don't ask me, hen, I don't smoke. There is no point. Unless you really want to get cancer.'

'Fat chance of that. Silk Cut Ultra. I'd get a bigger hit from a pot of yoghurt.' She takes another long, scandalised suck on the cigarette.

'You're lucky to find any fags at all, I'd have thought.'

'Ah, no. This is the emergency supply, from the days when Mr Smooth always had a packet in the flat lest his latest victim smoked.' She gives him a sarky, cheesy smile. 'Or didn't smoke but might whimsically fancy a post-coital gasper. Not a source of comfort to me, I have to say, when I was in New York and trying to believe his declarations of undying fidelity. Silk Cut Ultra, though, I ask you . . . Was it something I said?'

'Er, no. No. It's, well . . .' Graham purses his lips and nods reflectively, hoping she'll assume that he's been afflicted by the strangeness of this Robless gathering, whereas what he's really struggling to cope with is the thought that Silk Cut Ultra was the brand Jenny used to smoke. Isn't there anything that won't remind him of her? Can't there be any escape from her ghost? Because here he is now seeing a naked Jenny puffing away in bed, grinning contentedly beside some big, hairy Bluto who's got one arm clasped round her shoulder and another reaching down to . . .

Graham mumbles that he's going through to the living room. Where he finds a handy distraction in the form of Ian crouched over the glass table.

'Fuck me, what a surprise. Would that big line of powder consist, by any chance, of a cocaine–Ajax mix?'

Ian surveys his handiwork with approval. 'It's a fair cop, guv. Got me bang to rights. Hey – you fancy one, Graham? Come on, it's a special occasion.'

The latest, Silk Cut-inspired ache leads Graham to toy with the notion, but then he reminds himself that, on the handful of occasions when he's taken cocaine, he has felt only anxious and agitated, at the cost of instant diarrhoea, sweaty palms, a cardboard tongue, an itchy scalp, and a nose so blocked up the next morning that he had to breathe through his mouth, like someone from Birmingham. A bargain at ten pence a molecule. 'I'll pass,' says Graham, though he does join Ian on the sofa.

While Ian pushes a straw over both lines, Graham picks through the small pile of magazines that have been left fanning the coffee table's shelf. Mostly *Economist*s, but three issues of *Art Monthly* which come as a mildly intriguing surprise, a couple of *Vize*s which come as no surprise at all, a glossy magazine called *European Traveller* which last year had the fucking nerve to make him redo his illustration of a sun wearing sun-specs, and, sandwiched between a year-old *New Yorker* and an inexplicable *Elle*, Rob's curiously cheap-looking and skinny week-to-a-page diary.

'Heyheyheyhey,' says Ian. 'Rob's diary.'

Graham is too busy looking through the little black booklet to say anything sarcastic in return. Ian peers over Graham's shoulder for a very short while then, suddenly fed up with that game, gives up and breenges over to the other side of the room, to have a look through Rob's CDs and to sniff a lot.

Graham flicks through to this week's page. Only one entry and it's for today – 'L returns'. That Louisa, presumably. Next week's page? Blank. The week after? Blank. All the pages that follow – blank. Graham starts to flick back. Not counting today's, the diary's final entry is for the previous Friday – '8: FNC, Pig'. He turns back another page. Wednesday he met a J at 4. Friday there's the same – '8: FNC, Pig' (the night when they had the argument about Tony Blair and Eck did his usual Friday-night act, turning up after last orders). Graham flicks back another week. Sure enough, there they are again – '8.30: FNC, Pig' – and nothing else bar J for lunch at the Coach and Horses on the Tuesday. He tries to recall that Friday night – of course, the one here when Ian droned on about Barcelona's nightlife and Rob rolled those joints that made Graham feel he was being watched by a malevolent, supernatural power.

Graham riffles though another dozen or so pages. Not much in them, which is a bit surprising but also reassuring, because it's good to see that Rob's just about as unconscientious about that kind of thing as him, not that there's been too many top-level meetings and glamorous nights out for him to be not putting in his diary recently. Rob, though, he'd have put down as the meticulous type, but there's only a couple of entries a page. And the past few weeks, the ones that aren't the Friday Night Club are mostly afternoon or early-evening appointments with this J character.

Graham stares at the diary. Keep calm, he reminds himself. Keep calm. Then he forces himself to take another look, from the start. Quite a few Js earlier in the year, then a gap, then they appear every month or so, until the end of August. Then they start: '5.30: J's office', '6: J, Coach', '1: J, Dell'Ugo' . . .

Graham's throat produces a brief, low, constipated groan. J. Silk Cut Ultra. Her office handily placed a few hundred yards from this very flat.

J.

'That's me shooting the craw.'

'Graham. Are you okay?'

'Oh, aye, comm fucking pleetly tip fucking top. See you later, uh, Louisa.'

''Bye.'

''Bye, Graham. I hope you'll be all . . .' Alastair's farewell fades away, for Graham has already gone. The bedroom walls vibrate briefly as the flat's front door bangs shut.

Louise raises her eyebrows. 'I'm just guessing here but I think your friend might have left. Where's the other one?'

'Yo, guys, what's up, what's happening, what is occuring?' Ian marches in and bounces down on the end of the bed. He skims a hand over the duvet absent-mindedly then rubs his nose. He's clearly on edge. Well, no wonder. This is a strange and upsetting business.

'Incidentally, incidentally,' Ian announces. 'Found Rob's diary through there. Bugger all in it.' He glances at his watch. 'Shit. I'm late.' He jumps off the bed and gives them a thumbs-up. 'Talk to you soon Eck nice to meet you it'll be all right Christsake though 'bye.' Ian strides out of the bedroom. Two seconds later, the bedroom walls vibrate.

'Goodness,' says Louise. 'Is he always like that?'

'Well, he's obviously worried,' says Alastair.

'And wired.'

'Really? But it's only three o'clock.'

'Oh, well, goodness, I must be wrong, then.' Louise rests her hands on the duvet behind her and leans back. A little to his surprise, Alastair notices that he's noticed that this position emphasises the pertness of her breasts. 'Why did they both call you Eck?'

'Ahem. Well. It's just a nickname.' One of those things you're stuck with, he wants to say. Like being a bald ginge. 'Quite a common one in Scotland, although usually for Alexanders. Sometimes Alastairs as well, because the name Alastair is related to Alexander. Mind you, Alexanders are often Sandys. Or Alexes . . . Alecs . . .'

'Should I call you Eck as well?'

Alastair tilts his head in what he hopes is a take-it-or-leave-it way.

Louise smiles. 'Okay, Alastair. Now what would you say to a drink? Not including "Hello, drink". I think we could both do with a large, stiff one.'

Alastair, who was indeed about to say 'Hello, drink', nods feebly.

Louise slaps her thighs and pulls herself up with embarrassing grace. 'Come on, then. I really need to get out of this room.'

Alastair follows her to the kitchen where she heads for the fridge. 'This is weird,' she murmurs. 'Look at all this stuff. Fancy a pesto, raspberry jam and old broccoli omelette? Nice of him to leave a bottle of tonic, though.' Alastair is busy remembering all the times that he's stood in this kitchen, chatting away while Rob fetched bottles of beer or a bottle of cold white, when Louise offers him a tall glass clinking with ice. 'Flange,' she says.

'Flange?'

'Isn't that what Scots say?'

'Oh. Got you. *Slàinte*.' Alastair takes a sip of what is clearly not-quite-neat gin and coughs.

'Yeah, slange. So. What's the story?'

'Sorry, Louise. What's what story?'

'You three musketeers. Who are you?'

'Oh. Yes. Of course. Well, we're all friends of Rob from back home, basically. The Friday Night Club. Rob must have mentioned it. Kind of a joke thing really . . .' Alastair was going to explain how this is the second version of Friday Night Club, the title a knowing but fond acknowledgment of their shared past and one that this time round was christened by Rob, and maybe adding something if he possibly could about it being him, Alastair, who came up with the Friday Night Club title originally, when there were about a dozen of them one underage jamboree in the Harbour Bar and he dared himself to propose the name, ostensibly as a joke, but something in the way Louise is looking at him, as if he's just claimed that Paris is the capital of Germany, stops him short.

'Friday Night Club?' she asks.

'Yes. Oh . . . So he didn't . . .' You are an *idiot*, Alastair tells himself. For some reason, it's only now that it has dawned on him how strange and, to be honest, hurtful it is that she really doesn't know anything about the FNC or, to be more honest, him. 'It comes from schooldays,' says Alastair, soldiering on. 'It started in fifth year, I suppose. Not just us four, there was a whole crowd of us. All because of Rob, really, I mean he was at the centre of it. And it was called Friday Night Club because we'd . . .'

'Meet up on Friday nights, yes, I *think* I see. And you three and Bobby kept on doing it.'

'Not kept on doing it, not really. It, I mean this new version of the FNC, has only been on the go for five, six months, really since Ian returned from abroad, though we'd seen Graham occasionally after he came down here then split up with his girlfriend. And as it happens, the four of us did meet up in Munich a couple of years ago to . . .' Alastair lets the explanation tail off, because he's beginning to witter. Then it occurs to him that he'd have to witter a lot, lot more to explain the intricacies, the complexities of the various degrees of friendship at work here. Also, there is the fact that anything he wants to say at this point – about him and Rob being best pals since primary, despite the odd years when he and Rob didn't see so much of each other, about Graham and Ian being their own best pals rather than Rob's, about this Friday Night Club being quite different from the first Friday Night Club, because that had girls in it for one thing, and about the new Friday Night Club being something he often feels he has to put up with and not resent for having replaced nights out which had been just him and Rob – would sound distinctly ungrown up.

Louise seems too lost in her own thoughts to have noticed his lapse into silence. She purses her lips. 'Friday Night Club. Every Friday night?'

'Just about.'

'Goodness . . . Well, you bosom buddies must be wondering who the hell is the piece of work who appears out of nowhere and takes over the whole show.'

'No, no. Not at all.'

'You're a sweet man, Alastair, and a truly untalented liar.' Louise takes a good swig of gin and gives her head a shake. 'Boy, that hits the spot.' Then she strolls over to the coffee table, licks the tip of her index finger, dabs it on the glass and rubs the fingertip over her gums. 'So how bad's his habit, the energetic one?'

'Ian? I don't think he's got one, not really. He can't have, not on what he earns.'

'I'm right, though, aren't I?'

'About Ian?'

'No, silly. About me. More specifically, what you lot think about me.'

'Not at all. I mean, you musn't assume, that's to say I think we're all a bit taken aback because we didn't know about you, but I'm sure none of us resents . . .'

'Chill. Go on, then. Ask me who I am.'

'Sorry?'

'You heard me, Alastair.'

'Oh. Yes. All right, then. Well, um . . . who are you?'

'I'm the person who came back from the States because she thought she was, one, going out with someone, two, that the someone was called Bobby, and three, that the someone called Bobby was going to be someone she was going to be living with when they both sold their flats and moved in together.'

'He was going to sell this place?'

'Yip.'

'Move somewhere else?'

'Yip.'

'With you?'

'Don't sound too shocked. It's not like I've got a prison record or a secret penis or something.'

'But, but . . . but why haven't any of us heard about this? Or about you? Surely Rob would have said something.'

'One would have thought so, wouldn't one? One would also have thought that this note is not what one was expecting to find when one made one's triumphant return from exile. No.' She takes another slug of gin. 'That is definitely not what one expected. At least not this one.'

3

'ANY PARTICULAR REASON WHY
YOU MIGHT BE HERE, SIR?'

Sunday evening

Here's Ian, walking down St John's Wood High Street and lugging a Sainsbury's carrier bag filled with textbooks. Collecting these books is always a real pain – he has to stop by the empty school and let himself in with the keys he copied off a set he nicked from Moira's desk. But it's worth it because these course books are essential accessories for his weekly freelance assignment.

The woman in front has great legs and Ian bets himself that she's wearing stockings. Sheer, black material, with that shortish black skirt and on the legs of someone who looks like she spends a lot of money and a good part of each day at the beautician's. The kind of woman, come to think of it, that he expected Louise to be ... Yeah, got to be stockings. The woman scissors into a shop, so Ian decides to dawdle for a moment just in case she reappears. He pretends to examine the nearest window, an estate agent's. Nice little town house on offer – three bed, two recep, his for £720,000. With a twinge of pride at his worldly acumen, Ian starts to divide by three and a half to work out the salary needed to raise the necessary mortgage, but gives up as soon as he faces dividing £1,440,000 by seven. 'Course, he could always do it on his present income, as long as he could raise a deposit of ...

£680,000.

Until very recently, he would have postponed further thought about this arithmetic to some notional era in the future when he'd have an insider's knowledge of normal, adult life. But now that he is, ludicrously, forty months short of forty and six months away from becoming a parent, he's beginning to accept that the orthodox, adult world of mortgages, lawnmowers and insurance policies is destined to remain as distant and incomprehensible as baseball. This reflection soon gives way to a vivid image of him, Claire and some sulky, bulky schoolboy dodgemming around the flat in Vauxhall, but he manages to replace that with a vision of himself in about an hour's time, when he'll be ordering a celebratory double brandy in that pub across the road and then taking himself off to the pub's reliably quiet, clean gents'.

Still no sign of the stockingy woman. Ah, well. Assuming the air of a man with a mission, Ian crosses the road, takes a left and quickens his pace as he nears the mansion block where he will be giving his weekly private tutorial.

The building's main door has been propped open by a bucket of soapy water, so Ian saunters into the plush hallway, which boasts dark, panelled walls, an enormous and slightly worrying chandelier and a small, antique lift protected by wrought-iron gates. Ian wonders if he could afford the mortgage for the lift . . . Or the chandelier . . . Probably not even the bucket of soapy water. He hauls open the gates with needless force, steps inside, clunks them shut, presses an ivory button marked six and remembers, as he always remembers at exactly this moment each week, the even smaller lift that used to take him up to the apartment on the Boulevard des Invalides where he flat-sat for six months. Best thing about that Parisian lift was the manufacturer's plaque – '*Schindler: proche de vous partout dans le monde*'. 'Schindler's lift,' he'd joked, though nobody seemed to think it was funny, until that first date with Claire, when they'd gone to a screening of *Toy Story* on the Boulevard St Germain and she'd come back with him. 'Schindler's lift,' he'd pointed out, and she'd replied with a smile that shone and then with such a fit of the giggles that, by the time they stopped at the fifth floor, she'd had tears of laughter running down her wonderful face and he had realised, with something between joy and panic, that he was falling in love. This lift, though, is a British lift and therefore an ignoble, clanky object which seems too exhausted to do anything but give up halfway through its task and plummet to the ground. Powered, according to his fancy, by a rooftop team of well-whipped workhouse urchins cranking a colliery-sized wheel, the lift begins a slow and juddery ascent, until it comes to an abrupt, sickening stop at the sixth floor. As Ian wrenches the gates open and steps out on to the lushly carpeted landing, he reflects that anyone looking in on this bit of his life might predict that he's about to teach English to a diplomat or a sheikh. Definitely not the small, thin, young Spaniard suffering from rampant paranoia and rampant acne who awaits him behind the door of Flat 12.

Today, though, the door is opened by a teenage girl who is wearing only a pair of greying knickers that reach up to her navel. He notes her sallow skin and the blue-black sheen of her hair which tumbles down to her bony shoulders – as well, of course, as the disappointing breasts – and decides that this must be the man's girlfriend from back home and that he should therefore be ultra-smooth.

'*Hola*,' says Ian with his crinkly-eyed smile.

She glares at him as if his words taste of celery. 'Fook off,' she says in broad Yorkshire, and disappears into the nearest room, closing the door behind her with an authentically adolescent slam.

'Ah, Johnny?' Ian calls out in a singsong that reminds him of his mother when she used to announce teatime. Suddenly, the door next to the one slammed by the adolescent is flung open to reveal a scrawny youth with a pair of sunglasses slithering around on hair apparently rinsed in cooking oil and above a face as red and cratered as Mars.

'Johnny', for it is he, nods his head solemnly while signalling, with an O formed by his thumb and index finger, that he is pleased to see Ian and that he himself is, as ever, in control. Yeah, right. Mr Big. The man who thinks that wearing Ray-Bans on his head or calling himself Johnny (instead of Ramón, his real name, or at least the name on the passport that Ian once spotted lying beside the dusty bread bin), mark him out as a king of the streets, rather than, as Ian suspects Johnny/Ramón actually is, a daft middle-class twat who's using his stay in Britain to play at being a coke dealer. Still, he thinks as he follows Johnny down the flat's long and murky corridor, an upbringing, however privileged, in Vigo seems to have given the little twat a taste for one of the more lucrative Galician traditions.

'Hoakay, my frenn, we make the class here.' Johnny beckons him through to the rancid kitchen. 'Today we work hard, hoakay?'

'Yes indeed, Johnny.' Ian makes a great show of pulling books out from his carrier bag. Johnny nods in serious approval of this scholarly display, although Osborne & Foster, the *Let's Speak English!* workbooks and the *Advanced English Primer* are completely useless for his unique linguistic needs. Which is why Johnny turned up for three of the sixty-four lessons he paid for at the London Oxford School of English, before he treated Ian to a drink and a testing-the-water line in All Bar One and invited him to be his private tutor, one who could instruct him in the terminology of his profession and prevent his colleagues and customers taking the piss out of him behind his back. An impossible task, because even if Johnny spoke like Mad Frankie Fraser rather than Manuel in *Fawlty Towers*, he'd still be a twat, but Ian has been more than happy to address his charge's fear of ridicule by teaching him terms like 'deal', 'charlie', 'sorted', 'wrap' and 'gear'. After the second lesson, Ian had exhausted his own knowledge of Dealerese so he has taken to eavesdropping on

Vauxhall's teenagers. He's not quite sure about the subtle connotations, or basic meaning, of words like 'mong', 'dark' and 'yard', but it doesn't really matter because Johnny won't remember anything he's taught and, belying all the books Ian is piling up on the kitchen table, their lessons together will resemble lessons for, at most, five minutes.

Ian adopts a pensive expression and begins to pace up and down the kitchen because Johnny appreciates a pedagogical performance, no matter how absurd. 'Right,' says Ian. 'Today, we are going to revise words for the police.'

'Feelth,' says Johnny.

'Good, yes, excellent. And as we have already learned, there are many other words for the filth, so for this revision I have prepared a list.'

With some ceremony, Ian produces from his carrier bag an A4 sheet of paper. Johnny grabs it and scans what is a very short list with the grim dedication of a general assessing a decoded report. 'Rozzers, plods, old beel . . .'

'Bill.'

'Beel. Feds, peegs . . .'

'Pigs.'

'Peegs.'

'Pigs.'

'Peegs.'

'Excellent.'

'*Muy bien, muy bien*. Rozzers, feds, plods, old beel, peegs. Ah.' Johnny gives the sheet of paper a triumphant slap with the back of his hand. 'And feelth.'

'Excellent. Now. Let's return to the words we studied last week. How many pounds in a pony?'

'Ees ten.'

'Very close. It's twenty, remember?'

'Twenny.'

'Correct. And a monkey?'

'*Mono, sí?*'

'Exactly, *mono*. How many pounds in a *mono*?'

'Ten.'

'Almost. Good try. In fact it's five hun . . .'

'Good.' Johnny springs up from his seat. 'Ees good. Now conversation.'

'Yes. Conversation.'

Johnny prepares for this part of the lesson by taking a kitchen knife to a lump of cocaine he's conjured from a drawer and arranging it into two thick lines. Stretching out his arms like an umpire signalling a wide, he lets it be known that his is a generous spirit. 'My house your house, my frenn. Then we talk, hoakay?'

Two minutes later, the conversation segment of the tutorial is well under way, with Johnny talking animatedly. About what Ian isn't quite sure because Johnny is blethering in a heavily accented Galician dialect. There'll be another half an hour of this, then both parties will have deemed the lesson a great success. Johnny will rest content that Ian has increased his linguistic armoury. Ian will hand over £25 and Johnny will hand over two massively discounted grams. High and buzzing, Ian will clasp Johnny's hand in farewell, they will maintain the meaningful, manly eye contact which Mr Big seems to think confirms their comradeship and his own status as Mr Big, and Ian will relish the lift back down, perhaps imagining that a young and distraught Billie Whitelaw is pleading at him to return to her love-nest or that he's dodging the bullets of the Soviet agents who tried to ambush him in his glamorous bachelor pad. Then he'll take himself off for that double brandy at the pub with the nice gents.

Sorted.

Alastair grins wanly and shakes his head. The chances of him saying the right thing are, he estimates, slim. 'I couldn't say,' he says.

'Thirty-one.'

'Really?'

'You thought I was older?'

'No, the opposite.'

'So I look like a little girl, is that it?'

'Not at all,' says Alastair. He allows himself a silent sigh of exasperation. Why does she have to turn everything into an argument? Apart from anything else, it's just so exhausting. He puts on what he hopes looks like a polite smile.

'I'm sorry, Alastair,' says Louise. 'I'm all over the place about this, but God knows I shouldn't be taking it out on you. After all, he's dumped you as well, hasn't he?'

'Rob, you mean?'

'No, I was referring to . . . There I go again. Yes, Bobby, Rob, whatever he called himself. No, anyway, what I meant was he's left you in the lurch. Not that he split up from you or anything, but he was your friend.'

'Is. Is my friend.'

'Hmm. As you like. Far as I'm concerned, after this little stunt, it's was. *Was* my boyfriend. *Was* the man I *was* supposed to be coming back to.' She purses her lips and looks off into the distance. 'I can't tell you how stupid I feel. I mean, I really did think that this time it was going to work out. And chucking in my job, really, what brand of fool am I?'

Alastair nods sympathetically.

'Actually, I'm exaggerating a bit about the job. All I've done really is move from the New York office back here.'

Alastair is busy doing more sympathetic nodding when he is struck by an obvious thought. 'Sorry, Louise,' he says, 'but I don't even know what it is you do.'

'Advertising.' She scrunches her face. 'How exciting.'

'I don't know,' says Alastair, who is now desperately trying to think of anything positive to say about a job in advertising. Perhaps he could say something instead about his idea that advertising has changed from exploitative brainwashing into entertainment, thus reflecting the shift in capitalism itself whereby exploited workers have become consumers who have to be courted with things they might want rather than . . . Maybe this isn't the time. 'It must be fun.'

'Sometimes. Not recently. Tell the truth, I wasn't too unhappy to leave the States. I mean, most of it was great but the work . . . Jeez.'

'I suppose it must have been difficult. Trying to adjust to another culture and so forth.'

'The opposite. The accounts I was working on, they were all the same. Say what you like about the Yanks, but they're into their bowels.'

'. . . Really?'

'Laxatives, high-bran cereals, high-fibre breads, my whole working life was devoted to keeping Yanks regular. With the same ad, no matter what the product. Shot of young businessman dancing round office to soundtrack of James Brown singing "I feel good". Cut to young easy-shitting businessman's secretary looking surprised then delighted as her boss whisks her round in a whirly waltz. Cut to close-up of product. Deep, earnest voice-over – "Eezee-Crap Chocograins. Because you're full of shit." Collect salary at end of month.'

Alastair coughs. 'Was it in America that you met Rob, then?'

It's an obvious question to ask, given that Rob spent so much time in New York when he had his affair with the CNN reporter, but it seems to have stymied Louise. 'No,' she says after a moment. 'We met because I live in the flat below his. Funny. I had him down as just a City smoothie when I first moved here. But then one night he knocked on my door and it wasn't to barge in, smoke a joint and tell me all about his salary. This time he was quiet, thoughtful, got talking about his parents, how much he still missed his mother, all that, and it was like he was a different person.'

Alastair responds with an understanding nod, although

what he's thinking is that Rob's sudden double bereavement, what must be a dozen years ago now, is one of the few topics Rob doesn't like to talk about, him being the kind of chap who prefers to keep things light. Or so he had assumed. And to think that Rob had been so good about listening to him bang on and on when his own mother died. Why hasn't he, Alastair, returned that favour? It happened twelve years ago – can that really be a reason or even any kind of excuse?

I failed him, Alastair tells himself. There's a lump growing in his throat. I failed my friend.

This is fucking *useless*.

Over two hours now he's spent monitoring Jenny's flat and what has he found out? Fuck all, that's what.

Times he's peeked in on her flat before, that's all he's done – been in the area, taken a wee detour, sidled up and down her street a few times, had a keek in at her window, then sloped off, heart pounding, guts churning, brain very depressed. But this proper surveillance business is a completely different kettle of pish.

Over two hours of lingering and dodging about, of trying to look casual and normal as he has walked up and down her street, pausing briefly each time to check out the two front windows of her first-floor flat. And all that he's got to show for it is one terrifying glimpse of Jenny with her hair tied back, wearing a jersey and jeans, carrying a vase or something through to the kitchen maybe, and a couple of sightings of Megan, her fat flatmate, who seems bent on spending the entire day wafting around in a pink fucking kimono.

No sign of Rob – but he could already be inside, couldn't he? Rob could easily have spent the last two hours in the kitchen at the back, or in the bathroom, or – let's be fucking candid about this – in Jenny's bedroom, where even now he could be pawing her, slobbering all over her, shagging her, for fucksake . . . This is such a heinous idea, it seems ridiculous to

Graham that he can't just report his strong suspicions of this outrage to the police and that the police wouldn't respond by immediately surrounding Jenny's flat, breaking down the door, catching the culprits in the act and bundling them into a van with blankets over their heads.

That snooty-looking woman at number one has come to her window again. She's looking straight at him. Typical Notting Hill bitch, with her trendy wee glasses and her trendy big house. West eleven – hate it or loathe it, you can't help despising the whole fucking area and its stuccoed pillars and pastel-coloured houses and shitey new bars and nosey fucking bitches wearing trendy wee glasses. Why Jenny chose to move here after they split up he'll never fucking know. And now she's turned her flat into a love-nest with Rob. Rob, of all people . . .

Graham pushes himself off the wall because he's got to do something to halt that train of thought and because he's had enough of casting theatrical glances at his watch and taking discreet peeks at Jenny's place thirty yards up the road. He'll take another wander up her street, maybe find a new place to park his arse. Possibly even risk hiding out in that apparently derelict basement opposite Jenny's. Then again, he could . . .

'Can I *help* you, sir?'

Graham turns to reply to the voice behind him and comes face to chest with a dark blue uniform. As he looks up, his recent train of thought makes Graham wonder for a moment if this very large and obviously world-weary policeman has arrived to help him on his stake-out. Then it clicks that someone – probably the snooty bitch at number fucking one – has been on neighbourhood watch duty and alerted the authorities to the fact that there's a man in the area not wearing this season's colours.

'Any particular reason why you might be here, sir?'

'No. Well, yes, I'm . . .'

'Waiting for someone, is it, sir?'

'Ah . . . yes.'

'Only we've received several reports of a gentleman answering your description, sir, acting in a manner that could be seen as worrying to local residents, sir. Residents who are naturally worried, sir, about the remnants in this and nearby streets of, among other activities, the sale and purchase of illegal substances. Now, would it be one of the area's younger entrepreneurs that you were waiting for, sir?'

'Fucksake, all I was doing was standing here, minding my own . . .'

'Do I *look* like a cunt, sir?'

'. . . Sorry?'

'Do I look like a *cunt*, sir?'

'No. No, you don't.'

'Then there's no reason to fuck me around, is there, sir?'

'. . . No.'

'And possibly every reason why you, sir, might be best advised to move on.' The policeman's hands flutter by his side, as though he's shooing pigeons. 'At least to the end of Ladbroke Grove, sir, since that's where my beat ends, sir. Oh, and sir?'

'Yes?'

'Have a pleasant evening.'

When he's walked five yards away from the corner of Jenny's street, Graham looks back to see the policeman still standing where he was, giving him an encouraging smile and another shooing flutter. And behind the policeman that snooty bitch is at her window again. Fucking Notting Hill *cow*.

His heart's going like the clappers. His hands are damp with sweat. Keep calm, he tells himself. Keep calm. But it's in a daze of nervy panic that Graham walks through street after street of lavish houses until he reaches a junction and a row of shops. And, thank fuck, a pub.

The place is almost empty, and no wonder. It smells of stale beer, stale tobacco and stale air. And the carpet feels like it's been skooshed with Spray-Mount. Graham gets himself a pint and a big whisky (Teacher's, which goes to show the shiteyness of the gantry), gulps down both as quickly as he can, then heads for the door, steadfastly refusing eye contact with the pooch on the floor or the several old fucks gawping at their drinks. How many years until I'm one of them? he thinks, as the door clunks behind him and a cool breeze soothes his hot face. Ten? Five? One? That's what Rob and Jenny are doing to him. Giving him a big push down the chute towards the social garbage heap where he can spend the rest of his fucking life being a morose old fuck with nothing to show for his existence but a pint and a fucking leash. He has to do something about this, but what? Welcome to Shit Creek, here's your barbed-wire canoe and bon fucking voyage.

Graham digs out his mobile and pokes out Ian's number.

'Ian.'

'Hello?'

'Ian.'

'Eh?'

'Ian, for fucksake, it's Graham.'

'Sorry, you'll have to . . . Graham? Is that you, Graham?'

'Aye. Can you hear me now?'

'Where you phoning from? A wind tunnel? This is a terrible . . .'

'Notting Hill someplace.'

'On your mobile, right?'

'What? I said Notting Hill somewhere.'

'Man, I can hardly . . .'

'I'll call you back.'

'You'll what?'

'I said. Never mind. Fucksake.' Graham slaps his mobile shut and heads for the nearest phone box which, as sheer chance would have it, is actually working. And which, this being central-ish London, is decorated with dozens of hookers' postcards – 'Fully equipped Dungeon', 'Watersports nr Baker

Street', 'TV Transformation' . . . By Christ, does nobody want a normal shag in this town? Graham unearths a phonecard from his wallet, taps out Ian's number again and is trying to calm himself down by examining a card's line drawing of an Edwardian lady contentedly sitting on a prone gentleman's face when Ian answers.

'Yo, Graham.'

'Is this any fucking better?'

'Loud and clear, my man, loud and clear as a bell on a bright wintry morn.'

'Aw naw, you're wired.'

'No way, José.'

'You're off your face.'

'No way, no way, no way.'

'Fucksake. Okay. Look, Ian, have you got a minute?'

'Sure sure sure. So what is occurring in the vicinity of your area of occurrence?'

'Fuck*sake*, Ian.'

'Graham, you may think I spend all day every day charlied out of my head, but that's where you are very very very very wrong. I'm just in the door, right, and I'm about to start preparing for tomorrow's advanced class, if you must know. Verbs that take both gerunds and infinitives.'

'Eh?'

'I like to get up at eight.'

'What's that got to . . .'

'But I don't like getting up at eight.'

'Ian.'

'See the difference? Like plus infinitive – I like to go to the dentist – for something you think is good for you. Like plus gerund, the -ing – I like eating chocolate – for something you enjoy doing.'

'You really have just done a huge line, haven't you?'

'There's another example. I like taking cocaine, but I also like to be sensible about it.'

'Is Claire in?'

'Out with a couple of pals discussing placentas.'

'So you've definitely been at the marching powder. Look, Ian, can you keep a straight head for this? I need to talk. I'm going fucking insane here.'

'Talk away, talk away, talk away. I am all ears. I like talking with my friends and I also like to talk with them. Hey, are you okay?'

'No, I am not okay. Look, Ian, this is about Rob, all right?'

'With you so far, my man. Shoot.'

'This is fucking awkward, by the way. Did Rob say anything to you, I mean, there's every reason why he wouldn't have, but did Rob mention anything to you about . . . him and Jenny? Like, him seeing, being with, fucksake, shagging Jenny?'

'You mean Jenny? Jenny? Jenny Newman?'

'Aye. Jenny. Rob and Jenny. Jesus.'

'Rob's been shagging Jenny.'

'Fucking *hell*! You fucking *knew* about it!'

'Hey hey hey. I was only repeating what you said. Rob's been shagging Jenny.'

'Stop *saying* that, for fucksake. But you fucking *knew*.'

'Hey, let's just put the brakes on. This is the first I've heard of it, Graham, okay? Honest. Anyway, what makes you think Rob's been shagging Jenny? Sorry, I mean, that the two of them have been . . .'

'Ian.'

'Shagging.'

'Ian. Stop *saying* that. I just know, all right?'

'How, though?'

'It just adds up. There's the Silk Cut in his kitchen, the diary is full of Rob meeting J, he was always flirty with her . . .'

'Graham, you're making as much sense as one of my beginner classes.'

'That fucking diary, Ian, it was full of times he was seeing

Jenny. J at her office, J for lunch, J after work, J this, J that.'

'But J could stand for anything. Julia, Julian, June, Jane, Joan, John, Jonathan, Jonty, Jason, Jerome, Jeremiah . . .'

'Aye, but . . .'

'. . . somebody else called Jenny, or Jennifer, or Jack, Jackie, Jacqueline . . .'

'But how do you explain . . .'

'. . . Jessica, Jemima, James, Jim, Jimmy, Jimothy . . .'

'Jimothy?'

'That one I screwed up, but you get the idea.'

'Then how do you explain the Silk Cut?'

'I don't because I don't know what the hell you're going on about Silk Cut for. Look, Graham, you're taking two and two and making four.'

'Two and two do make four.'

'You know what I mean.'

4

'HELLO'

Monday lunch-time

'And there are four young girls. Giving me water from a vine leaf. Just dropping it on to my tongue.'

The bass is going to kick in after a few more bars of ethereal, plinky-plonky stuff. Normally, the sudden reappearance of the beat (BOOM cha, boom boom cha) – in Alastair's opinion, the greatest reappearance of a beat in the whole history of house stroke trance stroke ambient stroke dance music – would have him struggling not to skip through the carriage, arms waving in the air, hips shimmying. Today, though, even the first track of William Orbit's *Strange Cargo III* – usually a favourite for the soundtrack of his journey in – has lost all of its joyful, haunting energy. Actually, he can't be bothered with any of it. He presses the Stop button on his Discman during the plinky-plonky bit as the train slows down.

He looks out of the window at a Bangladeshi woman hanging sheets out on a brick-walled balcony of a horrible-looking council block. The train draws into Shadwell. Normally, the opening of the doors would have him primed to spot grown-ups stealthily muscling their way to the front seats, because this is the Docklands Light Railway and a driverless train, and front seats in the first carriage are much prized by a surprising variety of human beings, many of them over the age of ten, who like to play, surreptitiously, at being the driver. Today, though, even the sight of a banker type in his fifties and a young chap in paint-spattered overalls discreetly racing each other to the front scarcely registers.

It makes less and less sense. His trip this morning with Louise to Moorgate and Rob's lawyer wasn't at all what he expected. That chap, Jeremy Maddox, for a start. A sleazy individual, he thought, or maybe that's just his prejudice against any man wearing a double-breasted suit *and* one of those stripey shirts with a white collar. Pleased with himself too – sitting behind that old desk in his poky little office, claiming that he's a good friend of Rob's from the Coach and Horses, a pub that he has never even heard Rob mention before, and then telling them that Rob's instructions, imparted over the course of several lunches and appointments in the weeks before Rob left, were simple and clear – to arrange the sale of his MG and furniture and stuff, everything really, and then to put the Bateman Street flat on the market. And despite his alleged friendship, despite all those chummy meetings, despite those on-going financial arrangements, Jeremy Maddox maintained that he had no forwarding address for Rob, no knowledge of what Rob's up to or why he's up to whatever it is he's up to, and absolutely no idea where Rob has gone.

Their appointment had been for eleven. By 11.20, he and Louise were back outside on City Road and wondering what on earth to do for the rest of the morning they'd both taken off. They'd idled down Moorgate, then Louise had pointed out that they were only ten minutes away from the NatWest Tower. She hadn't known Rob's work number either, but she'd got going on her mobile, only to be bounced around by the switchboard. They'd decided they'd go to the Tower anyway – and hadn't made it past the security guy on the front desk. No Robert Mackenzie listed. Eventually, Louise had charmed the security guy into putting them through to Personnel, but Personnel could only divulge that they had no record of any employee called Robert, Rob or Bobby Mackenzie.

The train decelerates into Limehouse. At least Barry was nice about him taking the half-day. Mind you, Mondays are always

quiet. A bit of Books to do, some mucking about on Arts . . .
Blimey, he hasn't begun to think about the promotion business,
or about trying to teach the subbing basics to 007. No, all he
can think about is the same few questions which have been
whizzing round his head. Why didn't Rob ever mention Louise
to them? Or Jeremy blimming Maddox? Where has Rob gone?
What *is* he up to?

The doors close again and the train glides off. Normally,
he feels a twinge of excitement as the train nears Gotham
City. Today, though, Alastair looks out at a ghastly array
of grim, grimy houses and the huge, shiny tower ahead of
him, and he sees only a mess of deprivation and poverty
surrounding an oversized monument to stupidity and greed.
He feels . . . what? It's a peculiarly dismal, empty feeling. One
that reminds him too strongly of several very bad episodes in
his past – the worst being the combined Rhona split-up and
Cathy cataclysm of '88, the first being the time when the Friday
Night Club, the original Friday Night Club, ended up back at
Steve's house and he and Fiona were getting on brilliantly and
he was busy summoning up the courage to tell her that what
he most wanted to do right now was hold her and kiss her
and she abruptly confided that she'd just lost her virginity
to Steve and she knew she could tell him because she could
trust him and he and she were such good friends. Yes. This
is like then. So it's not only confusion or anxiety he's feeling.
Nor even loneliness, although that is part of it. No, more than
anything, what Alastair feels is . . . sort of chucked.

'So I thought I'd give you a bell, say I liked the phodocopier
vibe, see if you're into doing a liddle something for the
next issue.'

'Sure, Chaz. Fire ahead.'

'Sabout doing business in the EU. I'll, like, fax you the
thing, yeah?'

'Okay.'

'Only thing, keep it priddy straight, man. I mean, me personally I loved the dancing phodocopier, the vibe was cool, but *Business Madders* is, like, a priddy straight mag, yeah?'

'So no fancy stuff?'

'For real.'

'And the fee?'

'Same. Two hundred, yeah?'

'Okay. Just how straight do you want this, though, Chaz?'

'Priddy straight.'

'So if I did an illustration of, I don't know, two businessmen shaking hands across a dotted line for a border, would that be pretty straight or far too straight?'

'That'd be priddy much the vibe.'

Jesus Christ on a fucking bike. 'Okay. So I'll bring this one into the office?'

'Cool.'

'By Wednesday?' asks Graham, but the phone has gone dead. Fuck *off*. So this is what it's come to. Ten years ago he thought he'd done the last of those clichéd pieces of shite for business magazines. Fucksake, he was one of the people who helped make those clichés clichés – churning out all those drawings of risk-taking businessmen teetering on tightropes, of suddenly inspired businessmen standing under gigantic light bulbs (with optional dollar sign for the filament), of optimistic businessmen pointing to mountainous pound signs on the horizon, of fit, lean businessmen poised for a sprint. No. Drawing two fucking businessmen shaking hands across a dotted line for a border is *not* what he thought he'd be doing or what he fucking should be doing at this fucking age. This should be his fucking *prime*, and what is he doing? He's drawing two businessmen shaking hands across a dotted line for a border is what he's fucking doing.

The phone rings again.

'Graham, Jason.'

Oh, *just* what he needs. 'Mr Megabucks. How's tricks, Jason?'

'Tricks is great. Listen, I'm getting another little night out together here.'

'Where's here? Shoreditch?'

'Is there anywhere else in the world? 'Course Shoreditch. Cantaloupe or the Brickies, who knows? Friday night. You up for that?'

'I don't know, Jason. Fridays I'm usually booked up. And I've got a lot on at the moment.' A bare-faced lie, but the last thing he wants is a night out listening to Jason crow about his BT commission.

'You should try and make it. Audrey'll be there.'

Now why is Jason saying that? Maybe, just maybe, it's because Audrey really is keen and she's told him so. 'I'll see, Jason. I'll call you later in the week, all right?'

'Good man. Listen, I've got to run. This meeting to go to.'

Aye, right. The boy has this big, fucking important meeting. 'Good luck with it, Jason. Give them hell.'

'Oh, yes. See ya.'

Graham puts down the phone and tells it to fuck off.

Ian has his head halfway into his desk drawer when he hears a rap on his door.

'Ah, Ian, ah, I was ah.'

Never one to panic under pressure, Ian simply drops his straw on to the mirror, has a little sniff, lifts his head, and casually pushes the drawer shut. The act of a man who was just peeking inside his drawer. No problem, then, except he'll have to get through an hour of verbs that take gerunds and infinitives with a tantalising three-quarters of a line untouched and a metre away from his nose. 'Dr Foxsmith,' says Ian, as he gets to his feet. 'How can I be of assistance?'

'I believe you are, this, about to, this is, will be.'

'My advanced class, Dr Foxsmith?'

'Ah.'

'Yes, it's due to start in a couple of minutes.'

'In, that is, indeed. And with, I have, here is, are the two, ah, new.'

'Of course.' Ian inclines his head. 'The two French students who will be joining the advanced class today.'

Monique has turned up to occupy a substantial amount of the doorway. Foxsmith places an avuncular hand on her chunky shoulder and smiles at Ian. 'This is, ah, is, ah, Chantal,' declares Foxsmith. Monique is too busy blushing and simpering at her trainers to notice the error. 'And I gather, you already have, ah, have already met Monique.' Foxsmith shifts into profile to allow Monique's sidekick to appear. She steps forward and offers her hand. Ian retains just enough presence of mind to hold the hand, this cool, dry, slender, elegant hand, in his. She shouldn't be here, is his first thought. She should be busy appearing in adverts for cars or perfume. Or, come to think of it, for women. Twenty-one, twenty-two maybe, round about five eight, jackpot body since she's slim and 34C at an educated guess, excellent, long legs in soft blue jeans, rich, auburny hair that tumbles to her shoulders, and the kind of perfect face – oval shaped and containing a pair of large brown eyes beneath angular black eyebrows, a thin, straight nose, and a full, wide mouth – that makes any usual kind of face look like an inexplicable aberration.

'I'll ah, that is, leave you to, leave you, ah.' Foxsmith backs off and away.

'Chantal,' says Ian to Chantal with his crinkly-eyed smile. He remembers to release her hand. 'Hel*lo*.'

149

5

'THIS LION WALKS INTO A PUB'

Thursday evening

He can even remember what they were listening to on Rob's new hi-fi – Big Audio Dynamite. And there's Rob, nine years ago but still vivid, sitting cross-legged on the floor in his flat in Clapham, rolling what was to be Alastair's first-ever joint. He'd felt a bit strange to start with, then heavy limbed, as if it was the second half of extra time on a muddy pitch, and then he'd laughed until it hurt at the stories Rob told him about having sex with his secretary in the stationery cupboard then going to a meeting and a sheaf of Post-It notes falling out of his trousers. Alastair's first week in London, so he'd felt like a hopeless bumpkin as he marvelled at this racy new world Rob was showing him of illegal drugs and sex in the office. And they'd just picked up where they'd left off. As if that gap of three, nearly four years, when Rob had migrated south and proved so hopeless at returning postcards and phone calls, had never happened.

Alastair shifts his focus from the middle distance to the page proof on his desk. '. . . pinch sea salt,' he reads, character by character. '2 handfuls flat-leaf parsley, 1 tsp lemon juice, 66 tbsp extra-virgin olive oil.' Alastair is scoring a red line through the second 6 on his proof of Hugo's cookery column when he becomes aware of a commotion behind him. He glances over his shoulder and sees the editor, who must have loped past while he was concentrating on Hugo's recipe for chickpeas with Swiss chard, looming over Davina in Books. Davina is looking perplexed and the editor is looking very angry indeed.

The editor slaps the top of Davina's terminal.

The room goes quiet.

Alastair exchanges a worried look with Yvonne. Only James Bond seems oblivious to the on-going drama, for he rises from his seat and ambles towards his stepfather's partitioned office.

'But Jonathan,' Davina says, shakily, into the hush, 'this is an excellent piece by a leading . . .'

Now the editor is holding his right hand in the air, palm outward. 'Davina,' he barks. 'I have already spoken on this matter. When you wanted to commission David Allcock.'

'Derek Walcott. Who won the Nobe . . .'

'And what words did I speak when I spoke?'

'Jonathan, I really must . . .'

'I said that I wanted names. Big names. Not your obscure chums from literary parties.'

Alastair taps the Alt Screen key and sends a message to Barry: 'wot going on?' That done, he risks another glance behind him. Davina puts her elbows on the desk and starts to massage her forehead. The editor is leaning towards her, as if anxious about her health.

'This is the *Sunday Chronicle*, Davina. Not *The Times Literary Review*.'

MESSAGE is flashing on Alastair's screen. He gives the Receive key a gentle pat. 'big trauma re book review,' says Barry's reply.

'pls explain trauma,' Alastair messages back.

'So spike this piece of commie propaganda and get me an article by someone our readers will have *heard* of.'

'davina commissioned book review by prof called stuart hall.'

'Someone our readers will *like*.'

'stuart hall famous academic man? wot problem?'

'Someone our readers will . . . *read*.'

With a final slap on the top of Davina's terminal, the editor turns on his heel and strides past Alastair's desk, dislodging a set of proofed pages as he does so.

By the time Alastair has gathered the pages together again, MESSAGE is flashing on his screen. 'acc/ding b/bottle, ed thght d had got s hall broadcaster.'

'wot?' Alastair types back. 'it's a knockout s hall?' As he taps the Send key, he hears a series of dull thumps behind him. He looks round to see Davina banging her head on her desk.

'Spot on,' says Barry, forsaking messages now that the editor's gone.

'Blimey.'

'Now then, Al.' Barry scrapes back his chair and comes round to stand by Alastair's side. 'Let's leave poor Davina to her grief and turn the oil-tanker of our attention gradually round to Lifestyle and the special treat I have for you.'

'All righty. As long as it's nothing to do with Josh Todd.'

'Uncanny.'

'Oh, no, Barry. That'll be four Joshes running. That really isn't fair.'

'Al, my pal, be of good cheer. Derek's turn to do the actual subbing, as he's about to find out when he comes back from the tea run. But I thought you might want a look at a column of historic importance.'

'Historic how?'

'Because Josh Todd has found something to write about.'

'You're joshing.'

'I'm not but Derek soon will be. And he will be joshing with a Josh Todd column wherein our hero writes about . . . no, you're going to have to guess.'

Alastair ponders various unlikely answers. 'An issue?'

'There's no need to go over the top.'

'Sorry, Barry. Oh, blimey, I don't know.' Alastair tries to think of a slightly less unlikely answer. 'Somebody other than himself?' he suggests tentatively.

'Warm.'

'Then it has to be somebody important to him.'

'Warmer still.'

'Parent? Sibling?'

'Cooling very quickly.'

'Friend?'

'Getting warm again.'

'A close friend?'

'Hot, hot, hot. And how.'

Alastair reminds himself to close his mouth so he can start his next unfeasible question. 'Josh has a girlfriend?'

'Congratulations. You have won the chance to be the first person after Bluebottle, me and the editor, who, by the by, was anxious to look at a Lifestyle piece for the first time in his career, to read the touching account of Josh's romance. And, boy, do I mean touching.'

As Barry returns to his workstation, Alastair calls up the latest Josh Todd and begins to read the copy that has appeared on his screen.

I am waiting for the lady in my life to come back to my bedroom. She walks into my bedroom smiling and nude. 'Hi, Tiger,' she says to me and smiles. I smile back. Then I pull the lady in my life down towards me and soon I am kissing her. I am kissing her neck. I am kissing her breasts. I am carressing the insides of her thihgs. I am kissing her belly button. I am kissing the brilo pad of her pubic hair. I am kissing her labbia. I am probing with my tongue. I am tasting the inside of

Alastair looks over at Barry. 'We can't print this.'

'That's just what we're going to do. Bluebottle loves it. The editor loves it. They say they're looking forward to a huge mailbag from our readers.'

'Yes, from even more readers saying that they are cancelling lifelong subscriptions because of Josh Todd.'

'That's as maybe. But isn't it nice to think that Josh is no longer on his tod?'

'One thing, I suppose that can be our headline.'

'Tragically, no. Josh has already supplied his own and both Bluebottle and the editor love that as well.'

Alastair sighs. 'Just tell me.'

'"I used to think cunnilingus was an Irish airline."'

'No, really, Barry, what's the headline?' Alastair waits for Barry to crack but his expression remains steadfast. 'Oh no,' says Alastair. 'No, no, no, no, no.'

Barry nods his head. 'I'm really not joking.'

'Joshing.'

'My mistake.'

Absent-mindedly, Alastair scrolls down to the end of the copy. 'I can wait no longer,' says his screen. 'I am bursting into orgasm. I am feeling the spurting of my seed. I am COMING.'

'Blimey,' says Alastair.

'That is a very big one,' remarks Paolo. 'Very, very big.'

If he weren't sharing a toilet cubicle with an eighteen-year-old boy, Ian might have a little private smirk at Paolo's Carry On comments. Because he is, and even though he's fairly confident that there's nobody outside, Ian puts a finger to his lips.

To no effect.

'Possibly too big for me,' Paolo declaims. 'Because it is very thick and long.'

As Ian pushes the coke into two substantial lines on the cistern's top, he ponders the thought that, were someone to come in and push open the uncertainly bolted cubicle door, copping a blowjob off an eighteen-year-old boy would have to be his alibi.

Despite his alleged misgivings, Paolo takes first go and snorts his line with disarming gusto. He proffers his rolled-up note but Ian has his straw at the ready . . .

No more than a minute later, Ian and Paolo have side-shuffled out of the bog and casually rejoined the group upstairs in the Pig and Whistle. 'Right, then,' says Ian, rubbing his hands and suppressing a sneeze, 'who's for another drink? Paolo? Dieter? Stanislaw? Monique? Chantal, anything for you? No? Chantal? Positive? Just me, then.'

Since everyone else, with the exception of Paolo, is back on fruit juice or mineral water after their experimental halves of bitter, Ian orders a tonic, then relents and asks for a double brandy on the side. He necks the brandy at the bar and returns to the group with his nose twitching and his oesophagus on fire.

'No, no,' Dieter is saying. 'The present perfect tense is bad, naturally, but worse are the phrasal verbs.'

'Ah, come on, Dieter, come on, come on, come *on*,' says Ian. 'Verbs plus prepositions. Simple, simple, simple. You learn them through use.'

'Naturally, yes, but . . .'

'Put and up, for example. You can remember them by remembering examples. I put up with him, I put him up for the job, I put up the thing on the wall.'

Dieter holds his hands aloft in mock surrender.

'Come along, Dieter,' Ian says heartily. 'I put to you that you shouldn't put off using phrasal verbs. Don't put them down.'

'You see,' Dieter says. 'Put up, put on, put in, put down, and so many meanings. Impossible.'

Paolo stops twitching about in his chair, leans forward and says, 'Put out. A cigarette, yes? And girls.' He grins and raises his glass towards Monique and Chantal, who are both frowning at him with concentration.

Ian realises that he's wearing a similar expression. 'What do you mean, Paolo, put out girls? Oh, got you,' he adds, but too late.

'Yes, girls. She puts out. Also, she puts it about. Means

sex,' he explains to Monique and Chantal, who are both now frowning at each other. 'Or,' Paolo adds with a sarcastic-looking smile, 'she is lesbian and she puts off you.'

'Puts you off,' says Ian, who is busily wondering whether or not to explain the several meanings of putting someone off when he sees Chantal gathering her books together and Monique following suit. Damn damn damn damn *damn*.

'We are obliged to leave,' Chantal murmurs as she stands up and shrugs on her coat. 'We must to return to the landlady.'

'Who is putting you up,' Dieter says, much to his own delight and the consternation of the French girls.

There follows an awkward silence which is finally broken when Monique says 'Thank you, Ian' with her unfortunate simper. 'We enjoy the pub. We see you tomorrow.'

'Yes,' murmurs Chantal, 'tomorrow. Goodbye, Ian. And thank you very much,' she adds with a heart-breaking, groin-tingling, stomach-lurching stretch of those glorious full lips. It's too much to think about the body that must exist beneath the clothes, so Ian concentrates on that naked mouth. What he wants, more than anything else in the world at the moment, is to cover that mouth with his. But now she's going, and with her any point to staying here. He forces away a stare as Chantal leaves with a farewell wiggle of her fingers and Monique clomping along behind.

'Okay, chaps,' says Ian, drumming his fingers on the table-top. 'I'm sorry but I'd better go too.'

'Can't you put it off?' asks Paolo, who then lets out a coked-up yelp of laughter at this terrific joke.

Ian finishes his drum-roll and takes a last sip of tonic. ''Fraid not. See you all tomorrow.' He winks smoothly at Paolo. 'Enjoy yourselves.'

It's only as Ian marches out into Bateman Street that he realises he doesn't have anywhere to march to. Normally, his first move would be to get to a phone and see if Rob's in . . . But hey, that Louise might be around and, you never know, she might even be into partaking of a line or two . . . Funny how she's not what he expected and how that has made him realise that what he did expect was based on nothing more than a notion of Rob's type, some glossy kind of babe who'd fit into Rob's life of clubs and restaurants and in-crowd shenanigans. Someone not unlike, for example, Chantal, who really is a babe and no mistake. One of the great things about language schools – the way they offer up a regular supply of babes, and babes, moreover, who have to spend an hour or two a day lost in helpless admiration of their tall, dark and very handsome teacher.

Ian presses the bell below Rob's. The intercom crackles into life. 'Yes?'

'Hi, Louise? It's Ian. Rob's, Bobby's, Robert's pal. Can I come up?'

The door buzzes by way of a reply. Ian climbs the familiar stairs and stops unfamiliarly short at the first landing, where he sees Louise waiting for him just inside her open door. She's leaning back against the wall, her hands on her hips, her black Lycra skirt not quite reaching her raised knee, her right foot propped behind her in classic hooker's pose. 'Hello, sailor,' she says. 'You likee jiggyjig? Nice girls, clean girls.' She beckons him in. 'Love you longtime.' Ian follows her through a hallway decorated with old film posters and into a sitting room furnished with only a battered leather settee, a boom-box and a scattering of CDs on the wood floor.

'Is there some rule in this building that says you can't have a lot of stuff?'

'Feng shui,' she says. 'The room faces south and I'm an Aries, so any more clutter and I'd be looking at a very heavy, negative aura.'

'That right?' says Ian, mimicking mild interest.

'Well, it's always possible, I suppose, but I was kind of kidding.' She sits down, cross-legged, on the floor. 'I just haven't bought any furniture yet.'

'Right . . . When did you move in?'

'Getting on for three years ago. But I've been in New York for most of that time, remember?'

'Right.'

'But enough of this merry banter. Do you want to go up to Bobby's or what?'

'What, really. I was in the area, I thought I'd call in. To see how you were doing.'

'Ah, village London. Well, I'm doing excellently, given that the man I thought I was going to be with has apparently packed a few supplies into a red, spotted hankie, shoved the hankie on to the end of a stick and run away from home.'

'Right, right,' Ian says softly, in the hope that this sounds earnest and caring enough, as he lowers himself, a bit too creakily for his liking, on to the floor. 'So what I was wondering,' he says, 'was maybe you might want cheering up.'

She raises one eyebrow. 'And this proposed cheering up, what's it involve? You removing all my clothes and impaling me on your lance of manhood?'

'No. No. Absolutely not. No. No way. No.'

'That's a no, then?'

'Definitely.' But now that she's said it, the image of her slender legs astride him and her pushing slowly down is stuck in Ian's head. 'What I have in mind is Dr Murray's Medicinal Compound. Most efficacious. In every cay-ay-ase.'

'Let me guess,' she says. 'Would this be a curative that comes in powdered form?'

'Correct first time.' Ian produces his wallet and then a wrap from his wallet. 'How's about a toot?'

'Lawks a mercy. You really are quite the cokehead, aren't you?'

'Me?' She's only saying that because now he's brought out his little mirror, and just as well he had it, the only other available surface to chop a couple out on being the floorboards. 'Nup.'

'How much a week?'

'Dunno. A gram? Maximum.' He's placed the mirror on the floor and is cutting out a pair of, what, three-inch lines. Almost as long as the mirror, at any rate, so they should do the trick. He thinks about letting her go first, then thinks, hell with it, kneels down, whisks out his straw and gives his right nostril a blast. He pushes the straw and the mirror carefully over.

'Thank you.' She hunkers down by the mirror, tidy little bottom in the air. 'At the risk of sounding ungrateful,' she says, still hunkered down, her line still untouched. 'Liar, liar, pants on fire.'

'No way. My pants are made of asbestos.'

'Is that so?' She snorts up most of her line, then sniffs. 'I suppose I'm just wary of it, what with Bobby's days on the charlie. And me working with a bunch of powdered-up wankers. I mean, excellent treat but dangerous.'

'Sure,' says Ian, still lost in his idle assessment of her bottom.

'Just saying. Change of subject. You ever do anything like what Bobby's done?'

'. . . How do you mean?'

'When you were a kid.'

'Yeah. Not with a spotted hankie, though. One time I set off with my cowboy hat and holster. Silver revolver as well, like. Made it to the end of the street, then remembered I hadn't had my tea. You?'

Louise pinches her nose and shakes her head.

'Come on. Every kid tried to run away.'

'Disagree. Every *boy* tried to run away. Girls didn't do that.'

'Now look whose pants are ablaze.'

'True. Well, *I* didn't and none of my friends did.'

'You mean you never did the big bid for freedom thing?'

'No. Whenever things were really bad, I used to hide out with Mr Buggles. My rabbit,' she explains. 'I'd run to the bottom of the garden, get in the hutch with him for a cuddle and tell him all about it. A significant difference, if you think about it. Running away versus taking time out and being emotionally articulate.'

'Yeah, with a rabbit. How the hell did you squeeze in?'

'Oh, there was plenty of room. Until I filled out a bit when I was nineteen or twenty . . . Jeez, it's ages since I did this stuff. You forget how twitchy it makes you. And chatty. Oh my.'

'Just say the word if you want any more. There's the best part of a gram here.'

'God, no. I feel like I'm on intravenous espresso as it is. So,' she says, tapping her knees with her fingertips. 'Let's get down to business. What's your explanation for Bobby's disappearing act?'

Just for a moment, he feels tempted to say what he really does think – that some shit's gone down between Rob and this one, with the result that Rob's had no option but to get the hell out of it – but he'd prefer to avoid any kind of conversational heaviness and kick-start something a bit more frivolous and enjoyable. 'He's probably just stomped off with his cowboy hat and his holster. The man'll do the equivalent of remembering he hasn't had his tea and dawdle back in a day or two.'

'Well, it's a notion that does have the advantage of conforming to Turner's First Law.'

'What's that? Who's Turner?'

'Me, silly. And my law which is mine states that all men are effectively five years old.'

'Uh-oh. Feminism alert. Feminism alert. This is not an exercise. We are at Defcon three. We have a feminism alert.'

'Unfortunately, it really works. It's like science. When you know the basic secret – electrons, molecules, all that – then you can explain just about everything. No need for voodoo or witch doctors, just take the sample to the lab.' She holds a finger in the air. 'Similarly, the apparently impenetrable enigma that is male behaviour can be solved if you bear in mind the crucial fact that, to all intents and purposes, men are children. Everything falls into place. The football thing or really getting off on cars and gadgets – toys and games. Or the wonderful way you lot cope with illness. The fondness for farting. Crap attempts at deception. Sulks. Absolutely normal behaviour if you're four and or a chap.'

'Oh, how fair is that?'

'Then there's Turner's Second Law.'

'Turner's Second Law.'

'Which states that when analysing the actions of allegedly adult males, take the most cynical explanation possible, double it, and you might be in sight of the really awful truth.'

'Okay, Louise. So what's your cynical explanation about Rob's disappearing act?'

'That Bobby could have a relationship with me as long as I was safely tucked away on the other side of the Atlantic, but when I called his bluff and came back he couldn't handle the reality instead of his little fantasy so he took the easiest and daftest way out by buggering off.'

'A bit cynical, isn't it?'

'But strangely convincing, wouldn't you say?'

'Dunno. Hey – you got anything to drink? Needn't be alcoholic. Water, juice, anything.'

'Your whim is my command.' She jumps to her feet. A minute later she returns with two glasses and a bottle of Evian as large as her torso. Dry though his mouth is, the request was mainly intended to act as a diversion. Unsuccessfully, if the expression on her dial is anything to go by. She places the glasses and the bottle on the floor and sits down beside them. 'You know, I've thought about nothing else since I read that pissy little note. Obviously. And the only definite conclusion I've come to is that I really, really wish I was gay.'

Oh, super. Maybe if they have another line, she'll lighten up a bit. He gets out the gubbins again. 'Don't be daft. Just 'cause Rob's thrown a wobbly doesn't mean . . . well, anything much. Hey – what do you think . . . ?'

'Look at it this way. If I had a nice, warm, soft, loving girlfriend, there's no way I'd be having to put up with Bobby or whatever his fucking name is and whatever it is he's playing at. Incidentally, if one of those is for me, I'll pass. Where was I? Yes. Men. No offence, but Jesus. This is a Terry-Thomas impersonation coming up, by the by – you lot are an ebb-soh-loot shah.'

'You feel like that, go gay. Nobody's stopping you.' He snorts one of the lines. And then – hell with it – the other. Yes indeed, yes indeed, yes indeedydoody. 'Then you'd see what we have to put up with.'

'Oh, right. I'd be forced to have a relationship with someone I'd have to see more than once a month, someone who didn't snore and didn't go off in huffs or bang on and on and *on* about whether or not they should really be going out with you or, God, I don't know, all the usual *rubbish*. And then solving everything quite brilliantly by buggering off.'

'I think you might be doing what's known as generalising from the particular.'

'Uh-huh? Have you ever thought about how truly crap it is being a heterosexual female? All the things that nobody thinks to teach you when you're in first year at middle school and beginning to get all tingly about your Duran Duran posters. If only some wise woman had taken me aside and said, Okay, Louise, get interested in boys if you must, but remember that they won't have grown up since you last had any contact with them. And they will continue not growing up until the day they selfishly expire before you. The wise woman could also have pointed out the neat little catch that there are indeed men who are not only incredibly handsome and muscly and well dressed but sensitive and enlightened as well, but they're all only interested in other men. Thanks, God. Like, you want to buy a car, madam, well, certainly, madam, although I regret that madam isn't permitted to buy anything from the top range, but perhaps madam might consider this clapped-out Trabant.'

'Same for us.'

'Is *that* so?'

'Sure. You don't get to shag George Michael, we have to put up with all sorts of crap.'

'Like?'

'Okay. Periods.'

'I'll see your periods and raise you with shallowness.'

'Never being able to find your keys.'

'Complete and utter selfishness.'

'Not finding your keys because they're in your handbag and the handbag's got enough stuff in it, it's like you're going on your holidays.'

'Emotional dimness.'

'The whole palaver about *diets*.'

'Mindless violence.'

'Changing down a gear *after* you turn a corner.'

'Every crime against humanity.'

'Not being able to read a map, not having a clue which way's north.'

'Be serious. That's north.'

'Isn't.'

'Is.'

Louise gives her nose a quick, vigorous rub. 'I think you might be doing what's known as talking out of your arse.'

'*And*. How could I forget?'

'What?'

'No sense of humour.'

'Oh, don't be ridiculous.'

'True. Blokes get together and have a laugh. Fair enough, we might not always be having in-depth discussions about *relationships* or *love* or just *exactly* what our partner does in bed, but at least blokes are funny.'

'Ah. Of course. Women have no sense of humour. How right you are.'

'Think about it. 'Course women have a sense of humour but it is a bit dodgy at best and one thing you lot can't do is tell a decent joke.'

'Point one, I'm not entirely sure that makes up for millennia of oppression and evil. Point two, you're just plain wrong.'

'Yeah?'

'Yeah.'

'Okay, then, Louise. Tell me a joke.'

'Oh, this is ridiculous.'

'You see?'

'Utterly ridiculous.'

'I rest my case.'

'Right, then. A joke. Let me think . . . Okay. This lion walks into a pub. Barman says, "What'll it be, Mr Lion?" The lion looks at all the taps at the bar and says, "I'll have a pint of . . ."' She frowns.

Ian keeps a straight face. There's a beat. Two. Three. Four.

'. . ."a pint of Theakston's, please."'

Despite himself, Ian gives her a nod of patient encouragement.

Louise replies, with a sweet smile, 'And the barman says, "Why the big paws?"'

'. . . Right. Not bad. Kind of like the one about the panda who goes into the bar, you heard it?' And Ian starts to tell her the one about the panda who eats, shoots and leaves.

The back of seven, so that's a good half-hour since Ian went in. Either the boy has keys to Rob's flat or he's gone to see that Louisa. Why? Fuck knows. The only fucking certainty is that there's been no sign of Jenny, or of Rob, in the two hours so far that he has spent skulking around Bateman Street, loitering first of all with a couple of pints and a group of afternoon drinkers outside the Pig and Whistle and then the Carlisle, then hanging out beside the minicab office on the corner, and now sipping coffee in this daft wee café-bar-type joint whose studenty customers seem completely content to loaf around on the armchairs and sofas, playing Jenga and talking shite, apparently oblivious to the fact that the place does not possess a fucking *licence*.

Well, that's quite enough of that particular anthropological fucking experience. Time to wander back to Broadwick Street and the pub next to Jenny's office, though knowing her she'll be chained to her desk until it's long gone eight. Graham finishes his glass of now-cold caffe latte, hands over his six quid – six quid! For a few cups of coffee? They're taking the pish – and pulls his jacket collar up (just in case Ian has chosen this particular moment to stand at the window and look down on the street) before moving off and away to start the second part of today's surveillance programme – the tailing.

All goes to plan, here's what'll happen. He'll hang around outside her office, wait for her to appear, then follow her, in all probability to her rendezvous with the Judas who used to be his friend. And who, it's now horribly clear, has used that friendship to get at Jenny. To think that Rob was there, every Friday night, pally as you like and, the moment his back was turned, having a right good laugh. The Friday Night Club. What a joke. What a big fucking joke . . . Got to hand it to him, though, the boy knew what he was doing – using the Friday fucking Night Club to keep tabs on him then Saturday to Thursday screwing Jenny. The Judas. The fucking Judas.

Graham tacks through a series of side streets filled with puddles and beggars until he reaches the corner of Wardour Street and Broadwick Street. What he'll do, he'll keep on Jenny's office's side of the road so that he's less likely to be spotted if she glances out from her desk, which is – or at any rate used to be – right by a window on the fourth floor. And he already knows that she should be at the office rather than at a conference in some Moat House because he phoned the switchboard, asked if she was in today, got put through and immediately hung up. You cunning fox, Anderson, Graham says to himself, more as reassurance than anything else, because his heart's thumping like a bastard and there's a pre-runs buzziness in his guts.

Graham turns into Broadwick Street. He is thirty yards from the pub that will be his lookout base, twenty yards from the atrium of Jenny's office block, and just getting into stealth mode, when Jenny walks out into the street.

He stops dead in his tracks. In fact, his entire body seems to shut down for a moment. She seems both anonymous – thirtysomething woman in dark suit, carrying briefcase – and uniquely Jenny. His Jenny.

She's stopped too, her back to him, her briefcase between her feet, her hands on her hips. Her hips . . .

He forces himself into action. He scurries across the street and finds some sort of sanctuary in the doorway of an art shop. So there's his excuse if she does catch sight of him – okay, the shop's closed but he's just checking out the wares. He pretends to be pricing easels while he takes peeks round his shoulder. Jenny's still on the other side of the street. And now she's being joined by another woman in a suit who's just been slung out by the atrium's revolving doors.

Okay. This is the new plan. He waits here while Jenny has her chat, then he follows her. Simple. Graham takes a few deep breaths but he still feels nervous like he hasn't felt nervous since his Grade One violin, when he so very nearly wet himself. Now Jenny's picking up her briefcase. Are they about to move off or . . . ?

Oh, *shite*. Jenny and her pal are turning round. Shite, shite, *shite*. They look like they're about to cross the road. He is beginning to rehearse his lines about window-shopping for easels when a taxi draws up abruptly beside Jenny and her pal and between them and him. Well, thank *fuck* for that. Right. This is his chance to get out of the art-shop doorway.

Soon as he sets off, he realises that he should just have gone back the way he came. As it is, he's hurrying along on the other side of the road from Jenny and the taxi, hunched into his jacket and beginning to affect a slight limp. He decides against taking the first right into Poland Street because that's the way their taxi will probably go and continues scuttling along the interminable length of Broadwick Street to the corner of Marshall Street, where he ducks behind some kind of pottery shop. Only now does he risk a look back through the shop's right-angled plate-glass windows.

And sees Jenny. Still there. On her own. Why didn't she get in the taxi? *Shite*. She's crossing the road and she's aiming straight for him. Perhaps, he thinks, as he breaks into a trot, this is what your pulse is like at the start of a heart attack. He forces himself to keep up the jog, turning left and then right before slowing to a walk as he nears a pub on the corner. Panting as quietly as he can, Graham lingers for a moment among the office workers drinking outside, then checks behind him. And there's Jenny – still coming towards him. Fucking hell. Fucking *hell*.

Graham breaks into a jog again, down a little cobbled street. What is it with this fucking warren? He had no idea this bit of London existed. More to the point, he has no idea where he's going. Even more to the point, there's every chance that Jenny's about to round the corner behind him. Fuck*sake*. Graham takes the next left and finds himself in a narrow passageway. He slows to a fast walk until he reaches – aha! – Carnaby Street, then panics at the sight of so many people wandering around, for who's to say one of them might not be Jenny if she's taken some short cut he doesn't know about? He dodges past a slumped wreck of a tramp who's holding up a single copy of the *Big Issue* and turns into the first open shop he sees.

'Can I help you, sir?'

Graham looks round. A wee serving girl is looking up at him with a gummy smile. Time to resort to his polite fuck-off tactic, the one he uses for market-research birds with clipboards. He puts on a puzzled expression and unleashes his one German sentence: '*Ich verstehe nicht.*'

'*Kein Problem. Moechten Sie sich unsere Sonderangebote anschauen?*' She gestures towards a shelf of miniature Big Bens and toy police helmets. Only now does he register that this shop is packed to the rafters with leather jackets, unfunnily logoed T-shirts, football scarves, general shite for tourists and, beside the cash till, a sign whose second-top line carries a German flag and the declaration '*Man spricht Deutsch*'.

'Nine,' he says.

She's not going away and she's still smiling. '*Schauen Sie sich nur um. Gefällt es Ihnen bei uns in den Ferien?*' she says.

Keep it simple, stupid, he tells himself. He shakes his head decisively. 'Nine,' he says.

For some reason, the wee serving girl looks a bit worried by this, so Graham nods reassuringly and gets the fuck out of there, having momentarily forgotten why he went into the shop in the first place but instantly remembering when he sees Jenny ten yards to his left and leaning down to give the *Big Issue* boy a coin. The sensible thing would have been to have gone back into the tourist shop, but he thinks of that only after he's beetled away in a panic along Carnaby Street, through a well-timed throng of possibly Italian youngsters. When he reaches Liberty's on the corner of Great Marlborough Street, he risks another glance behind him.

She's still coming this way.

Maybe, he wonders, she's taking the pish. Nah – how would she have known? . . . Fuck*sake*, though. He takes advantage of a pedestrian crossing and a gap in the traffic to cross over towards a crowd of people gathering outside the Palladium.

And looks behind him again. She's *still* following him. Where the fuck is she going?

The Tube. Of course. The Tube. Central line from Oxford Circus. If he can only get to the top of this street and turn right into Oxford Street, he'll be safe. Unless she's going shopping . . . He'll have to take that chance. He weaves in and out of theatregoers, then some drinkers outside a pub, and then a clutch of dithering schoolgirls, until he can finally hang a right.

Ten, twelve paces into Oxford Street, Graham stops at a kiosk and pretends to examine the rack, like he's a connoisseur of chewing gum.

There's Jenny now. Turning left and away from him, thank *fuck*, and heading towards the Underground entrance. He looks on, his panic replaced by a horrible yearning, until Jenny disappears into the crowd.

6

'JUST BE COOL AND IT'LL GO AWAY'

Saturday afternoon

Here's Ian, flat out on the bed and staring at the cracks which trail across the ceiling like rivers seen from orbit. Next door, the television is on with the sound turned down and page 311 on Ceefax relaying the news to an empty room that, four hundred miles to the north, Raith Rovers have just drawn o–o at St Mirren. It'll be another hour before Ian knows this, because he has another hour to go of this all-afternoon stint, not of painting the kitchen as he promised and intended, but of staring at the cracks which trail across the ceiling like rivers seen from orbit. And of trying to evade the Fear.

It's only because he had four hours' sleep last night. And his system is probably run down. Plus he's feeling a bit crap about not painting the kitchen.

But no matter how hard he tries to persuade himself otherwise, he knows the Fear is still there, skulking in the undergrowth, waiting for the right moment when his guard is down and it can pounce.

As long as he keeps his cool, he'll be all right. And one thing he's learned from past experience is that the Fear can be thought off.

So think.

Right. He'll think about the view from the flat on the Boulevard des Invalides . . . The view fades quickly away . . . He'll concentrate instead on his real, specific worries. First – money. He has none. Okay. Second – Claire. Who is still treating him as if he's suddenly acquired BO, but that's a phase, probably hormonal mood swings, and it'll pass, and soon they'll be having a laugh and a good time just like they used to. Maybe . . . Anyway, third. Well, third is Chantal. So why is he bugged by Chantal? Because . . . because she's started to occupy a place in his life, not only as yet another girl to fancy and flirt with but as an upsettingly beautiful reminder of all the upsettingly beautiful girls who are going to turn up in the future when he'll be stuck in a world of buggies and Huggies and crying. Which leads to worry number four – that the party that has been his adult life to date is winding up, with even the hardcore drinkers in the kitchen beginning to drift off into the night, and soon the music will stop and the lights will come on and he'll have no option but to stumble away . . .

Ian turns on his side and hugs himself tight. It's only a coke comedown, he tells himself, and four hours' sleep, and not painting the kitchen, and Claire being off with him . . .

But it's no use. He could be losing it here, for the thinking hasn't prodded the Fear away – just encouraged it to edge closer and closer. Because the Fear can sense his weakness.

He has to show it he's strong. Otherwise the undergrowth will rustle and next thing he'll know the Fear will have pounced.

'Just be cool,' Ian pleads into a pillow. 'Just be cool and it'll go away.' Claire. He'll think about Claire. Beautiful, beautiful Claire. He'll remember the way she looked at that party on the rue Monge when she wore a turquoise dress that showed off her tan. Or her fit of the giggles in Schindler's lift . . . So why is he not doing the right thing by her now? A beautiful, funny, adorable woman and he's not doing the right thing with her because he's scared, scared that this time he's made a mistake he can't ignore or leave behind. He feels a sharp stab of envy of Rob. The others still seem bamboozled by it all but what's happened is glaringly obvious. Louise put him under pressure to settle down, Rob's thought, hell with it, and made his great escape. Why? Because Rob could. Whereas he . . .

'Oh, Jesus,' Ian moans into the pillow. 'Jesus Christ almighty.' A mistake he's going to be stuck with for the rest of his life. A mistake which is going to deprive him of money, sleep and freedom. A mistake which will do the opposite of disappear. A mistake which will grow and grow.

The undergrowth rustles.

Nil-nil. Well, at least they kept a clean sheet. He'll get a match report when he phones his father tomorrow. By which time both his pow-wow with Louise and his night out with Ian and Graham will be in the past and all the better for it.

Alastair shoots the TV with the remote and returns to the back bit's Victorian table, where he has set out his photograph albums – twelve identical volumes covered in black, velvety material and each containing thirty stiff pages with clingfilmy covers. It had taken the best part of three consecutive weekends a couple of years back to fill these with the snaps that had been lying in an appalling jumble in a kitchen drawer until he applied chronological method to this ungoverned madness and out of chaos created order.

Perhaps, Alastair considers, the next step should be to construct some sort of index and reference system. Ah, but that would discourage browsing, and browsing through these twelve albums, as he has rediscovered this afternoon, can be really fulfilling. Flicking through album after album for photos of Rob, he's dallied over countless other images from throughout his life, recalling a host of Sunday car rides to the Lomonds or the coast, family holidays in Morecambe and Llandudno, teenage parties with the FNC, the trip in '82 to watch Scotland in Spain, weddings, dinner parties, more weddings, holidays in France and Italy and Morocco – a festive miscellany populated by friends and family (and, very occasionally, Alastair himself), squinting into the sun or carousing with devilish, red eyes.

Rob makes his first appearance in volume three, as a happy,

blond boy wearing school blazer and shorts and standing beside a forlorn, ginger-haired runt who is, fortunately, mostly hidden by the football he's clutching as though it is a lifesaver. Which, Alastair reflects, is exactly what it turned out to be, for it was the discovery that he could pass and dribble and shoot that propelled him up the primary-school social scale, from bullied geek to rarely tormented star winger. That and, of course, the friendship of Rob, after Rob moved in six doors up the road. There's no photo to commemorate the occasion, of course, but he still has a clear memory of how it began – Rob sidling up to him in the street while he was concentrating on his keepie-uppie with a ruined, grey tennis ball and Rob asking, in the exotic Lancashire accent which he was soon to discard, if he, Alastair, wanted to go hunting (oonting, he said it like) for Jerry soldiers in the woods. And that was it, the start of the era when he and Rob were inseparable, building gang huts, stalking spies, playing football, going to the football . . . and finding in each other the companion neither of them had had. For, like him, Rob was an only child, although, unlike him, confident, extrovert, with even a touch of wildness in that willingness of his to take a risk, put on a show.

Volumes four to seven and ten to twelve feature Rob so often that a casual peruser would assume these albums are his. Alastair opens number five at random – and finds Rob in Aviemore and a pair of tartan bondage trousers, so that'll be from the Friday Night Club's summer trip of '78. He turns a handful of pages and sees Rob starring in four pointlessly similar group shots of another FNC, each snap showing everyone making faces at the camera, Rob and Steve in the front, lying on their sides and propped rakishly on their elbows, like Edwardian footballers. Alastair's heart sinks as it dawns on him where and when he'd taken those group shots – Steve's party, towards the end. So even while he was taking those photos, he must have been summoning up the courage to importune Fiona, and very soon after he took those photos he was going to be rewarded for his ridiculous presumption by her devastating him with her news about her and Steve.

With some haste, Alastair slams volume five shut and puts it down. He picks up volume six and lets it fall open. To reveal Rob in the kitchen of the flat they shared in that first year at uni, pointing to the beer-mats that covered one wall. Over the page and there's Rob and a nameless girl at a party, above Rob in Seville, the '82 World Cup, wearing a Scotland flag like a shawl. And opposite, Rob at Steve and Fiona's wedding, the one photo Alastair could bring himself to take of that day. Rob's kilted up and doing a joke sword-dance, arms aloft and mouth forming a silent hooch, socked legs poised on tiptoe around the X formed by two large, silver, inexplicable fish.

Alastair looks at the ceiling while he picks a page earlyish in volume seven – where a grinning Rob has his arm around Rhona, carbon-dating that snap to the first half of '85, before Rob's parents died and Rob moved to London. Eight and nine are Robless, of course, but he starts to turn up again in ten, and here he is, at the wheel of his MG, somewhere south of the Pyrenees, the summer of '90 when the pair of them drove down to visit Ian and that woman he was with – Caroline? Christine? It's bad he can't remember, and that could well be the marijuana to blame – in Madrid. Then it's Rob, Rob and yet more Rob until the most recent entry in volume twelve – Rob in the garden, a couple of months ago, toasting the camera with a can of Stella and a ginormous spliff.

But where is Rob now?

When will Rob come back?

. . . Will Rob ever come back?

She's a hundred yards in front and still heading towards Ladbroke Grove. Maybe she's going to the florist's on the corner. No. She's reached the corner but she's ignoring the flowers. She's waving to someone up the street. No. *Shite –*

she's hailing a taxi. Graham ups the pace and gets to the corner of Ladbroke Grove just in time to see the back of Jenny's head getting smaller and smaller as her cab trundles south.

There's a taxi with its light on coming down towards him. But now it's stuck behind a bus. It's overtaking the bus. Anyone hails this fucker before him, there's going to be fucking trouble. Graham sticks out a hand, the taxi pulls up, and he hurries to the opening window.

'Yes, mate?' The driver is a large individual aged between twenty-five and fifty.

Graham points down the road, where Jenny's taxi has – thank fuck – drawn up at the lights. 'Follow that cab,' says Graham.

'Ewe tine a piss?'

'Seriously,' says Graham, pulling the door open and getting inside before the driver can refuse. 'Just follow that cab. At a safe distance, by the way.'

'So which is it?'

'Which is what?'

'MI5 or jealous asbund?'

'MI5.'

The cabbie switches on his radio. Graham hears a few seconds of a programme where the presenter is trying to interrupt someone who has phoned in to say that he's sorry but she deserves a proper monument, before the cabbie reaches behind him to slide his window shut. Graham sits back and tries to calm down but he's too full of adrenalin and anxiety.

Could Jenny have seen him get in? Fuck off. Who looks behind them when they're in a taxi? Will he manage to keep track of her cab? Fuck knows, but so far, so good – they're almost at Holland Park Road and up to now there's been enough traffic to provide cover, not enough to make tailing too difficult. Things get only slightly trickier as Jenny's cab nudges along towards Notting Hill Gate, shifts into the right-hand lane and then swings down Kensington Church Street. Where in the name is she going? He's not going to find out at this rate, because his cab's still stuck at the junction, waiting for a filter right.

Is this worth it? He can recite the answer by now. Yes, because this way, and unlike Ian and Eck, he's actually doing something about tracking Rob down. If he keeps following Jenny, Jenny will eventually lead him to Rob, who's gone into hiding to avoid confronting the wronged parties in this affair, i.e. Louisa and good self. And yes, that's not the only reason he's doing this because yes, it's the Jenny bit of the Jenny and Rob thing that bugs him, and yes, this is a way of regaining some sort of control over a situation that clearly threatens to get completely out of fucking order.

Finally, the lights change and his taxi bounces down an abnormally clear road. They pick up Jenny's cab again down at the junction with Kensington High Street. It's heading a short queue to turn left. With some astute lane-dodging and racing of amber lights, his cab keeps Jenny's in sight all the way along, past the Albert Hall and Kensington Gardens, to Knightsbridge, where Jenny's taxi pulls over and Jenny gets out.

Fifty yards behind, Graham raps on the window, hands over the fare plus a twenty-pence tip and manages to sneak out in the middle of a handy three-lane jam. He reaches the pavement just as Jenny starts to cross the road. Graham watches as she weaves through the throng of cars and people.

Oh, fucking great. That's him drawn another blank. Because that's her going into Harvey fucking Nichols. Well, shopping was something he refused to do when they were together, so he's fucked if he's going to start now.

Jenny goes inside. Graham crosses the street, has vague second thoughts about following her into the shop, dismisses them and heads off to the Tube.

7

'YOU TAKING THE PISH?'

Saturday night

He's the first to arrive. Ian thinks about getting himself a drink but then he has a far better idea. Okay, so it'll be breaking his rule, this being a Saturday, but there's a little bit left in his second wrap and the second wrap is in his wallet and he'll be stocking up when he goes to Johnny's tomorrow and a toot will dramatically improve what has been a horrible, terrible, dreadful day. Took a heroic performance just to keep going after the Fear episode. But did Claire see it like that? Woah no. You'd have thought that he'd spent the afternoon in bed with her mother the way she went on. Or, to be more accurate, didn't go on, because not painting the kitchen seems to have been yet another terrible crime which must be punished by pained selflessness ('Really. That's fine. As you please.') and, well, pregnant silences.

Ian takes the stairs down to the shunkie. Mere moments later, the world seems a much more encouraging place. He catches his reflection in the mirror and narrows his eyes. Looking good. Feeling good. Yes, oh yes, indeed. Anyway, what's the big deal? He's having a night out with his pals, she with hers, and could he really be expected to remember that this is the day when Briony celebrates her twenty-fifth with a 'dinner' 'party'? No way, especially with Rob's disappearance still unsolved, as he pointed out to Claire, who seemed mutely content to accept his point that he just had to cry off the Briony thing and attend this high-powered meeting with Graham and

Eck instead, although he reckons it won't be a high-powered meeting at all but simply another meeting of the FNC – with only a seventy-five per cent attendance, mind you, and on a Saturday and in a subdued atmosphere, the three of them coming to terms with the obvious reality that one of their mates has had to take drastic steps to escape from a relationship he didn't want.

Ian sniffs, rubs his nose and takes the stairs back up to the bar, where Graham has appeared. Bang on time for once, so either the man is taking the Rob business seriously or he's gagging for a pint. What are the odds?

'Here, I'm just ordering. Pint of lager?'

'Yip, yip, yip, yip, yip.'

So that's Ian useless. Graham drums his fingers on the bar. There are times, and this is one of them, when Graham wonders if there's any way to split up from your friends, find a new and better set. (It's just that I need some space, Ian . . .) Mean to say, how is it possible to have anything like a conversation when Ian's ripped and his eyes glow with daft, chemical enthusiasm? Fucking student. Come to think of it, that's just what Rob has done – betray one of his best mates and fuck off. Arm in arm with Jenny. The image brings on a rush of horror which leaves Graham trying very hard not to gasp. Or sink to his knees and lie curled up on the enormous ashtray that is the floor, sleeping tight until he can wake up to find Jenny beside him and the world normal again.

They carry their drinks over to the wall covered by old brewery mirrors. Graham makes sure he's facing back towards the bar. 'By Christ,' he murmurs, as he examines his Guinness, the brown foam churning. This feels exactly like anticipating the first pint of the day, which only goes to show the effects of his hour-long ramble through Mayfair after he treated himself to three badly needed nips and two troubled pints in a small, snotty, braying pub in Knightsbridge. 'Am I gagging for this.' He takes a long, two-gulp pull on this pint, turns to Ian and does a swift double-take. 'What are you grinning at?'

'Nothing,' says Ian with an innocent look. Then he has another smile at his lager.

Graham's face suddenly quivers into a mask of wide-eyed fury. 'You taking the pish?' he says between gritted teeth.

'Nup. No way. Fucksake, calm down, man.'

'Oh, blimey, I'm really, *really* sorry. I called in on Louise, you see, and didn't realise the time until . . . actually, until I happened to look at my watch, completely by chance, and I had no idea, I mean, it seemed I'd only been there for five minutes but it had already gone half eight and I couldn't believe it. Anyway, I am really sorry.'

'Cool, my man.'

'Nae problem, Eck.'

Alastair finds an excellent spot at the bar, right by the till, but that makes no difference to the three young chaps behind the bar, who ignore him and his twenty. Eventually, when the three chaps have served every other customer, washed every spare glass and conducted a surprisingly heated debate about the wonkiness of the till's buttons, Alastair catches the eye of one of the barmen, who seems quite nonplussed by this turn of events, and orders a round.

While Alastair waits for the barman to pour the drinks, and to take a well-earned break from this toil by adding a lengthy footnote to the wonky-till discussion, he mulls over the information he and Louise have collated. There's hardly a lot, but even so his thoughts are in such a jumble that he tries to simplify matters by itemising the key points with blobs, like they do in the Comment section.

- Rob has been going out with Louise for nearly two years, without telling her about them or them about her. Or telling anyone about his allegedly great drinking buddy, Jeremy Maddox.

- Whatever he's done, Rob has been planning this for some time, what with getting Maddox to sell his flat and stuff.
- Judging by the note and Jeremy Schmeremy's evasiveness on the issue, Rob has concocted a new identity for himself, maybe like in *Day of the Jackal*, taking on the name of a little boy his age who died, or something.

Stick to the facts.

- Rob seems to have been deleted from the NatWest's personnel records.
- The police aren't concerned or even vaguely interested, mainly because Rob doesn't appear to have committed, or been the victim of, any crime.
- Louise is probably right, and the only way they're going to discover anything about what's happened is by buying professional help – i.e., hiring a private detective.

Which seems such a drastic step, and not only drastic but desperate, intrusive and, yes, seedy, that it makes Alastair feel just hopeless that he can't find stuff out on his own. If this was a film, with, say, Sandra Bullock as Louise and him played by ... God, it'd probably be the one who's George on *Seinfeld*, then Sandra and George would progress from being stumped to gradually unearthing clues by hacking into computer networks or stumbling across an intriguing 555 phone number hastily scrawled on a book of matches advertising a strange club or bar where they'd go and they'd meet an acquaintance of Rob's they didn't know about who'd give them another lead and they'd follow that up and ... But this isn't a film, and he and Louise do not possess a single clue or the slightest idea of how to go about finding one. So Louise's idea does make sense, and she does know of someone who could help, an investigator type hired by a chap at her work whose dippy daughter was embroiled with a crack dealer. Well, even though the detective won't be a glamorous, wisecracking dude in a hat but some fat bloke who probably spends most of his working life looking into adulteries and dubious insurance claims, at least the fat bloke might come up with an explanation to better and kill off all the thriller-inspired explanations that have been flying around in his mind – Rob has unearthed some financial scandal and has had to go on the run, Rob belongs to a covert security force and has had to go on the run from terrorists, Rob is not Rob but a sleeper agent run by a covert security force, who has been under deep cover disguised as a normal citizen, since the age of eight.

His stubby fingers straining around the three glasses, Alastair joins the others, who are both oddly quiet. Hardly surprising. He doesn't feel much like it's party-time himself. Well, maybe so, but he knows from experience – specifically, the one, protracted experience of coping with his mum's decline into a fearful imbecility which ended only when she took her rattling last gasp – that all you can do when bad things happen is keep going and hang on in the hope that the bad thing will, in time, get less bad. Hope, mind you, not expectation, because, for all the wonderfulness of modern life, the benefits of having a washing machine or a vote don't matter when it comes down to grief and sorrow – or they do matter, to the extent that given the choice of being distraught and watching colour TV or being distraught and having so little to do that the visit of a pedlar is the highlight of the year, then he'd opt for being distraught with the colour TV. But, far as it goes, that only goes so far, and even with all the advantages of living in an enlightened, prosperous, peaceable democracy which is part of a Western world whose technology, infrastructure, knowledge, expertise and sheer prosperity are such that it dwarfs every preceding civilisation, like in *Independence Day*, where the city-sized flying saucers are but tiny adjuncts of a mother ship so vast it could cause an eclipse, life comes with no guarantee of anything but its own extinction.

'Hey,' says Ian into the silence. 'Knock, knock.'

'Fucksake,' says Graham, who shakes his head and swigs his beer.

'Who's there?' says Alastair.

'Diana,' says Ian.

'Diana who?' says Alastair, with some misgivings because it's only been a couple of months and he's never seen the appeal of topical bad-taste jokes.

'Ah, how quickly you forget,' says Ian.

There's a pause before Alastair realises that this is the punch line. 'Hah,' he says politely.

8

'SHOOSH, SHOOSH'

Monday morning

A stone's throw ahead, Jenny turns left, her long raincoat
billowing in a gust of wind. He flies up to the corner of the
street, in time to see her opening her front door. As soon as
she shuts the door behind her, he scoots up the street and starts
to hover outside her flat. No sign of her, so he wheechs round
to the back garden and looks in on her bedroom. There she is.
Lying on the bed and already naked. And now she's holding
out her arms to a man standing out of sight in the doorway. It
has to be Rob. He peeks in her bedroom window. He watches
as Rob moves forward from the doorway, takes off his jacket,
kicks off his shoes, leans down to remove his socks, unbuttons
his shirt, unzips his trousers, pushes down his boxer shorts,
and stands there, admiring the knobbled weapon that is his
vast erection, clutching it in both hands, like he's a flag-bearer
heading a march. Graham screams and pummels the window
with his fists. Neither Jenny nor Rob pays him the blindest bit
of notice. Only now does he realise why he can fly through the
air and hover twenty feet above the ground. He's dead. He's a
ghost. And this is how he's going to spend eternity, hovering in
midair, pummelling Jenny's bedroom window, and watching
her beg to be skewered. 'Please,' she begs Rob. 'Please, please,
please.'

'Thirty-three.'
     Alastair focuses on the bit of floorboard directly below him.
His arms straighten and lock. He takes a deep breath.

And then he thinks, Why? What on earth is the point? Alastair flops down on to his stomach. The floor is squashing his left cheek. He is gaping at a grey smudge of dust on the corner of the skirting board. Give it up, he thinks. Give up this ludicrous regime. Hire a cleaner. Phone in sick. Quit geeing himself on to keep things going, keep up the whole pathetic pretence that it's somehow worth it. This is as much as he'll ever have. For all his wittering to himself about this part of his life being a period of quiet recovery after trauma, it's actually been nearly a decade when he's done nothing while everyone else has been playing and winning at the mating game, getting together, getting married, having children, finding some purpose to their lives. Not him, though. The first half of his life has already been and gone, and what has he got to show for it? Nothing. No soul mate. Nobody to share his life with. He couldn't even hang on to Rob. And no wonder. He's small, he's bald, he looks like a cartoon of Jimmy Johnstone, and he's pathetic. So just what *is* the point?

There is no point. But that's not the point. And it will not be an excuse.

Alastair places himself back in position, then slowly, so slowly that his arms shake with the strain, he lowers himself down, until the tip of his nose almost touches the rug, then up until his arms straighten and lock.

'Thirty-four.'

Two more. Come *on*.

Sticky eyed, furry mouthed and fuzzy headed, Ian is standing in his tiny, shambolic kitchen and staring morosely at the kettle as he waits for . . . the water inside the kettle to boil.

'Oh dear.' It's Claire, still in her nightie. She's holding on to the door and looking decidedly groggy.

'Hey,' says Ian. 'Are you all right?'

She shuts her eyes and shakes her head.

Ian goes to her, strokes her shoulders, then holds her in a

gentle hug. 'Ah, Claire,' he says. 'Don't you worry. It'll pass in a moment.'

'Mm,' she says into his chest.

He nuzzles her blonde crop with his chin. 'Shoosh, shoosh,' he mumbles sleepily. 'Shoosh, shoosh.' Behind him, the kettle clicks off as the water inside comes to the boil. He can feel the strange little thickening of her tummy now for she's relaxing into a proper cuddle. 'Better?' he says.

'Mm. Much better.' She gives his chest a peck, and another, and another, then she rises on tiptoe and her mouth moves towards his. There's a moment when her lips stay an inch away from his and he feels a rush of exquisite longing. And then they kiss. He savours it all, the softness of her lips, the tender flickering of her tongue. He cups her bottom in his hands, pulls her towards him. They should have enough time, if they skip breakfast, and when did they last do it? Nineteen hundred and . . . Okay, fair enough, two weeks ago, but it seems a distant memory.

'Claire,' he whispers into her ear. 'Claire. Let me take you back to bed.'

She groans. He can feel her pubic bone grinding against the base of his dick, which he's sure is going to burst very soon, like an ineptly cooked sausage.

'That'd be nice,' she says.

'Oh yes,' he says.

'Just for a cuddle, though,' she says. 'I do feel a bit queasy still, and I've got to meet Briony in half an hour.'

'Eh? Why?' is what Ian says, although what he's thinking is that the way he's feeling this deadline would still give her twenty-eight minutes to get herself ready.

'Oh, she's got some baby stuff from her brother that she wants to give us. Clothes mainly. Maybe a cot as well.'

'Right. A cot.'

'But there's always this evening,' she says, nuzzling his chest again. 'After the AFP.'

'AFP?' Ian says to the top of her head.

'The tests. At the hospital. Five-thirty. We're going together, remember?'

'Ah.'

'Oh, Ian, you haven't forgotten, have you?'

'No. 'Course not. I just didn't realise it was today.'

'But you can make it?'

'That's the thing. I've got an extramural trip with the advanced lot this evening.'

'Oh, Ian.'

'I'm sorry, Claire, I've got my days muddled up. And I've already told Foxsmith that I'm doing it.'

'Oh, Ian.' She's pulled away from him. She's crossed her hands in front of her breasts. Her eyes are squeezed shut and her mouth is stretched into a taut, thin line.

9

'HE COULD HAVE MADE AN ACCIDENT'

Tuesday afternoon

'Graham, my boy, hi, it's Nige at CDQ.'

'Ah, Ni . . .'

'How are you, good, excellent, top man, thing is, Gray, my main man, the thing is, this is a bit awkward, but what it is, we have a bit of a problem here at Calder Davies Quinby with the exhibition.'

'What kind of problem?'

'Basically, in essence, a timing problem. Nothing to do with you, logistics that's all, no reflection on you, your work or anything. What it is, Saul Quinby was over in Prague last week, bumped into Brian Eno, and Saul was sold on this scheme of Eno's, so what it is, the period CDQ allocated for your thing has been reallocated.'

'What do you mean, Nigel?'

'Again, don't get me wrong, this is not a cancellation and it's certainly not in any shape or form a rethink about you. As I said, Eno's got this installation.'

'Uh-huh?'

'It's a kind of interactive Internet thing, very cutting edge, very multimedia, very now, very exciting.'

'Sounds, ah, exciting.'

'Yes, we're all very excited about it, everyone at CDQ's very up for it, very excited about it, and since we've got the chance to host an Eno event, we can't pass it up and of course, as I said, Saul and Eno go way back, so there you are.'

'But where is that?'

'Say what, Gray?'

'Where does that leave my exhibition?'

'As I said, we're going to host the Eno event for a non-defined period, a timeframe which means that we can't host your exhibition at the same time. What it is, we're going to have to rethink the parameters.'

'You're postponing it?'

'Exactamundo.'

'Till when?'

'That's out of my hands, Gray, I mean, that's a real fifth-floor job, and as I said, we'll be re-examining the situation after the Eno thing, reassessing the schedule, with a view to letting you know the outcome at that point in time.'

'. . . Well, Nigel, I realise the problem, and I quite see, with Brian Eno and everything . . .'

'Yes, well, we are all very excited about it. Top man, Gray, top man. Okay, so we'll be in touch, okay? As I said, we'll be hosting the Eno thing for at least a year, so we'll be in touch in the fullness, okay? You take care, Gray, my main man. Laters.'

'Goodbye, Nigel.'

There's a clattering noise as Graham replaces the phone while he gazes at the wall, and then there's only the background mayhem of the drills and thumps of the Thames Water crew out in the street.

This is bad. This is very, very bad. Very, very, very fucking *bad*. Unless he's misunderstood and Nigel was only talking about a postponement. Ahah. Of a year. At least. And then what? Nah – he's definitely being shat on here.

How long can things go on like this? When is he going to get a break? Just one fucking break. Is that too much to ask? A break. That's all. Not world peace or a win on the lottery or a shag off Liz Hurley. Just a break.

What's he doing that's so wrong?

And what the *fuck* is it with Brian fucking Eno? And Damien fucking Hirst and Tracey fucking Emin and all the rest of that fucking bunch of *fucks*. With their commissions and their exhibitions and their TV appearances and their tents and dung sculptures and fucking fish in fucking formaldehyde. Who the *fuck* are they? What makes them so good? And him so cancellable? Eh? Come on. What's the fucking difference? What's the fucking magical quality that they've got and he hasn't?

By Christ, he's had better ideas than that Sensation lot. He had better ideas than them when he started on this six months ago, and he jettisoned them all, because the idea he has is so much fucking better than the other ideas and especially their trite shite which is only the kind of fucking garbage that you'd expect from a bunch of fucking *students* . . .

Graham pushes back his chair and stumbles through to the bedroom, where he stares at the nearly completed installation in a dwam of disbelief. He has an impulse to wreck the whole thing, tear down everything, tear it into shreds, sweep everything on to the floor, rip it all up, stamp on it and keep on stamping and ripping and shredding until it's all no more than litter.

No. He's not going to do that, and he's not going to do that for the very good reason that this time there's a real chance that he has hit on something. His every instinct tells him that this work just *has* to be good. Not because the alternative would be such a calamity – although it definitely would be, no two doubts about that – but because he's put in so much effort and time and emotional fucking energy into this, and it's such an excellent concept, so bold and, basically, brilliant, there's no way this should fail. No *fucking* way . . .

And what about that thing about good art being born of torment? *My Struggle* by Damien Hirst? Fucking *settle*. But him? His career's hit an iceberg, his overdraft's a joke, and the woman he loves is getting screwed by his best friend. Okay, second-best friend, but who's fucking counting. Aye, he's struggling and no fucking mistake, and this work comes straight from the fucking heart. Fuck the lot of them. Fuck Eno. Fuck Calder Davies Quinby. Fuck Rob. Fuck fucking Jenny.

Fuck them all.

'He should have used a knife.'

'Oh, yes indeed. Stanislaw?'

'They ought to have driven slowly.'

'*Good*. Dieter?'

'They should not have swam so far.'

'Swum, Dieter. Swum swum swum swum swum.'

'Swum.'

'Paolo?'

'She needs to lose weight and go to the Versace shop.'

Ian glances down at the row of cartoons in his teacher's copy of *Let's Speak English! Volume Four*. These cartoons depict, from left to right, a man hacking at bread with a spoon, a car upside down in a ditch, two children waving forlornly amid a storm-tossed sea, and a matronly figure wearing a triangular frock and a top hat. 'Very funny, Paolo.'

'Thank you.'

'But remember we're using modal verbs. Should have, would have, could have. What *should* she have done?'

'Okay. She should have eaten less food and she should have bought a hat by an Italian designer.'

This brings a cheer from the rest of the class, apart from Chantal and Monique, who continue to stare anxiously at their textbooks. Paolo leans back in his chair to exchange a high five with Dieter.

'Very good, Paolo. Let's move on to the second set. Could have. What *could* these people have done? So we're making a guess about them. Chantal. What could this person have done?'

Ian spends the puzzled silence that follows by examining Chantal's tumbling, shining, auburn hair as she leans over her book and the cartoon of a man lying in bed, mummified by bandages, all four limbs hauled into the air by pulleys, a pair of skis improbably propped against a wall.

'He . . . could have . . . made an accident.'

'That's excellent, Chantal. Excellent. Really really really good.' Lesson 36, the modal verbs, the constructions of second guesses and second thoughts, of regret and recrimination – he should have done this, he could have done that, he would have done the other thing, given another chance – has never been one of his favourites. Today, though, he's in a fine mood and on sparkling form, and even the modal verbs seem dedicated to benevolent advice and benign reflection. No doubt about it, this sunny ebullience has been inspired by the sight of Chantal but two metres away. Plus, to be fair, a pre-class pick-me-up. Ian swallows a sneeze and checks out the next drawing, where a footballer is holding his arms aloft and being hugged by his team-mates. 'Who's next? Monique?'

'The man could have . . . could have . . .' Monique shakes her head.

'Okay, Monique, good try. Anyone? Yes, Paolo.'

'Obviously,' says Paolo. 'This guy is celebrating his transfer to Juventus.'

'Could have, Paolo.'

'Where he could have the chance to play good football.'

I could have had an even bigger line, thinks Ian. And I should never have got pally with that little wanker.

Alastair shuts his eyes and gives in to an enormous yawn. He arrived at work so late that he was just in time for the lunch break, but it's been a busy old morning nonetheless. And a long one, what with him forgetting to shut the bedroom door last night, allowing Susie to nudge her way in and wake him early, at 6.24 to be precise, by clambering all over his face. However. Sweet. And he'd been able to have a good go at the garden before making it down to Holborn for the eleven o'clock with Louise and the detective she knew about.

A grander office than Alastair had expected – all thick carpet, glammed-up receptionist and pastelly abstracts, and nothing like the Portakabin-style cubicle he'd so confidently pictured. The detective, Mr Hilton, was another surprise – neither a wisecracking dude in a hat nor a fat, sweaty bloke but an imposing, suited man in his late fifties with the studiedly formal manner of an old-school ex-cop who has had to train himself how to be polite to the public. That, at any rate, was how Alastair interpreted his fondness for sirring, mistering and mizzing. And Mr Hilton was so ready to reminisce about his days on the Flying Squad that the three of them managed to exchange a mere sentence or two about other, minor issues, such as Rob's disappearance. Well, Alastair had thought, perhaps that was as much info as Mr Hilton needed at this stage, as he'd tried to tell a rather downcast Louise over coffee afterwards. A quick hug outside the coffee place and a tortuous journey east on account of a suspect package at Liverpool Street, and that had been the morning gone.

And now it's one of those post-lunch-time lulls. Despite his late arrival, Alastair can think of only three things that he has to do – wait for James Bond to return from the tea run, digest the canteen meal which is sitting in his stomach like a brick, and regret his decision to bypass the salad bar for once in favour of a plate of what looked like deep-fried sock and chips. Alastair has another yawn. He's worked in offices for . . . it must be fourteen years now, but he's never got used to the fact that working in an office invariably means being forbidden to have a little lie-down after lunch. He'll have to rest content with this moment when the phones aren't going and the other subs have yet to return.

Alastair takes a deep breath and tries to summon one of his daydreams – about the ramshackle gîte he could do up, or the mansion in Fife he could swap for his two-up, two-down in

Finsbury Park. Instead, he finds himself remembering the time in Primary Three when Rob told his new classmates that his family had just moved up from Lancaster so that his father could continue developing his hovercraft design, and Alastair was so proud to be best pal and desk-sharer of this assured, awe-inspiring newcomer. 'Hovercrafts, is it?' his own father had said with a smile when he told his dad all about Rob's revelation that evening. 'And there was me thinking Nairn's made lino.'

Come on, now, Alastair tells himself. This won't buy the baby a new bonnet. He gives his head a quick shake, turns to his screen, and scrolls down the Lifestyle files. Ah, Tamara's copy has arrived. Well, that'll certainly keep him busy for a while. He calls up the file and skims the intro.

Was I deeply pissed of or what. Imadgine my horror when for the first time in my life I had to turn right when entering the airoplane. Fare enough, it was a 12-seater island-hoping byplane but still you would of thought there would of been a first class but no and nor was there any room for my lugage

Alastair taps on the Alt Screen key and types out a message to Barry, who is returning with Derek, the pair of them holding their stomachs and groaning theatrically, James Bond following sullenly behind and brandishing a grey cardboard tray of drinks. 'strordinary news. tamara just filed on time. and the first par has only one deeply. shall I do her or'

His phone rings. Alastair tucks the handset between his ear and his shoulder, like a maestro with his violin. 'Subs,' he says, while he adds 'do you want' to the message to Barry.

'Hi, Alastair.'

'Hello, Louise.'

'Here's your tea, Alan.'

Clamping a kidnapper's hand over the phone, Alastair looks up to thank James, then ungags the phone to add, 'How are you doing, Louise?' Then he types 'to have a go 1st?' and presses Send.

'A bit better. I still don't know about that Hilton, though.'

James Bond shoves the Styrofoam cup down on top of a very precarious pile of marked proofs. 'We could always try someone else,' says Alastair as he reaches out to rescue his tea and approximately ten hours of collective work.

'Shimply shooper,' Derek says to James, who's handing him his tea.

'We-ell, yes, Alastair, I suppose we could.'

'Shooperb.'

'But, thing is, I've already made another appointment.'

'Mmmm. Moasht shatishfying.'

'I know it's a bit rash but I felt I had to do something and if we had another time fixed I thought that might gee him along.'

'A taisht shenshaishun.'

'Friday at two. Can you make it?'

Friday. Lifestyle's press day. 'Difficult, Louise. It's our busiest day, you see.'

'Let me gesh. PG Tipsh?'

'And Canary Wharf is so far out it's technically part of Amsterdam. Shit. I really wanted you to be there with me.'

'Or Lapshang Shooshong?'

'Bloody hell, Derek. Give it a bloody rest.'

'Shorry.'

'I'm bloody serious, Derek.'

'I don't think I'll be able to make it, Louise.'

'Damn.'

'Well, I'll be with you in spirit and you can call me as soon as it's over.'

'I'll do that. You're a good man, Alastair Carr.'

'Don't be daft, Louise. Talk to you later.'

'You will indeed. Oh. I almost forgot. Remember you mentioned that Bobby had been in New York?'

194

'Yes?'

'When was this?'

'A couple of days ago.'

'You what?'

'When I mentioned it. No, sorry, Louise, that was a stupid joke to make. Let's see. Ninety-four, ninety-five, something like that. When he was seeing . . . staying at the Paramount, as I recall. Why do you ask?'

'Because that *shit* told me that he couldn't come out to see me in the States because he was on some Yank blacklist.'

'A blacklist? You mean he said he was banned from the States?'

'More or less.'

'Did he tell you why?'

'. . . Yes.'

'Louise?'

'. . . He said it was because he'd once been arrested when he was on a demo about Nicaragua outside the American embassy.'

'Are you joking?'

'Nope.'

'Only that Rob would be as likely to, I don't know, join the Salvation Army or something as go on anything like a demonstration. Far less get arrested for it.'

'I don't know about that. He threw an egg at Mrs Thatcher, didn't he?'

'Not that I know of, Louise. To be honest, Rob's never been into politics.'

'Don't be silly. What about the SNP thing?'

'What SNP thing?'

'Him being a party member thing. Him working in the SNP campaign office thing.'

'. . . Blimey.'

'I see. Maybe you and I should have another session comparing notes about Robert Mackenzie. Don't you think?'

'It does seem that way, yes.'

'Next you'll be telling me you didn't know about Bobby being a scoutmaster.'

'What?'

'That really was a joke. Not the rest, though. Damn, the other phone's going. I'd better dash, Alastair. Talk to you later.'

'Okay, Louise.'

'Pip pip.'

'Pip pip.'

Frowning to himself and moving in slo-mo, Alastair replaces the phone. He turns to his computer and sees MESSAGE flashing on his screen. It's from Barry. 'gd news abt tamara. you have a go 1st if you want. also s/thing to report re 007. and wot you smiling abt? hot date? lucky swine.'

'yes. she won't leave me alone, that cindy crawford. wot to report re 007?'

Barry starts thumping away at his keyboard. A moment after the thumping stops, Alastair's screen flashes MESSAGE. 'gd news and bad news, al. gd news is that b/bottle has decided 007 won't be with us for long but will go to Arts to write bits n bobs. so we won't have to put up with derek and his bloody connery act for much longer. bad news is that dep chief sub plan is no more. aplgies.'

That's it? aplgies? To his own surprise, Alastair realises that what he is feeling is very pissed off. 'Barry,' he types, using a capital letter because this is not going to be a friendly message. 'Not only do I resent the fact that the offer of my promotion has been withdrawn, I also object to the way that you have informed me of this withdrawal. I deserve better and you know it.' He gives the Send key a biff before he can think twice.

After a few moments of silence, Barry pops his head up over his terminal. 'Bloody hell, Al,' he whispers. 'What's got into you?'

Alastair's not quite sure what the answer to that question

is himself. Refusing to meet Barry's eye, he stares steadfastly at his keyboard. 'I am sorry, barry,' he types, but then he tells himself not to be such a wimp. 'Actually, that's not true,' continues the message, partly to Alastair's own surprise. 'Messaging me like that, it isn't good enough.' Alastair presses the Send key.

Barry starts thumping.

'bloody hell. i know, al, and i really made a balls up. I hate doing things like that so I tried to do it chummily and it was wrong. I am sorry. Truly.'

'thanks, barry.'

Barry pops his head up again. 'Al,' he says. 'How can I make it up to you?'

'Actually, Barry, there is something.'

'Fire ahead.'

'I'm going to take a long lunch break on Friday.'

'Friday? *Fri*day? Don't be absurd.'

'I'm not being absurd. You're always saying you owe me one. Well, now you definitely do owe me one, and that one is a long lunch break on Friday.'

Barry holds up his hands in mock surrender. 'All right, all right. Take the long lunch. I trust it's with a pretty damsel?'

Alastair smiles. 'As a matter of fact, it is.'

'Should have said so in the first place. Can't stand between a man and the eternal mystery that is lurve. Now, as a further peace offering, I can give you a real treat.'

'Which is?'

'Josh Todd.'

'Oh, no, Barry, not . . .'

'Don't you fret. It's Derek who's earned another Joshing. But I thought you might like a sneak preview.'

'His copy isn't in, though. I just checked the Lifestyle files.'

'When?'

'About ten minutes ago.'

'Aha. That's your problem right there. The new Josh arrived

about nine minutes ago. I've got it on-screen, so call it up on Read. Should put you in the mood for your Friday lunch.'

'I doubt it.' Alastair quits Tamara's latest and replaces it with a copy of the file labelled JToddnew.

I see the lady in my life waiting for me at the bar. I walk over. I say 'hello' and then I order myself a drink. I decide that I want a gin and tonic with ice and lemon and I tell the barman that this is what I want. The drink arrives. I hand over my money. I take a sip of the drink.

Josh seems to have rediscovered the gift of tedium, thank goodness. There's room on the screen for only one more paragraph, so Alastair orders himself not to scroll down, otherwise he'll just get annoyed and want to edit the worst of the rubbish and, before he knows it, he'll be subbing Josh again.

I take another sip, and another, then another, and soon I have finished the drink. 'Lets go,' I say to the lady in my life and she agrees. Soon I am leading her out of the bar on the fifth floor of Harvey Nichols and out to the street. I hail a taxi. We go back to Notting Hill where she lives where I immediately grasp her from behind and pull her back towards me. She twists round to face me so I unbutton her coat and I kneel down in front of her and then I am burying my face in her lap. Then I am lifting up her skirt and taking down her pants because she is wearing stockings. Then I put my mouth on to her groin and soon I am tasting her vagina as I lick it with my tongue.

Oh dear, thinks Alastair. Oh dear, oh dear, oh dear. Dearie, dearie me.

'Derek?' says Barry.

'Yesh? Sorry, yes?'

'Have I got a treat for you.'

10

'HAPPY NOW?'

Wednesday evening

Here's Ian, swerving through the crowd of post-work drinkers and heading towards the back of the pub and the door marked 'Fir'. He pushes the door open with a creak. The place is empty, apart from the person occupying the one cubicle. Oh, super. Ian marks time by taking a piss, directing his stream round and round the blue puck of disinfectant, then blasting the sucker with a final burst that lasers down, slap bang on its centre.

Still no sound from behind the locked door. Ian zips up, wanders over to the basin, starts washing his hands. A faint rustling noise from the cubicle but no more than that, so he adopts Plan B. Taking quick, small steps, he moves back to the door, pulls it towards him with a creak, shuts it again, and returns with a heavy, clomping tread to the urinal. He waits there while he counts to twenty, then he clomps over to the basin where he ekes out some more time by running the hot water and examining his reflection in the small, mottled mirror.

Looking good. Ian tweaks and pats a couple of his less ruly black curls. Yip. Damned good.

The luck of it. Think how different his life would have been if he didn't look like this. One thing, he'd probably have settled down a lot earlier, it being one of his theories that what gets and keeps many or most relationships going is not desire but need and fear. How else do you explain the pairing of, for instance, his employer and his employer's spouse? Desire couldn't enter into such an arrangement, what

with Foxsmith being a ferret-faced arsehole and the good Mrs
Foxsmith, who made the mistake of once visiting the school,
turning out to have, surprise, surprise, the body of a weeble
and the face of someone who, as an infant, must have run
headlong into a sturdy wall. Don't try to tell him that they
actually wanted each other. They were just delighted at finding
another person ugly enough to be flattered by another ugly
person's interest in them. Reason for marriage, and cue two
lives of unimaginably hopeless masturbation.

Whereas he . . . well, he's been able to go for women he's
fancied, hasn't he? Granted, this gadding about has had
drawbacks, and his sexual CV (which is, let's be frank, long)
includes more than its fair share of tears and trauma (though
not for him, obviously, his energies having had to be spent
on a variety of elaborate pretences, all of them constructed to
spare the soon-to-be-ex partners a basic truth – 'I have been
/ I will be sleeping with someone else. She is prettier / sexier /
newer than you. So that's me off and you dumped') and he
has no doubt that his name is Ian Mud in selected circles in
a clutch of European cities.

Yeah, but all that goes to prove is another of his theories,
which states that men like him get a bad rep only because,
one, they have the wherewithal and the gumption to follow
their restless, roving instincts, and, two, because the instincts
of females – for stable relationships, nest-building, kids, all
that – are seen as moral only because they're convenient for
society. Patriarchy? Don't talk to him about a patriarchy. If
this were a patriarchy, if men got to do what they really
wanted to do, there'd be an anarchy of mindless rutting – no
candlelit dinners, no foreplay, no cuddly stuff afterwards, just
grab, grope, ride, then on with the trousers and shut the door
behind you. So although he has acquired a score of eighty-four
shagees (though down to seventy-eight if the criterion is actual
penetration), even that impressive score is but a tiny fraction
of his unrequited lusts. And any self-respecting gay guy would

think a score of eighty-odd not just crap but completely sad. Like when he compared tallies with that gay guy who taught at the Oxford School in Barcelona – little chap, not good looking or anything, camp, but funny, palled about with that porker from Dublin (the pair of them corroborating that joke – Why do poofs exist? So fat girls won't feel lonely), Rih, Rah, Roh, yes, Roger, appropriately enough, tried it on with him when they first met, gave him that gay guy's pouty, big-eyed stare a couple of times, before he put him straight – and it turned out that, in the course of that year alone, and it was only September or October, Roger had nearly bested his lifetime score, which must have then stood somewhere in the mid-seventies. Gay guys, what are they like? Well, that's just it – they're like what straight blokes would be like if straight blokes didn't have to obey rules made by and suited to women. Compare and contrast gay guys to gay women. No bathhouses or cottaging for lesbians, oh no, none of that rampaging for them, just support groups and couply-douply trips to furniture shops.

There's a flush, then the cubicle door opens and a suited youth emerges, rubbing his nose. Aye, aye. Ian takes his place. Ten seconds later, he is hunkered down by the toilet bowl, head bent over the lidded toilet seat, left index finger pressed against his left nostril, right hand angling a straw over a thick, three-inch line. Ian snorts half the line up his right nostril, switches to his left, discovers this passage is so blocked that he might as well try sniffing through his feet, switches back to his right and sucks up the rest of the powder.

Ian pulls the flush, for protocol's sake. He packs the wrap and the straw into his wallet and steps out of the cubicle, remembering as he does so that, according to the story he told Claire, he should be rejoining Graham to talk about Rob. Well, it's not really a lie, since he would be about to rejoin Graham and maybe talk about Rob, had Graham not cried off.

Still nobody else around, so he treats himself to a rattling good sniff. See, that was the thing about Claire, because she offered a way out of what appeared to be the cul-de-sac that his thinking had led him into. There's a moment when he struggles to remember just what that thinking was. Yes. If straight men had the same licence as gay ones, then he would have spent his entire life sleeping around – flingettes, two-night stands, or, more likely, encounters that would last the time it took to chat a girl up and give her one before sloping off for the night bus. And, let's face it, he would be happy to oblige, say, one in five of the women he meets. Push came to shove, like in that game fuck-or-die, then the proportion would have to go up to a third or even a half, even more, since he doesn't come up against too many Brionys, women he would simply refuse to have, unless for an enormous fee or under the threat of expertly applied torture. So that's one problem which, he came to acknowledge, would face him in any relationship – that a good part of the time he'd be checking out other women, wondering how they might compare to the present incumbent, what they'd be like under their clothes. Factor in the threat from the élite – your Isabelle Adjanis, your Sophie Marceaus – and your everyday extras, like the piece of work with the ridiculous breasts he's spotted working in the Krazee Kost-Kutter Klothes Kompany, and he really did have a problem, because even with a good-looking woman like Cristina there were always those subversive, taunting reminders – on billboards, on telly, on the covers of women's magazines (now what is *that* about?), or merely passing him in the street – that there were women out there who were much sexier than the one he was with, so how could you do the equivalent of settling for an all-right house in Kirkcaldy when you could have the equivalent of a stonking great big apartment in Paris?

He'd thought he'd solved the problem with Cristina, when the initial falling-in-love bit of the relationship had been amazing, like having a bright light shone in your face, so that he just didn't notice anything in the background, just as he didn't pay any heed to her nipple-circling, am-I-special? routine. For weeks he'd wandered around Madrid, oblivious to that city's miniskirted, sloe-eyed minxes, entirely unbothered by the vamps on billboards. Then those weeks passed, the odd row started appearing, and he learned the occasional eyebrow-raising fact about Cristina, notably when she confessed that she really couldn't be doing with oral sex. And, slowly at first, the bright light had waned and the figures in the background had re-emerged into focus.

Old enough by then to do a post-mortem on the bashed mess that was the Cristina relationship – shit, marriage – he had concluded that the only reasonable thing he could do would be to concentrate on the élite, casual stuff apart. Cue several years of casual stuff. Then along came Claire, bringing with her a light so massive and powerful she could have staged evening fixtures. A light that shone at him so brightly that everything else would stay in the background for ever and ever.

Well, that was the theory. He checks the mirror and gives a stray curl a tweak. Then he's out back into the body of the kirk, swerving through the crowd of post-work drinkers until he reaches his companions for the evening.

'Can I get you girls another drink?' Ian asks. 'Monique? Chantal?'

'What can I get you?'

Pint of Guinness and a quadruple tequila, is what he badly wants to tell the barman, but he has to keep a clear head, so he says, 'Mineral water, please,' and, trying to ignore a twinge of desperation at this denial, tells himself that it's just very dull to spend an evening without alcohol. Or anything else, by the way – no distractions, no chatting, just mineral water and fuck all.

Three hours he's been waiting in this pub. Three fucking hours. Three hours of sitting on his own, reading the *Evening Standard* (never a sign of a happy, busy time), doing the *Standard* crossword (ditto, and some), pretending to be waiting for someone, then giving up on that pretence and becoming what he was – the sad bastard on his own in the corner – while he toyed with glass after glass of mineral water. Man of steel, though. Man of fucking steel.

This all started when he phoned the switchboard at Jenny's work and, by cunningly claiming to be a client, secured the information that she was away for two days at the conference she was organising in Hampshire. Which was all he fucking needed, by the way – to be immediately assailed by images of Rob waiting for Jenny in her hotel room, wheeching off her knickers then impaling her. Also, it put the kibosh on his half-formed plan to have another, better go at following Jenny after she left her office.

Then he had his brainwave. Megan. The fat flatmate. He'd follow Megan instead – and bump into her, accidentally, as you do, make polite chitchat and ask her politely, with an air of kind concern, as though enquiring about the health of a distant, elderly relative, about how Jenny was doing these days. Was she okay? Was she seeing someone? That's great. Good for her. Anyone he knows? . . .

Simple, yet brilliant.

But things had not quite gone to plan. Not a fucking tall to plan, in fact. Although everything had gone fine to start with. He'd had to hang around for only ten minutes outside the twee little office where Megan did whatever the fuck Megan did in the exciting world of restaurant PR, before Megan had appeared. Looking like the kind of person who'd describe herself in lonely hearts ads as a bubbly, vivacious blonde – i.e., a dumpy wee fat bird who likes her drink. Easy enough to follow her, though, as she waddled her way towards the Tube, despite her lack of height, because her frizz of yellow hair made for an excellent marker, even in Covent Garden's usual milling gaggle – tourists, fire-eaters, jugglers, some cunt dressed as an android, a couple of women holding babies and placards that announced in scrawled capitals that they were hungry and from Bosnia. Uh-huh. Bosnia. Tinkers, more like. So the idea at this stage was to bump into Megan casually in the Tube – perfectly natural, folk meeting at a Tube platform, going the same way, having a wee chat, easy fucking peasy.

Aye, but Megan being Megan, she had swung away from the Tube station, hoiked a right and headed down Long Acre, towards Great Queen Street and all those shops selling masons' shite, then trundled into a pub, one of those new-fangled Oirish joints where you can have all the time you like to admire the buckets of nails on the gantry and the antique road signs to Tipperary because you're being served by a moron who's just off the plane from Auckland and is pouring his first-ever pint. Packed to the rafters, like, but he'd still heard Megan's shrieks and managed to catch a glimpse, as he ambled past, of the commotion as Megan met up with Megan's pals, a yelpy squad of Megan look-alikes. On for a session, it seemed, so he'd dodged across the road to a normal pub – or as near to normal as you can find in London – on the corner and settled down to keep watch and stay sober. Three and a bit fucking hours ago.

He's about to crack and order a Guinness and a whisky chaser when he spots Megan coming out of Mickey O'Fenian's or whatever the fuck it's called. On her own and clearly pissed. He waits for her to pass his pub on her way back to Covent Garden Tube station, but instead Megan suddenly veers east, swerving a bit as she walks by the weird row of masons' shops. The fuck is she going now?

Ah, Holborn Tube station, just down the road, Central Line direct to Snotting Hill. Fuck. And she's got a good hundred yards' start.

Graham hurries out, crosses the road, narrowly avoiding death by taxi, and trots along behind her. When a side street appears on his left, he decides to take a gamble – run up the side street, hang a right if there is one, hang another right if there is one and not a dead-end, and stroll down Kingsway where he'll bump into Megan coming towards him. That doesn't work, he'll double back and get her in the Tube.

Graham jogs along his detour, which, rather to his own surprise, does indeed lead him into Kingsway. He stops on the corner for a moment to recover his breath, then starts to mosey south. And that's her now.

'Megan!'

It takes her a few bleary seconds to get him into focus. 'Oh, hello. Where you going?'

Way ewe gown. Christ. 'Just . . . down the road here. So. How's Megan?'

'Good, good. Bit squiffy, to be honest.' Wee flicker of a smile there.

'Excellent. Girls' night out, eh?'

His heart sinks as soon as the words are out of his mouth but she doesn't seem to notice his blunder. 'Asswipe,' she says cheerily enough, though he still needs a moment's thought before he realises that she's agreeing with him.

He nods encouragingly and remembers to keep smiling. 'Still living with Jenny?'

He couldn't have been more casual or chummy, but the very mention of Jenny seems to remind Megan that she should be frosty with him. 'Yes,' she declares. ''Bye, then.'

'Hold on, Megan. I'll walk you to the Tube.'

'That's the opposite direction for you.'

'Nah, not really. And I'm a gentleman.'

'Hmm,' says Megan as pointedly as it's possible to make a hmm. She makes a move to go past him. Graham responds by turning side-on to accompany her.

'And how is Jenny? She doing all right?'

'Fine.'

'I hear she's seeing someone.'

No reply.

'That's great, I think. Really good. I mean, I'm really pleased if she is. Seeing someone, like.'

No reply.

'I just hope she's happy, that's all.'

Megan keeps on walking.

'Always difficult, isn't it, to start up another relationship. If that's what it is . . . No, really, I'd be happy. For her. If she's seeing someone.'

'I'm going to cross the road now. Goodbye.'

That's it. He's had enough of this shite. He grabs her by a flabby arm and hauls her back. 'Just tell me, all right? Jenny. Jenny and Rob. What the *fuck* is going on? When did it start?'

Megan studies the hand that's gripping her flesh. 'If you don't let go,' she says softly and pleasantly, all trace of squiffiness gone, 'I am going to scream for help. Then I'm going to start crying. And those two big blokes coming up behind you look very gallant.'

Graham lets go of her arm.

Megan nods once. 'That's better. Now. For the second time, goodbye. Or, should I say, fuck off.'

'But you've got to tell me. I know you know. Jenny is seeing someone, isn't she?'

Megan puts her hands on where her hips might be and sighs. 'Yes. She is. And well done her, is what I say.'

'It's Rob, isn't it?'

She tuts and looks to the orange night sky.

'Fucksake, all you have to do is . . .'

'I tell you what. If you get down on your knees, clasp your hands like a good little boy saying his prayers, ask me nicely, I'll tell you everything I know.'

Out of the corner of his eye, he can see two burly young men in suits looking at him as they pass by. He lowers himself down until he's kneeling on the pavement. He puts his hands together and says, 'I'm begging you to tell me, Megan.'

'Please.'

'Please.'

'Pretty please.'

'. . . Pretty please.'

'You have no idea how much I'm enjoying this. Okay, so all I know is this. Jenny is seeing someone. He's very keen on her, you'll be pleased to hear, and he is called Jay.'

Graham frowns at Megan's podgy knees. 'Jay?' he says.

'Yes, Jay. I don't know his full name. That's his initial.'

'J?'

'J.'

'J?'

'J.'

'But that's what Rob calls her in his diary.'

'Who *is* this Rob?'

'And she can't call him J because he'd be R. Or B, I suppose.'

'I haven't the foggiest what you're talking about. Oh, I can tell you one other thing.'

'What? What?'

'The one other thing I know about this guy, and I just know this will cheer you up, is that Jenny met him through one of your ickle chums. And that's your lot. Happy now? You can get up if you want.'

Graham lurches to his feet, feeling woozy as he does so, whether from the change in altitude or the befuddled state of his brain he's not quite sure. He takes a deep breath and stares uncomprehendingly at a blob of chewing gum fixed to his right knee. 'So it's someone called J something who's screwing her, not Rob. You sure it's not Rob?'

Megan rolls her eyes.

Graham's stomach lurches at the terrible thought which has just filled his brain. 'Jason! Fucking hell, it's Jason! Jason . . . She must have met him through Col. It fits. Col's the friend. She knows Col. Jason . . . It's Jason . . .'

'Well, there you go. Goodbye.' As Megan steps round him, she shows him a fist, then steadily raises her middle finger.

'Jason,' says Graham.

'Blimey,' says Alastair. He stubs out the roach and flops back into the comfiness of the candy-striped sofa. Susie seizes the chance to jump up and lie on his stomach. 'Good grass,' says Alastair. This strikes him as a very cool thing to say. Then it strikes him that, right now, anything would strike him as a cool thing to say.

'Where would I be without grass?' Alastair whispers to Susie. 'In an even bigger neurotic mess, I suppose,' he whispers back. As it is, he's mustering a smile as he remembers the incident on the DLR this evening, when he was astounded to see, farther along the carriage, standing with his back to him and reading the *FT*, Rob. Before he'd had time to think, Alastair had rushed over and, just as he began to reach out, realised that he was about to hug a stranger. Nice chap, fortunately. Financier from Stockholm. Lars. And he didn't seem at all bothered. Quite the opposite, in fact, and by the time they got to Bank, Lars was asking him if he knew of any good bars in the Earl's Court area . . .

Blimey, thinks Alastair, for it has just occurred to him that maybe Lars was gay, and maybe even chatting, him, Alastair, up. Oh well. Oh dear. Oh well. He tries to banish his embarrassment by concentrating on the Discovery Channel documentary he's been half watching about the CIA.

Not too bad, reckons Alastair after a minute or two, but he still switches it off, because it's going to be a whole programme of American-sponsored ghastliness and that will only depress him in the end. It was bad enough even half watching the carpet-bombing in Vietnam, the coup in Chile, the Bay of Pigs fiasco there in black and white, the poor old Guatemalan banana-growers, and then the Contras and Reagan pretending they were freedom fighters. 'As if Cuba was a threat,' he scoffs at Susie. Or even the Soviet Union – a country where folk had to queue for bread and drank shoe polish. But maybe people'll think the same kind of thing in twenty years' time, when they look back on the great baddies of this decade and wonder why the big fuss about Libya or Iraq or whatshisface in Belgrade. Anyway, what are they compared to the old days, when watching the news was like supporting Scotland and the best to be hoped for was the avoidance of catastrophe? That's why he can now be such a smiley optimist about democracy and world peace and so forth – because he grew up in the seventies and the firm expectation that civilisation was about to end in a mushroom cloud as big as the planet.

Same syndrome, come to think of it, as supporting Scotland, at least since the '78 World Cup, when he, along with an entire nation, learned to aim low and avoid disappointment. Keeping your hopes down – it's an approach that has come naturally to him and has usually worked quite well. Even with sex. So he's always, or almost always, managed, fairly instinctively it seems, not to think about girls who were out of his reach, from Kirsty Barclay onwards. And, over the past nine years of singledom, he's definitely found that it's easier to cope with not having sex if he doesn't have any expectations of having any sex. And that's not difficult. After all, when did he last get a glimmer of having sex? Okay, fair enough, this summer, at the *Chronicle* party, when Antonia, the rather attractive (he thought) temp on the picture desk, seemed to be chatting him up. But how could anything happen when Antonia was supposed to be living with a website designer? Anyway, not to forget that it was also bad form leaving Jenny to fend for herself for a noticeably ungallant half an hour . . .

That kind of rare incident apart, he's become so accustomed to the lack of sex that he can go for days at a time now, and almost not think about sex. And it's certainly become odd to think that he has had sex in the past, that there are four women in this world who have had sex with him.

Now, is he stoned enough to go through his short list of

exes? 'I'll give it a shot,' Alastair whispers to Susie, although she seems to have fallen asleep on his lap.

- Carol, 1982. Final year at uni, when he was swotting like crazy, never going out, hardly ever seeing Rob, who in any case had begun to hang out with a hippie crowd, but a rare night out had somehow ended up with him back at Carol's and Carol encouraging him to lose his virginity.
- Angela, 1982. Two months after the one-night stand with Carol and, on a roll now, he got off with Angela at a post-exam party. Sweet, nice-looking Angela, who turned out to be a real demon in bed. Only four months they went out together, before they graduated and went their separate ways, but long enough for him to learn a variety of surprising moves.
- Pat, 1985. A *Scotsman* leaving do, he got off with Pat, a fellow sub, and, amazingly, got away with having an office affair for three weeks, until Pat cut it short because it was in danger of becoming serious. Well, that's what she said, but at least it was good of her to do it gently.
- Rhona, 1986–8, the nearly three years which in hindsight have to be seen as a golden era, one to rival that of the first FNC. Nearly three years when he was blessed with his longest-ever relationship *and* a vigorous social life (even though Rob had disappeared down south by that time, taking with him those great nights out in the Café Royal) – what with his *Scotsman* pals, Rhona's lot, Jenny a bit, before Graham and Jenny also decamped for London . . . and Cathy.

Cathy, whom he'd got to know through Rob but who stayed on as a friend after Rob left. Yes, as a friend, he'd reassured Rhona, and himself, every time he arranged to meet Cathy for a drink or a curry. But he could make those reassurances only because he hadn't got past acknowledging that Cathy was way out of his league, Rangers to his Cowdenbeath. Even so, that supposedly innocuous friendship definitely contributed to the real reason he and Rhona split up – that he wasn't actually in love with Rhona. Whereas he could easily have fallen in love with Cathy. With her eventually unavoidable loveliness. Not that there was any chance of Cathy reciprocating. As he soon found out. Less than a month Rhona had been gone, and Cathy had taken so much trouble to make sure he was all right, checking up on him, treating him to an evening at the Kalpna, and how had he repaid her kindness? By getting drunk back at her flat and asking if he could go to bed with her. Appalling. Appalling, appalling, appalling . . . Cathy, of course, had turned down the bumbling, crass proposal, which broke the rules of their friendship and, effectively, ended it. Over ten years on and he'd repeated the Fiona catastrophe – starting off by being grateful just to be in a beautiful woman's oxygen space, then becoming friends, then making a disastrous pass, thus destroying a friendship and himself in the process. Brilliant.

'Nine years ago,' Alastair whispers. 'Nine years.' Nine years of celibacy – it sounds a horrifyingly long period of time, though lately he has begun to wonder if maybe he's not that abnormal, if maybe lots of people aren't having sex, if maybe most people he knows don't have much or any sex. Gadabouts like Rob excepted, of course . . .

Not that Rob's ever gone on too much about his gallivanting – no names, no pack-drill, and no indiscreet details. Rob's innate tact would be the reason for that, Rob just lapsing occasionally into mentions of a pick-up at a club or another affair with another bored secretary or besotted housewife.

Alastair sits bolt upright and Susie springs off his lap. 'Louise,' he says, for only now has it dawned on him that every time Rob has had one of his escapades, he must have been two-timing Louise . . . Well, there's another good reason for Rob not to brag too much.

11

'YOU SEE MY PROBLEM?'

Friday lunch-time

'Hi!'

   'Hello?'

   'Graham!'

   'Speaking.'

   '. . . It's Audrey.'

   'Oh, hi there, Audrey. How are you?'

   'Oh, you know. Same old, same old. There I was, thinking haven't seen you, you haven't been around, dah dah dah dah dah, and yes, there was the Cantaloupe thing but we didn't get a chance to, like, and all the rest of it, so on and so forth, blah-di-blah-di-blah, so I thought I'd whatever. So. How's the exhibition coming along?'

   'Aye, well, not so good.'

   'But that's the way it happens, isn't it, the ups and the downs of the creative process, the this and the that, the blah blah blah, and you've just got to keep at it, keep going, dahdahdahdahdah.'

   'Aye, I know what you mean, Audrey, but it's more than that. They've been bum-licking Eno at CDQ so they've got some installation by him instead.'

   'Oh, *no*. Oh, but Graham, that's just, those *swine* . . . What about Marty?'

   'What about Marty?'

   'Col, or maybe it was Hermann, whatever, was like, Marty's got this big space on D:Zine's ground floor and he's on for turning it into a kind of gallery thing, exhibitions, installations, dahdahdahdahdah.'

'And you reckon he might be on for hosting mine?'

'Sure. He knows you, he's on the lookout for whatever, he needs art in there, blah blah blah. Why not?'

'That is brilliant news.'

'Glad to be of, you know, whatever. You can buy me a free drink at Jason's studio thing tonight.'

'Studio?'

'See, that's you in Finchley, out of the Shoreditch thing. Party, celebration, launch kind of thing for the BT campaign thing Jason's been doing. At his studio. Jason was like, it's open house, party-time, let's all celebrate my fantastic success, blah-di-blah-di-blah, so why don't you come along?'

'Oh, aye. He never told me it was in the studio. What time?'

'Well, seven or eight, whatever, but I've got another thing I've got to go to rehrehrehrehreh, but later, yeah, and it'd be great to see you, talk about the Marty thing, catch up, whatever.'

'I'll be there. And thanks, Audrey. Really.'

'Oh, blah-di-blah-di-blah.'

'See you tonight.'

'Ciao.'

'Honestly. Don't worry . . . I'll remember. Honest . . . Okay. See you later.' Jesus. Ian places the phone back on its cradle and wonders if his life is ever going to be the same again, or whether this really can be the start of decades of chores, tasks, responsibilities, things to do, things to remember to do. Don't panic, Mr Mainwaring, he tells himself. It's only a trip to Superdrug. Still, though, but. Ian wanders along the corridor to the common room, which is empty, so he is mulling over whether or not he could risk chopping one out when somebody appears in the doorway. Chantal. Smiling uncertainly and looking good enough to eat.

'*Bonjour*,' Ian says, and follows this up with a crinkly-eyed smile. '*Fais comme chez toi.*'

'*T'es trop gentil.*' Chantal props her dinky bottom on the edge of the orange-coloured armchair.

Oh, most fortunate edge of the orange-coloured armchair. 'How are you, Chantal? *Tout va bien?*'

'*Oui, assez bien.* Well enough.'

'Excellent,' Ian says, while racking his brains to find something to talk about. The weather? The landlady? Monique? Toulouse? . . .

'I want to ask a question about the class today.'

'Great! I mean, good. Ask away.'

'Like. I do not like like.' She makes a face, as though like were sour. 'It is so difficult. I like to do this but I do not like doing it, I detest the dentist but I like to go . . . Bof. Terrible.'

She's wearing a skirt that shows off the inch above her knees and her skin is the colour of caramel. Ian has another go with the crinkly-eyed smile. 'Yeah, it's a difficult one, Chantal. Okay, gerund first. Ing for enjoying. What do you really like doing?'

'I like . . . eating good food?'

'That's it. What else do you like doing?'

Little bait being dangled there but she doesn't bite. 'I like seeing my friends. I like . . . holidays. No, a moment. I like going on holidays.'

'There you are. Now, like to. You like to do something that is good for you. But you might not enjoy it. For example, I like to, oh, I don't know, I like to get up at eight, but I don't like getting up at eight. So what do you like to do?'

'I like to . . . I like to study English.'

'Oh, Chantal.' Here's another chance to flirt and he isn't going to pass it up. 'Don't you like studying English?'

She crosses her legs to reveal a perfect triangle of slim,

caramelly thigh. 'I like studying English with you.' She puts on a face of mock seriousness. 'Mr Murray.'

Ian laughs. 'Excellent attitude. You may call me sir.'

Chantal uncrosses her legs, places her hands on her knees in good-girl pose, then treats him to a glance of playful coyness with those big, almondy eyes. When she speaks it is with the hint of another pout and at a level just above a whisper. 'Sir,' she says. Then the pout disappears and that wide mouth slowly widens farther.

'Subs.'

'Alastair?'

'Jenny! What can I do you for?'

'Oh, Alastair, I know I said I'd call you and it's not as if I haven't wanted to. Only . . . well, I . . . it's . . . I'm sorry, Alastair, but do you have a moment?'

''Course, though I have to leave at one to see a detect . . . Blimey, you won't know about Rob, will you?'

'Rob from Kirkcaldy? What about him?'

'It must sound crazy but Rob seems to have gone AWOL. That's where I'm off to, a private detective who's trying to trace him.'

'God. And Rob's disappeared? But then he's always been a bit odd, hasn't he?'

'Has he?'

'Kind of. That suave, sophisticated act of his . . . I'm sorry, I know he's your friend. I only knew him a bit, because of Graham. Although that didn't stop him trying it on soon as Graham and I split up.'

'. . . Blimey.'

'Not that he got anywhere, I assure you.'

'Blimey.'

'Anyway, Alastair, why I'm phoning, I was wondering if you could do me a favour.'

'Blimey . . . Yes, Jenny, of course.'

'And tell me something about this Sunday's Lifestyle.'

'I thought as much.'

'What?'

'You're a spy from the *Telegraph*, aren't you?'

'Oh. I see. Yes. Foiled again. The thing is, Alastair, I am spying but for myself. What I want to know is . . . It's about . . . Oh, this is just appalling. I can't believe . . .'

'Jenny, are you all right?'

'Not really, Alastair, to be honest. The thing is, I need to find out what's in Josh Todd's column for Sunday.'

'Josh Todd? Don't tell me you're a fan.'

'Not exactly. I just want to know if his column on Sunday is going to be anything like last week's.'

'Oh, yes. It's the usual drivel about nothing, really. Josh blethering on about him and his new girlfriend.'

'And is there anything about him and this woman having sex?'

'Blimey, yes. Cringe-making stuff. Maybe even worse than last week's. Apart from anything else, I feel really sorry for the girlfriend. Oh, no, wait a minute. That's why you're phoning, isn't it?'

'I'm afraid so.'

'You know her, don't you?'

'Well, that's a matter for debate.'

'Is it anyone I know? No, no, don't tell me. It'd be unfair on her. And if I ever met her, I just wouldn't be able to look her in the eye.'

'Alastair, I do hope that isn't the case, otherwise you and I will never see each other again.'

'Sorry?'

'Please don't make me say it.'

'What? Oh . . . Oh, God.'

'You see my problem?'

'Oh God. Yes, I . . . Oh. Ahem. I see. Ahem . . . So . . . how did you meet him, Jenny?'

'At the *Chronicle* party.'

'Oh, no. Oh, God. But then this is all my fault. Oh, Jenny, I am so sorry.'

'Don't be daft, Alastair.'

'But it's my fault. If I hadn't taken you to the party, you wouldn't be . . . you wouldn't have met Josh.'

'Alastair, you are not to blame for this. And I did have a great time with you at the party.'

'Oh, blimey.'

'There was a bit towards the end when I lost track of you. He came over, we got chatting, and he seemed quite nice at first. And I suppose I was kind of flattered. I mean, I've got to the stage when I walk past a building site and hope to hear wolf whistles.'

'I cannot believe that for a second.'

'True. So there I was being chatted to if not up, and it was a bit of a morale-booster, that was all. I mean, I didn't flash my knickers or give him my number or anything. But then I bumped into him a month or so back. I was having lunch at the Ivy . . .'

'Very posh.'

'Work, I needn't add. He was there waiting for me when I went to get my coat. He asked me out for a drink and it seemed too much bother at the time to say no, so I said yes, so we went for a drink and that was okay, so we had another date. And the rest you know. As do millions of *Chronicle* readers. Thanks to that incredibly stupid, selfish, ghastly *wanker*.'

'Circulation's down to six hundred thousand, if that's any comfort.'

'None whatsoever, Alastair, I assure you. When I read his column on Sunday . . . I simply couldn't . . . I had to . . . Of all the . . . Basically, I've never been so angry with any man in my life, and for an ex of Graham Anderson's that's saying something, believe you *me*. Apart from anything else, he's making most of it up so that he sounds like some kind of demon lover, although he's one of those clueless types. Clitoris, oh yes, the capital of Lithuania. But I can't even put the record straight because that would mean . . .'

'. . . Is that what you wanted to tell me when you called before?'

'No. No, I was trying to keep it quiet. And now look.'

'He doesn't name you. There is that.'

'And you won't tell anyone, will you?'

''Course not, Jenny.'

'Promise?'

'I promise. Blimey, though, it must be awful for you.'

'Thanks, Alastair. And, yes, it is. Beyond awful. As I told Josh when I also told him that if I ever saw him again, it would be through the cross-sights of a machinegun.'

'If you want a hit-man, any of us on the subs desk would do it for free.'

'I'm keeping that job for myself, if you don't mind. So how bad is this week's?'

'Ummmmm . . . Bad.'

'Oh God . . . Could you maybe fax, no, bike round a print-out?'

'Not according to the rule book. But this is different, and it's not as if you're going to be showing it around.'

'You're right about that.'

'Well, if you've split up with him, the silver lining is that this'll be the last column he writes about . . . about you.'

'I really hope so. After all, we only had two proper, you know, fully fledged dates. The second and last was on Saturday, because the next day I read his shitty little column.'

'Yes, this one's about Saturday. I can tell you the thrust, I mean the gist, of it now, if you want. All that happens is that he meets his unnamed girlfriend at Harvey Nichols, and then they both go back to her flat.'

'What about the party?'

'Nothing about any party, thank goodness. This is all about Saturday afternoon.'

'Not Saturday night?'

'No.'

'Oh shit.'

12

'WHICH WAS REALLY BIZARRE'

Friday night

Pine tables, leather chesterfields, an exhibition of not bad black-and-white photographs of rural pylons on the wall, menus folded around little glass vases all holding a single small iris in full bloom, a blackboard detailing the day's specials in faultless italic, a list of specials that includes the words crostini, seared and teriyaki . . . No way is this pub a pub. An art gallery with tables, maybe. A restaurant that sells beer, possibly. But a pub? No way.

Ian dips his crusty bread into the saucer of olive oil. So when did this all happen? When did British pubs start being so cool and civilised they could almost be Dutch? What happened to fizzy beer and flock wallpaper, a menu that stretched to one cellophaned roll filled with a rectangle of processed cheese and a large, violent ring of onion? Young guy over in the corner, he's sipping from a stemmed bowl of Leffe and reading a book on post-structuralism, if you please. Had Ian tried that when he was a student back in late-seventies Edinburgh, when you were considered a poof in bars like the Diggers and Drummonds if you didn't smoke or still had two ears, he'd have been able to finish the book at his leisure and in the peace and quiet of the Royal Infirmary.

'Which was really bizarre,' Ben is saying as Ian turns his attention back to what has to be, please, the end of Ben and Ruth's account of their experiences at this summer's Womad festival – a heady day out which featured, Ian now knows, Ben and Ruth particularly approving of a Malinese dance troup and a Hasidic rap artist, Ben and Ruth finding themselves gratifyingly adept at the tabla workshop, Ben and Ruth joining in the mass jeering as Concorde flew overhead, and Ben and Ruth returning to the carpark to find that the windscreen of their Peugeot 206 was one of several which had shattered on contact with Concorde's sonic pollution.

'And then we had the most amazing journey back from Reading,' says Ruth. 'Didn't we, Ben?'

'Yeah, it was bizarre, actually, because . . .'

Oh, for goodness' sake. Ian nudges the saucer of olive oil over to Claire. She replies with a tiny shake of her head and a slightly less tiny smile, which could be anything from cool politeness to naughty complicity. Who knows? Not him. Not any more. This pregnancy business is turning a transparent, happy-go-lucky girl into an inscrutable woman of mystery.

'. . . decided to avoid the motorway because of the windscreen and go by the B-roads instead, so we . . .'

When's she going to turn back to being nice, loving Claire again? How much more of this . . . apartness does he have to take?

'. . . on the radio that the M4 was jammed solid. So our route was much quicker, wasn't it, Ruth?'

'Definitely quicker. I mean, why they have motorways ruining the countryside when they just get clogged up . . .'

'Yeah. It was really . . .' Ben furrows his brow as he searches for *le mot juste*.

Please, God, thinks Ian. Strange. Unusual. He realises that he's digging his fingernails into his palms. Surprising. Disconcerting.

'. . . bizarre,' says Ben.

'Ah, young James,' Barry announces heartily. 'Did you manage to find out what was happening in Design?'

'Yes.'

'And what was that?'

James Bond twitches his left shoulder. 'Not much.'

'Did you ask about the cover?'

'Yes.'

'And what did you find out about the cover, James?'

'Doesn't like it.'

'Oh, bloody hell. Bloody *hell*. The editor doesn't like it?'

'Yes.'

'What doesn't he like?'

'Hasn't heard of him.'

'David Beckham? He hasn't heard of David Beckham?'

'Says he's too obscure for the Lifestyle cover.'

'Oh, *bloody* hell. But what the bloody hell could Blue, Richard find as an alternative? Al, any ideas?'

'Well, there is the piece about Vivienne Westwood. The editor might have heard of her.'

'Possible. Unlikely, but possible. Sorry, James, what were you going to say?'

'Says he likes the Josh Todd article.'

'That's good, but I'm more worried about the cover, James.'

'Says he might want Josh Todd on the cover.'

'Do what?'

'Says he might want Josh Todd on the cover.'

'Bloody, bloody, bastarding, fucking hell. I'd better have a word with B . . . Richard about this. He can't put Josh on the cover. He can't, he can't, he just can't.'

'Says he'll make a decision on it when he gets back.'

'Gets back from where, James?'

'Oswestry.'

'Eh? What?'

'Gone to do a thing for Sky News.'

'Right. Osterley, you mean. Even so, the editor might as well be popping up to Shropshire, the state of the traffic, and it's right out by Heathrow. Gone ten now, so it could be midnight before he gets back. Unless he phones in. Or . . . Oh, bloody hell, this is going to be a late one. A very, very late one.'

A week ago, in a previous lifetime, Alastair would have tried to reassure Barry at this point, at least offer to stay with him until the bitter end. But as it is, Alastair says nothing and resigns himself to the inevitable.

In fact, Alastair doesn't mind at all the prospect of endless hours waiting for Lifestyle to go to press. With Friday Night Club suspended and little to do in the way of work, except come up with the occasional remaining caption or headline, he can take this chance to have a good think about the second meeting with Mr Hilton – and the aftermath, when he was saying goodbye to Louise and she suddenly stepped forward, put her hands around his back, and began to sob into his chest.

Graham licks the salt scattered on the back of his hand, downs another tequila, sucks a slice of lemon, shudders, coughs. 'Fucking get in,' says Graham, then he looks around the studio for a buckshee beer chaser.

There's an unopened bottle of Budvar on Col's workbench. In fact, the first thing he noticed when he arrived several hours ago was two dozen unopened bottles of Budvar chilling in a bucket beneath Col's workbench, but by now Graham is far too drunk to recall their existence. Invigorated by the tequila, he lurches over and grabs the Budvar before any other bastard can get to it. Hah! He opens the bottle, takes a swig and surveys the scene.

Col is chatting with Tim over by the high window that looks out on to Curtain Road. Sue's with a group of half a dozen children Graham's never seen before who are solemnly smoking a joint. Hermann's at the back of the room, sitting on what was, once upon a time, Graham's desk and chatting up an improbably tall, thin girl who may or may not be some kind of model. A quartet of Jason's pals are beginning to dance around the boom-box. Jason's nowhere to be seen. The bastard.

Audrey hasn't turned up yet. Aye, well, fuck it.

Time for a slash.

Graham pushes himself off towards the studio door, then down the corridor to the bogs. Just think, he thinks – four years back, I used to do exactly this walk every time I wanted a dump. Until I had to sack myself. How low can you get? Losing your job as a freelance illustrator, that's got to come pretty fucking close.

Graham shoulders the door and stumbles into the toilet. Where he sees that Jason is scrubbing his hands in a basin full of soapy water. Fucking *poof*. Wanker probably puts a towel over the fucking bedsheet before he shags her. Big pack of fucking Kleenex on the bedside table.

'Well, well. If it isn't Jason,' announces Graham before lining himself up in front of the urinal.

'Graham. All right?'

Awe wigh? His pish batters at the urinal. 'So, then,' Graham shouts over his shoulder. 'That's you washing yourself nice and *clean*, eh, Jason?' Graham tucks himself back in, failing to notice as he does so that his conspicuously laundered chinos are acquiring what will soon be a New Zealand-shaped stain.

Graham makes his way over to the row of basins and stops a foot behind Jason. Graham leans forward so that his reflection appears alongside Jason's in the small, cracked mirror. He feels quite pleased with himself at having inadvertently created this cinematic moment. But now he has to say something else.

'Having a good wash, eh? Ya *bastard*.'

Jason peers at Graham's reflection. 'What's this?' he asks.

'What's this?' says Graham. 'What's this? *This* is what this fucking is.'

The idea was to clout him across the ear. But by the time Graham has drawn back his fist and taken a swipe, Jason has swerved out of harm's way. Jason turns and grabs him by the shoulders.

'Graham. What the fuck are you playing at?'

'Oh, aye. Playing, is it?' Although he's never tried it before, Graham feels a surge of confidence as he tenses his neck then delivers his head-butt.

A small fraction of a second before he makes contact, it occurs to him that the proper target for a head-butt might be somewhere about the top of an opponent's nose, not the brickwork of an opponent's forehead. As it turns out, Jason ducks to the left so that Graham catches him a glancing blow on the side of his temple.

'Ow!' says Jason.

Graham says nothing, for it would have needed many, many more tequilas to block out the confusion of pain in his skull. And now a sickening dizziness which has him clutching his head and reeling from side to side.

Jason, by contrast, seems to have suffered damage that can be cured with a little light rubbing. 'What the hell was that all about?' he says. 'Jesus Christ, Anderson, you drunken *idiot*.' For further emphasis, Jason pushes Graham in the chest. It's not a big push but Graham's on his heels and off balance and the push propels him backwards towards a cubicle.

'Jason. The fuck you doing to Graham?'

It's Col, standing in the entrance and staring in astonishment as Graham staggers into the jamb of the open cubicle door. Graham's first reaction is heartfelt gratitude, because there was a moment there when he feared that he was going to keep on staggering into the cubicle and down on to the lidless and seatless toilet, coming to rest as though he's in a cartoon about dysentery, the back of his head against the cistern, his arse slumped from view and his legs dangling over the side of the bowl. His second reaction is to notice the pain.

'Graham, Jesus, are you all right?' says Col from somewhere far away.

Part Three

1

'TALKING IN MY MIND'

Saturday morning

'Thirty-four.'

Blimey.

'Thirty-five.'

Alastair closes his eyes, takes a deep breath and lowers himself down again. Then he pushes himself back up, his arms trembling as they straighten and lock. 'Thirty-six,' he gasps, then he staggers to his feet to do the stretching. He does twelve bends to the right, twelve to the left and twelve where his palms have to touch his toes. Then he straightens up and shakes himself loose.

Twisting his neck from side to side, Alastair makes his way to the bathroom, where he steps on the scales. Ten stone two. Say what you like about upsets, but they're pretty good for the waistline. Alastair squeezes Colgate out on to his toothbrush and starts to scrub his teeth. Rob, he thinks, now that he doesn't have anything else to think about. Rob . . .

Alastair spits, rinses and waggles the toothbrush at his mirror image. 'Come on, now,' he tells himself. 'This won't buy the baby a new bonnet.' So. Here's what he's got to do. One, not obsess about what Rob's been up to. 'Two,' he says, as he puts the toothbrush back in its beaker, 'make the most of the Saturday.' Which means ignoring the fact that he was subbing Lifestyle until 2.30 in the morning. And that means having a plan of action. Which will also help him not think about Rob . . . So. Bit of brekker, shower, shave, all the rest of it. Then off to Marks for the weekly shop, maybe pop into the garden centre for a look-see, back here to clean the place up. And, no getting out of it, give the windows a going over with hot soapy water and last week's Comment section. Then the results, then off to the Pig and Whistle for the summit meeting with Ian and Graham, tell them his news. About Rob. Why? Why on earth would Rob . . . ?

'Soo-zee,' Alastair calls out in a minor third to distract himself. He lets the minor third elide into a couple of bars from one his current favourites, 'Everytime' by Lustral. Whoever she, he or they are. 'Can you hear me? Talking in my mind,' sings Alastair to cheer himself up as he makes his way down to the kitchen, his cup of Earl Grey and his orange juice.

Graham is following Jenny as she hurries down St Martin's Lane towards Trafalgar Square, her long raincoat billowing in her wake. Just before she reaches the end of the street, she turns abruptly left and into a very narrow and very dark alley. He breaks into a trot. But by the time he has reached the alley's entrance, Jenny's nowhere to be seen.

He can hear her, though. She's somewhere near by and she's moaning. 'Oh, please,' she says. 'Please, please, *please*.' He takes a few steps into the alley and immediately realises that he's been lured into a trap. There's a faint light at the other end of the alley, but he knows he won't reach it in time. He spins round to see a figure standing in silhouette. The face remains in darkness but he recognises only too well the swot's side parting, the hunched stance, the looming rectitude.

'Got you,' says Gordon Brown.

Sticky eyed, furry mouthed and fuzzy headed, Ian is standing in his tiny, shambolic kitchen, blowing his nose into a wad of toilet roll while he waits for, oh Christ almighty, the water inside the kettle to come to the boil.

When it does, Ian chucks the damp wad of loo roll into the bin, pours water over the ground coffee pouched in a beigely unbleached filter paper, rescues the two slices of bread which are starting to blacken under the grill, then smears them with butter and marmalade. Balancing the plate of toast on two mugs of coffee, Ian picks his way back to the bedroom, where Claire is sitting on the edge of the bed, elbows on her knees, head in her hands and her T-shirt riding up to reveal a patch of her smooth, taut back.

'You okay?' asks Ian as he hands Claire her mug and her toast.

'Oh, God. I don't know if I can face it.'

Now, a lot of men at this point would make the mistake of thinking that she's talking about the toast, but Ian is too well versed in the ways of women, plus he's seen far too many crap French comedies (Comic hero to gendarme: 'I've lost my dog.' Gendarme: 'Name?' Comic hero: 'Fifi.' Gendarme: 'Okay, Monsieur Fifi') to make that schoolboy error.

Ian places his mug on the floor, sits down beside her and rubs the exposed small of her back. 'Don't worry, sweetheart. Don't worry.'

'Oh, Ian, I just can't stand the thought . . .' She sighs into her hands.

'I know, dear. I know. But we'll work something out, you'll see. And maybe it'll be different when the baby arrives . . .'

Claire takes her hands away from her face and nods thoughtfully at the middle distance. 'I'm talking about breakfast,' she says.

2

Saturday evening

'You know what's going to happen now.' Ian nods towards Alastair, who's bobbing up and down behind a crowd standing three deep at the bar of the Pig and Whistle.

'What?'

'Herds of wildebeest will migrate across the Serengeti, wide-eyed children will become wizened pensioners, entire civilisations will rise and fall, and Eck still won't have been served.' Ian drains the very last of his lager and slumps. 'Might as well get comfortable. We're in this for the long haul.'

Graham shifts in his seat. Not much chance of him getting comfortable, unless he could give himself a jab of anaesthetic. His head is aching, his left arm is badly bruised, his back is just sore all over and he seems to have wrenched something in his neck. So here he is, sitting like Whistler's mother. And whenever he wants to look to either side, he has to swivel like a fucking robot. Anyfuckingway, never mind all that. This is his chance. 'Ian, there's something I've got to ask, all right?'

'Ask away.'

'Who do you know with a first name starts with J?'

'I don't understand.'

'Perfectly fucking simple question.'

'Okay, well, in that case, Jenny.'

'Don't get fucking smart here.'

'Serious, man. And I thought that you thought that J was Jenny. In Rob's diary.'

'Nah. Turns out that the person she's seeing is called J something as well.'

'Not Rob, then?'

'No, not fucking Rob. It's someone who knows someone I know and his initial is J. All right? So who could it be from your pals?'

Ian frowns at his empty pint glass. 'To be honest, I don't know anyone else called J. Wait . . . No.'

'What? Who?'

Ian grimaces. 'No, sorry, Graham. I mean, I know a Jean-Pierre in Paris, and there are two Juans I used to pal about with in Madrid, but I've only been back here a few months so it's not as if I have this great social life full of Joes and Jacks and Jebediahs, you know what I'm saying?'

'Have a think, though, eh?'

'. . . Look, Graham, you want my advice?'

'No.'

'Forget about this J business. And say you do find out that Jenny is seeing somebody called J something or other, then what? Telling you, man, let it go.'

'Oh, aye. Easy as that.'

'I'm not saying it's easy, Graham, but you have to do it. And after all, it was you that split up with her. And it has been over a couple of years now.'

'So?'

'So, maybe you should stop worrying about what Jenny's up to, start worrying about yourself. Maybe it's time to move on. Fresh fields, pastures new.'

'You've tried this shite before and I'm going to give you the same answer. Just what the fuck would you know about it? Twelve years me and her were together. Twelve fucking years. That's not something you can forget about like that.' Graham finishes the sentence with a contemptuous snap of his fingers, then winces as another current of pain shoots up and down his neck.

'You all right?' asks Ian after long moments of silence.

'Twisted my fucking neck, that's all.'

'Bad one.' Ian taps his fingers against his pint glass. Boy seems stuck for something to say but Graham's fucked if he's going to help him out. Time to move on, eh? There speaks a man who can leave entire countries on a fucking whim. Who walked out on that Spanish bird after about half an hour of marriage. Who expects a Duke of Edinburgh Award for staying with Claire for all of two years.

'So,' says Ian at last. 'How's it going with Audrey?'

'Audrey? All right.'

There's another long silence, then Ian has another go. 'You any idea how Louise fits into all this?'

'How do you mean?'

'Her thinking that she's Rob's girlfriend. And Rob being a bit of a one for the ladies. That.'

Graham shrugs then winces.

'What I was wondering,' says Ian, 'was maybe Rob didn't have all those girls on a paternoster after all.'

What the fuck is he talking about? 'The fuck you talking about?'

'Remember? The paternoster of oiled bimbettes.'

'. . . Oh, aye.'

'Or he did have the paternoster and just lied to Louise.'

'I suppose.'

'But here's the thing, Graham. Rob talked a good game, always banging on about the women he was chasing after and chatting up and shoving out of his bed. But did you ever actually see Rob with any girls?'

'Oh, aye, Ian. All the time. Me, Rob and one of Rob's birds. The perfect set-up for a perfect night out. What am I? His chaperon? Some kind of professional fucking gooseberry?'

'Okay, okay.' More tapping on his glass. 'What do you think to Eck's news about Rob?'

Rob, Rob, Rob, Rob, Rob. Fucking Rob. Aye, he's still really pissed off with Rob, and not just because he has spent far too much time thinking that Rob was cheating on him with Jenny to forgive and forget and not be pissed off with Rob for being exactly the kind of flash fuck who would have had no qualms at all about getting Jenny into his bed. 'I don't have a scooby,' he says, after summing up the will to remember Eck's news about Rob. 'Eck's found out that Rob told Louisa he wasn't allowed in America? So what? Rob was spinning her a line. And Rob didn't tell her about us or us about her. What's the big deal?'

'Yeah, but there's also the thing about Rob being over-drawn.'

Graham shrugs his shoulders and swallows a yell. 'Aye. Bit out of order, though, Eck and Louisa going through the man's financial stuff like that.' No, he's still really pissed off with Rob because he has also spent a lot of time remembering how Rob encouraged him to leave Jenny when things were getting rocky and he was taking a first good look around London and the scene in Shoreditch and the women, all those women . . . Not that Rob said anything. It was just the example he set – the bachelor boy, always out on the town, chatting up dolly birds and screwing around and living the life of Jason King. Back in the real world, though, life without Jenny turned out to be just that.

'Way hay,' Ian says into another silence. 'Here's the wee man now.'

Alastair places the three glasses carefully on the table and sits back down. The other two are looking at him expectantly. He offers them a smile that he's sure comes across as weak and sickly. In fact, his stomach does seem a bit queasy – a symptom of his not-good feeling about how the final bit of his report is going to go down. However. And there are a few items on the agenda before he gets to the crunch. Oh God, though.

Alastair clears his throat. 'Another thing that's odd,' he says, 'is Rob's passport. That it's still there, for a start, so what we're assuming . . .'

'Oh ho,' says Ian. 'We now, is it?'

'Nothing like that, honestly. So what we, Louise and I, are assuming is that Rob's got a new passport and the thing he said in his note about him getting a new name and so on and so forth is real. But what it is about the old passport as well is that there's only a couple of pages that are stamped. And he's had it since ninety-one.'

'Aye, Eck, but you don't get it stamped when you go abroad these days.'

'Only the EU, Graham. And maybe it's slackened off a bit this year but Rob used to have to go all over. The States, Japan – he was always out in Japan. Brazil. Singapore. Mexico. On top of the European trips. But his passport was nearly blank.'

'What did they say at his work?' asks Ian. 'Maybe the bank did the visas or something.'

'I don't think it works like that,' says Alastair. 'But that's another thing. We checked at his office and they don't have any record of Rob.'

'That's ridiculous,' says Ian. 'Where was he working, then? He must have been doing something to pay for the flat and the car and everything.'

Alastair has been puzzling over exactly this question ever since he and Louise went to the NatWest and found themselves back out on the pavement after three minutes. The only answers he can come up with (Rob used the NatWest job as a cover while working for MI5, for a hush-hush arms dealer, for a drug baron) are still ones which he hopes owe far more to hours he's wasted gazing at movies on cable than unsuspectedly honed intuition. 'I just don't know,' he says. 'That's one of the reasons why, and I know this sounds stupid but there didn't seem any other option really, so what we've done, I mean it wasn't my idea originally, it was Louise who really made the running on this, but I must say, I do think it's quite sensible if you think about it, so what we've done, you see, is hire a, well, a private detective.'

'Fucksake.'

'Christ.' Ian gives him a little smile. 'And what's your dick like? What has your dick told you? What have you learned from your dick?'

'Ah, well, you see, he's only just started but we, Louise and I, saw him for an update yesterday and he's already found out something about that chap Maddox, the lawyer. Concentrating on him, you see, because Maddox probably knows more than he lets on, and maybe could even have helped Rob get a new identity, if that's really what Rob's done. Anyroad up, Mr Hilton, that's the detective, he drew a blank with an official approach, a phone call that is, but then he went undercover, you see, and caught up with Maddox in the evening, in the Coach and Horses. He got talking to Maddox, got Maddox talking about Rob, and it turns out that Maddox thinks he knew Rob rather well. Although he didn't even know him as Rob. Maddox kept calling him Mac.'

'Mac?' says Graham. 'Fucksake, that's even worse than Bobby.'

'I know. Mac.' Alastair's shoulders give an involuntary squirm of distaste. 'But from what Mr Hilton gathered, Rob was part of a crowd that went to the Coach and Horses and then often ended up back in Bateman Street. For a smoke. Apparently, Rob was well known among Maddox and his buddies for his high-strength grass.'

'Aye,' says Graham. 'He got that right, at any rate.'

Alastair squeezes his hands between his legs and leans forward. 'But did either of you ever come across Maddox?' he asks, anxiety pitching his voice up an octave. 'Surely we'd have met him, or at least Rob would have mentioned him if he was this big drinking and smoking pal?'

'Boy never said anything to me about any Maddox,' says Graham. Ian just shakes his head.

Alastair gives his hands another squeeze then takes a deep breath. Here goes. 'Another weird thing that came out of the conversation is that it was only recently Maddox realised Rob was in banking. Presumably when Rob asked him for whatever legal help Maddox has given him. Most of the time Maddox has known Rob, though that can't be long, he has thought that Rob was . . .' He's going to have to say it. '. . . some kind of artist.'

'You what?' Graham looks as if someone's just said something very nasty about him. 'What kind of *artist*, exactly?'

'Well, Maddox seemed to think that Rob was . . . of the struggling variety.'

'Oh, aye? And what kind of thing was he supposed to be struggling at?'

'Maddox seemed to think Rob's most recent project was a way-out, experimental thing about his bed or some such.'

'Really? Really? Is that right.' Graham frowns at his pint. 'So did this Maddox say anything else about Rob's artistic career?'

'Er, yes.'

'Aha?'

'What Maddox said is that Rob did give the impression that he made ends meet by . . . doing illustrations and things for magazines . . .'

'Fuck*sake*.'

'. . . and sometimes teaching English as a foreign language . . .'

'Jesus Christ almighty.'

'. . . which, according to Maddox, Rob had first done to get by when he lived in Paris . . .'

'Jesus.'

'. . . in a flat off the rue de la Réunion . . .'

'Christ.'

'. . . with a girl called Claire.'

'Woah.'

And to think that he had been only a bit pissed off because he might not have a trendy flat in Soho to visit any longer. And that there's still this part of him that envies Rob as well, just to screw with his head even more.

Ian nudges open the cubicle door, back-heels it shut, takes out his wallet then the wrap in his wallet. Yes, all right, this is a Saturday, but it's a one-off and bollocks to the rule in the first place. He sorts out a line on his mirror and leans over it, straw at the ready. Hell with it . . .

. . . What it is, what it is, what it is is that Rob needed to boast and clearly thought his own life didn't sound exciting enough, so he nicked the artist bit from Graham and got the rest from him. Naturally enough, for who else could provide such a rich supply of impressive exotica? And, given that he nicked Claire for a mention as well, erotica. And there was him assuming all these years that Rob must have been running up a tally of conquests like a Test match score, Rob never having been keen on anything that might smack of the long term. But maybe not, though. Maybe not, maybe not, maybe not. Backing up the new theory about Rob's empty paternoster.

Ian sniffs. Time to get back. 'Poor guy,' he whispers, smiling as he packs away the gubbins. 'That poor guy.'

3

'OH, SURE, EVERYTHING'S COOL'

Sunday evening

Is he making a mistake here?

No. He's phoned Eck, Col, Hermann, Tim, even Marty, and drawn a complete fucking blank with the lot. The more he's thought about it, the more he's certain it has to be somebody Ian knows. One of his teacher mates, maybe. Or, and this is the favourite theory, one of his unwashed fucking hippie neighbours from Bonnington Square – doubtless the kind who tries to impress women by teaching them how to fucking juggle. Aye, right – soon as he finds out who it is, the boy'll be having his balls to play with, that's for fucking certain.

Graham is hunched over the steering wheel of the decaying Golf as if he's driving through a heavy snowfall, although it's a crisp, clear evening, and he's not driving anywhere because he's parked outside a big, red mansion block in St John's Wood, and he's leaning over the steering wheel so that he can just see the mansion block's main door where, if Claire's right, Ian should be appearing in a few minutes.

Sundays used to be great with Jenny. Lie-in, coffee and croissants in bed, read the papers, a shag maybe, then a bath and out for a walk, or just muck about and watch stuff on the telly. He assumed they were merely normal at the time, but now all those uneventful Sundays with Jenny are pangfully cherishable, highlights that he had no idea were going to be highlights until after they'd happened, highlights he has to replay again and again and again.

Graham has another peer through the windscreen at the mansion block's entrance – nobody there – then tries to relax back in his seat, because his neck is giving him terrible gyp. Nearly a quarter of an hour he's been sitting here in the Golf, waiting for Ian to come out – fifteen minutes that have managed to be both boring and fraught, but very much of a piece with a day that has been, in stark contrast to those remembered Sundays with Jenny, utterly fucking shite. Having started with a panic attack a second after he awoke, today went from worse to worst. The first couple of hours he tried desperately hard to be normal – made himself breakfast (which reminded him of Jenny), bought *Scotland on Sunday* and the *Chronicle* (and left both unread, since reading the Sunday papers would have reminded him of Jenny), went for a walk (which reminded him of Jenny) – but by midday he'd run out of steam, and it was all he could do to sit down in the kitchen and brace himself for what he knew would be a dark afternoon of the soul. Which it certainly was . . . Until he finally managed to get his head out of his hands and his arse into gear and have another go at finding out who this J is.

Ian's answerphone was on, but Graham was determined to leave the flat, so he'd risked the car and driven down to Vauxhall anyway. Then waited outside Ian's place for a full hour until Claire turned up, carrying two bulging Sainsbury's bags and looking none too chuffed. She's all right, Claire, if you like the pointy-nosed, boyish type. No idea what the body's like, though, because every time he's met her she's been wearing a floaty dress or a smocky number, just to add to that chorister look. So he'd given her a couple of minutes, then invited himself in, coming up with the line that he had to see Ian to return fifty quid he owed him. Aye, *that* would be right. She'd been okay about it, a bit distracted, come to think of it, but happy enough to hunt through Ian's battered notebook for him and find the address where he'd be doing his regular freelance teaching stint. The first Graham had heard about any such thing, but he'd kept cool, because you never knew with Ian, and no way was Graham going to be the one who fucked up and alerted Claire to what could be Ian's regular freelance bit on the side. Aye, he'd kept his cool, said he'd have to dash and got the fuck out of Bonnington Square's strange wee hippie ghetto, gunning the Golf up Vauxhall Bridge Road until the engine began to rebel and the speedometer almost touched thirty.

Fucking car. Still, better to be sitting in it than hanging around outside waiting for Ian to . . . That's him now, marching out with a poly bag slung over his shoulder. And heading this way.

Ian still hasn't noticed the car or him inside the car when Graham stops him in his tracks by the simple method of swinging the door out in front of him, making Ian do a sudden Riverdance step to the side.

'What the . . . Jesus, Graham, what the hell are you doing here?'

'Waiting for you, the fuck do you think?' It strikes Graham that he's at a vague disadvantage sitting in the car with Ian looking down at him like this. Trying to ignore the fact that his body obviously doesn't want to do it, Graham clambers out. 'It has to be someone you know,' he says.

'Graham, I've told you . . .'

'J. Somebody you know whose name begins with J.'

'Yeah, you did mention this before, and I've . . .'

'You hoakay here, my frenn?'

There's this dodgy-looking boy come out of the same mansion block and right up to Ian. He must be the freelance assignment although he looks more like an apprentice waiter than someone over here to improve his vocabulary. Trying his best to look hard, though, coming right up, planting himself in front of him.

'Oh, sure, everything's cool,' Ian says. 'This is Graham, he's a friend of mine. Graham, this is Ram . . .'

'Johnny,' the waiter says, and starts to return his stare.

'Johnny, is it? Johnny. Well, very nice to meet you, *Johnny*.'

Ian has three grams of coke on his person and he wouldn't put it past his pupil to have a knife on his. Two very good reasons for him to step between the two of them before this develops into anything. 'Now, Graham,' Ian says, as he makes a move forward, but that's all he has time to say before Graham pushes him back while keeping up his playground staring match.

'You never told me you had a friend called *Johnny*. So how's your sex life, *Johnny*?'

Johnny looks understandably puzzled by the content and tone of the question. He continues to examine Graham's eyes, then he says, with worrying calm, 'Very good.'

'Is *that* right? And what's the name of the lucky lady? It is a lady, I presume.'

'*Qué?*'

This, Ian notes to himself, has to stop now. 'Get a grip, Graham,' he says. 'You're making a . . .'

'Just having a wee conversation here about your friend Johnny's romantic life.'

Graham steps forward. Jesus Christ, the two of them really are squaring up. Before he can have second thoughts, Ian darts behind Graham and puts his arms around him, as if he's executing a Heimlich manoeuvre or an abrupt rear entry. Ian has just enough time to register Johnny starting to smile and, in the background, Johnny's sulky girlfriend shuffling out of the main door – and wearing, Ian notices, clothes – before he feels Graham's elbow thump him below the ribs.

'Huh,' Ian hears himself say as he feels the air rushing out of his lungs, then his feet giving way beneath him. Next thing he knows, he's sitting on the pavement and forgetting to breathe. Ian coughs, splutters, grabs air in his throat with the long, dry gasp of a dying man, and gathers his wits just in time to look up and see Graham suddenly stagger back, clutching his face and yelling incoherently, into the side of the car.

'*Muy bien*,' Johnny says, nodding approval at the silver canister in his right hand. 'You hoakay?' he asks while he helps Ian to his feet.

'Sure, fine,' gasps Ian.

'Your frenn, huh?' Johnny smiles at Graham, who is still leaning back against his car and moaning behind his hands.

'Yeah . . . yeah, my friend.'

'Mad man. Hey. You.' Johnny moves over to Graham and shakes him by the shoulder. Graham replies with a high squawk. 'You wanna know my girl? You wanna know? See.' Johnny beckons the sulky girl towards him, before grabbing her by the elbow and pushing her towards Graham. 'See. My girl. You like her? You wann her? Eh? Eh?'

Graham seems to be too busy swearing and rubbing his eyes to respond at first, but after a few moments he risks a brief squint.

'And now, my frenn, you are nice and say hello, yes? Thees ees Heidi. Heidi, thees ees mad man. Say hello to Heidi, mad man.'

Graham manages another squint. 'Heidi?' he says. 'Heidi?'

Johnny pokes Graham's shoulder. 'I ask you before, mad man. Say hi.'

'Heidi. Hi.'

The sulky girl lights up a cigarette. 'Fook off,' she says.

There's a nature programme on BBC2 until seven, then the news on Channel 4, Spanish football on Sky Sports One . . .

Alastair lets the TV guide fall to the floor. Clunkingly ironic, but the only thing he can think of which might just have a chance of shaking him out of this dark mood would be a phone call to Rob, arrange to meet for a quiet drink in Soho, maybe saunter up to a Pizza Express for a *quattro formaggi*.

How many nights have he and Rob spent exactly like that? Fifty? A hundred?

'A lot,' Alastair announces to the spurned TV guide. 'Specially before Friday Night Club started up again.' But what was Rob up to all those other nights when they didn't meet up? Alastair forces himself off the sofa and begins to pace the room. 'I have no idea,' he has to confess to a Doisneau poster. 'No idea whatsoever.'

So why is that? Is it just because they're blokes, like Louise said? ('So what exactly have you pair of bosom buddies been talking about for thirty years if you don't have the foggiest idea what he's up to?' she'd asked that first afternoon at Rob's flat when she was upset and got a bit snippy. 'Football? Really, *men* . . . There *is* more to life than Range Rovers, you know.' 'Raith,' he'd replied as pointedly as he'd dared, because he'd felt frustrated by her falling back on a stereotype. 'Raith Rovers.')

No, the bloke thing is a lame excuse, because of course there are men who seem able to conduct deep, candidly confessional friendships with other men. Gary, for instance, who was only a year at the subs' desk before he got that cushy job on a glossy travel mag, but who spent so much of that year describing the troubles then breakdown of his marriage that Alastair felt he'd known Gary all his life. Gary, who had to wipe away the tears at one point when they met up last month and discussed how devastating it was for Gary to see little Amber only once a week. Gary, who seems to have a clutch of mates he can rely on and talk to and cry in front of.

So he can't just blame not knowing about parts of Rob's life on being a chap. Nor can he blame it on his own shyness. Nor another potential excuse he's mulled over – one that tried to make something of the way Rob's always had of presenting himself so completely, with a casually debonair assurance, and turn that into a reason for not doubting Rob or quizzing him for further details.

No. Enough with the excuses. It's him, Alastair, who's to blame. Because right from the start, from the moment when Rob came up to him in Torbain Street and wanted to play, he, Alastair, has been so grateful for the fact of the friendship that he hasn't asked or tried for more, not having had the least expectation of getting what he's got. And, it's now pretty obvious, because all the time he's been telling himself that he values Rob, he has never sat down and really thought about Rob. Except maybe when Rob suddenly took up with the hippie crowd at uni, or when Rob upped sticks for London and went his own way for several years, failing to return calls, not relaying new numbers or addresses, while he, Alastair, fretted over and over about what he could have said or done or not said or not done to have caused offence. There. You see? Thinking, really thinking, about his friends is clearly something he does only when things go wrong. Taking everything for granted the rest of the time. Like electricity. Being alive, even.

Now that he does have to think about it again, what he always blithely assumed was a best-pals thing with Rob clearly emerges as amounting to not much more than mucking around together, the adult equivalent of hunting for Jerry soldiers in the woods. Fair enough, Rob was good about it two years back when Alastair got upset a few times after his mother died, but that was Rob being good about it, and, for all their three-decade heritage, that was also Alastair asking a lot of Rob and probably in rather an embarrassing manner. Not that he didn't appreciate it, of course he did. But when Rob wanted to talk about his parents' accident, who did Rob talk to? Louise. Not him.

However. There is this in his defence, that it does seem more natural to open up to a girl. Rob must just be like him and find it easier to talk seriously to women. Who've always seemed to him somehow more . . . *evolved* than men – graceful, white-robed Athenians to his own tribe of bearskinned barbarians.

Typical mummy's boy, he thinks as he enters the kitchen – worshipping women. So much so that, even though he has always admired Rob – marvelling at Rob's success, being amazed at Rob's latest romantic escapade or the size of Rob's Christmas bonus – that doesn't really compare to the complete adoration he has felt for Fiona and Cathy. And he's told them stuff he'd never tell Rob. Look at when he was at school, how he talked to Fiona, not Rob, about his secret ambition to do English at uni. Or, much later, how he blurted it all out only to Cathy about not really being in love with Rhona.

Alastair brings out the little wooden box from its hiding place behind the coffee jar. He pauses before he opens it because he's reminding himself not to rewrite his past here. For all that he's just gone on about his great openness with Fiona and Cathy, he has to remember that there was something else going on with Fiona and Cathy, and he wasn't at all honest and open about that something else with either of them or himself . . .

Alastair shudders. Yes. Sometimes it's only right to have low expectations.

4

'IT'S LIKE JEFFREY ARCHER'

Monday evening

'I live in Warsaw but I am living near the station of Dalston Kingsland.'

'Very good. Miroslav?'

'I live in Bratislava but I am living in Shepherd's Bush.'

'Excellent. Sayuri?'

'I live in Yokohama but I am living in Hendon.'

Of course Hendon. Who'd've thought that London would have a thriving Japanese community and that it would be based in Hendon? Not Ian, that's for sure. And why Hendon? Having studied the map – because he always does in a new city, to avoid looking like a bamboozled tourist – he has come up with a theory about this, which states that the first, intrepid Japanese colonists had to keep going, past Kilburn, Kensal Rise and Brondesbury, past Willesden and Harlesden, beyond Cricklewood and Dollis Hill, to find sanctuary in the first bit of London they could stay in and pronounce.

Two minutes to six. 'Excellent, Sayuri,' says Ian. 'Well done, everybody. We will continue with the present tenses tomorrow. Workbook exercises seven and eight for homework, please. See you all at five tomorrow.'

The eight members of the new intermediate class have just trooped out when Chantal appears in the doorway. She's wearing a bright, white T-shirt, a little pinkish cardigan thing that emphasises her breasts' upsetting promise, and a tight black skirt that stops short of those knees, so cute he could draw a face on them.

'May I come in?' she asks with what could be a coquettish smile.

'Of course,' says Ian, who has already scraped back his chair and sprinted round to the front of his desk. He props himself up against it, his hands behind him, in an attempt to look cool and casual. Chantal, meanwhile, has shut the door behind her and sashayed forward, then does her own leaning-against-the-desk manoeuvre. A nanosecond's glimpse is all Ian needs to check out the sheen of her auburn hair, the elegance of her profiled nose, the well, the everything about her. What a complete and utter babe. A complete and utter . . .

'Thank you for the lesson today,' she says. 'Now I think I understand "like".'

'That's good,' says Ian, despite the fact that his mouth seems to have lost all its saliva and that, behind his back, her fingertips seem to be touching his. If his hand remains absolutely motionless, she might not notice and this moment will continue.

'Now I like to study like,' she says. 'And I like studying it.'

'Good.'

'So I want to say thank you.'

There's a chance he's got this hopelessly wrong, but if he had to bet on it, he'd have to say that the tips of her fingers moved a fraction of a millimetre against his just there. And again. She can't think his hands are a book or part of the desk, surely? Surely? Ian turns slightly towards her. Chantal turns slightly towards him. Her fingers are still touching his. Now he looks her in those big, brown eyes. She returns the look, and, as she holds his gaze, her soft, full lips part. And, no mistake about it, her fingertips are moving, with startling delicacy, across his knuckles.

Oh, Christ, Ian thinks. Oh Jesus Christ almighty. She's still holding his gaze when, somehow or other, their hands suddenly clasp each other and, somehow or other, her eyes get closer and closer to his, and he feels his lips meet hers. They are soft and warm and sumptuous.

The door clicks.

They jump apart and stare at the door as if it has burst into flames.

'You did close it, Chantal?'

'Yes. I am certain I . . . It is the wind, perhaps?'

'Yes. Yes, maybe the wind.' What with one thing and another, Ian can feel his heart banging away at his ribcage. If that was somebody at the door and that somebody was Foxsmith, then he could be in a bit of bother. Although it happens all the time, language schools have to keep up the pretence of going through the motions of frowning on teachers getting off with their charges. A nice quartet of phrasal verbs there, Ian finds himself noting. Still, it wasn't as if they were spotted, if indeed they were spotted at all, shagging on his desk. He glances at Chantal. Now that, thinks Ian, is one hell of a thought.

Chaz has assumed the air of an art director who's been around the block a few times, a veteran who can appraise an illustration when he sees one. He performs another close inspection of the businessman standing underneath a light bulb.

Some time later, Chaz delivers his verdict. 'Yeah,' he says. He scratches the side of his orange Lycra top and nods once. 'Cool,' he says. 'Yeah, I'm into the . . . the vibe, yeah?'

Breathing in. And breathing out. 'Good,' says Graham.

Chaz turns to his twelve-year-old assistant. 'Wotchoo think, Tamsin, man?'

Tamsin scratches the back of her T-shirt. 'Yeah,' she says. 'Yeah, it's got that, that . . .'

Chaz examines the drawing again. 'Vibe,' he declares.

'Vibe,' agrees Tamsin.

'Yeah, I'm into the . . . yeah, this is a vibe I can big up to.'

. . . eight, nine, ten. 'Good,' says Graham. He's about to

add that he'll be sending Chaz the invoice but thinks better of it, because that would be an oration which would obviously mark him down as a real fucking has-been . . . And keeping calm, keeping calm. 'See you later,' Graham says, and he tries to shake Chaz's hand – with no success, because Graham's conventional move is confounded by the angled palm of Chaz's soul-brother clasp.

Graham hirples out of the *Business Matters* office, stroking his sorer left eye, trying very hard not to move his neck or goad his back, and feeling as young and with it as a golf commentator. He negotiates a urine-scented flight of stairs and steps out on to Camden High Street.

'Speh some chynge?' immediately drones a slumped urchin.

Just fucking tremendous – accosted by a . . . human being with real problems. And one who is providing another test of the new resolution. The new Graham. 'Sure,' says Graham. He fiddles in his trouser pockets and gingerly lowers a fifty-pence piece on to the urchin's sleeping bag. 'Good luck.'

'Chairs, mite.'

You see. That wasn't so bad, was it?

He is pondering what life must be like for the sort of folk who are always being nice to tramps – expensive, presumably – and picking his way through burger-bar debris when he is approached by a small, old man vibrating inside a greasy pin-stripe suit.

'Thing is, pal,' says this raddled creature to the person standing invisibly behind Graham's left shoulder, 'ah wantay buy a submarine. Could you see your wye fur tae contribyootin a wee . . . contribyooshin? Towards the cost, like?'

The tramp with the allegedly amusing line in patter was one of the old Graham's pet hates. But this is the new Graham, and the new Graham should be thinking at this point that at least the guy is putting a bit of effort into his job. Graham rummages inside his trouser pockets again. He brings out a pound coin. Oh well. He places the coin on the old man's blackened palm, wishes him luck and, having narrowly failed to avoid the outskirts of a remarkably large, coiled, possibly human turd, has to rub the side of his shoe against the edge of the pavement before resuming his trek to the Tube.

Sudden and heavy raindrops are beginning to add their own stains to the pavement's pocks of old gum. As he ups the pace, Graham finds himself wondering just how the citizens of Camden achieve that distinctive Camden look. It must be a co-ordinated effort so that everyone knows when and which dustbins should be emptied on to the streets. Probably through some fucking rota from the fucking council . . . Stop that.

Okay. So.

Keep calm.

Keep calm and be nice.

'Seer. Oh, seer.'

A dishevelled woman, carrying a baby and wearing an unlikely number of dull-patterned skirts, has materialised in front of him. She's thrusting a piece of cardboard at his face. 'Homless form Sarajevo,' claims the scrawl on the cardboard. No, no. That is not on. Graham shakes his head and pain clobbers his neck. Fucking *hell*. When he opens his eyes again, the woman's still standing there. Well, you never know, he thinks, resigning himself to it. She might really be a refugee. And even if she is part of a beggarly mafia, she's clearly not doing too well. He shoves his hand in his pocket and gives her the rest of his change – a few coppers and two 5p coins. The woman mutters what he trusts is a thank-you. The rain is getting heavier.

'Skews may.'

It's a teenage girl standing in the doorway of a trendy hairdresser's. Her own hair is spiky and sort of green. She's also got the regulation torn army fatigues and, to complete the image, she's holding a thin, black dog on a leash of string. 'Goh any cheh hange?' she whines.

Crusties. Another of the old Graham's pet hates. What with

crusties being lazy wankers whose great protest against society is not having a bath. And who obviously have a way of looking at him and seeing some fucking old guy with a sad, orthodox, humdrum life. 'I'm not some fucking *suit*,' he always wants to explain to crusties. After pinning them up against the nearest wall. 'I'm an artist, for fucksake. An *artist*. What do you want? A smock? A fucking *beret*?' But this is the new Graham. He forces himself to offer this one a rueful smile. 'I've run out,' he says.

The crusty girl scratches the dog's ears. Then she looks up and returns his smile. 'I hope you get cancer,' she tells him sweetly.

Fretting over this several hours later in the relative safety of the flat, Graham will conclude that he just wasn't ready for a fight, that this was a blow that simply caught him unawares, like the punch that killed Houdini. As it is, he stands there, gazing forlornly at the still-smiling girl for what feels like minutes, the surprised hurt growing into a sense that he's utterly, abjectly on his own here, abandoned in this endless, endless city teeming with millions upon millions of strangers.

He blinks away tears. Move on, he tells himself. Move away. He heads towards the Tube in a capsule of misery, all but unaware of the rain, the mêlée at the pedestrian crossing, the nudge from behind that forces him to step into a roadside puddle, the sweeping, flailing arms of the two down-and-outs who launch themselves into an infuriated and inept fight near the Tube entrance, the throng at the Tube entrance, and the old biddy sporting a Biggles helmet who veers wildly through the throng, stops abruptly in front of him, jabs at his ankles with her shopping basket's wee wheels, mutters, 'Rude, rude, rude,' and, when he replies with a baffled 'Sorry', hisses, 'Bloody Scotch' and fends him off with a final sharp shove of the basket into his shins.

His automatic pilot guides him towards the ticket machine. He has no change.

He'll try the ticket machine that takes notes.

The ticket machine that takes notes says 'EXACT MONEY ONLY'.

The ticket booth is besieged by a gang of excitable youngsters who might be trying to ask for travelcards in what might be Italian . . .

The escalator is blocked by a group of triangularly obese Americans.

The concourse at the bottom of the escalator is extremely crowded.

The electronic display says that smoking is forbidden but gives no information about the next High Barnet train.

A grey-faced official emerges and warily yells out the news that there has been an incident at Euston so all Northern Line services have been suspended indefinitely.

Jenny, thinks Graham as he stands in the shifting mob, his shoulders slumping as he gives in at last. Jenny. Where are you, Jenny? Maybe if he stands here long enough – a month, six months, a year – Jenny will pass by . . .

Carried along by the outraged scrum, Graham is swept back up the escalator and out into the rain.

Credit to Davina, she's not giving up yet. 'But I do think,' she says, only a slight tremble in her voice, 'that this is a superb review. Extremely well written, very acute, funny, I mean, yes, it is negative, but . . .'

'But nothing,' says the editor. 'Who is this reviewer anyway?'

'John Updike? He's, he's, he's one of America's . . .'

'A Yank, eh? I might have known it.'

Like every one of his co-workers, Alastair is looking at his screen but eavesdropping on the heated literary debate taking place behind him. Making only the slightest clicking on his keyboard, he gently types out a message to Barry – 'any idea wot this is abt?' – and tenderly presses the Send key.

'As far as I can see, Davina, this is a prime example of you and your literary chums ganging up on someone out of sheer snobbishness and jealousy.'

'Really and truly, Jonathan, I don't . . .'

'Davina. I have spoken on this matter. Several times now. So you will put this review in the bin where it belongs and find me a critic our readers will like. A critic our readers will *understand*. A critic our readers might just have *heard* of.'

MESSAGE has flashed up on Alastair's screen. He gives the Receive key a soft push. 'big trauma re review of new j archer,' starts Barry's message. 'god knows how but davina managed to get john updike to do the piece. only trouble is, updike has slagged off j archer s/thing rotten and last nite ed was at his 1st j archer party – shepherd's pie and krug, acc/ding to b/bttle. so ed wants updike rev spiked, nice rev of book by his new best friend in its place, and d threatening to resign. again.'

'But Jonathan,' says Davina with a plaintive, dying fall.

'Spoken.'

'I.'

'Spoken.'

The next thing Alastair knows, the editor has breenged past his desk, dislodging sheaves of layouts in the process, so Alastair is busily gathering these together when his phone rings. 'Subs.'

'Alastair, it's Louise. Is this an okay time to call?'

''Course. Hold on a moment, though . . . Right. There we are. Any news?'

'No. No news. I was having a bit of a relapse, so this is me just phoning up for some TLC.'

'I'll do my best, Louise. What's the matter?'

'Oh, only everything. It's like splitting up with someone. Well, it *is* splitting up with someone, but with an extra little twist to make you feel even worse. I mean, I try to keep up the chirpiness when other people are around, and that does help, like putting on a smile can make you feel there's something to smile about. Sometimes I can even kid myself that I'm coping. But then I get back to that flat and it all hits me. I mean, why am I even in that flat? The work could be a drag and I had a commuting relationship, at least that's what I thought I had, but I did love it in New York. I had this lovely little apartment on MacDougall, right in the heart of the Village . . . But here, I get back to Bateman Street, as late as possible, and I close the door behind me. And I feel like throwing up. Really. I mean, it's a physical thing. Why does nobody warn you about this when you're a child? That it'll be so bad it makes you physically ill? Oh, Alastair, where's Mr Buggles when I need him?'

'Sorry, Louise, Mr?'

'I forgot. That was another musketeer. Silly me. But that's what I am, isn't it? Just plain *silly*.'

'That's about the last adjective I'd use to describe you.'

'I dunno. Dictionaries of the future should illustrate the word "schmuck" with little pictures of me. Yes. A real mugshot. I mean, how could I be taken in by such a pathetic liar? Fair enough, if the man was an international criminal or a master of disguise, then, you know, fine, I was conned by an expert and what can you do? But what really gets to me is that I was quite happily taken in by a twit.'

'Rob isn't a twit, Louise.'

'No? What kind of person pretends to be a great globetrotter and, according to his passport, never leaves his own postal district? Or who explains that despite being this great globetrotter, he can't come to see me in New York because he's wanted by the FBI? A twit, that's what kind. So how come I didn't suss him out as a twit? Because I must be an even bigger twit.'

'I know what you mean, Louise,' says Alastair, and indeed he does, having spent several nights lying awake until the wee small hours, the pillow itching, the alarm clock ticking louder and louder, the thought running round and round his head that he used to know, deep down, that Rob was at least embellishing the truth when he said his dad had invented a new kind of hovercraft or that Daleks were real and he'd seen one in Lancaster. But when Rob had boasted about having a steamy affair with a sexily boss-eyed CNN reporter or getting off with a woman who had a surgically enhanced bottom in Brazil, then he, Alastair, had believed that this was what had happened. Which has led him to what seems, particularly at three in the morning, the terrifyingly clear conclusion that his own perceptiveness and judgment peaked when he was eight and have been on a downward curve ever since. 'But,' Alastair continues, remembering how his subsequent pep talks to himself have gone, 'it's not us being twits. If someone tells you something, you believe them. Unless the person tells you that they're Elvis or that they've just come back from Jupiter, and then you know they're mad.'

'But Bobby's lies were so rubbish, that's the thing.'

'Yes, but my point is, not really unbelievable rubbish.'

'That's exactly what they were.'

Alastair is trying to think of a way to continue his argument when Davina stomps past, muttering theatrically to herself. Aha. 'It's like Jeffrey Archer,' he says.

'Great. I've been going out with Kirkcaldy's answer to Jeffrey Archer. Not a comfort.'

'Listen, though. Jeffrey Archer's got away with all manner of terrible lies. About going to Oxford, about that prostitute, about that story he copied, anything. The ironic thing is that the crap lying has helped Jeffrey Archer get to the position where he's rich and famous and a target for investigation. But if the lying is done by someone like Rob, and the lies aren't outrageous, then who's to suspect anything's wrong?'

'You've been concocting this over a few joints, haven't you?'

He decides not to let on about his three-in-the-morning frets. 'Well, yes, as it happens.'

'Lucky man. This is a bit cheeky, but I'm going to suggest it anyway.'

'Suggest away.'

'You still on for Wednesday evening?'

'Our confab? Absolutely.'

'Would you mind bringing round a little bit of your grass with you?'

'Delighted.'

'First few days of this I tried drink, then coke with your friend Ian, so now I'd like to give hash a bash.'

'Worth a shot, I'd say.'

'Thanks, Alastair. You're a brick.'

'You too, Louise. See you Wednesday.'

'Another hot date?' says Barry, who popped his head over the top of his terminal as soon as Alastair put down the phone. 'Al, you dog.'

'Just good friends, Barry.'

'Aaaaaah, of course.'

5

'IS THAT A COMPLIMENT?'

Wednesday evening

Of course, this is exactly what he needs. Absolutely superb. Thanks, God.

'Most, ah most, to be, as it were, regretted. Very.' With a final, sorrowful shake of his head, Foxsmith leaves the classroom and Ian staring at the sheet of paper on his desk – a course assessment form handed in by Monique, who has suddenly left the school a week early, stomping off to Heathrow and a plane back to civilisation.

What has he done to upset her? Clearly something bad, going by the stuff she's written in the Remarks bit and the series of vitriolic zeroes she's awarded him. And this after he went to all that trouble reorganising her digs. Jesus.

The only explanation he can come up with is ridiculous – that Monique has clomped off in a huge huff because she got wind of his flirting with Chantal. Which means that Monique did have a crush on him *and* she thought she was in with a chance. Either that or she and Chantal were embroiled in a lesbian love pact. No, not that. Definitely not that. Maybe Chantal told her about the kiss. After all, girls tell girls everything. So Monique throws a wobbly, chucks in the school and runs back home. Making damned sure in the process to put him in the shit by telling Foxsmith that Ian Murray is the worst teacher in the world and the very spawn of Satan. Cheers, Monique. You troll.

When the door clicked. That might have been her, or someone she knows – someone anyway, and spying on them . . .

Well, however it happened, it's happened and the consequences are far from good. Foxsmith is bound to have reams of desperate teachers' CVs lying around his office and, unless he failed to interpret Foxsmith's meaning correctly, that's him now one mistake or one bad report away from being kicked out and replaced. And sent scurrying off to one of the really shitty cowboy schools where he'd be lucky to get five quid an hour doing the present perfect thirty, forty hours a week. She has pissed on his chips (recent action). She has pissed on his chips (in the past and time not specified). She has pissed on his chips (action that started in the past and continues into the present). Yeah. That little witch has pissed on his chips, all right.

Don't panic, Mr Mainwaring, he thinks. This is a blip, no more. He'll be fine, everything will be all right . . .

No it won't.

It's the Fear. Oh Christ. It's been stalking him. And now it's beginning to close in.

He's got looks and he's got brains and he's got fluent French, excellent Spanish, good German . . . And Claire's beautiful and . . .

Ian hugs himself tight. He could have a line, that might work. Or it could just sharpen the dread.

He can't stay here. He has to go. But where? Where can he go? Where will he be safe?

Rob's . . . He can't go to Rob's. Rob's gone. Maybe this is what happened to Rob. He got the Fear and had to run off. If that's it then he's not going to cast any blame on the poor guy because nobody can mess with the Fear. You think you're fine. You think you're in control. Then along comes the Fear . . .

Oh Christ. Oh Christ. Oh Christ.

He's got to get out of here.

A friend of someone he knows and his name starts with J.
A friend of someone he knows and his name starts with J.

A friend of someone he knows and ... Whoever it is, the bastard is screwing Jenny, and for that the bastard will pay. Initial J. Initial J ...

Stop that. He has a job to finish off. And he is a man of steel. He forces his attention back to the nearly finished drawing on his workbench. The drawing stars an inspired-looking gent in a stripey suit, holding a finger to his chin and standing below an enormous, floating light bulb with a pound sign for a filament. A day's work and it'll mean half a page in the December issue of *Management Monthly* and, more to the point, a cheque for £150. He tries not to compare that figure with the sums on his invoices eight, nine years back when wheelbarrows of cash were being tipped into his lap, morning, noon and night. Aye, well ... He was about to remind himself that money doesn't grow on trees, but that's exactly what money did in the grand old days of yore, when he took all of thirty minutes to do the new logo of the Oakham Building Society (an oak above a squiggle), thereby achieving his best-ever rate of £6,000 an hour.

The phone rings.

'Hi, Graham, I've got some very good news for you.'

'Audrey. How are you?'

'Oh, the usual, you know. So thing is, I ran into Marty last night at the Cantaloupe and I told him about you having an exhibit and so on and so forth, and he's on for it, really up for it, really keen, all the rest of it.'

'That's excellent, Audrey.' Not that it's easy to tell, but it sounds like Audrey's being normal, so either she doesn't know about his fight with Jason, or she has heard about it and Jason's getting the blame. 'So what did Marty say exactly?'

'Oh, most of it was the usual blah-di-blah-di-blah, but he does want to host your thing in D:Zine's reception.'

'Really? Great. When?'

'Starting next Friday if you can manage it. Could be up for

a while maybe and Marty'll lay on a launch do, party-type thing, get a sponsor for the drinks, blah blah blah.'

'Fucking hell. Thanks, Audrey. Thanks a lot, honestly.'

'Oh, whatever.'

'No, I really appreciate it. I don't know how to repay the favour.'

'Oh, blah blah *blah*. Tell you what, buy me a drink if you want. You doing anything Saturday?'

'Buying you a drink. How about eight at the Cantaloupe?'

'Sure.'

'Maybe we could get a bite to eat as well.'

'Sure, sure, whatever. And, you know, give Marty a call.'

Moments later, Graham is making two entries in his normally barren diary. 'Skibble dibble dip dibble,' he sings to the tune of 'What A Difference A Day Makes' as he turns back to the drawing of the businessman underneath the sterlinged light bulb. 'Skeeble dee dibble deedoo.'

'. . . Oh, blimey, have I been bogarting this?'

'Ta. No, you haven't. Lawks a mercy, it's strong, though. What is it?'

'Home-grown mixed with some stuff I got from Rob. Bobby. Mac . . . Mac, I ask you. Anyway, him. Kind of skunk, I think . . . What were we talking about?'

'Can't remember. Hold on . . . Half the Cabinet being Scottish, Scottish accents on adverts . . . there being ways of telling someone's Protestant or Catholic . . . Yes, what on earth was that all about, Alastair?'

'. . . Ummmm, right. Got it. Well, back home, things like your name or which school you went to are giveaways. Even looks. So, in Scotland, most of the actresses and newsreaders and so on are called things like Annemarie Rafferty or Madeleine Murphy or . . . or Isabella Ravioli, because the good-looking people are Irish or Italian. Hence the ET joke.'

'What ET joke?'

'All right, Louise, I'm going to tell you the ET joke. This is it coming up, all right? The ET joke. Starting now. How do you know ET is a Protestant?'

'Okay. How *do* you know ET is a Protestant?'

'Because he looks like one.'

Louise frowns and takes a deep breath. 'Right. So Mackenzie was fanciable because he was Catholic, is that the kind of thing you're saying?'

'... Rob is Protestant, Louise. Otherwise he'd have gone to different schools. And wouldn't have a name like Mackenzie.'

'... Oh. So why did he tell me he was Catholic?'

'Did he?'

'Yip. Lapsed, but Catholic.'

'Who knows? ... Maybe he thought Catholic was more interesting. Why did he come up with any of his stories? ... Mind you, fair enough, he has cheekbones so he doesn't look terribly Protestant. Me, I'm more typical.'

'... You know, Alastair, I think you might almost qualify as an honorary girl.'

'Is that a compliment?'

'Usually. Not sure in this case because I was referring to ... yes, your less than high self-esteem. Most men I know, they think they're God's gift, but you, you're like one of us, talking yourself down, assuming everyone else is better than you, all that. Here. Take this.'

'Eh thang yaw. That's not low self-esteem, Louise. That's me not being completely crazy.'

'Tish and tosh, Alastair Carr. You're a catch.'

'And that's definitely the grass talking.'

'Possible because I am feeling nice and woozy, but the fact remains. A catch.'

'Don't be daft.'

'Not being. For a start, unlike most men your age, you're not burdened by a wife and two veg. Or fucked up by an ex-wife and two veg. And you're sane, normal, solvent and straight.'

'Yes. Shame about being a bald, ginger runt.'

'Honorary girl, Alastair. You're nice looking, you're in good shape, bald, yes, but at a curious time in the history of men's fashion when it's cool to have no hair. I bet you're a right little heartbreaker on the quiet.'

'Just to show that you're well meaning but completely wrong – exactly the opposite.'

'Uh-huh? What about the women in your office? Or your chum's ex you were talking about? The one you took to your works bash?'

'You mean Jenny? Well, I didn't do her any favours by taking her to that party, I can tell you.'

'Why?'

'Oh, complicated. It was a real shame, though, not just because it worked out badly for her in the end. I was kind of hoping . . .'

'To fuck her?'

'. . . 'Scuse me, Louise. Frog in my throat. No, no, Jenny's way out of my league. No, just that there was a time when we were getting to be quite good friends. And I kind of hoped that we could be again.'

'You don't have any dastardly designs on her? What a man.'

'That's hardly a reason to give me a gold star.'

'Disagree.'

'Blimey, have I been bogarting this?'

'Don't think so. Thanks. Now where were . . . Who can that be? See, that's living in Soho, the one part of London where you don't have the normal London advantage of being spared people popping in on you. I'd better pass this back. Hold on . . .'

'So I was at a loose end and I thought I'd pop in on you. Eck, my man!'

'Hello there, Ian. How're you doing?'

'Oh, you know. Hey, that a jazz cigarette you're smoking?'

'Yes.'

'Okay if I join you kids? But, hey, I wouldn't want to be interrupting anything.'

'Not at all.'

'Find yourself a bit of floor and join Alastair and me in our drug-crazed orgy.'

'*Vraiment formidable.* You have no *idea* how welcome this is.'

6

Thursday evening

'Bog,' Ian explains before heading for the stairs to the basement.

Right, then. This is his chance to have another go with the wee man. He puts on a nice, friendly smile. 'So, Eck, how's it going?'

'Not bad actually, Graham, although I must say that I've been a bit taken aback because according to some of Rob's diaries . . .'

He tunes out as Eck drivels on about his ridiculous investigation, tormenting himself with an image of Jenny's mouth poised over a salami-sized penis, until he forces himself to tune in to Eck again. '. . . for at least five years without any of us knowing.'

'Aye,' he says, nodding sagely, since that seems the kind of thing to do, guessing by Eck's tone. Okay. Now.

Graham's head is going like one of those toy dogs that used to live on the back shelves of cars. It's only a quarter past eight but it's obvious from his reddening face and bellowing voice that Graham must have been raiding his own drinks cabinet before he came out. At first, Alastair had felt rather chuffed that Graham wanted to tweak the routine again and go for a Thursday evening in place of the regular Friday bash, thus giving him, Alastair, the chance, second week running, to have a proper night out rather than one that involves racing over from Canary Wharf to arrive in time for last orders. But now it doesn't seem such a great favour, especially with Rob painfully conspicuous by his absence, Graham drunk, Ian popping up and down to the loos as though his bladder's a walnut, and Alastair beginning to suspect that Graham has some sort of agenda on the go.

'So, then,' says Graham through an ugly, forced grin. 'You heard from Jenny recently?'

'Jenny?' So that's the agenda. Blimey, Graham's looking rough these days. Which only makes him wonder what Jenny saw in Graham in the first place, because, no denying it, he can come across as just a great big galoot. 'Yes,' Alastair says. 'We talked on the phone not so long ago.'

'You seen anything of her?'

'Not for a while.'

'Ever introduce her to any of your pals?'

Well, thinks Alastair, bang goes any pretence of subtlety. 'No,' he says, not, strictly, untruthfully.

'To be a wee bittie more specific,' Graham continues, apparently trying to focus on the ashtray, 'did you ever introduce her to a pal of yours called J something? Like John or Jim. You ever do that, Eck?'

Alastair takes a moment to reassure himself that he won't be lying. 'No, Graham. In fact, I can't think of anyone I'm friendly with whose first name begins with J. Apart from Jenny.'

Graham's glaring at the ashtray now. When he speaks it is with a dangerously clenched tone. 'Taking the pish? Just answer the question, all right?'

'Okay, Graham,' replies Alastair as steadily as he can and hoping that he doesn't sound like a kindergarten teacher. 'No, I have not introduced Jenny to any friend of mine called J something.'

*   *   *

'Hey,' says Ian. 'I've just passed Graham on the stairs. What's with him?'

'Jenny,' says Alastair. 'One minute he was interrogating me about Jenny seeing some man, the next he was stumbling off. To the loo, I presume.'

'Yeah, he didn't say much to me either,' says Ian, choosing to pass over the detail that the few words Graham did utter on the stairs were that Ian was 'fucking charlied up', which is only partly true, him having chopped out only the merest tiny thread on the cistern, just to keep alert. 'By the way, by the way, by the way,' Ian says, 'that was an excellent little time last night at Louise's. I haven't been so stoned since I last had Rob's skunk. And it was very well timed, I can tell you.'

'Trouble at the school, you said.'

'Yeah, big trouble at the school. A student dissed me in a report and they've landed me in the shit.'

'I bet it was a girl who had a crush on you.'

'A gel? With a cwush on me? With *my* weputation?'

'That's *The Fast Show*, isn't it?'

'Didn't know you were a fan, Eck. Hey, how did you guess it was a girl? Apart from my reputation?'

'Because you used they for one person.'

'I did?'

'You did. One student, you said, but *they've* landed me in it. And people unconsciously use they in the singular when they want to avoid an incriminating he or she.'

'Or or or when people don't know the sex of the person. Like when the telephone voice says that the caller refused to leave *their* number.'

'Because there's no equivalent in English of a neutral pronoun, like *on* in French.'

'Eck, you really are quite the cunning linguist. I didn't know.'

'Well, that's one reason I like subbing, I suppose.'

'Kind of like my job in a way.'

'Yes . . . I hope you don't mind my asking, Ian, but is this they an annoying they or an important they?'

'You really want to know?'

7

'CIAO'

Friday afternoon

'Right, then,' says Barry. 'Who's doing what? Derek?'

'Finishing off Josh.'

'Yvonne?'

'Checking Hugo's recipe for pumpkin soup.'

'Alice? Bloody hell, where's Alice gone?'

'Emergency appointment with her reflexologist,' says Yvonne.

'Oh, bloody hell. Al?'

'Trying to get a headline for the latest instalment of Tamara's Caribbean epic.'

'Any luck so far?'

'Well, I have got "No, she went of her own accord" but I don't know if that's rubbish or any good.'

'The former, I think, but don't bin it yet. Any sign of double oh bloody seven?'

'Bond, James Bond?' says Derek. 'I think he's still busy writing his little piece for Arts.'

'So much for our extra bloody sub. How Bluebottle and all the rest of them bloody expect us to do all the bloody work on the shallow end of this bloody paper with only five, make that four, bloody subs I do not bloody know. Okay, then, team. Bottoms on seats, backs to the wall, noses to the grindstone, and we'll all be out of here by Monday.'

Alastair returns to staring at the list of headline ideas in his notebook. Should he even bother to jot down 'Jamaican funk'? No. What he really wants to do is give her another call. It felt so good, talking to her earlier in the week, after he'd dared himself to phone her up. Alastair reaches forward but then his palm stays on the handrest while he gives himself a pep talk. It was great just having that chat, and, yes, of course she is very fanciable but he's not going to let himself fancy her. He's going to behave himself. Because he is quite content as he is and he's fought long and hard to get to the stage where he is quite content as he is. Because if he starts hankering after her, the result will either be unrequited longing or a traumatising no-thank-you. And because there's a very good chance that they could become really good friends – the very thing he needs. And seeing her could provide an antidote to his glooms about Rob, those three-in-the-morning glooms when he's been lying awake and convincing himself that his own attempts at friendship are obviously rubbish. So he wants to be her friend. Yes? Yes. And he's got a good reason for calling her. Yes? Yes.

'Jenny, hi, it's . . .'

'Alastair. How are you?'

'Bit frantic. Not just at the moment, though.' Ignoring his own instructions about bottoms and seats and noses and grindstones, Barry pops his head above his terminal and gives Alastair a scandalised look – eyebrows raised, eyes boggling, mouth pursed as for whistling. Alastair shakes his head and takes cover behind his computer. 'The thing is, Jenny, I thought I should let you know that I saw Graham last night.'

'Oh? And how was he?'

'Well, mainly very keen to quiz me about the chap you were going out with, see if I knew who it could be.'

'Oh God . . . You didn't tell him, did you?'

''Course not, Jenny. But I thought I'd better warn you that Graham's on the case. However. All he knows is that it's someone whose first name starts with J.'

'Yes, Megan told him that, the stupid girl. That must be

from when I mentioned that the one thing you-know-who and I had in common was that our Christian names started with the same letter. Thank goodness I never said anything else about him. If Megan had known, I'm sure she'd have been delighted to tell Graham I'd become the Mata Hari of the *Sunday Chronicle* ... You don't think there's any way Graham'll read any of you-know-who's stuff, do you, and realise it's supposed to be me?'

'How would he realise if nobody tells him?'

'You're right, Alastair. Oh God, though. I just feel so terrible about all of this.'

Alastair takes a deep breath. 'Look, Jenny, if you ever want to get it off your, have a chat about it, just say the word.'

'I might take you up on that offer if you really don't mind.'

This is good, Alastair tells himself. This is going well. So this is no time to bottle out. All he has to do is keep going here and he'll be fine. 'Tell you what, Jenny.' He has to clear his throat. Okay. Keep going. 'First free date in your diary, why don't I cook you supper? Or maybe it'd be wiser if we ordered pizza.'

'As I recall you used to be a dab hand in the kitchen, Alastair. Anyway, it's another unwise offer. You should see my diary. Tumbleweed drifting across it.'

'Nonsense.'

'True.'

Maybe it's only because she's belittling herself but he feels the confidence growing inside him. 'I'm going to call your bluff, Jenny. An evening at my place first free date you have.'

'Tomorrow, Sunday, Monday, Tuesday, no, not Tuesday, but ...'

'See. Tuesday, you're booked ... Tomorrow, then.'

'You sure you're not having to cancel some five-star gallivanting for my sake?'

'Positive. Eight o'clock be okay with you?'

'Perfect. See you tomorrow, Alastair. And thanks. Really.'

'Least I can do. See you tomorrow, Jenny.'

His mouth twitching into a smile, Alastair puts the phone down, fetches out his diary, almost forgets to notice that there's no FNC marked for tonight, and in tomorrow's entry scores a line through 'Gary and Co., Star of India, 8.30' and below it writes 'Jenny, supper at house, 8'. Which is all it will be. All he wants it to be. And the last thing she needs is some other dolt drooling after her.

Alastair turns back to his computer, calls up the unsubbed version of Josh's latest column, and dares himself to reread as much as he can of one of the offending paragraphs.

The lady in my life is looking so gorgeous that I decide their and then that I must have her. Rising from the chair and adjusting the long black skirt, I lead her away to a quiet nuke where I start to carress her breasts with my hands although she is wearing a blouse and a bra. I fall to my knees in front of her and I keep carressing her breasts with my hands while I press my face against her skirt and I am feeling that I

No thanks to the prose, Alastair is visited by a vivid image of Josh kneeling and trying to bury his face in Jenny's crotch. It is a picture that makes him feel like he's just drunk old milk. However. At least this'll be Josh's final ode to sexual joy, what with him getting chucked the day after this party, immediately after Jenny read his first column about her. And it is rather gratifying to know, from their promising chat on the phone earlier this week, Jenny's version of events on this particular evening – namely, that Josh invited her to a do at his parents' house in Belsize Park, got himself squeaking drunk, dragged her off to the conservatory, tumbled over a pot plant and hugged her knees while declaiming that it was his intention to make love not to her but with her. At which point, Mrs Todd had appeared, asked Jenny if she was all right and sent Josh to bed. 'Without any supper,' Jenny had added. 'Or me.'

Not that Josh has admitted to any such anticlimax in his latest column, which gives the distinct impression that he'd sent the lady in his life soaring high above alpine peaks of carnal bliss. Alastair scrolls down to the end of the text, fails not to register the finale – 'I am sweating. I am spent. I am repleat.' – and closes the file.

'Okeydokey lemonsmokey. Now let's try some phrasal verbs with get. Anyone? Dieter?'

'I am getting into British food.'

'Excellent. Is that true, Dieter?'

'Naturally, no.'

'Okay. Stanislaw?'

'I take a Tube to get to the school.'

'Yes, yes, yes. To get to somewhere. How about, let's see, Chantal? Do you have an example with get, Chantal?'

'I . . . I . . . I get up in the morning?'

'*Excellent*, Chantal. Very, very good indeed. Anyone else? Paolo? Do you have an example with get?'

'*Sí.*'

It's only now, halfway into the lesson, that Ian realises Paolo hasn't been acting the idiot as usual. 'And would you like to tell us what the example is?' Come to think of it, the little tosser's hardly said a word all class.

'*Sí,*' repeats Paolo, who is apparently trying to make some sort of a point by staring at him and not doing any blinking. 'To get off with a girl. To get it on. Means sex,' Paolo explains to the others while maintaining steady eye contact with Ian.

'Wow, that's very impressive,' says Ian brightly, pretending to ignore the fact that Paolo is now making a real show of shoving his books and pens and paper into his doubtlessly expensive leather bag. 'Right, everyone, let's move on to look. Look into, look up to, look . . .'

Paolo scrapes back his chair and stands up. Back to performing his hard man's act, he hoists his bag up on to his shoulder and marches up to Ian, who doesn't budge. They're standing almost nose to nose in front of the silent class. 'I am getting out,' Paolo announces. 'And you will not get away with what you do.'

Ian musters a puzzled smile which does nothing to appease Paolo, who turns to the rest of the class, waves goodbye like a child to a passing train, gives them a '*Ciao*' and marches out, making sure to slam the door behind him.

Is that better? Graham takes a step back and looks long and hard at the slightly rejigged arrangement. Yes, he decides. That's closer to the informal effect he was after. Certainly feels better this way, and what else does he have to go on apart from the way it feels? Answer: fuck all.

He reaches for the can of McEwan's, finishes it off with a couple of gulps, crumples it in half and lets it fall to the floor. Will all this have the same effect in D:Zine's reception? Well, that's the fucking question . . .

Maybe he could fit in one more drawing on the left?

Probably not. In fact, he's fairly sure it's just about done. What he'll do, though, he'll treat himself to another can and have a think about it. Then a quiet Friday night in, the FNC having apparently died a death, and he'll be all set for Audrey tomorrow.

8

'I HADN'T EXPECTED CHAMPAGNE'

Saturday night

Here's Ian, sitting in a pub in Vauxhall, drinking lager and marvelling at the fact that it'll be closing time in half an hour. Christ, even Scotland's figured out that letting people drink beyond eleven doesn't mean night-long brawling on vomit-splattered streets. Yeah, well, what do you expect? Welcome to England, where the time is 1897.

Not entirely true, he has to concede, and this pub's clientèle offers an awkward reminder of London's often startling hipness. This place is crammed with cool-looking twentysomethings all set to give it large in what Ian has gathered are Vauxhall's surprisingly jumping clubs – the all-niter for gay bikers just over the road, the joint near the MI6 building that's supposed to be at the cutting edge of trance, the fetishy place underneath the arches . . .

'Excuse me. Is someone using this?' A guy whose lime-green T-shirt says 'Aceeed' is pointing at the little wooden stool next to him.

'Go ahead,' Ian says, and he swirls lager round his glass to look busily unconcerned as the Aceeed guy drags the stool over to a group of lean, laughing boys and lean, up-for-it girls who all seem keen to display their flat tummies and jewelled tummy buttons. So that'll be him being the old geezer in the corner, then, the one on his own, nursing his lager and his memories of the Blitz.

Well, it could be worse. Because right now, at this very moment, he could be up in Crouch End, listening to the green blethers of Ben and Ruth. Which is exactly what Claire'll be doing and what he'd be doing too had they not had their worst-ever row earlier this evening. Soundtrack to his life right now – the repeated crash of doors being slammed in his face. By petulant youngsters, and through no fault of his that he can see, unless he's to blame for Chantal having a crush on him rather than that little Italian tosser, or it's suddenly a huff-making offence to dare to mention the slight drawback about going to Ben and Ruth's for a tofu bake or a beansprout soufflé – the distinct possibility that Ben and Ruth might be there.

Thank the living Christ that he didn't tell Claire about being fired yesterday. Mood she's in, she'd've executed him. Fucking Paolo, though. Little tosser. Defeated in a game of lust, he goes for revenge by telling Foxsmith that Mr Murray is crap at teaching modal verbs but excellent at supplying his students with charlie. 'Ah, Ian, ah, one has no, that is, not to blacken the school's as it were, ah, but no option remaining but to, ah, given the um, less than, ah, so all for the best if, ah, yes.'

And that was it. Goodbye London Oxford School of English, goodbye view of the Krazee Kost-Kutter Klothes Kompany, goodbye 240 notes a week, hello cowboy joint in Soho, eight hours a day, three days a week, six quid an hour, starting nine o'clock sharp Tuesday. Utter, utter crap, and the worst of it is that he has to count himself lucky to get even that. Cheers, Paolo. So that's what he gets for giving – giving, mind you – the little tosser a couple of lines. What do you call an Italian boy with a grudge? A little Eyetie tosser, that's what . . .

'Time's up,' calls the barman.

Ian finishes his lager. Crap flat, crap job, crap city, zero money, girlfriend pregnant and in a permanent strop. Yeah, time does feel like it's up.

'Anyway.' Jenny props her elbows on the table and gives him a smile.

'I didn't realise,' Alastair says. 'I suppose I'd always assumed that it was Graham and Jenny and that was that. You know, as you do with couples. I mean, you'd been together since just after student days . . .'

'Yes. I suppose I was like that as well. Not taking it for granted exactly, because that was never an option, the way he was carrying on, but not being able to see past it. To think that there could be life outside that relationship.'

Alastair purses his lips, trying for a solemn expression although an unworthy part of him is delighted. Because this is the kind of conversation he's been wanting to have with her. And because it shows they're getting on. No other reason. 'Absolutely,' he says, attempting now to look empathetic, although being in a relationship and not being able to think about life outside it is something he last felt not very pressingly and nearly a decade ago.

'So I think that I have to accept some of the blame too.'

'That's ridiculous. That's like the police saying someone chinned them in the fist. Come on, Jenny. How on earth could it be any fault of yours?'

'Okay. I know that I didn't force Graham to be an emotional – what's the right word? – twerp'll do. Although of course I did think that for a long time. No, I just mean that I had to be stupid to put up with it for so long. Putting up with it for five minutes would have been bad enough but . . . I'm sorry, Alastair. Here I go again. What I should be doing is saying thank you for dinner.'

'Don't thank me, thank Delia.'

Alastair is wondering if he might add a little line of patter here. Delia be praised, perhaps, or hallowed be Delia's name, but then Jenny gives him a breathtaking smile and says, 'My compliments to both of you.' Probably just as well. 'Any news about your friend Rob?'

Keep it simple, stupid, Alastair reminds himself, because this is exactly the sort of situation when he can find himself blethering rubbish, lots and lots of it. 'Not really,' he says. 'We've hired a detective to find out what's going on and we've got another appointment, a third appointment in fact, to see him on Monday afternoon so ... Well, we'll see.' Alastair coughs. 'Sorry the food was nothing very fancy.'

'Alastair, it was a triumph. And I get quite enough of mango risotto and seared humming-bird during the week.'

'How *is* work?'

'Completely ideal if you want to spend half your life setting up overhead projectors or explaining to some executive how to open the minibar. No, I'm still enjoying it really. Though I could do with less dashing around now that I'm getting middle aged.'

Alastair smiles and shakes his head in what he hopes is a rueful way. But maybe he got that slightly wrong too. It probably came across as patronising. Why can't his face behave itself? He caught a glimpse of his reflection in the kitchen window when he went through to serve up the salmon and this pouch-cheeked daftie glanced back at him, a silly grin stuck to his face like a false moustache. So that was what he looked like when he was having a great time. An epsilon-minus nincompoop.

Whereas Jenny ... well, Jenny is looking terrific. Dangerously so.

Alastair tops up her glass. As he does so, he reminds himself of all the points that make it rather a good idea for him not to notice the down on her forearm or, let's be honest about this, the way her chest pulls at her jersey.

- Jenny is Celtic to his Lochgelly Albert. Hanker after Jenny? Hmm, good idea. While he's at it, he could start lusting after Emmanuelle Béart as well. Who looks a bit like Jenny in a way – similar shape of face, and something about the mouth as well. Though Emmanuelle Béart's lips are much fuller, of course. Some might say too full. Anyway.

- Jenny is Graham's ex, so falling for her would be like marrying a cousin – not exactly illegal but still somehow dodgy.
- Jenny is in recovery, first from Graham and then from the *Chronicle* business, as Alastair now wants to call it, since it seems something like obscene to put Jenny and Josh Todd together in a phrase.
- Also. He has learned from past mistakes and he's not going to blow it this time. He's not going to fall for her, he's not going to make a pathetic, doomed play for her, he's not going to do anything that'll end up with her upset and him humiliated. Especially because
- he's got the chance here of having this amazing and, yes, lovely woman as a friend. Someone he can have a great chat with. Muck about with. Go out with. Well, not go out like that go out, obviously, that's the point, but go to places with. Which, to be openly selfish about it, is something he's going to need in his life, if it really is going to be Robless . . .

But she *is* lovely.

'Mm,' says Jenny, inspecting her glass. 'And this is a real treat. I hadn't expected champagne.'

Neither had Alastair, but when he'd taken her coat and seen how she looked in her black jumper and black trousers, her nut-brown hair pinned back with a little tortoiseshell comb, second thing he'd done, if you count as one the managing to control his stomach's sudden tightness and his knees' threat to buckle, had been to sprint into the kitchen, rummage frantically in the fridge and unearth a bottle of Moët. On the grounds that giving the vision sitting on his, Alastair's, candy-striped sofa a slug of the just-uncorked Chardonnay would have been like offering Audrey Hepburn a bite off a Curly Wurly.

Next item on the agenda had been to excuse himself, do another sprint, up to the bedroom this time and on tiptoe. Halfway up the stairs until it dawned that the glee on his face together with his high-stepping dance would do just fine in a very bad impression of Tom sneaking up on Jerry. Then a quick-change act to replace the dark blue polo shirt and black jeans – the kind of outfit which he'd thought would be appropriate for an evening of pally morale-boosting but which he now suspected made him look like he'd just done a stint in the garden – for his best white Ted Baker and a pair of Armani trousers. Another sneaky prance down the stairs and for the next hour it had been the pair of them perched at either end of the sofa, her looking terrific and him trying to sit cross-legged as uninelegantly as he could without the pins and needles in his right calf becoming too unbearable, and feeling that this was a cocktail party he'd thrown for some unthinkable reason and Jenny had been the only one compassionate enough to turn up.

'But what about you, Alastair?' Jenny asks. 'Are you seeing anyone at the moment?' She takes another sip of champagne, for all the world as if she's genuinely curious, though she might as well be asking if he's played for Scotland recently.

'No,' he manages to reply, with what he hopes could resemble a straight, serious expression. 'No, I'm not seeing anyone at the moment.'

'I should take you along to my book club,' she says. 'Ten women, two married, one gay, the rest manless and on the Häagen-Dazs. Five minutes in and you'd be having to fight the girls off with a stick.'

This can only be intended as a nice tease, since the alternative explanation is that Jenny has suddenly turned into the kind of person who delights in asking if your dog is still dead, but even so. Alastair clears his throat, then smiles at the table while he tries to think of something to say. Something that will provide a smooth segue to another subject. Any other subject. Something funny, by preference. Definitely something light and witty. 'Well,' he hears himself saying, 'I hope I wouldn't have to resort to a stick.' Oh, *brilliant*, he yells inside his head. You blithering *idiot*.

She leans down to give him yet another peck. But then he feels her tongue poke at his lips so he opens his mouth for politeness' sake. A loose strand of preposterous purple hair flops on to his cheek. His penis is a chipolata, slumped forlornly on his itchily moist pubic hair. Her tongue twitches around inside his mouth, like something he's eating that's suddenly come alive.

'Mm,' she says after she's finished her kiss. 'I need a drink.' She leans back until she's upright and resting a considerable part of her weight, comfortably for her presumably, on his balls. 'I'll get us a glass of water.'

'Good idea,' says Graham as she – thank fuck – gets off him and out of the bed, although he could do with something stronger. A bottle, for example, of tequila. She jiggles over to the door, where she unhooks her dressing gown. He hadn't expected that orange peel at the top of her thighs. And her skin smells strange – kind of like almonds. Not like Jenny. Jenny had a scent like vanilla.

It's as if somebody flicked a switch in his head the moment he finished coming. Up till then, just the kind of evening he would have asked for. Couple of drinks and a shared snack of chunky chips at the Cantaloupe, just him and her and her being encouragingly positive when he told her about the installation. So that was good. And it had been such a long, long time since he'd done anything like this, he'd been going mental with anticipation. And everything had been fine. More than fine. Excellent, really. Exactly the kind of date he thought he'd be having every week after he and Jenny broke up. So next thing they were snogging like teenagers in the Cantaloupe, then hopping in a taxi back to her flat in Stoke Newington. And now this. What the fuck has happened here? Well, long as she doesn't go all snuggly-wuggly when she gets back . . .

She reappears at the doorway of her bedroom. She rehooks the dressing gown and jiggles back towards him carrying a full glass of water. Graham reaches out for it, but she brings the glass up to his mouth and carefully tips it forward. Prone, he can manage only a sip before water pours back out of his mouth. She places the glass on the floor then lies down beside him. She throws an arm round his neck just where it's sorest. Graham grimaces. 'Mm,' she says into the side of his chest. She presses his neck. This time he can't prevent himself taking a sharp intake of breath. That is fucking *sore*.

9

'HE STILL DOESN'T KNOW, DOES HE?'

Monday afternoon

'. . . how to deal with lawyers like that in the Flying Squad, I can tell you.' Mr Hilton opens the slim manila folder marked 'Mr R. Mackenzie' and pats it flat on his desk. 'Nevertheless,' he says decisively. 'Two lines of enquiry have born fruit. The first concerns your friend's career. Perhaps I was mistaken but you did say that Mr Mackenzie worked as a banker?'

'That's right,' says Louise.

'In the City,' Alastair explains.

'In so far as the bank was situated more or less in London, yes, Mr Carr. Your friend was employed, as you thought, by the NatWest Bank. But, to clarify matters if I may, first of all at a NatWest in Leytonstone, and then, until he was made redundant earlier this year, at a branch in Theydon Bois.'

So that's how you pronounce it, Alastair finds himself thinking in the middle of his bewilderment.

Louise gives Mr Hilton a disbelieving look. 'What on earth was he doing in banks out there?'

'In each location, Mizz Turner, Mr Mackenzie was a member of the customer services team.'

'. . . You mean he was a cashier?'

'Precisely, Mizz Turner. In fact, Mr Mackenzie remained in this post and at a grade-nine salary level for his entire term of employment with NatWest. In its way, quite an achievement. But then your friend was no high-flier at his previous employer, the Bank, my apologies, the *Royal* Bank of Scotland, was he?'

'No,' says Alastair. 'But this was the early eighties. Rob and I were about the only people we knew who had any kind of job at all. And nobody gets going when they're young, unless they're a pop star or something. So Rob was doing all right, even during that stint at the Newington branch. In Edinburgh,' he adds for Louise's benefit. 'But he got fed up. That's why he came down here in eighty-five and joined the NatWest. In the City.'

'And what exactly did Mr Mackenzie claim he did in . . .' Mr Hilton holds up a pair of index and middle fingers. They pat the air twice. '. . . the City?'

'Corporate investment,' say Alastair and Louise in chorus.

Mr Hilton replies with a sorrowful smile, as though they've just come up with a particularly unconvincing alibi.

Alastair takes a deep breath because he's decided that he really has to set things straight. 'Look,' he says. 'I'm sorry, Mr Hilton, but I think you've made a mistake. Perhaps you've got the wrong records. Maybe there are two Robert Mackenzies at the NatWest. Or more. I mean, it'd hardly be surprising, it's not that unusual a name. No, the Robert Mackenzie we want works, or worked, in banking. Not *a* bank. Banking. In the City. In corporate investment.'

Mr Hilton leans back in his chair and gives Alastair an is-that-so? nod.

Alastair squeezes his hands between his knees and frowns. 'All right. Let's say for the sake of argument that Rob did work as a cashier. How do you explain his car or his flat, for instance? I don't know what a NatWest cashier earns but it's not going to be enough to buy an MG and an apartment slap bang in the middle of Soho.' Alastair shrugs helplessly. 'You must have got the wrong man.'

Mr Hilton clasps his hands behind his head. 'Might I ask, did he talk about his work, your friend?'

Alastair and Louise exchange a glance. 'Not in any detail,

if that's what you mean,' says Louise. 'But that only proves Bobby wasn't one to bang on about work.'

'Indeed. But if you'll bear with me for a moment, I'd be willing to put a small wager on my guess that neither of you ever actually visited Mr Mackenzie at his place of employment.'

Alastair looks at Louise. She shakes her head. 'Well,' says Alastair, 'it does seem that neither of us did . . . But that's hardly unusual. A corporate investment department isn't the kind of place you call in on, is it? I mean, it's a busy office.'

'I imagine so. But now I'm going to take another little punt here and suggest that Mr Mackenzie was probably very anxious about not being phoned at work either. Perhaps he said something about personal calls being forbidden?'

Louise is looking thoughtful. 'No,' she says. 'He didn't give me a work number. I'd call him on his mobile or at his flat. And we used e-mail a lot when I was in New York.'

'To conclude, then,' says Mr Hilton, 'the only evidence either of you had for your friend's career as an investment banker were a few signs of his apparent wealth. So when you, sir, said how did I explain his car and his apartment, for instance.' Mr Hilton's fingers pat out another pair of inverted commas. 'That was in fact the start and the end of the list.'

'Hold on,' says Alastair, who's busy assessing the thought that maybe his far-fetched, TV-movie-inspired notions may not have been too far fetched after all. 'Are you saying that Rob pretended to have a job in the City as a cover for something else? Drugs or crime or spying, something like that?'

'I favour a simpler explanation, Mr Carr. It seems to me that Mr Mackenzie's alleged job in the City was a cover for his actual job as a cashier in Theydon Bois. An odd commute, I'll give him that.'

Alastair has a picture of his brain fizzing and sparking like a wet socket. 'But if Rob worked as a clerk in a bank, how do you explain the money?'

'Very easily, Mr Carr. His inheritance.'

'No, I'm sorry,' says Alastair with a smile of tolerant disbelief, 'but you really have got this completely wrong. Rob's parents were not exactly landed gentry. His dad was a foreman in a linoleum factory.'

'If I may.' Mr Hilton lifts a sheet of paper from the manila folder and gives it a brief appraisal. 'Let me take you back to the summer of 1985 when Mr George Mackenzie of Torbain Street, Kirkcaldy, suddenly retires from his employ at a kitchen-flooring manufacturer. The same week that Mrs Joan Mackenzie receives a cheque for two hundred thousand pounds.'

'Two hun . . . ?'

'The couple seem to have kept this good news quiet, as such lucky people often do, and quite sensibly so in my book, but they do celebrate their good fortune by taking a month's holiday in Yugoslavia as was. Two days into their dream vacation, they take a coach ride to Trieste, the coach driver fails to negotiate a hairpin bend, the coach plummets into a ravine, killing everyone on board.'

'You're right about the coach thing,' says Alastair.

Louise seems too stunned to say anything.

'Your friend loses both parents in the tragedy but as their only child he does inherit the sum of two hundred and four thousand pounds and twelve pence. Two months later, he leaves his job in Edinburgh and moves to London.'

Alastair tries to catch Louise's eye but she's still staring into space. 'So how come Rob's parents had all that money?' he asks.

'Premium bonds, sir.'

'*Premium* bonds? That's where Rob's money came from? His mum had a win on the premium bonds?'

'Initially, yes. It seems that Mr Mackenzie Junior then set out to be a freelance capitalist. His initial dabblings in the stock market were . . .' Mr Hilton waggles a dubious hand.

'But he did happen to do rather well in the property market for several years, buying, renting out and then selling flats in Highbury . . .'

'That's right,' Alastair interrupts. 'He had a place near the Arsenal ground.'

'. . . Kentish Town, Archway and Brixton.'

'Blimey. Really?'

'With the profits from which he purchased outright the Bateman Street property in 1990.'

Alastair looks at Louise, but she's still too busy staring in front of her. She looks even more shocked by this than he is. He shakes his head as if to clear it. 'Then what was he doing as a bank teller if he was this big-time property mogul?'

Mr Hilton holds up a warning index finger. 'Not quite big-time, Mr Carr. Certainly not big-time enough to be full-time, if you follow me. And however modest his salary – eight thousand pounds a year when he returned to work in eighty-nine – it did provide a steady income at a time when your friend's various fiscal ventures were of a nature that he might as well have taken a suitcase of notes and thrown it in the Thames.' Mr Hilton opens the manila folder again and reads from another sheet of paper. 'Eighty-six, he invested heavily in a Kenyan ostrich farm which was declared bankrupt six months later. Early eighty-seven, he came a real cropper with an ill-fated venture into the futures market. Later the same year, he had another try at the stock market and came a real cropper on Black Monday. And so it goes on. Until last year, when he switched most of his remaining capital into Far East stock and . . .' Mr Hilton gives them an encouraging nod.

Louise still seems incapable of making any response. 'Came a real cropper?' suggests Alastair obligingly.

'When the Korean economy went into freefall barely a week later. Precisely. If you don't mind my saying, it's just as well for NatWest's corporate investment arm that your friend didn't work there, because he did have an extraordinary talent for losing money. So much so that he had to remortgage his flat. In fact, from the documentation I've seen so far, Mr Mackenzie had bankrupted himself.'

There follows a silence which Alastair ends with a dry cough. 'You mentioned that there were two fruitful lines of enquiry. Can I ask about the other one?'

'Indeed you can, Mr Carr. It concerns Mr Mackenzie's present whereabouts.'

Alastair feels his heart suddenly banging at his ribs. 'You know where Rob is?'

'Indeed I do.' Mr Hilton consults the manila folder. 'He's going by the name of . . .'

'Stop,' commands Louise. 'Don't say any more. Or say what you have to say to Alastair. I don't want to hear it. I'm going outside. Call me in when you've done.'

She's right, thinks Alastair. He holds his hand in front of her to stop her getting up. 'No need,' he tells her, then he turns to Mr Hilton. 'From what you know do you think he's okay? I mean, are debt-collectors going to break his knee-caps? Or the police, are they after him? Is he in any danger?'

'Neither line of enquiry gives any indication of that, sir.'

Alastair stands up. 'Then that's all I want to know too. Thank you for all your hard work, Mr Hilton.'

'Much appreciated, Mr Carr, though in all fairness it was very straightforward, routine work. When I think of some of the cases we had on the Flying Squad . . . Yes. Well. I'll bid you goodbye, then. If you could settle the bill with Mizz Maguire in reception.'

Alastair offers his hand to help Louise up. 'You're right,' he tells her. 'We'll leave him alone.'

Louise is staring at the manila folder as though it's just called her by name. Alastair puts an arm around her and leads her out of the office. You're coping, he says to himself, and you're doing jolly well. But then he shuts the door to Mr

Hilton's office behind him and, all of a sudden, it seems like he's just smoked one of Rob's specials. In an unthinking daze, he monitors his signature being written on a bill's dotted line, then the approach of a flight of stairs, then the opening of a pair of glass doors.

He pushes open the doors, to be roared at by the traffic. He feels a tug on his arm. Louise is pointing at a nearby coffee bar. They walk towards it and in. Louise orders two double espressos. Following her example, as if she's guiding him through a complicated ceremony, he places his coffee on a long counter and perches on a high stool. Then he realises that she's just asked if he's all right. Come *on*, he shouts inside his head. Get a *grip*. He brings Louise into focus and takes a deep breath. 'Fine,' he says. 'I'm fine.'

Louise lights a cigarette and smokes in silence. They both gaze off into space. Alastair is trying to rewrite Rob's life, to discard the established version of Rob as a whoop-de-do ladykiller, high-flier, go-getter, and put in its place a Rob who was . . . ordinary. Who had an ordinary job. Who didn't have a big salary or a lavish expense account. Who didn't travel the world. Who may not have spent most evenings of his life wining and dining and chatting up girls at the latest in places. He tries to imagine Rob taking the Tube out east each morning, spending his days counting out other people's money, squandering the money that fate had given him, a fortune, really, especially to a bank clerk in 1985 . . .

Why, though? Why did he feel he had to lie all the time? Why couldn't he just have told the truth? What would he, Alastair, have done if he'd known that Rob was a cashier with an accidental nest egg? Spurned him? Hardly. Though that's probably missing the point . . . But it does mean, however it's looked at, that the trajectory of Rob's life has been quite different from the one he's always assumed it to be, the straight line arrowing ever upward, from school to university to financial apprentice to lavishly rewarded City mover and groover. In fact, the trajectory seems to have been a long slide downhill for Rob from what could now be seen as his peak, when he was sixteen, seventeen, at the centre of everything, liked by everyone and looking foward to a life of adventures . . . Maybe that was one reason Rob was so keen to establish the FNC second time around, because it evoked his glory days . . . Another thing – how easy it was for Rob to take off like that, how it took over a week for anyone to notice that he'd gone . . . And how would it be different for him, Alastair, if he wanted to disappear? There'd be his father to consider, of course, and before all this happened, he'd have cited Rob too, but, as Mr Hilton would say, that's the start and the end of the list.

Louise takes a quick puff of her cigarette. 'Did you have any idea about any of this?'

Alastair rouses himself. 'None.'

Louise shakes her head. 'You lot. You're just middle-aged teenagers, aren't you? I mean, for goodness' sake, the Friday bloody Night Club . . .' She sucks at her cigarette, spits out smoke. 'Funny. This seems worse than anything even I've come up with . . . You know what I think?'

'Um . . . no.'

'We both know that he was keen on his spliff. So many blim burns on his shirts and his dressing gown it was like he'd been shot by a twelve-bore. I mean, I just used to think that the dope thing was one aspect of his rich and multifarious, whizz-bang life. But now . . . now I think that was the only aspect there was. I think Robert Mackenzie was nothing more than a pathetic stonehead.'

'I don't . . .'

'Something I noticed when I was wandering round and round his flat the other day. Or actually something I noticed wasn't there. The only things missing that I can see. His little box was empty.'

'Not with you, Louise.'

'His dope box. The one with the fancy carvings. Nothing in it. So those were his two indispensable items of luggage. His bag of skunk and his king-size Rizlas.' Louise takes another brief puff of her cigarette. 'All that time I spent in New York worrying if I could trust him, wondering which club he'd be going to that evening, which restaurant with which scheming, gold-digging bitch. You've seen his diary. About as empty as his passport, hardly anything in it apart from his good chum Jeremy and you and the musketeers. There was me worrying myself sick about what he was up to and what he was up to was coming home after a day's slog at a bank in the burbs and rolling a big, fat one. To spend the rest of the night rolling more big fat ones, chain-munching Hob-nobs and dreaming up rubbish. How for me he'd be this rich City boy with a sob story about . . . and about how he'd be this rich, all-singing, all-dancing, party-time bachelor to you lot. An impoverished, avant-garde *artiste* to his great chums we never knew existed in the Coach and Horses.' Louise smiles at her cigarette and gives a short, joyless laugh. 'And there was me thinking I couldn't have been more stupid.'

'What do you mean?'

'When I'd been assuming all along that Bobby upped and went because of me.'

'But he did, Louise.'

'Right. He was broke. Beyond broke. His high-flying job was a sham. His whole life was a pretence. He was due to be rumbled. It was nothing to *do* with me.'

'Come on, that's just not true.'

'Okay, but only because my return meant that it was going to get harder and harder for him to keep everyone in their different boxes. Keep those different fantasy worlds apart. But I wasn't even his downfall. I think his downfall was the fashionable flat in the middle of Soho. Any other part of London he might still have got away with it. But Soho, people pop in on you.'

'Maybe that was why he was always asking us to phone him first. I always . . .' Thought that this was in case he'd be interrupted in mid-seduction, is the rest of the sentence, but Alastair decides not to say it out loud.

Louise looks off into the distance and smiles. 'Honestly, what a pathetic little scheming dopehead liar.'

'Come on, Louise,' says Alastair, although he's started to wonder just how many of the things Rob told him were made up. The CNN reporter, for example. The Brazilian girl with the bottom. The three-in-a-bed adventure with the sisters from Milan. Maybe he never even played strip poker with Kirsty Barclay.

Louise stabs her cigarette out on the saucer. 'You don't see it, do you, Alastair? Just how rubbish he was. And just how thoroughly he took the piss.'

'No, I . . .'

'I thought I was his girlfriend, you thought you were his best friend. But you know what we really were? We were members of his audience. For two of the different parts he liked to play. If we'd mattered to him, he wouldn't have lied to us, would he? And he'd still be here, wouldn't he? But he could leave us behind like he left everything else behind. Apart from his precious grass.'

It's understandable, Alastair reminds himself. She's bound to be wound up and bitter. Not that he can say such a thing, but how could she not be? 'I'm sure there's more to it than that.'

'He *used* us, Alastair. And you know why? One, because he was a sad, self-centred prick and two, because we could be used. The pair of us were only too willing to believe any old rubbish he came up with. Me because I was so worried about the relationship that the last thing I was going to do was demand to see his P60. You because you're . . . you. And I was conveniently stowed away in New York, while you were always there for him. When it suited him.'

Can that be right? Possibly, Alastair concedes to himself. Sort of. A bit . . . It could fit in with a few episodes in the past. Starting with the way that Rob did seem to drop him when they both went to big school and Rob began to hang around with the hard men. Until Rob hoved back into view in fifth year, and perhaps it could be argued it wasn't coincidence that by then he, Alastair, was not only in the school football team but was also pally with the Bill-Fiona-Steve set whom Rob was keen to co-opt into what would become the Friday Night Club. There was also the time when Rob drifted off at uni. And, granted, Rob certainly showed that he was no returner of phone calls or postcards after he moved to London, so that the two of them hardly ever saw each other until he followed Rob south four years later . . . Rob's enthusiasm for the second version of the Friday Night Club, wasn't that a bit suspect, given that these group nights out suddenly seemed to replace their one-to-ones and on what is for him, Alastair, the worst night of the week? Even Rob's last communication – those two ten-pound notes – maybe that wasn't Rob being decent and doing the right thing by a friend but Rob just squaring an account, dusting his hands and thinking that was that, discarding his friends like he left behind his furniture and his toothbrush . . .

Alastair gives his head a quick, impatient shake. This is just him feeling sorry for himself. 'I don't think so, Louise. I think maybe it's a bit different for me. You see, Rob and I have been friends for nearly thirty years.'

'Please don't give me that.'

'But it's true.'

'So you're saying that he could exploit a newcomer like me but not his best buddy and old pal Alastair Carr.'

'No, but . . .'

'His great chum who shares this enormous *heritage*, this *bond* that's so strong from knowing so much *stuff* about each other, like, oh, let's think of an example – yes, that his parents died in an accident umpteen years ago.'

A very good case in point, Alastair notes to himself. 'No,' he says, then he coughs. 'I'm not saying that.'

'Uh-huh?' Louise leans towards him. 'Okay, I didn't know about his parents' accident. Because his story to me was that his mother had been struggling with the infirmities of old age.'

Alastair shakes his head sadly.

'Until she died early last year.'

Alastair gives his head another shake and sips his coffee.

'Of Alzheimer's.'

The cup is stuck to his lower lip. Black and sticky and surprisingly hot liquid dribbles down his chin.

'A very moving account he gave of it. And I have to admit that it proved very effective as a seduction tactic.'

Alastair manages to replace his cup on its saucer and wipes his mouth. 'Fucking hell.'

'Quite . . . Something else that occurs to me. The way he kept puffing himself up, first of all by boasting and telling me what turns out to be a pack of lies, and then by putting me down. How he was the one with the glitzy lifestyle and the terrific salary, how I was so lucky to be going out with him. But in real life I was the one with the job and the big pay packet and the office with a view of Central Park.'

Alastair dabs at his chin and the dark spots on his chest. He'll have to buy a new shirt on the way in to work . . . He's in such a daze that there's a moment when he has to remind himself what he's doing here with this woman he doesn't really know. Come on now, he tells himself. Snap out of it and think through what's happening here.

So. Louise is obviously looking for solidarity and he'll give her as much as he can. But he's got to stick to his guns and not do it at the expense of rewriting his own emotional history. This malarkey may have shown that his friendship with Rob wasn't quite what he used to think it was, but it'd be going much too far to blame Rob for things he just didn't do. Okay, so Rob might have boasted a bit but he never put him, Alastair, down. 'I couldn't say, Louise.'

'I can't believe you're still sticking up for him.'

Alastair smiles wanly. 'It's bound to be different, though, isn't it? A relationship and a friendship.'

She shakes her head. 'You mean he was always this great, positive force in your life?'

'. . . Yes. Of course.'

'Oh, come on, Alastair. Haven't you ever noticed that you've been better off when he wasn't around?'

'I haven't, no.'

'Really? What about your relationships?'

'What about them?'

'Something that struck me after our heart-to-heart the other night. Every relationship you talked about. The girls you went out with your final year at college, the same final year at college when he wasn't around because he'd taken up with a new set. Rhoda or whatever her name is, when you were still in Edinburgh but after he'd upped sticks for London. Far as I can tell, Alastair, your love life has happened only when he hasn't been around.'

She's still looking for him to enlist and he really does want to offer her some support here. And joining in by blaming Rob for all the world's evils might help quell the hurt that's still growing inside him at the idea that Rob actually stole his own bereavement for a chat-up line. And he really does want to offer her some support. On the other hand . . . well, on the other hand, she is talking nonsense. As off the mark as the convolutedly fanciful analyses people come up with when they've been converted to therapy. 'That's coincidence, Louise. And me being not exactly a ladies' man.'

'Maybe. And maybe it's coincidence that he also latched on to you when you split up with Rhoda, Rhona, whatever, lured you down here and got you started smoking grass the moment you arrived. I mean, what better way to keep you docile? And happy enough to dodge around at home on your own? At his beck and call, always ready to be impressed by the latest story to make him look great and you feel small?'

This is worse than therapy. This is astrology. 'No, Louise,' says Alastair. He is surprised by the firmness in his voice.

'Uh-huh. So you're telling me that he never held you back? Never put you down?'

'Rob was my friend, Louise. No.'

'You sure about that? ... Eck?' She looks at him with a grim smile. 'Because what I'm sure about is that he held *me* back, he put *me* down all the time, and my life is going to be a lot, *lot* better now that I don't have to deal with that devious, pernicious, cowardly, selfish, lying, stonehead *bastard*.' She lets out a high, strangled yelp, hides her face in her hands and starts to sob.

'Oh, Louise,' murmurs Alastair. He reaches over and strokes her hair. 'Oh, Louise.'

'But, you know, like I say, I *was* kind of like, yeah, I'm expecting him to call.'

'Audrey, I really am sorry. And like I've said, I was going to call you today. I mean, it's only Monday.'

'Yeah, yeah, boy time, of course, I forgot. Boy time. It's a classic men are from Mars, you know what I mean?'

No is the answer to that one, but Graham gives her a non-committal 'uh' instead.

'You know, and it *is* specially kind of, like, weird, even with boy time, the Mars–Venus thing and the blah blah blah, not to call when, you know, you were, like, goodbye, and it's, like, four o'clock in the morning. Yeah? I mean, you know.'

He had his way, the phone would be in smithereens right now. This can't go on for much longer, surely? He checks his watch. Five-thirty. So that's her been yapping away for over an hour now. Fucking price he has to pay, though. Hefty price, mind, time-wise – about ten minutes' yap for every minute's shag. He should have called yesterday and avoided all this shite. Just as well he's only got a couple of tweaks, if that, to do for the exhibition and zero on the illustration front, bar a crappy little commission to do an Earth covered in a spider's web for *Computing Now* with a Friday deadline. 'Look, Audrey,' he says, 'I'm sorry, right? Like I've said a hundred times already, I couldn't sleep. I'm sorry.'

'Yeah, right, yeah, I know, but, you know, four o'clock in the morning and then no phone call Sunday, no phone call today, I'm, like, what's going on? You know?'

Here they go again. How many times, how many fucking *times*, do they have to go round this short loop? 'Yes, I am sorry, Audrey, but it's just . . .' What? What can he say here that he hasn't already said? Maybe he could tell her the truth. Audrey, while you were sleeping, whistling through the crust in your nostrils and stinking of marzipan, I stared into the darkness, gagging for a drink, even of water, and thought not about you but about Jenny, and wondered if Jenny'd been doing what I'd just done and, if so, who with. End of story. '. . . It's just that things are complicated at the moment, Audrey,' says Graham. 'What with the exhibition and everything . . . Look, I'd better go. I've got to get this work done before the courier arrives . . . Audrey? . . . Audrey? You still there?'

'. . . Yeah.' This tiny, pathetic voice.

'I've got to go, okay? . . . All right? . . . Okay?'

'. . . Is that it, then?'

'I've got to go, Audrey. Honestly . . . I've got to go . . . Okay, so, 'bye. I'll talk to you soon, all right?'

'. . .'

'I've got to go now, Audrey. Sorry, but I've really got to go. 'Bye, then . . . 'Bye.'

Graham bangs down the phone. 'Jesus,' he says. 'Jesus fucking *Christ* on a fucking *bicycle*.'

They're about to turn the corner into Bonnington Square when

Ian remembers that the flat'll be in a mess. But that's good, because it'll back up the impression he may have given her that he lives on his own. Ian lets go of Chantal's hand and rubs his nose, not because the nose is its usual troublesome self – in fact the nose has been feeling good today, not running, not itchy, not too blocked, not anything really, despite a couple of nice little lunch-time lines – no, not because the nose was giving him the usual bother but because it gives him a reason to let go of her hand. You never know – someone might be looking out of a window at exactly the wrong moment, and that someone might be someone Claire has got talking to at some point or other, for some reason or other. No, you never know. And one thing Ian's learned over the years, when it comes to situations like this, you cannot be too careful.

They've reached the main door. Nothing to see here, he thinks. Just him with a friend, that's all – couple of pals popping in for an afternoon coffee or an afternoon spliff. All very innocent. He shuts the door and takes Chantal's hand again to lead her up the flight of stairs.

He's fiddling with the keys when she taps him on the shoulder and beckons him forward to kiss her again. His mouth melts into hers again. He's holding her shoulders but – he can't help it – his hands roam down to her hips then cup her dinky bottom. He gives her one of his best moves – the one where he concentrates on a corner of the mouth, a surefire winner. His wilful fingers begin to spread over the soft-denimmed bottom and are about to start clutching.

He forces himself to hold back. All the time in the world for that once they're inside – or, more accurately, all the time in the world until, say, seven o'clock, because Claire's due back at eight after a day up in Stanmore with her folks. Still, that gives him a good three hours with Chantal. Who, on top of everything else, told him over lunch that she was gym champion of her lycée. Her eyebrows lifting a fraction as she said that, to let him know. His groin fizzing at images of how she might hoik her long, pliable legs. Not too easy to eat a mozzarella-and-tomato ciabatta after that. In fact, he'd given up on food, swigged his Badoit instead, then taken himself off to the loos of the trendy little café in Greek Street for an adjustment of the boxers and another quick line.

Now he ushers her into the main room, where he checks for any telltale signs of Claire – none, really, apart from her pink-edged trainers, but they're hiding over in the far corner – and then he's with Chantal on the sofa and kissing the corner of her mouth again.

'*Un moment*,' he says when he eventually summons up the willpower to disengage his lips from hers. '*Un moment. Reste ici.*' Ian limps through to the bathroom, where he runs a tap and flushes the loo – like he could use it in his state: maybe just, if he had ten minutes to spare and could place the bowl halfway up the bathroom wall – while he sets about hiding the stuff that's unmistakably Claire's, shoving her potions and lotions and salady-sounding pots into the bathroom cabinet. Then it's through to the bedroom, where he stashes some *Cosmo*s and a nightie under the bed.

That's all he has to do. It's so easy. But that's only in keeping with this assignation, which has gone like a wet dream – from the moment Chantal agreed that they should meet to the moment when she told him she'd be leaving at the end of the week and went all meaningful on him. Allowing him to up the romance, in reassuring French, by stroking her hand and murmuring, '*Alors, nous avons seulement ce moment.*' Corny, but it worked, as corn has a surprising way of doing with women, in his experience. Although he has a theory that that's maybe just because he doesn't have to try too hard. Or, in this case, at all.

But that's what he means – everything's been so easy. Which only goes to show that this was somehow meant to happen. And in any case, where's the harm? This is a one-off, she'll be back in Toulouse by the end of the week, and as long as Claire doesn't find out – and how on earth would she find out? – then this'll be a treat, nothing more than that, like having a final, pick-me-up toot at the end of a party. Plus, come on, what red-blooded man could pass up the chance of an afternoon sesh with a quality French babe gymnast? Not Ian Murray, that's for sure.

He's returned to the main room, where she's waiting for him on the sofa. He sits down beside her, puts an arm around her shoulder and pulls her towards him, ready to start the kissing build-up all over again, because he's bound to have lost a bit of momentum here. She, however, thinks otherwise, judging by the way her free hand has come to rest on his trousers' pleasingly prominent bulge.

'I like kissing you,' she murmurs into his ear.

'And I adore kissing you,' he murmurs back, choosing English now that things are getting serious – the safe option in such circumstances, even for someone as fluent in French as he is. He gives her his best crinkly-eyed smile. 'Let's go to bed,' he says, taking control now.

He stands up, pulls her upright, leads her through to the bedroom. He back-heels the door shut behind them, leans forward to nuzzle her ear as a token distraction, and peels off her jacket. Next to go is the pink cardigan, which he slips off her shoulders and down her svelte, tanned arms. She takes a step back. She tilts her head. She smiles. She holds his gaze as she crosses her hands and begins to pull up her T-shirt. Very, very slowly. Revealing inch after inch of perfect, brown flesh. Eventually, the first glimpse of a lacy white bra. This, he thinks, is about as agonisingly gorgeous as it gets. And this is only the start. He stands there, transfixed. More lace now, the suggestion of rosy nipples underneath the lace, the white of her string-thin bra straps, the smooth, lighter brown skin of her underarms as she ducks into the T-shirt and yanks it over her head and her thick auburn hair.

Only now does he take a step forward and pull her towards him. Then it's time to kiss again, while his left hand buries itself in her hair and his right sidles round her back to find the bra clasp. Girl her age, she probably won't be expecting the sheer smoothery of this, he thinks, as he nibbles her full lower lip and prepares to undo her bra one handed. She's making little straining noises in her throat. His fingers are easing out the clasp and . . .

And there's a noise at the front door. Which cannot be. That cannot be happening. But it is. It is happening. Someone is opening the front door.

'. . . them tomorrow instead.' Claire. It's Claire. 'I don't know what I'd do without them at the moment, I really don't.'

Ian and Chantal stare at each other, their hands by their sides now, but the pair of them rooted to the spot. Chantal's mouth opens in a silent 'What?', or it could be '*Quoi?*'

'Oh, absolutely.' That's Briony. Her unmistakable whine. Fucking, fucking Briony. 'Maybe we could do an afternoon film or something. Have you got a *Time Out*?'

'On the table, I think. Or maybe in the bedroom.'

Briony walks in on them and yelps. A moment later, Claire appears behind her. She doesn't say anything at first, just takes in the scene. He blurts out something about it not being what she thinks, that he can explain everything. How? Saying what? This girl from the school was feeling faint so he took her home, loosened her clothing and was about to call the doctor . . . Claire replies with a sneer then sprays the room with an Uzi. He can see it all.

And that'll be it. No more Claire.

No more Claire. For all his vague envy of Rob's walk-off, for all his occasional little daydreams where he finds himself by himself somehow, in a bar in Le Marais or a flat with a rooftop view of the *sixième*, he has never really thought about what no more Claire would actually mean. Only now, as he stands there in the bedroom, listening to Claire and Briony next door, looking at but not really seeing a plainly terrified Chantal, sickly saliva trickling down his throat, does the reality dawn on him. Claire. No more Claire. What'll he do? Where'll he go? How'll he cope? What'll be the point of anything if there's no more Claire? And the baby? Christ, the baby. His baby.

'Here it is.' Claire. Still in the main room. She must have found the *Time Out*, thank Christ. 'Any suggestions?'

'*Women on the Verge of a Nervous Breakdown*, that might be appropriate.'

'Yeah, right.' Claire again. 'Or *Clueless*. Something something.'

'He still doesn't know, does he?'

'Oh, he doesn't know anything about anything.'

'But you haven't told him, have you, Claire?'

Is he the he they're talking about? And told what? What hasn't she told him?

'Because I haven't decided for certain. Something something Stanmore.'

'But, Claire, you've said yourself that it's hopeless. Bad enough being totally poor and living in this . . . this *tip*, but he's never there for you, he's the opposite of supportive, he's making zero effort, he doesn't help you, he's horrible to all your friends, his first reaction to the baby was to ask about an abortion, and he hasn't got much better since, from what you've said yourself. And he seems to have no *idea* what you're going through.'

'Something something something.' Claire, muttering.

'I know. And at his age.' Briony's voice coming over loud and clear, Briony having a foghorn where human beings have tonsils. 'And do you want a cocaine addict as father of your child? I don't *think* so.'

'I know.'

'Look, Claire, you'll be much better off with your parents,

even if it's for a little while, and if he still doesn't see any sense, then you've empowered yourself, you've made the first move.'

'I know. You're right. I just don't feel very empowered, that's all.'

'No, you feel ill. Look, Claire, it's not only yourself that you have to think about now. And you can't keep on fainting in supermarkets. On your own.'

'I know, Briony . . . Oh, Christ, let's just get out of here, shall we?'

Ian risks breathing for the first time in what feels like years. Chantal hasn't so much as blinked. Petrified, he finds himself thinking. She's petrified.

'We could go up to Leicester Square and take pot luck, what do you think?' Claire, near the front door.

Yes, Ian pleads inside his head. Yes. Leicester Square. Right now. Do not pass go.

'Wait a minute, please, Briony.' Claire again. A slight rummaging sound, then a chink, of keys maybe, or coins. 'I'd better take my specs. Now where? . . . Ah. I know. Bedroom.'

10

'WHAT DO YOU RECKON?'

Wednesday evening

'No, really,' says Graham. 'I'm delighted.'

Fionnula, Marty's new and controversially female assistant, nods keenly. 'Good,' she says. 'It's . . . exciting work,' she adds. She's quite sexy, Graham has decided, even though she's on the plumpish side, could do with sending herself to the dry-cleaner's and has five silver rings dangling from her left ear.

'Yo, Graham. Sup.' It's Marty, looking as svelte and as somehow untrustworthy as ever. Today he's wearing a pair of baggy beige breeks with enormous pockets on the sides, and a blue fleece, zipped up so that Marty can tuck his chin into the collar and nuzzle it for something to do when he's not speaking. He untucks his chin again. 'Early doors, I know, but, still, good few people here. And the work's looking . . . good.' Now it's Marty's turn to nod. 'Good.'

'Good turnout from the press as well,' Fionnula tells Marty.

'Who?' asks Graham.

'*Blueprint* and *Design Week* said they might come. Guy from the *Ditch* has just arrived and, best till last, the *Sunday Chronicle*'s here.'

'The *Chronicle*?' asks Graham. 'Where?'

'Over by the desk. Chatting to that man with the stubble.'

Graham squints around a group of standard-issue trendy freeloaders. It's Eck and Ian. 'You mean the wee baldie bloke?'

'Guy in the black Armani, yeah.'

305

Graham flinches. 'Naw, that's a mate of mine. Works at the *Chronicle*, like, but that's it.' *Fuck* it. Typical Eck. Trust him to turn up early. And spend all of a minute gazing at the installation, smiling half heartedly and stammering the blandest praise before launching into a long, wandering monologue, with a lot of sorrowful head-shaking, about what he'd discovered about Rob. Apart from the pools win, nothing Graham hadn't really known – after all, he has become so used to thinking of Rob as the man who betrayed him, lied through his teeth and used and abused the FNC for his own nefarious ends, that it couldn't come as any great surprise to be told that Rob had done all of those things, if not quite in the way that he had once thought. But Eck had said his piece like he was reporting a death in the family, happily mistaking Graham not giving much of a shite for grim acceptance of this supposedly terrible bombshell. Then Eck had fallen into conversation with Fionnula, that being an obvious thing for the pair of them to do at a time when the only other people in the room were Marty and himself, and Marty and himself had both become occupied at the table of freebie drink. What did Eck expect, though, turning up at quarter past for a 6.30 kick-off? Mind you, the place is still only half full, but that's good going for a quarter past seven. Isn't it? Come on, 'course it fucking is. And reactions so far have all been good. Well, they would be, wouldn't they? But they have. All been good, that is. The reactions so far.

By fuck, he could go another beer.

'Six quid an hour?' asks Alastair.

'Six quid an hour,' says Ian.

'Blimey.' It occurs to Alastair that Ian would earn more cleaning people's houses, but it also occurs to him that it might be a bit tactless to point this out, so he makes do with what he hopes is a sympathetic-looking headshake.

'I'd probably earn more asking people if they want fries with that.'

Alastair directs a dry cough into his fist. He's had a thought. 'This is only a vague idea, Ian, okay?'

'Okay.'

'Just a suggestion, I mean, nothing more.'

'With you so far, my man.'

'Well, you know how you know about grammar?'

'Uh-huh.'

'And you can spell.'

'Ye-es.'

'And you worked on that magazine in Paris?'

'Well, I don't think that doing little things for a hippie English news-sheet . . .'

'And you can work a computer?'

'Sort of. Depends.'

'Never mind, Ian, I mean, that's easy enough to pick up, and I could give you the rest of the basics, like how you do a delete sign or what thirty-six point means . . .' Alastair stops himself. He's getting carried away here, because it seems such a brilliant idea. Yes, but then there must be something obviously wrong with it. It's probably of no interest to Ian anyway. And possibly very presumptuous of him to be thinking of this at all.

'You're talking about subbing, right?'

'Well, yes, but it's only a . . .'

'But I'm not trained as a journalist.'

'Nobody's trained as a journalist these days, Ian. Even subs. Once you've got the basics and you know how the language works, then subbing's one of those jobs which you can only learn by doing it. And there are jobs going for subs. I know of at least two chief subs on magazines who need staff. One of them, Gary, he's quite a good friend, so I could put a word in for you if you want. There's even a job going at the *Chronicle*, although Barry'd probably be looking for someone with experience. But the *Indie*, say, you might get shifts there, they'd take anyone. God, sorry, Ian, I didn't mean . . .'

'No, that's fine.'

At least Ian looks vaguely intrigued rather than outraged. Although he's also noticeably subdued, and 'subdued' isn't one of the words he associates with Ian. Even so, Alastair judges it time to change the subject. 'So what do you think?' he says, nodding towards Graham's exhibition. This occupies the far corner of the reception area and consists of one work or piece or installation or whatever the right noun is. One part of it is on the floor, a white but slightly stained and rather crumpled-up duvet, on which are scattered a weird variety of objects – here an empty bottle of whisky, there a paint-brush, and everywhere scrunched-up sheets of paper which occasionally reveal little squiggles, and which, according to Fionnula with the earrings, are meant to be opened up by members of the audience who'll then see that each sheet of paper contains a pen-and-ink self-portrait. So far, the scrunched-up pieces of paper have remained pristinely scrunched, but Alastair reminds himself that this is an opening party attended by a lot of arty types who'd doubtless think it very unhip to engage with Graham's whatever-you-call-it. Anyway, the objects on the ground are far less striking, to his eyes at any rate, than the second part of the whatsitsname, which takes place above, on one of the white walls. And this second part consists of seven rows of photographs, twelve in each row, which curve in a rainbow over the duvet. And which, more to the point, at least as far as he is concerned, are all the one colour snapshot of Jenny, kneeling pertly on a tartan picnic rug in a field somewhere sunny, smiling up at the camera and, because she's wearing only a bikini bottom, displaying surprisingly large breasts with surprisingly big, pink nipples. He wonders if Jenny knows about any of this. If she doesn't, and he can't see how she could, and if she had she'd surely have mentioned it, how will she feel about her latest starring role? Not best pleased, reckons Alastair. Not best pleased.

When he arrived – as early as he possibly could to tell Graham about Rob, and because the couple of times he's dared hold anything like a party he's spent the first couple of hours panicking about people not turning up – he'd taken a good long look at the thingummy while Graham was engrossed in chat with the thin chap with the weaselly face who keeps on ducking into his fleece. Once he'd got over the initial shock of seeing eighty-four reproductions of Jenny and Jenny's bare chest, he had done his best to be mature and objective and assess the whole thing – and completely failed. Hard enough to figure out anything from the world of contemporary art, a world which seems as trendily remote as fashion – both being worlds, as far as he can see, run by a handful of people in the know telling people not in the know that apparently silly things are actually very important and exciting, although few people in their right minds could surely want to put those things on their walls, just as you'd never even think about wearing a hat made from shrubbery – but completely impossible when it features eighty-four reproductions of Jenny and Jenny's bare chest.

He can't even judge whether this whole do is going well or not. There's maybe fifty people here, but is that normal, good or bad? And there's still only a few of them paying any kind of attention to the actual exhibit – is *that* normal, good or bad? Alastair looks over at Graham, who's currently shaking someone's hand and laughing heartily, but all he can decode for certain is that Graham has already had quite a few drinks.

Alastair takes another sip of his Japanese lager while Ian, who really does seem quite under the weather, takes another look across at Graham's thingummyjig. 'Really, Ian,' says Alastair. 'What do you think?'

* * *

'I think we get the hell out of here, Alastair.'

'Are you feeling all right?'

'Fresh air would be good. But mainly I think we should just get the hell out of here. Come on. Follow me.'

Ian sidles through the small throng towards Graham, mouths 'See you later' at him because Graham's ensconced with a couple of people, sticks up a thumb just as Graham turns back to his conversation, reaches the door and then the cool of the early-evening air.

'Phew,' says Ian.

'Phew indeed,' says Alastair.

'You fancy a wander? Maybe a drink if we stumble across a not crap pub? If there is such a thing around here.'

They set off down a narrow street featuring warehousey-looking buildings with hoist things coming out of some upper-storey windows, and leading God knows where.

'You didn't think much of it, did you, Ian?'

The pair of them come to a halt and gaze up at the gable of a derelict building. Ian sighs. 'No. No, I didn't think much of it . . . Oh, who knows, it might be brilliant, and he might get rave reviews and what we've just seen might be the start of a new and spectacular career for Graham as an installation artist of great and trendy genius.'

'But?'

'. . . But I wouldn't bet on it.'

Alastair puffs out his cheeks and raises his eyebrows. 'Well,' he says eventually, 'do you suppose Graham's happy with it?'

Ian shrugs his shoulders. 'I think Graham doesn't have a clue. Not that that singles him out.'

They move off slowly down the street. 'This could be bollocks, of course,' Ian says after they've sauntered another couple of yards. 'But I remember reading somewhere that there are now more people in Europe working as artists than there were people alive in Renaissance Italy. Pub over there that doesn't look too appalling. Fancy a pint, Alastair?'

11

'LITTLE HICCUP ON THE LUNCH FRONT'

Thursday afternoon

'Waldemar?'

'. . . The woman is buying cloazez.'

'Good.' He has to have another quick check of the class diagram on his desk. Then he looks up again at the dozen people crammed into this tiny room with crumbling walls and a sink at the whitewashed window. More or less what he'd expected, in fact, from a place calling itself the International Oxford English School. In Lisle Street. Above a minicab office. 'Miroslav?'

'Thee boy. Eez eating. Thee ice gream.'

'Very good.' Damn, he's forgotten the next name. And it's far too warm in here. Only another fifty-three minutes until his lunch break. He takes another peek at his diagram. 'Boris?'

'Barees.'

'Barees.'

'The man is playing the golf.'

'Good.' Oh, bugger it. He glances back down at his class diagram. 'Natsuko?'

'*Sumimasen.* You say Natsko.'

'. . . Right . . . Natsko.'

'the sun-kissed slopes of the Andalusian sierras, where earthy peasant cuisine and the'

Alastair is trying to concentrate on Hugo's piece about tomatoes. Not an easy task, and one that's made even harder when he sees the editor lumbering this way, accompanied by a chubby-faced and bespectacled young man who looks like he would be much happier swanning about a campus or minding a second-hand bookshop than picking his way through the shallow end's shambles of workstations. The pair of them weave towards and then into Bluebottle's office. There's something familiar looking about that young man. Something about the glasses, maybe . . .

Josh Todd. Blimey, it's Josh!

He goes to Alt Screen and hurriedly taps out a message to Barry. 'wot josh here for? and why with ed? and why ed down here? wot going on?' Alastair presses Send.

'delightful news, al,' starts the reply, 'ed and b/bottle taking josh to lunch to discuss recent brilliance of josh's columns.'

Alastair studies the message then sticks his head round the side of his terminal. 'Barry?' he whispers. 'Are you being serious?'

'Oh yes,' Barry whispers back, then he ducks his head back down and starts hammering away at his keyboard.

Soon Alastair's screen flashes MESSAGE. 'just to make you even happier, al, i shd add that b/bottle planning to invite 007 to lunch as well so b/bottle can push 007 forward as new bright young theatre critic for arts section which is wot 007 wants to do, and as far as b/bottle concerned, wot 007 wants 007 gets.'

Alastair is wondering if there's anything he can type in reply to this terrible news when his phone goes off. One long ring – an internal call.

'Hello?' says Alastair.

'Alastair Carr? Front-desk security here. We have a Graham Anderson in reception to see you.'

What? Graham? Here? 'Ah, yes, okay, I'll come and collect him.' Graham? Here? What? Alastair scrapes back his chair. And Josh Todd in the office at the same time? Oh God. Could Graham have got wind of Josh? Oh God. 'Back in a minute, Barry.'

'Be quick. Lunch-time soon.'

Okay. This is the plan. Keep calm, act nice and normal, spin Eck the line, take him to the nearest pub, if there is a nearest pub in Canary Wharf, sandwich, couple of drinks, and take a more subtle approach. Because the more he's thought about it, and he's thought about it only all the time, the more he's convinced that it's got to be someone she's met through Eck. Because Jenny and Eck have kept in some sort of touch, unlike Jenny and Col or Jenny and Ian. And because he can't come up with any other feasible explanation. So get Eck talking about his pals, people at his work, then suss out anyone Eck mentions who has an initial J. Because he's got to find out. And if he wasn't trying to find this out, Christ alone knows what he'd be doing with himself. No, he's got to find out.

There's Eck now. Looking like he feels – i.e., like someone's died on him but he's doing his best to soldier on.

'Hi, Graham,' he says, still with this air of smiley desperation. 'Congratulations again on the exhibition.'

Shows how much the wee man knows. Graham shrugs, as though modestly. 'Aye, well . . .'

'So,' Eck says into the gap, 'what brings you to this neck of the woods?'

'Afternoon appointment,' Graham replies. 'With the art director of the colour supplement,' he adds, gesturing to the portfolio he's lugged all the way from Finchley to back up the spiel. 'So I was wondering if you wanted a cheese roll and a couple of pints somewhere near by.'

He couldn't have been more laid back and pleasant but Eck gives him an anxious stare. 'Yes, well, that'd be nice, Graham, but . . . but, you see . . . the thing is, we usually all just pop over to the canteen.'

'Nae bother, Eck. Canteen it is, then.'

'. . . Sure, sure. Um, I'll have to get you a pass.'

Like a pass is a fucking jar of plutonium. 'Fine.'

Eck proceeds to fuck around for a few minutes, in a particularly Eckian fashion, with the security bloke, who seems exactly the sort of bloke a security bloke would be securing an office against. Eventually, the security bloke beckons him over to sign his name and collect a plastic-covered sign that announces VISITOR. Graham clips it on to the breast pocket of his leather jacket, an action which makes him feel, for some unfathomable reason, a bit of an arse.

Eck does one of his wee coughs. 'If you don't mind, then,' he says, 'we'll just head straight to the canteen.'

'Right you are,' says Graham, then he notices that Eck is staring at him in horror. Must be because there's a gang of suits coming towards him and he's blocking the way. He moves to his left, but only slightly because he's fucked if Eck's going to have him bowing and scraping to a bunch of suits. Having themselves on that their lives have some fucking purpose and picking up a big cheque at the end of every month. Fucking suits. Although, to be accurate about it, the two younger blokes of the four aren't wearing suits and one of the other two is jacketless. Aye, but they're still salarymen, that's the fucking point. The suit who's actually wearing a suit has given the Eckster a brief nod. The other three just ignore the wee man.

'See you later, Richard,' Eck says to the suit's back. Richard. Can't be him, then. But whoever he is, he's obviously got the knack of soothing Eck, who's switched from something like panic to something like normal.

'So, Eck, you not going to show me around?' Graham asks, now that the wee man's got rid of his fear grin, and because maybe a quick tour might give him the chance to ask Eck about people he mucks about with here.

'Um, well, yes. If you want. A good time to do it, actually, because it'll be quite quiet.'

Right. He'll have to do it slightly different, then, if nobody's around . . . He'll think of something. 'Who're that lot?' Graham asks, on the grounds that he might as well, although anyone would think it's a devilish trick question going by Eck's sudden fretting.

'Oh, um, well, that was Richard Marshall, who edits the Lifestyle section. And the chap in the shirtsleeves was . . . the editor. And the thing is, you see . . .' And that's Eck gone off on one again, as they set off towards a pair of double doors, stammering drivel about calling an editor an editor. Or some fucking thing.

Graham tunes out as he takes in his surroundings – typical newspaper office, or at any rate very like the ones he used to visit when colour supplements really were commissioning him, except none of them had a view of France. They head off through a right old mess of desks and computers and garbage and towards the only people left in the office, a clutch of nerds in the far corner. Then something happens which he really was not expecting. One of the nerds suddenly puts a foot on his chair, throws his arms wide and bursts into song. 'Hi ho,' he bellows, 'hi ho.'

Big bloke beside him takes it up, miming that he's got a mike. 'It's off to lunch we go.'

The female's turn. 'With a spade and bucket,' she sings. Then she and the two blokes turn towards *him* and point. What the *fuck*? Ah, she's pointing to Eck.

'And that girl from Nantucket,' Eck sings back as they approach the karaoke crowd. The other three give Eck a brief round of applause, then all four of them do the 'Hi ho' bit again. What in the name of *arse* are they like?

'The subs,' explains Eck with a what-can-you-do? smile. 'I'll introduce you. Maybe we could all go to the canteen together. Does that sound okay?'

No it does fucking not is what he's thinking as he returns the smile and nods, but then he remembers why he's come and the nodding turns sincere.

Before he does the introductions, Eck goes into all this detail about them both being members of the fucking Friday Night Club. As if all the . . . well. Boy's an embarrassment.

No Js, as it turns out. So no fucking point to this after all.

'So,' the bald one says heartily, 'you'll have to give us the gen on Al here. The inside info on the famous FNC. Al's secret life.' Cunt gives him a wink.

'Aye,' he replies. 'Ha ha. Right enough.'

A bit of faffing around and then they're all heading back the way he's just come. They're about ten yards from the double doors when these swing open. A large man strides towards them. It's the big bloke in the shirtsleeves, one of the editors Eck was going on about. And he's followed by those three others. The big bloke in the shirtsleeves is muttering to himself and looking grim. The other three are looking a bit sheepish. The big shirtsleeves bloke stops and turns round. 'For God's sakes, Richard,' he says. 'I mean, for God's sakes, why didn't you *say* something? Wait here.' He strides past, leaving the other three lingering there like farts in a trance.

That Richard raises his eyebrows as they approach. 'Little hiccup on the lunch front, Barry,' he says softly. 'Editor forgot his jacket.'

'Aaaaaaaaaaaaaaaaah,' says this Barry meaningfully, drawing it out for so long that he's about growling by the end of it. And that it's now no longer the thing for the two groups to pass each other. 'So where are you off to for lunch?' the Barry bloke continues.

'MPW.'

'Very nice.'

'I'm certainly working up an appetite for it.' More of the eyebrow raising.

Since it seems to be the thing here to exchange significant looks rather than actual words, there follows a long and awkward silence. Which gives him the chance to check out this younger pair, although it's only as he offers his hand to the one nearer him that he remembers that neither of them had paid Eck any attention when they passed by before, so this has to be a complete waste of fucking time. 'Graham Anderson,' he says nonetheless, having to raise his voice to make himself heard over a sudden outburst of coughing from the wee man.

'Oh,' says the one nearer him, clearly taken aback by this new-fangled fucking procedure of introducing yourself by shaking someone's hand and telling him your name. 'James Bond.'

At first Graham is too busy controlling the adrenalin which has surged through him at the thought that this arsehole's taking the pish. But after he's steadied himself, he realises first that maybe somehow the arsehole isn't taking the pish, and second that if he really is called James Bond then he's a J.

'Right, then,' announces Eck very loudly. 'We'd better leave you to it, Richard.' Eck taking a step forward now. And the fear grin has returned.

Graham ignores Eck's attempt to get them all moving and offers another handshake to the second younger one, buying a bit of time to figure out what's going on with the James Bond arsehole.

'Graham Anderson,' he repeats.

'Josh Todd.'

Another J. And that name sounds familiar. 'Ah,' he says, pleasantly, like, keeping up the charm, 'you're the one that writes those articles in Style.'

'Lifestyle, yes.'

'I should have recognised you from your picture,' he says, while frantically searching his brain for a way of quizzing this pair of Js further.

Eck's grabbed his arm. 'Really, Graham. The canteen.' Eck's giving him this pleading look. The boy's all over the shop. Now why would Eck be in such a state?

He shakes off Eck's hand and stays his ground. 'I don't suppose,' he says, sensing his mouth twitch as he tells it to adopt a smile, 'that either of you know Jenny? Jenny Newman?'

'Yes, of course. Jenny Newman. Ho, Jenny *Newman*.'

It's the other one of the editors, the big one, who has arrived at his side and is clumsily shrugging on his jacket. Graham turns to face him. 'Jenny Newman?' he says, the Newman coming out in a falsetto. 'You know Jenny Newman?'

'Yes, yes, yes,' the editor bloke says in a booming voice. 'Marvellous. Phwoar. Always had a thing for Jenny Newman.'

Eck's tugging at his arm again. 'I'm, I'm, I'm sure,' he stammers, 'that the editor is . . .'

'Graham,' says Graham, smiling and holding out his hand. 'Graham Anderson.'

'How remiss of me,' the Richard man says. 'This is the editor of the *Sunday Chronicle*. Jonathan Witherington.'

'Jonathan, eh?' Graham says through his teeth.

So this is the man who has been fucking Jenny. *His* Jenny. He lets go of the cunt's hand and feels his own hand curl into a fist so tight that his entire forearm is like an iron bar. 'Is that fucking right?'

'Graham!' he hears Eck shout.

As if that's going to stop him.

12

'YOU REALLY THINK I SHOULD?'

Saturday night

'Go for it, man. Seriously.'

'You really think so, Ian?'

'Definitely. Look at today's result, even. The force is with you.'

'I suppose . . . You really think I should?'

'Absolutely. Hey, Alastair, we've been over this a hundred times.'

'I'm sorry, I know. And I really appreciate all the . . .'

'Hey, least I could do. Just go for it, all right? And by the time I see you you'll be completely sorted. Honest.'

'Oh God.'

'See you tomorrow, Alastair. Good luck.'

'Thank you, Ian. I'll need it.'

'Not at all. See you tomorrow. 'Bye.' Ian puts the phone down and gives it a thoughtful look. Does Alastair have any chance? Maybe. She was daft enough to get off with Graham all those years ago, wasn't she? And he's told Alastair during his pep talks how to do it – play it safe, give her his own best chat-up line, the one that strikes an endearingly diffident note and, in the unlikely event of failure, provides room for a dignified retreat. Oh, Alastair can do it. Or, remembering that this is Alastair he's talking about, maybe not . . . He'll find out when he sees him tomorrow.

'Course, it will be odd spending a Sunday evening at Alastair's house instead of Johnny's flat, but not going to Johnny's flat is something he's going to have to get used to.

And he's looking forward to the sesh with Alastair – if it's anything like the impromptu lesson they had after Graham's exhibition, it should be good fun. No, fair play to Alastair, because the Carr crash course, as Claire has christened it and as they all now call it, looks like it could already have paid off – as long as he doesn't screw up his second interview at *European Traveller* magazine. Now who would have thought that he'd get such a break and that it'd be courtesy of Alastair? Not so long ago, he'd have said Rob was the only break-giving kind of guy he knew – before Rob turned out to be such a galling disappointment.

The thought of Rob's sham life threatens to become depressing, so he distracts himself with the daydream he has been constructing, one where he's working in the surprisingly cool, almost glamorous office he had a brief look at yesterday when he met up with Gary, the chief sub who knows Alastair. He sees himself at a desk, one with a computer, a mug of pens maybe, and a telephone, studying a page proof as it's called, scoring out a mistake and, with a certain suave confidence, making one of those curvy delete marks in the margin. Then glancing out of the window at the planes gliding above and the bustle of Carnaby Street below. He'd never have thought it possible, but he really wants to work in an office, or at any rate that office, with its trendy furniture and its laid-back buzz.

Not to mention the salary – twenty grand a year, near as damn it, plus any fee he'd pick up if he gets the chance to do an article, and as Gary himself said, Ian does have four languages and an insider's knowledge of various countries, so it wouldn't be beyond the realms of possibility that he could soon be enjoying the occasional freebie to Rome or Barcelona or . . . Time permitting, mind you, because he'd only go if Claire was okay about it . . . Or, and here's a thought, if he could wangle a joint trip. Then take the baby as well. Write an article about what Rome's like with a toddler, where's good for kids in Paris . . . God, it's going to be great – if he gets the job. If he gets the job. Looking like a good if, though.

Ian checks his watch. Quarter to eight. 'Claire,' he calls out. 'We'd better be going soon.' A night out with Ruth and Phil, Ruth's new boyfriend, Phil having stepped in as soon as Ben announced that his father had pulled a few strings and got him into the MBA course at Harvard so that would be Ben off, then. As the man himself would say, bizarre. Or, come to think of it, maybe not so bizarre after all. Oh, tonight will be okay – at worst, another evening ticked off without the charlie. Not that going without charlie has been at all bad. He's had a sense of loss, occasionally, but about as much as the sense of loss he feels at the passing of the FNC (i.e., not much). Definitely nothing like as bad as it was giving up ciggies. 'Claire,' he calls again.

'Through here,' she calls back. From the bathroom, by the sound of it.

Ian goes through and finds her still wrapped in her blue towel, standing in front of the washbasin and examining the mirror.

'This is terrible,' she says. 'Even my face is getting fatter. Look.' She turns and puffs out her cheeks. 'I mean, I *am* Oliver Hardy.' She blows a raspberry and her cheeks deflate.

'Claire, even Françoise Hardy looked crap compared to you.'

'Singer, right? Nice-looking singer or enormous soprano kind of singer?'

'Very nice looking.' He takes in the sight of her smiling back at him, turning that towel into a designer frock. To think that if she hadn't rummaged around in her bag one more time, if she hadn't found her specs . . . And if he hadn't been given the chance to realise how much he wants this child . . . Or if he still didn't know how crap he'd been, how ill and lonely and scared she'd been . . . Well, none of it bears thinking about. As it is, she's responded brilliantly to the new, improved him, her initial come-off-it wariness soon giving way to amazed relief then eager affection. Just like it used to be. Better even. 'But not half as nice looking as you.'

'I bet you say that to all your girls,' she says, and Ian keeps up his smile. She prods at the towel where it covers her stomach. 'Getting as big as a bus,' she says.

'Nonsense. You're lovely. I love you.'

She replies with a smile, then untucks the towel's fold above her breasts. The towel drops to her feet. 'Oops,' she says. 'It's come undone.' She steps over the towel and comes closer and closer until she's almost standing on his shoes. She circles her arms around his waist. He strokes her soft, warm, just-out-of-the bath skin and nuzzles her wet hair with his chin.

'Claire,' he says, 'we'd better be going soon.'

'Really?' she mumbles back into his chest. 'The thing is . . .'

'Aha?'

'I'm feeling a bit peaky.'

'Are you, love? But according to the book, the queasy spells should be over by now . . . Anything I can do?'

She gazes up at him, putting on the look of doe-eyed innocence that always creates havoc in his boxers. 'Well, yes, Doctor, I think there might be something.'

'Um, yeah, but what about . . . ?'

'I hope you don't mind, but I phoned Ruth and cancelled. While you were at Sainsbury's. Because I've been feeling like this all day.' She goes on tiptoes and caresses his stubble with her mouth. 'Kind of tingly,' she whispers. 'Hot.' Her mouth moves to his ear. 'Bothered.'

'Goodness,' Ian manages to say. 'Sounds serious.'

'Yes,' she breathes into his ear. 'So I thought maybe I should lie down for a while. In bed. All nice from the bath. No clothes on . . . What do you think, Doctor?'

Claire turns in his arms so that they're facing the mirror together. She sways her bottom gently, slowly, to and fro. His hands move down to stroke the firm little bulge of her tummy. 'Of course,' she says, raising her eyebrows at their reflections, 'you go out if you want. Saturday night, after all.'

'I don't know,' says Ian, shaking his head and pursing his lips. 'Girl in your condition, you shouldn't be left alone.'

'Maybe after the lie-down,' says Claire, 'I might feel better. Then we could have a party on our own, couldn't we? The two of us.'

He strokes her tummy. 'Three,' he says, because it's too good a line to waste. 'The three of us.'

Graham is standing in the crammed hallway. The flat's really too small for a do like this, but he wasn't to know that so many people would come – not only the old studio crowd but a huge squad of arty hangers-on who've emigrated from Shoreditch for the occasion. 'Where'll I put this?' asks Col, holding up a bottle of champagne. 'Through there,' says Graham, nodding towards the kitchen and a large black bin full of ice and bobbing bottles. Someone pats him on the back. It's Marty. 'I rather think,' he says, 'that Saatchi's going to up his offer.' 'Mr Megabucks,' says someone else who's sidled up behind him. Graham turns round. It's Chaz, who seizes his hand and shakes it.

The doorbell rings. Graham glances over and smiles, because he knows that'll be Jenny behind the frosted glass. 'I'll get it,' he shouts, as he squirms past some of Marty's anonymous pals. Keep calm, he tells himself, then he opens the door.

'Not prudent,' says Gordon Brown, who takes a step forward and inspects him with slack-jawed disdain. 'Not. At all. Prudent.'

Graham jolts awake. He stares along the surface of the kitchen table, taking in the whorls of the pine, then the silence of the flat, and then the soreness of his back and his neck. Very slowly, he lifts his head off the table, and sits back in his chair. He blinks a couple of times. Then he reaches for the bottle of Johnnie Walker Black Label and fills the tumbler again.

'Fuck,' says Graham.

Ian's told him how to do it and if anyone knows how to do it then it has to be Ian. Yes, of course, he has qualms – that's only natural because it's a nerve-racking business. But all he has to do is follow Ian's instructions and he'll be fine. And if Louise is anything like right, then even Rob no longer being around is a good omen. Not forgetting also the point that he's got nowhere by not having a go, so if he does have a go and fails then he'll be no worse off. So he's got nothing to lose. Has he? No. Well, then.

His resolve quivers again as soon as Jenny walks into the kitchen. 'I thought so,' she says, holding up the cover of *Northern Exposure.*

Alastair nearly drops the bottle of champagne he's trying to open. 'Is it all right? I can easy put something else on.' As Ian said, it's a Saturday night. A hot date. The second Saturday night she'll have been here. So, as Ian says, that means she's keen . . . But would she be wearing that long black dress, would she have pinned her hair up again with the tortoise-shell comb, if she really were after something non-platonic? That long black dress, that tortoiseshell comb, very becoming though they both are, aren't they the kind of thing she'd wear in the expectation not of being pounced on but of being treated in a friendly, civilised manner? And doesn't everything about what it was like the time she was here before, and now this first ten minutes of her being here again, indicate that pouncing on her might be a very wrong thing to do? Or not? Oh God. Oh dear. Oh God. But if he does it Ian's way, he won't come across as a moustache-twirling lech, so even if she does turn him down it won't necessarily be a catastrophe. Will it?

'No. I like it.' She studies the CD cover and gives it a couple of twirls. 'Any word of Graham?'

Far from having had any word of Graham, Alastair has spent much of the last two days trying very hard not to think about Graham as he's psyched himself up for this evening. But now he can't stop his memory presenting a sudden still of Graham about to punch the editor, and James Bond, who arrived in what turned out to be a brown belt's blur, at Graham's side, gripping his arms and standing hip to hip, holding Graham there for this paused image as if to begin some salsa shimmying, before flipping him over, with speed and skill that would have impressed his namesake. 'Not since Thursday. I haven't known whether to call him or not.'

'Well,' says Jenny with a rueful look, 'a little light bruising isn't usually fatal.'

Alastair tries very hard to think of something else to say and fails.

'Any more news of Rob?' asks Jenny just before the pause gets awkward.

'No. No more news of Rob.' He's never been a world champion at small talk but now it seems as impossible as figure skating. And if he can't handle this, then how on earth is he going to cope with giving her the chat-up line? Even if he can not think about Graham or, more accurately, Graham's attempt to duff up the editor, and that's a big if, can he really follow Ian's advice? Trace a finger down her cheek and say, 'Jenny, I wonder if you'd mind if I made a pass at you?' Ian might be able to bring that off, but when Alastair has practised it in front of the mirror – 'Jenny. I wonder if you would mind if I made a pass at you?' – he's seen only a gawky eejit failing to be smarmy. He tries to concentrate on thumbing the cork out of the bottle and prays that Jenny will say more words very soon.

'Oh yes,' she says. 'Something else I've been meaning to ask you. Why did your editor say he knew me?'

The champagne, he wonders with a jolt of panic. Isn't that a bit over the top? A sign that he's trying far too hard? Or not? Oh God. He clears his throat. 'The editor's not very good with names, you see. We haven't found out yet who it was that he confused you with. Barry at work's started a book on it.' He manages to stop before he starts to witter about Nanette Newman being the evens favourite but him going for Jenny Agutter at two to one. That's a good sign, the not wittering, because that shows he's got his nerves under control. All he has to do now is thumb this cork up without breaking a window or seeing half the contents disappear in an explosion of foam.

Alastair eases the cork out with a restrained pop and, with a steady, dry hand, fills two champagne flutes with white froth. Okay, he thinks. He's in control. He's going to do it. Which means, he acknowledges with surprising calm, that this is one of those rare moments in life when you know that, one way or the other, life is about to change.

He tops up the champagne. When should he do it, though? Is now too early? Shouldn't he wait until much later, at least until after the meal? But who knows what kind of tizz he'll be in by that time. Why not now? While he's feeling confident. Yes.

Jenny. I wonder if you'd mind if I made a pass at you. Now.

'Jenny?' He offers her a flute with an almost steady hand. She smiles. 'Yes?'

'Jenny, I wonder if you would mind . . .' He breaks off to clear his throat. And as he does so he realises that he is being completely ridiculous. What does he think he is doing? Who does he think he is?

She's still giving him a heart-rendingly fond smile as she waits for the rest of the question. Yes, fond. Not yearning or lustful. Fond.

'. . . chives in your salad,' says Alastair, his voice falling to a whisper.

'Chives would be good.'

'Right you are,' he mumbles. 'Back in a tick.' He finds himself doing a poor impersonation of someone picking up a pair of scissors, walking across a kitchen, opening a back door and heading towards a herb garden.

He's reached the chives. He hunkers down as if to examine them. How idiotic can he be? Once bitten, twice bitten, thrice bitten – brilliant. Hasn't he learned anything? And not only from the Fiona and Cathy disasters, but also from Rob?

Alastair gazes at the snipped chives he's holding. Each one a short straw, he thinks, but then he orders himself not to be so self-pitying. He's old enough now to accept what he and his life are like, not to make Rob's mistake and kid himself on that he's something he's not, that his life can be something it won't.

As he sits on his heels and stares at the chives, he tries to acquire a new resolve – to behave himself and be mature about this. This time there will be no embarrassing, humiliating fiasco. He will recover the situation. With luck, she will be his friend. And he'll be happy with that.

'Alastair?'

He looks up to see Jenny standing at the kitchen window. It's a sight that provides him with another terrible moment of clarity. He really has fallen for Jenny, completely fallen for her, and he is not going to cope with that just as he didn't cope with falling for Fiona and Cathy. And even if he does cope with it, what would that coping amount to? Him pretending to be untroubledly chummy with a woman he secretly adores, claiming to himself that it's perfectly fine as she tells him about some date she's gone on, some man she's in love with . . .

Well, he reflects ruefully, at least he's become more efficient with age, having managed to condense the whole process – self-delusion to unrequited longing to abject misery – from a couple of years down to a couple of dates. Oh, well done, him.

'You all right, Alastair?' Jenny has come out of the kitchen and is coming towards him.

'Yes,' he says. 'Thank you.' He straightens up and has to rock back on his heels to keep his balance.

'Careful,' says Jenny. Her hands clasp his shoulders to steady him. So that's what her touch feels like, he thinks.

'Alastair?'

Her hands are still on his shoulders. 'Yes?'

'Aren't you going to kiss me, Alastair?'